THE SHADOW KING

Book 3 of The Raveling

ALEC HUTSON

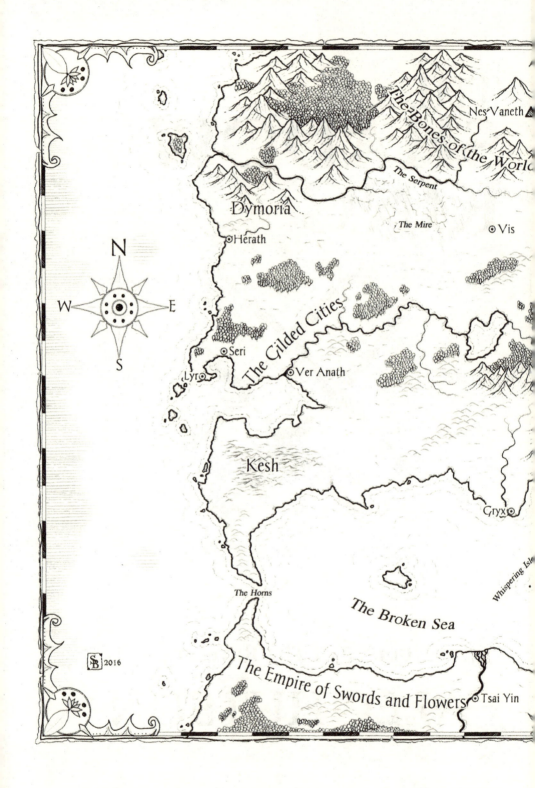

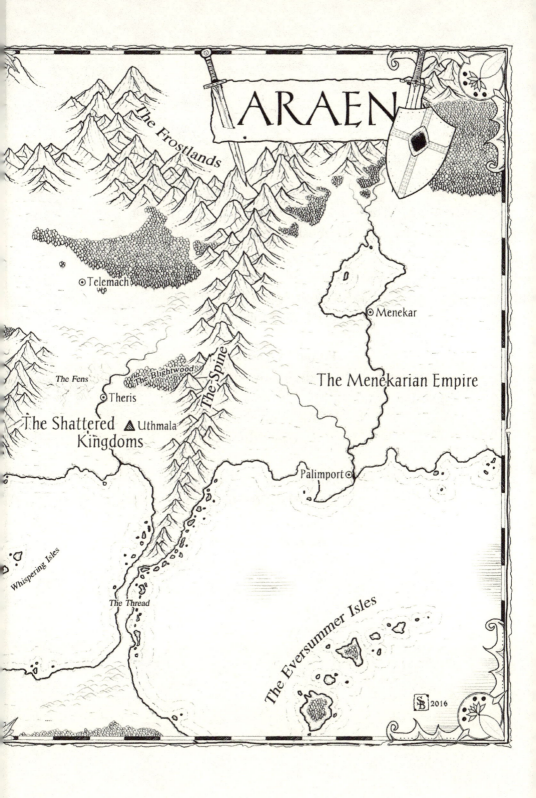

The Shadow King © 2019 by Alec Hutson
Published by Alec Hutson

Cover art by John Anthony di Giovanni
Cover design by Shawn King
Map by Sebastian Breit

Edited by Laura Hughes
Interior layout and design by Ampersand Book Interiors

All rights reserved
First Edition

ISBN: 978-1-7342574-0-3 (print)
978-0-9982276-9-6 (ebook)

Please visit Alec's website at
WWW.AUTHORALECHUTSON.COM

For my brothers, Justin and Silas

WHAT CAME BEFORE

THE HISTORY OF sorcery is scribed in blood.

The seekers of the Reliquary say that the first men to draw power from the beyond were born in ancient Menekar, the Mother of Cities, in the years that its armies swept across the white plains. Most tribes knelt in fear before their glittering power, awed by this sign of the god Ama's favor. Those who dared resist were consumed and left as ash to be trampled beneath the boots of the marching legions.

For a time, the first sorcerers were content to serve Ama and the emperor. But the hunger for power that comes with a mastery of sorcery is insatiable, and when no more cities remained to conquer the sorcerers turned back towards Menekar. The emperor was cast down from the alabaster throne, his broken body hung above the Malachen Gates, and the Warlock King rose in terrible glory. In his court, those touched by sorcery were venerated as holy and those without the gift seen as barely more than animals. All manner of depravity was condoned.

Ama was not so easily ousted, however. There arose during the darkest time a champion infused with the divine light of his lord – the monk Tethys, first of the Pure, bearer of a white-metal sword. Immune to the ravages of sorcery, he led a crusade that destroyed the Warlock King and his monstrous court and returned Menekar and her empire to the sheltering radiance of Ama.

But the knowledge of sorcery could not be suppressed. Across the mountains of the Spine, in the shadow of the decaying wraith kingdoms, walls were being raised against the wilderness. In the fertile lowlands Kalyuni was founded, and soon the first Star Towers thrust towards the sky. Sorcerers now had a new sanctuary to pursue their art, and one by one the Mosaic Cities of the south were bound into a great Imperium. At the same time, in the far north, the holdfasts of Min-Ceruth emerged deep within the towering peaks of the Bones of the World. The wraiths were beaten back into their mountain sanctuaries, and the queens of Nes Vaneth ruled with a merciless splendor.

For centuries the history of Araen was shaped by the rivalry between these three great powers: the holdfasts of Min-Ceruth, the Mosaic Cities of the Kalyuni Imperium, and the vast and etiolated empire of Menekar. The Pure – the paladins of Ama – had taken as their divine task the liberation of man from sorcery and all the evil it brought into the world, but the power of sorcerers was great as well, and for an age the strength of these three realms remained in balance.

The Pure were right to warn against sorcery. When the princess of Nes Vaneth was murdered by a diplomat from Kalyuni, her grieving mother set in motion an ancient spell the sorcerers of the north had long ago constructed as a final devastating strike upon their rivals to the south. The waters of the Derravin Ocean surged over the western mountains and flooded the lands of the Mosaic Cities, creating the Broken Sea. Yet even as the churning water climbed the gleaming walls of their Star Towers, the wizards of the Kalyuni Imperium unleashed their own cataclysmic spell, bringing black ice and endless winter to the Min-Ceruthans.

Two great empires perished that day, entombed within ice or drowned beneath the waves. Menekar wasted no time, dispatching its shining legions and the Pure over the Spine to restore order in the devastation and cleanse what remnants of sorcery remained. Treaties were signed at the point of a white-metal sword between Menekar and the kings and archons and padarashas of the western realms. Sorcery was renounced and any surviving practitioners given over to the paladins of Ama for swift and brutal judgment.

Menekar was not long without a rival, however. For decades the Shan and their Empire of Wind and Salt had wandered upon the waves, fleeing a devastation in their own lost homeland. Now, even as the north convulsed in the aftermath of the cataclysms, the Shan set about recreating their glorious empire in the lands south of the newly formed Broken Sea. They erected towers for their warlocks from the bones of the turtles that had ferried them across the ocean, built mighty cities in the ruins of the Imperium, and once again their brilliant culture flourished as they sought to forget the Raveling that had devoured their ancient lands. An age ended for the Shan, and The Empire of Wind and Salt gave way to the Empire of Swords and Flowers.

For a thousand years afterwards the pulse of magic faded like the heartbeat of a dying man. Until once more it began to quicken . . .

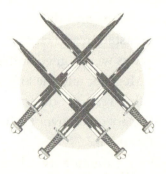

THE STORY SO FAR:
THE CRIMSON QUEEN

KEILAN IS THE son of a fisherman from a tiny village on the shore of the Broken Sea. His mother, who had been plucked from the sea during a storm, was accused of sorcery and put to death by the frightened villagers. His father was nearly broken by this tragedy, numbing his sorrow and rage with drink. Keilan's own power begins to awaken during this time, and while using his sorcery to hunt for fish he accidentally brushes against a vast and terrible presence slumbering beneath the waves. His brief disturbance of this creature brings him to the attention of Dymoria's Crimson Queen, who is the first great sorceress born since the cataclysms. She dispatches her servants to claim him, but a paladin of Ama, Senacus, discovers Keilan first and takes him from his village. Like all children found with the taint of sorcery, Keilan will be brought to Menekar to be cleansed, in the hope that he will rise again filled with the holy light of Ama.

But the queen's magister, Vhelan, and his knife, Nel, rescue Keilan from the Pure and flee. After a harrowing escape from dark sorceries that still lurk in one of Kalyuni's ruined cities, they join a caravan traveling along the ancient northern road. Among their fellow travelers is the seeker Garmond, a scholar of the Reliquary, and his Fist guardsmen. One of the Fist brothers, Xin, becomes friends with Nel and Keilan, and begins to teach them the secrets of his sword fighting. Also among the caravan is a Shan by the name of Cho Yuan. He claims to be searching for something important that was recently stolen from the Empire of Swords and Flowers.

The caravan is attacked by wraiths under the command of a shape-changing monster. Cho Yuan is slain, and Keilan unleashes sorcery that wounds the monster badly enough that it is forced to flee. In order to discover more about the demon that attacked them they descend into the Barrow of Vis, one of the world's great libraries. There the spirit of the Barrow bequeaths several ancient tomes to Keilan, though at the time he does not understand their importance.

With a Visani escort they soon arrive in Herath, the largest city of Dymoria and the seat of Cein d'Kara, the Crimson Queen. Keilan pledges himself to her and joins the Scholia, her school for sorcery. When the queen realizes the depth of Keilan's power she enlists his aid in unlocking the memories of the sorcerer Jan, who has recently arrived in her court and claims to be the last of the vanished Min-Ceruthans. With Keilan's help, Cein passes through the barriers in Jan's mind and discovers he was part of a mysterious cabal of sorcerers who orchestrated the cataclysms that destroyed the old world – all so they could use these deaths to power a spell that would render them immortal.

Even as these truths are laid bare a trap nested by the sorceress Alyanna within Jan's mind is tripped, and a surge of sorcery nearly kills Keilan and the queen. When Keilan awakens soon after, he discovers the queen barely alive and goes to find aid, only to be captured by another of the ancient sorcerers, the swordsinger Demian, and Senacus, the paladin who first took him from his village. While Demian stays behind to interrogate Xin and Nel, Senacus takes Keilan from the palace. Before they can flee the city, however, Keilan reveals that he saw Demian in the memories of Jan, and that the swordsinger is in fact a sorcerer. Shaken by this revelation – though it does confirm his own suspicions about Demian – Senacus abandons Keilan at the gates of Herath.

The next day Keilan discovers that Xin is dead, slain by Demian, who has now disappeared. Nel and Keilan intend to chase after the paladin in the hopes that Senacus can lead them to the vanished swordsinger.

JAN is a farmer in the Shattered Kingdoms. He is plunged into grief after his wife dies of a sickness, and in the depths of his sorrow something happens that awakens long-suppressed memories. To his shock, he realizes he is in fact an immortal sorcerer, though most of his past still remains lost. The incident that triggered this revelation was a murder committed by some sort of supernatural creature near his farm, and Jan comes to believe this was done to wake him. He follows the creature's trail, until he arrives in the pleasure gardens of the Menekarian Empire. There he meets Alyanna, who claims to know him, though his own memories of her are indistinct. She tells him magic is returning to the world, and that a great sorceress has arisen in the far west: Cein d'Kara of Dymoria. Alyanna promises to restore his lost memories if he investigates this Crimson Queen for her. Jan asks about the creatures he has chased across the plains, and Alyanna tells him they are her new servants, recently freed from imprisonment in Shan. Despite his wariness, Alyanna convinces him that they are firmly under her control.

Jan travels to the kingdom of Dymoria, and Cein d'Kara quickly unmasks him as a powerful sorcerer. Curious about his missing past, she agrees to try and break through the barriers in Jan's mind. During the ceremony, a magical trap laid by

Alyanna is triggered and the queen and Keilan are nearly killed. In her anger, Cein decides to imprison Jan until she can be sure that he is no longer a pawn of Alyanna.

ALYANNA is an immortal sorceress who has lurked in the shadows for over a thousand years. It was her magical brilliance that crafted the spell that rendered a secret group of wizards immortal, including Jan and Demian. To her distress, she finds that the potency of this spell is fading, and she has begun to age again.

In recent years, Alyanna has posed as a concubine in the pleasure gardens of the Menekarian emperor, hoping to unravel the mysteries of the Pure, though she has become intrigued by her new servants, the Shan demon-children that call themselves the Chosen. She heard them calling from their prison inside the bone-shard towers of Tsai Yin and freed them in return for their servitude. Alyanna learns from the Chosen that a demon hunter from Shan is searching for them, and that he wields a weapon capable of imprisoning their spirits again. She dispatches another of her servants, the shape-changing genthyaki, to slay the demon hunter Cho Yuan. He is traveling with a merchant caravan to Dymoria because he believes it was Cein d'Kara who liberated the demons. During an assault on the caravan Cho Yuan is slain, but the genthyaki is badly wounded by the sorcery of the boy Keilan. Alyanna learns from the dying genthyaki that Keilan is a Talent, a rare and powerful breed of sorcerer. Hoping to use Keilan to recreate the spell that granted her immortality she sends Demian west to capture the boy.

Meanwhile, Alyanna forges an alliance with the dreaded kith'ketan shadowblades, enlisting their aid to destroy the Crimson Queen before Cein can become a true rival to her power. Alyanna's web of plots comes together on a single night, as the trap she laid within Jan's mind is triggered by Cein just as Demian and the shadowblades invade the queen's fortress in search of Keilan. Alyanna transports herself inside the palace and challenges the weakened queen, but is defeated when the Chosen refuse to obey her commands. She is forced to flee back to Menekar, where she is captured by the genthyaki she thought had perished. Now the creature serves the Chosen, having been succored back to health through their dark magics. He is consumed by the desire to inflict suffering upon his former mistress.

THE STORY SO FAR:
THE SILVER SORCERESS

CHO LIN IS the daughter of the Shan demon hunter Cho Yuan. While training on Red Fang Mountain, she is brought word that her father has been slain in the barbarian lands when hunting the Betrayers – the demons that ushered in the Raveling that destroyed the ancient homeland of the Shan. Shocked to hear that her father is dead and that the demons are loose again in the world, she travels to her family's compound and is told by her crippled brother about the shape-changing monster who slew their father. He gives her the famed sword of her family – the weapon that bound the Betrayers a thousand years ago – and she departs for the northern lands to find the demons and avenge her father.

In the Shan port city of Ras Ami, Cho Lin is recognized by a childhood friend and invited to her manse. While drinking wine, Cho Lin is poisoned, and she discovers that her old friend has been corrupted by the Raveling, the death cult that worships the Betrayers. Using her training to overcome the effects of the poison, Cho Lin slays her once-friend. Trusting no one, she leaves her family's soldiers behind and sets sail for the northern city of Herath. According to her brother, a powerful northern sorcerer freed the Betrayers from their prison in the city of Tsai Yin, and the warlocks of Shan suspect it was the newly arisen Crimson Queen of Dymoria.

After the long voyage to Herath, Cho Lin begins her investigations by sneaking inside the queen's great fortress of Saltstone. Once inside, she discovers that her sword can sense the residue of the Betrayers, and she follows this trail to a locked room in a ruined tower. Inside she finds the sorcerer Jan, imprisoned for his accidental role in Alyanna's attack on the queen and her Scholia. Cho Lin frees him after he claims to know the whereabouts of the Betrayers, and they flee the city, though the magister Vhelan catches up with them before they get too far. Realizing that any attempt to recapture Jan would end in bloodshed, and believing that this is something the queen would not want, Vhelan allows them to escape.

While traveling along the Wending Way, Jan slips away from Cho Lin and journeys into the Frostlands. Incensed by his betrayal, and realizing that only he can help her find the Betrayers, Cho Lin follows him. She is saved from a pack of wraiths by a Skein warband, and she learns that Jan is traveling to Nes Vaneth, the ancient, ruined city of his people and now the seat of power of the barbarian Skein. Cho Lin also learns that a civil war has recently happened among the barbarians, with several tribes from the north overthrowing the Skein king because of his perceived weakness. She arrives in Nes Vaneth and finds Jan has become an honored guest of the new king.

Jan tells her that after the attack on Saltstone his lost memories came flooding back, and he now remembers that beneath Nes Vaneth the Min-Ceruthan queen forged a great sorcery to protect her child from the black ice called down by the southern sorcerers. This child may also be Jan's child, as he was once the queen's lover. The sorceress Alyanna had effaced these memories from his mind long ago when he came to her for help in freeing the child from its prison of ice.

They descend beneath the city, and after discovering that the ice child is gone they are ambushed by the Betrayers and the Skein. One of the barbarians is revealed to be a powerful sorcerer, and Jan and Cho Lin are captured.

The immortal sorceress **Alyanna** is languishing in the catacombs beneath the Selthari Palace, tortured by the inquisitors of Ama and the shape-changing genthyaki. Her old servant has taken the form of Menekar's Black Vizier, and by his orders she was Cleansed: her sorcery has been cut away, and into the hollow left behind was poured the holy light of the Pure.

After months of torture, her ancient ally Demian penetrates the catacombs and rescues her. They flee across the white plains, but are hunted down by paladins of Ama. Demian is badly wounded in the fight, and he convinces Alyanna that they should seek shelter with the kith'ketan, a mysterious order of assassins that dwells beneath a mountain in the range known as the Spine. He lived among them for centuries, and believes that their leader, the Daymo, will aid them. Alyanna is surprised to learn that the mountain fastness of the kith'ketan is the same place where she performed the ceremony that resulted in her immortality a thousand years ago.

Demian recovers, and they are summoned by the creature worshipped by the kith'ketan, which dwells deep beneath the mountain. When they arrive in its presence, it offers to restore Alyanna's sorcery if she can fulfill the promise she made that first secured their alliance against the Crimson Queen – bring a great Talent into its lair and sacrifice the sorcerer. Rather than leave to hunt down the boy Keilan, as Demian suggests, Alyanna stabs her old friend. The creature under the mountain inhabits his dying body, then restores Alyanna's lost sorcery. Without allies, and fearing the threat of her old servants – the genthyaki and the Chosen – Alyanna reaches out to the Crimson Queen and offers a truce and an alliance.

Grieving the death of his friend and mentor Xin, **Keilan** and Nel and a troop of Dymorian rangers pursue the paladin Senacus south after the attack on Saltstone. The Pure is the only link to those who perpetrated the assault, which nearly killed the queen. They catch up with Senacus just outside the gates of Lyr, one of the Gilded Cities, but the commander of the Lyrish guards takes them all into custody, fearing what would happen if Dymorian swords slew a paladin of Ama just outside the city gates.

The ruling archons of Lyr summon Keilan before the Council of Black and White to discover why this has happened and what they should do, but they are interrupted by an emissary from the famed Oracle of Lyr. She leads Keilan, Nel and Senacus to the coral temple of the Oracle, where they are given a vision of one possible future that the Oracle wishes to avoid. In this vision, demonic children battle a sorceress in the ruins of Menekar, and the rest of the world has been laid waste. To Keilan's surprise, he realizes that the silver-haired sorceress looks very much like his mother and also one of the sorceresses that he saw in Jan's memories, when Alyanna's ancient cabal performed the ceremony that granted them immortality. The Crone of Lyr, one of the most powerful women in the city, convinces Keilan that the reason the Oracle shared this vision with him was because she wants him to find this sorceress who can challenge the demon children. She suspects he must have some connection to her.

Keilan, Nel, and Senacus set out for Keilan's village, hoping to find some clue about his dead mother that will help lead them to the sorceress. Along the way, they stop in the Reliquary of Ver Anath and see their old friend, the scholar Garmond. From him they learn about the Raveling, the great cataclysm that destroyed the old lands of Shan, and the demon children responsible for bringing down that tragedy.

They travel the Iron Road, finally arriving in Keilan's village. There they discover that once, when in the grip of a fever, his mother spoke of a famed pirate lord, who has retired on an island in the Broken Sea. They travel to the island, Ven Ibras, and learn that Keilan's mother lived there briefly before fleeing when strange robed creatures came searching for her. The same creatures seek out Keilan, and bring him to the island of the immortal sorceress Niara, where it is revealed that she is his grandmother. She takes him on as an apprentice, alluding to the great things they must someday do together, and he learns about her life work of helping mankind avoid the fate of all the other intelligent species that came before. She also reveals that long ago the warlocks of Shan sought her out to help craft a weapon that could destroy the Betrayers, which she is still in possession of.

While Keilan is learning sorcery, his childhood friend Sella discovers a room full of strange dolls, one of which warns her about Niara. The sorceress's servants imprison Keilan's companions for the theft of the doll. Senacus escapes and confronts Niara, and the sorceress is enraged when he reveals himself to be a paladin of Ama. In the resulting fight, Keilan is cut by the knife imbued with the blood of the Betrayers, and when trying to save Senacus he accidentally kills Niara. He is distraught as they return to Ven Ibras with the weapon, but resolves to bring the knife to the only person he knows who can wield such an artifact: the Crimson Queen.

THE
SHADOW
KING

PROLOGUE
12 Years ago

PERCHED UPON THE dead man's face, the raven dipped its head towards where Algeirr knelt in the snow, as if asking for his permission before feasting.

No, not permission – it paid homage to the one who had delivered up this bounty.

Algeirr traced the jagged rent in the dead warrior's ringmail hauberk, forcing himself to look – truly look – at what his actions had wrought. His nephew's patchy yellow beard was crusted with ice; his eyes, blue as the northern sky, were wide and staring. Upon his pale cheeks, the bird's claws left faint indentations. The wind gusted, ruffling the dead man's wolf-fur cloak, stirring his lank hair.

Beneath the links of his armor a blacker iron glinted. Algeirr's fingers sought and found a tiny hammer scrawled with silvery runes, strung on a thread of wraithgut. A heavy sadness filled his chest. Algeirr rubbed the amulet between his thumb and forefinger, murmuring the Stormforger's lament for the slain, the ruined city around him receding as he reached for his god.

His nephew had still believed. His nephew had held fast to the old ways, despite the Gray King's heresies.

The raven pecked at the dead man's eye, tearing loose a clot of glistening tissue. Algeirr lashed out at the bird and it rose into the air, shrieking.

"So the raven feasts upon its own," came a young man's voice, faintly mocking.

Algeirr tucked the amulet back under the dead warrior's roughspun tunic and raised his head. The fighting in the city must have ended, for around him had gathered the great Skein lords of the southern Frostlands: thanes of the Wolf, Bear, and Stag, men who pastured and sowed and raided across the tumbling Serpent. And beside them, slightly apart as was their wont, were the thanes from the harsher north, Iron and Ghost and White Worm clansmen, paler and more gaunt, their lips set in thin lines. Some had been wounded in the day's fighting and leaned exhaustedly upon greatswords streaked with dried blood. Others stood tall, cheeks flushed from the battle's savage thrill. Their breath ghosted the frozen air.

Algeirr stood, wincing as his knees protested, and faced the speaker. Agmandur the Young Bear met his gaze briefly, then looked away, his smile fading.

"Do you mean me, stripling, or the bird?" Algeirr said bitterly.

The Thane of the Bear forced a chuckle. "The bird, Priest. The bird."

Algeirr gestured at the dead warrior sprawled in the blood stained snow. "This was Svartun, my nephew. He used to clutch at my leg and beg for tales of Brigga Bluespear and Gorm One-Eye. I whittled for him his first wooden sword so that in the dark he would not fear the Nightfather."

The Wolf lord, Hert, tall and gray and lean, stepped forward and laid his hand on Algeirr's shoulder. "We know the burden you bear, old one. It is almost finished."

"Yes," Algeirr said, turning from the thanes and squinting up at the mass of stone looming above them. "The end is near."

Just one final, terrible task remained. No man was more cursed in the eyes of the gods than the kinslayer – yet what if that deed was done to save the gods themselves?

They stood in the shadow of the Bhalavan, the Hall of Heroes, where dozens of Skein kings had felt the cold kiss of the blackbone crown upon their brows. Cracked pillars flanked massive bronze doors covered by the squirming runes of fallen Min-Ceruth, the mysterious writing half obscured by snowdrifts that piled twice the height of a man.

Countless times Algeirr had slipped inside and found his clansmen seated at long tables, being served great haunches of aurochs and bear by shuffling thralls, hefting stone pitchers brimming with mead as they laughed and boasted and sang. But there would be no song inside the Hall of Heroes this day; the men he had feasted with and loved as brothers were dead, motionless in the snow like Svartun, feathered with the blackfletched arrows of the Ghost clan, or with their iron helms riven by double-bladed Stag axes.

A wave of dizziness washed over Algeirr, almost driving him to his knees again. What had he done?

"W-w-wait!"

Algeirr paused, his hand on the greening bronze of the door, and turned back to the city. An elder and a young boy were threading their way between the corpses scattered across the great square, a small flock of carrion birds taking wing as they passed. With a cry the boy stumbled, collapsing in the snow, and the graybeard hauled him to his feet.

Beyond them the city of Nes Vaneth spread in all its broken, tumbled glory – an endless vista of shattered stone and ice, its crumbling buildings sunk in snow, sundered arches curving together like the ribs of giants, and the jagged remnants of pale green crystal towers stabbing the sky. Smoke billowed from beyond the distant gates, smearing the cloudless blue. Not long ago Algeirr had stood and watched as the warriors of the gathered Skein clans had pulled weeping women and children from the Raven longhouses and then set the buildings aflame, trying his best to harden his heart against their screams for mercy. But it was impossible. Despair continued to grow inside him, an emptiness gnawing at his certainty that this was what the gods demanded.

He waited with the thanes at the Bhalavan's great doors.

"Who are you, old man?" said Kjartan of the Stag when the graybeard finally reached them, the polished bone of his helm's tines flashing in the sun.

"M-m-my n-name is—is—"

"Onndar," finished Agmandur, and he looked little pleased to see his clansman.

"A skald," said Hroi, his voice whisper-quiet. Though Hroi was barely more than a boy, Algeirr sensed that the White Worm thane was the most dangerous of the gathered Skein lords. From his shoulders hung the checkered cloak of the Skin Thief, the blackest of the Skein gods, and it was rumored that one of those cured swatches belonged to his own father, the old thane of the White Worm. "He comes to see a king cast down, and another raised to take his place. Every song must have an ending – right, singer?"

Onndar nodded, visibly relieved to be spared the struggles of an explanation.

Hroi's bloodless lips curved into a slight smile. "The Stammering Skald – even at the edge of the barrowlands we have heard of you."

"And this one?" the Wolf thane, Hert, asked, his mouth tight with anger, pointing at the wide-eyed boy.

"M-m-my ward, my s-sister's child."

"This is not a place for babes," Hert said disdainfully. "Nor for singers."

But Algeirr knew why the skald had joined them. There would be many a lay composed about this day, and Onndar wanted *his* song to be the one on the lips of every singer in the

Frostlands. The Raven thanes had worn the black-bone crown for nearly seven hundred years, and having it pass to another clan would have seemed a rank impossibility only a few years ago. After all, many of these same lords had sworn fealty and stood shoulder to shoulder with the Gray King four years past at Icebridge during the Red Thane's rebellion, when the upstart Fox clan had been extinguished and the Raven's primacy reinforced. Yet, somehow, the seeds of their destruction had been planted that very day, as it had been during Gunmunder's long convalescence from his wounds that his strange heresies had been born.

Onndar had come to see a king unmade ... and to see who would be bold enough to take up the fallen crown.

Algeirr cleared his throat noisily and spat. "Enough prattle," he said, then entered the darkened hall, pausing after only a few steps so that his eyes could adjust. The massive iron braziers that had once blazed night and day were dead, the cook pits filled with mounded gray ash. It seemed the hall had not hosted many celebrations in recent days. A bone-deep chill filled the room, and something else as well, the sense of being watched ...

There. Movement beneath one of the long feast tables, among the shadows. Algeirr strode closer, gripping the hammer hanging around his neck, a demon-banishing prayer upon his lips, but stopped when he saw what huddled there. Only a girl, clutching a ragged purple shawl around herself – some thrall from below the Serpent, her dusky skin marking her as Myrasani, or perhaps from iron-walled Vis. She shrank back from him, murmuring something in her lilting tongue, and he snorted and turned away.

"What's that?" asked Gerdin, the hard-eyed thane of the Iron clan, peering past him. All the thanes had by now assembled inside the bronze doors, though none had ventured very far into the cold and forbidding hall.

"The spoils of war," Agmandur said, making a show of adjusting his belt. "And I've half a mind to despoil this spoil here and now." Laughter rumbled among the Skein.

Algeirr beckoned for them to follow him deeper into the hall. "The Stormforger watches us, do not doubt. Let us show him we are true warriors of the Frostlands."

"True warriors would have the girl and *then* kill the king," Agmandur muttered behind him, but Algeirr ignored the Bear thane and led them past the feast tables and into the far shadows of the Bhalavan, where strange shapes reared out of the darkness. Great stone warriors resolved from the murk as they approached, the long-dead heroes or kings or gods of Min-Ceruth – Algeirr did not know which. They watched the intruders with empty gray eyes, swords and lances upraised. On the shoulder of one perched a falcon, wings spread, its head a nub of chipped stone, and around the forearm of another a serpent coiled, scaled with strange designs.

Beyond the statues an arched passage curved away into blackness. Algeirr drew forth a torch, and after a few long moments of striking flint to stone, a spark finally caught, and firelight pushed back the dark. His hands were shaking badly. *Ageran, Stormforger, give me strength!*

He led them through twisting corridors that sloped downward, deeper and deeper into the Bhalavan. They passed entrances to cells where the Jugurtha, the warriors whose axes had been sworn to defend the Raven King unto death, had once slept – Algeirr had been surprised to see their black-horned helms earlier, in the pitched battle near the Winding Stair, where the spine of the Raven defense had been broken. The Jugurtha would not have left the king's side unless commanded by Gunmunder himself. Why send them away? Did he think the Raven powerful enough to defeat the combined strength of six other clans? Or did he know himself damned and mercifully allow his sworn axes to die defending hearths and wives instead of a madman's folly?

Burning gobbets of fat dripped from Algeirr's torch, hissing briefly upon the cracked stones before vanishing. *Like the souls of men. Flaring bright for a brief moment and then swallowed by darkness.*

Such thoughts! They did not befit a priest of the Stormforger. He shook his head to clear it of blasphemy – any Skein who had stayed true to the gods and died in glorious battle would be carried in the beaks of the dark-winged flock to the High Halls, and be feasted by those who had already journeyed into the Nightfather's shadowy realm. So it was written in the epics.

The corridor jagged left and opened into a large room, its ceiling lost in shadows and the floor beneath the strewn rushes a mosaic of blue-and-white glazed tiles. The straw scattered about was dry and brittle, and clearly had not been changed for weeks, and the pallet looked as if no one had slept in it for at least as long. Where was the magnificent silver bear-pelt blanket that had swaddled Gunmunder during his long sickness? Algeirr had knelt beside this same bed for weeks, lost in prayers to the Green Mother, watching his sleeping king's ashen face twitch and grimace. The demon had been whispering to him then, in his dreams, he now knew. Seducing him. Had the king succumbed easily, weakened by his sickness, or had Gunmunder turned his soul into a battlefield, fighting against the false promises and poisoned words? Was there a part of him that resisted still?

"Where now, priest?" growled Kjartan, glancing around the empty room. "If Gunmunder has fled the city while we've been standing around his bedchamber, I'll have your ugly head."

Algeirr stalked to the far side of the sleeping pallet and gestured for the trailing thanes to follow him. A few gasped when they saw that he stood at the edge of a black pit crudely hacked through the ancient tiled floor.

"It is as you told," Ferrin Oathsealer said, crouching beside the opening and lowering his gleaming ebonwood bow into the darkness. Before the man-tall bow had completely vanished, it struck stone, and the Ghost thane glanced up at Algeirr, who struggled to meet the albino's unsettling eyes. "Only five spans deep," Ferrin said, frowning.

"At first we must crouch," Algeirr said, his mouth suddenly dry. "But the passage grows larger quickly."

Hert kicked at a loose chunk of tile, sending it tumbling into the black. "For so many centuries this was unknown to those sleeping above . . . what squatted down there, listening in the darkness?"

Algeirr fought back a shudder. The ancient Min-Ceruthans had been a sorcerous people, and none knew what abominations their magics had birthed. They had raised Nes Vaneth and her sister cities from the womb of the world, shaping stone like a potter might clay, twisting the very fabric of these lands to their whims. The southern traders had told him that the Iskannatum, the black devouring ice, had been the dying counterstroke of another race of sorcerers, the magi of the drowned Mosaic Cities, but Algeirr still preferred the tale he had heard as a child around the hearth fire – that the Stormforger had destroyed the Min-Ceruthans for their presumptions. Sorcery was a vile and wicked thing, and the gods could not abide those who aspired to make themselves the equal of the divine.

They stood at the edge of the pit, shifting their feet and glancing at one another, until Hroi stepped forward, his mirthless laughter echoing.

"What frightened women we are!" he cried, drawing his famous sword, Night's Kiss, the clouded amber blade hissing like a serpent as it slid from its sheath. "If you wish to wait here, I'll bring back the black-bone crown, but it will be on my brow and you'd all best bend the knee!" With a derisive snort he leaped into the darkness, his mottled cloak flaring behind him.

Agmandur cursed and followed, his great shoulders barely clearing the edges of the hole. He reached up to help Algeirr climb down, and then the others followed, though less gracefully, not as limber as the two young thanes.

Before and behind them the passage vanished into blackness. Adjusting his sweaty grip on the haft of his torch, Algeirr pushed his way past the younger thanes and led the way forward, his other hand clutching the Stormforger's amulet. The hammer's iron seemed warm to the touch. He did not turn to see if the others followed him, and for a brief, terrifying moment he imagined that he crept alone through the tunnel. Then he heard Agmandur curse again when his head bumped the low ceiling, and other sounds soon reverberated in the tight passage: boots scuffing on stone, the clink of mail and weapons, the labored breathing of those who had suffered wounds.

"Ageran's black hammer!" Kjartan suddenly bellowed, and Algeirr turned to see the huge Stag thane looming over the aged skald. He had left his tined helm in the chamber above, and Kjartan's long red braids swung as he furiously shook his head. "Tell the whelp to keep his hands to himself!"

The boy's eyes, round and white and terrified, peered from behind Onndar.

"Th-the b-b-b – child – w-will be more c-c-care—" the skald began, but before he could finish, Kjartan waved him silent and rounded on Agmandur, his disgust plain.

"How did your father stomach *this* one? I'd have torn his tongue out years ago!"

The Young Bear shrugged, and then he said, grinning faintly, "He sings beautifully."

Kjartan muttered something unintelligible, and Algeirr turned away so the thane would not see his own smile.

They continued on, the Stag thane grumbling to himself, down a steep flight of stairs and past wall sconces carved into the faces of leering demons, the passage swelling until they could all comfortably walk upright. Algeirr heard the trickle of running water, and once something scurried over his boot, disappearing before he could see it clearly. Soon after, Hert stumbled and then had to lean upon Ferrin so he would not fall behind. The Wolf thane had taken an arrow between his shoulders earlier, and now his breathing rasped loud and wet. They all knew that the Nightfather waited in the shadows for him, but Hert's face was grim and determined. A true Skein, the old Wolf. He would have been the perfect choice to take up the crown; Algeirr worried that none of the other thanes could claim the Frostlands without further bloodshed.

A blue glow arose at the far edge of his fading torchlight. Almost there. He had returned to the place of his nightmares, with the greatest champions of his people behind him, and yet his heart did not swell with joy and righteous anger. Fear. He felt fear again, as he had the first time he followed Gunmunder down into this abyss to gaze upon the abomination hanging cold and blue in its prison of ice. He remembered the dread wonder thrumming in his veins . . . three years had passed since that cursed day, yet the memory was fresh and immediate, while the intervening seasons seemed lost in mist. Endless days trudging between halls, pleading and cajoling and threatening the thanes so that an alliance could be forged to save the old ways, before the demon they had discovered here in the bowels of Nes Vaneth could devour the very gods themselves.

The glow strengthened, until Algeirr cast aside his guttering torch and rounded on the Skein following him. Blue light limned their armor and weapons and gave their faces the pallid color of frozen corpses. They watched him expectantly.

"Three years ago," Algeirr began, reaching for the voice of his god, the crash and rumble of Ageran the Stormforger, "Gunmunder brought the priests of our clan to this place and demanded that they cast aside the gods and embrace his mad new faith. Instead, each repudiated him, and in return the Raven King collected their heads with his sword, soaking the ice with their blood in an attempt to wake that which slumbered. Only I was spared, despite my own refusal." Algeirr let his eyes linger on each of the faces before him. "Now I have returned, the old gods are triumphant, and the final blow is poised to fall. Let us strike quickly and mercilessly."

Muttered assent followed as he turned again to the glow creeping from around the bend in the passage before them. He moved forward, and was swallowed by the light.

They stood at the entrance to a vast chamber filled with stone statues carved with the same exacting detail as above in the Bhala-van, except here they writhed in contorted agony, shielding their faces, knees buckling as if confronted by some blinding horror. Tiered stone steps climbed the space before them, and upon the final dais a massive wall of ice rose, seamless and gleaming. The light that filled the chamber emanated from the ice itself, flickering like a flame without heat, casting shadows that coiled and danced across the stricken figures.

And there he was. The Gray King, Gunmunder, standing tall and crooked upon the final step, a black stone set into the roiling blue light of the ice behind him. He leaned upon the storied runesword Kalikurvan of the Raven thanes, much of the blade's silvery length lost behind his great beard. The king's head was bowed, as if he slept. The curved talons of the black-bone crown glittered, clawing the air.

A few steps below him sat Horth Wraithsbane, the last of the Jugurtha, a notched bastard sword set across his lap. The massive warrior scowled when he recognized Algeirr, glancing up at his king. The old priest felt a trickle of apprehension. Here was the greatest champion of the Raven, famed across the Frostlands. As a boy, Horth had been part of a hunting party that lost its way in a blinding snowstorm and was set upon by a pack of wraiths. One by one his clansmen had died, until only he remained. But as the shadows closed on him, they found not hot blood and soft flesh but the hard kiss of steel. After his sword had snapped in the bitter cold he slew the final wraith – a great bull with flaming red eyes and blue talons – by plunging his hunting knife into its breast as it hugged him close and crooned its dark song.

"Brother," rasped the old king, raising his head.

Cold dread closed around Algeirr's heart. Blood trickled from the sunken pits where once Gunmunder's eyes had been, following dried black paths that veined his cheeks.

"You have returned to us."

Algeirr tried to keep the tremors from his voice. "Yes, Brother. As I said I would. But how can you see me? What have you done?"

Gunmunder's answering chuckle was bone-dry. "I see far more, Brother, than I ever did. Before, it was only in my dreams that I could glimpse the glory of this place – now, it surrounds me always."

"Madness," hissed Kjartan.

"Madness," repeated Gunmunder, though Algeirr did not know how he had heard the Stag thane, "is the refuge we crawled into after the light failed and the darkness came swirling down." The Gray King's voice echoed in the vast chamber. *Down, down, down . . .*

"Like a corpse upon the bier we placed coins over our own eyes, hoping that this would be enough to pay our passage through the Night and into the Dawn." Gunmunder made a plucking motion over his empty sockets. "I was the first to glimpse the light around the edges of our blindness, but I will not be the last. My awakening came too early, perhaps, but in time you all will see what I have seen."

"And what do you see?" Hert asked.

Gunmunder lifted his head higher at the Wolf thane's question. "The world as it was, and what it could be again."

Algeirr remembered the first breathless descriptions Gunmunder had given when he had finally awoken from his long fever dreams. Avenues of shining white stone strode by men in lacquered masks, the living city answering to their world-cracking voices. Beautiful maids sailing upon the wind with butterfly wings. The towers whole and unbroken, wrapped by vines studded with bright blossoms. Nes Vaneth's vanished glory, reverberating through the ages.

A lure with honey-sweet promises. What man, squatting in furs and iron among the ruins of such ancient grandeur, would not be tempted to trade away his soul for a taste of what had come before?

"Enough of your babbling," Hroi said, shouldering his way to stand before the Skein. "We who live in the shadow of the Worm have glimpsed the past as well, yet we know it is dead and rotted, and we do not yearn to return it to shambling life." Night's Kiss fairly crackled, a shimmering haze surrounding the sword's strange metal. Hroi laughed and cut the air with the blade. "She's hungering for your blood, my king. She smells the stink of Min-Ceruthan sorcery upon you."

Horth rose ponderously to his towering height, taking up his own sword, and slowly began to descend.

As if an unspoken agreement had passed between them, the two Skein heroes rushed each other, Hroi bounding up the cracked stone steps, silent as a hunting wraith, while Horth barreled towards him bellowing a war cry.

The Raven champion chopped down with his sword but Hroi caught the blow with Night's Kiss, and with a terrible shrieking sound Horth's blade shattered, fragments spinning away into the gloom. The huge warrior's momentum carried him hurtling down the steps and the White Worm thane twisted away to avoid him, lashing out as he tumbled past, his sword biting deep. Without a sound, the last of the Jugurtha crumpled at the base of the steps, his face a bloody ruin.

Shocked silence, and then the Gray King spoke. "Is this what you want?" cried Gunmunder, holding aloft the black-bone crown.

"Take it, then," he finished, and flung it toward the thanes. The crown rang sharply upon the stone floor, but did not shatter, and came to rest at the feet of the Young Bear. The thanes converged on him, all speaking at once. Hroi hurried down the steps and pushed into their midst, jostling for space.

Above them, Gunmunder slowly turned away and moved towards the glistening blue wall. Algeirr abandoned the thanes to their argument and climbed the steps as fast as his old legs would allow, until he stood panting upon the final dais. The ice loomed over him, alive with dancing blue flames, and he glimpsed shapes recessed deep within, some man-like, others not. Coldness radiated from the wall like heat from a fire, stinging his exposed flesh. The Raven king seemed not to notice the chill, his bare hand touching the ice and his head lowered as if in prayer. Algeirr approached him, the soft scuffing of his boots lost beneath the heated babble of voices from below.

Yet Gunmunder still heard. He spoke without turning from the wall. "Kill me, Brother. Send me to her arms."

It was then that Algeirr noticed the shape hanging within the ice, just beyond where Gunmunder's fingers touched the slick surface. A babe's blue-tinged body, its eyes closed and tiny mouth open.

Revulsion filled Algeirr. He remembered the steaming blood of old Berand Godsinger splashed upon the ice, Gunmunder imploring the child to wake as he stood over the headless corpses of the Raven priests. The madness of that day still haunted his dreams.

"I thought by now you would have cut into the ice," Algeirr said, drawing forth his dagger.

Gunmunder leaned forward, resting his forehead against the wall. "I could not," he said softly.

Algeirr nodded. He understood his brother. What if the babe was nothing but cold, dead flesh? Algeirr stepped forward, poised to slip his dagger between the gaps in his brother's armor, but Gunmunder stilled him with a word.

"No," he murmured, thrusting out his sword's hilt. "Use Kalikurvan. I would die by the sword of my ancestors, wielded by my closest kin. It is a fitting death."

Algeirr's gnarled fingers closed around the runesword's hilt, smooth metal carved into a falcon's likeness, its outstretched wings the crosspiece. Shimmering runes were incised down the blade's silvery length. How many years since his father had let him touch this sword? He remembered that day, his older brother boasting to him that eventually he would wield Kalikurvan and rule all the Frostlands, and then his father's indulgent laughter filling the Bhalavan. A lifetime past.

He lifted the blade and brought it down upon his brother's bowed neck. The spell-forged steel passed through flesh and bone without the slightest hesitation. Algeirr closed his eyes, not wanting to see Gunmunder's corpse slide to the floor and the gouts of blood that would flow across the stone. He felt no joy, only a sense of closure, and a great weight being lifted. He could turn the blade on himself now if he so chose, end the line of Vesteinn Croweater and join his ancestors in their eternal feasting upon the Stormforger's high benches. His grip upon the sword's hilt tightened. He imagined the cold point sliding through his belly, bringing release and freedom from the tragedies of this world, his limbs slackening in the Nightfather's comforting embrace.

No. There was still something he must do.

Exhaustion washed over him as he opened his eyes. Algeirr stepped over his brother's corpse and faced the thing hanging in the wall. He raised Kalikurvan and smashed the runesword's pommel against the ice. Cracks webbed the surface, shards falling away . . . again and again he struck, gouging chunks from the wall until one tiny foot extended into the chamber. Carefully, he scraped more of the ice away, marveling at the softness of the babe's flesh despite its centuries of imprisonment. Finally, the child slid free into his arms, cold and blue and dead.

Algeirr brushed closed the babe's purple lips. It had been a girl, he could now tell. All the terror, all the tragedy had come from this, and yet really it was just a small dead thing, some innocent victim of eons-old sorcery. What madness, Algeirr thought, clutching the tiny corpse to his chest.

And it moved.

He nearly dropped it when he felt its leg twitch, and before he could dismiss it as some trick of his tired mind, the babe drew in a shuddering breath and wailed. Tiny fingers groped for him, tangled in his beard. Pale blue eyes opened and found his own. *Impossible.*

His first instinct was to swaddle it in furs, to shelter this spark of life in the desolate frozen hall, but his mind screamed at him to dash the babe against the ice. *Demon!* Algeirr raised the squirming body, his arms trembling.

But then he knew. He felt the god's voice, gentling his soul, purging him of his hate and fear. The whispers boomed within him. Twice before, Ageran had spoken to him: once when he had been a boy crouched over his first steaming kill, telling him that he had been chosen to take up the hammer and drink of the blessed mead; and the other time in this very chamber, as the blood of his fellow priests coursed along the cracks threading the ancient stone floor, revealing what he must do, the hard path he must follow. And now it came again, showing him the way forward, like a lightning strike on a moonless night.

Algeirr lowered the babe, cradling it in the crook of his arm as he turned from the wall. Below, the knot of arguing Skein quieted as he descended the stairs, the silence broken by the shriek of the runesword's tip scraping stone.

Onndar the skald was the first to speak. "He-he's d-d-dead, then?"

The thanes shrank away as he reached the final step – all except Hroi, who actually leaned forward to better see the unnatural child he held.

"My brother is dead," Algeirr said, shielding the babe from the gaze of the White Worm thane.

"And what will you do with *that*?" Hert hissed through teeth gritted with pain.

"The Stormforger has told me." Algeirr strode across the chamber and laid Kalikurvan across the outstretched arms of a cowering stone maiden. "I will leave you thanes to choose a new king to rule in Nes Vaneth. Where I go, I must go alone. Do not follow me. And never speak of this day, nor of what was drawn from the ice."

"Algeirr—" Ferrin began, but the old priest held up a hand to silence him.

"Swear on your clan's heartsblood, lest the Nightfather's shadow darken your hall."

Algeirr waited until he heard mumbled promises from all the thanes and the ancient skald, and then with a final, lingering look upon the dread chamber, he carried the ice-child into the twisting passage that led upward, to Nes Vaneth and daylight.

1: CHO LIN

SHE MOVED AMONG the dead in a chamber of ice. The corpses watched her with frost-rimed eyes, traceries of blue veins sunk beneath their pale skin. Some of the dead were clad in ancient, ornate armor, runes carved into black-metal cuirasses, while others wore the tattered remnants of once-fine dresses, tarnished silver torcs and bracelets hanging loose around their withered limbs. Many had raised their arms, as if in an attempt to ward away the doom that had come swirling down from above.

Cho Lin found herself at the base of the tiered dais that dominated the vast, silent hall. She began to climb the steps, and the scrape of her slippers on the stone sounded unnaturally loud. Before her loomed the wall of ice, its depths illuminated by a cold blue light. She shivered, her lungs burning with every gasping breath she took of the frozen air. Cho Lin glanced down, and was surprised to find that she wore only the red tunic and black breeches of an apprentice daisun monk. How foolish, to journey into the far north dressed like this. Her father would have chastised her.

Cho Lin reached the top of the dais. Shapes roiled deep within the ice, blooming and then wilting. She concentrated, trying to discern their true nature, but the effort only left her dizzy, and she had to put her hand on the surface of the ice to steady herself. The wall was not seamless – a hole had been crudely hacked at about eye level, and gleaming shards were scattered on the floor. There had been a babe here once, she had been told, placed within the ice long ago to protect it as the sorcery of the Star Towers had consumed the holdfasts. Cho Lin approached the wall. Who had drawn the babe from its prison? Had it survived, as the Skein king had claimed?

Wait – there *was* a tiny body inside, entombed deep within the wall. She could see a pale blue arm, its small fingers curled into a fist. Her heart hammering, Cho Lin reached inside the hole, until her shoulder bumped against the wall. The tips of her fingers brushed the babe's hand, and the prickling coldness almost made her recoil.

But she did not, and beneath her touch she felt the child twitch. Its small hand clutched at her finger.

Pain.

Cho Lin screamed, trying to withdraw her arm, but it was held fast. Her other hand pushed frantically against the surface of the wall; the thing inside was too strong, though, and she was pulled forward, her body ground into the ice. She felt a pop as her shoulder slipped from its socket. The agony was unbearable; it was going to rip off her arm. Sobbing, her legs collapsed, yet she did not fall; the unnatural strength of the thing within the ice kept her upright.

She fought against the blackness that threatened to carry her away. Sharp, stabbing pain enveloped her wrist. She struggled to understand what was happening, her mind unable to accept the horror. Her hand . . . her hand was thrust down the throat of the babe – its mouth had grown, its jaw distending like a snake as it began to swallow her. Cho Lin moaned as the needle-sharp teeth crept up her arm. Where they had passed, she felt nothing.

She could see the babe's features more clearly now. Black veins writhed beneath its pale skin, and behind its tangled hair she could see that its eyes had been gouged out . . .

Cho Lin woke.

She lay on stale rushes scattered over stone. The cold she had suffered in her dream was real – her limbs tingled, and she could barely feel her fingers and toes. With some effort she pushed herself into a seated position, brushing away the dry blades of grass tangled in her hair. She coughed wetly, spitting out flecks of the sickness that was clogging her chest and making her breathing ragged.

Cho Lin crept closer to the edge of her cell. No food had been left as she slept – the few bones strewn beside the black iron bars were the same ones she'd been gnawing on for the last two days. Her stomach clenched as she examined them yet again, hoping she'd missed some tiny morsel of flesh or forgotten to crack one open for the marrow within. Nothing. In frustration she hurled a rib through the bars, clattering it against the far wall.

At the noise, a shape stirred in another of the cells.

"Jan?" Cho Lin cried hoarsely, grabbing hold of the bars – but only briefly, as the intense cold of the iron soon made her let go.

The gray light suffusing the prison's lone window did not illuminate the deeper reaches of the chamber. In the gloom, Jan was just a featureless mound, and she couldn't make out very much. But still her heart leapt to see him move, ever so slightly. For the past day he had not responded to her, and she'd feared he had died.

"Jan, speak to me."

No answer. He'd been delirious after the Skein had thrown them in here, maddened by the pain of losing his eye. A moment of clarity had briefly returned, and she'd convinced him to try and clean the wounds made by the demon's claws with a splash of the spirit their captors had brought one evening. The memory of his screams still haunted her. He'd been growing weaker since then, barely touching the scraps tossed inside his cell. The last words he'd spoken had been a rambling, fractured apology to a woman named Liralyn, begging for her forgiveness.

Cho Lin slumped, struggling to keep her despair at bay. Where was the hope? They were prisoners of a cruel and savage people. Even if they escaped these cells, safety was a thousand *li* away, across a harsh and frozen land. And the Betrayers were here, worshipped by the Skein as avatars of their darkest god. The demons knew who she was; they would never let her leave this place. She had failed.

"Jan . . ."

Wood scraped on stone. Cho Lin's stomach twisted as the prison's iron-banded door opened, the film of ice that had formed along its hinges and edges cracking. Food.

But it was not their gaoler, and when she saw who had come, she couldn't hold back a whimper of fear. It was the stranger, the one garbed like a southerner. He wore only a thin linen doublet, frilled where it hemmed his wrists and neck, and breeches that left his ankles bare above his leather shoes. Simple clothes like a tradesman might wear in warmer lands. No furs, no heavy wool.

He should be dead from the cold.

And yet there was no sign that it bothered him at all. His face was not empty; a hunger lurked in his eyes. His cheeks were sunken, his hair lank and ragged, and his hands constantly twitched and clenched, as if he had to restrain himself from reaching for her. Or, at least, that was what she had seen before. Today he carried something, and that tiny flame of hope she'd been nurturing nearly flickered out.

The Sword of Cho. Its scabbard rested in the crook of his arms, laid so that its black-dragonbone hilt could not touch his flesh. He held it gingerly, away from his body.

Her attention was so focused on the sword that at first she did not see the other figure that had entered the prison trailing behind the southerner. He was pale and slightly stooped, wrapped in a gray robe, and so emaciated as to almost resemble one of the corpses she'd seen in her dream. His unnatural eyes were a vivid shade of blue she had never encountered before. Yet despite the intensity of his stare he looked to be younger than her, and she had not yet seen her twentieth winter.

Lask, the shaman of the White Worm.

His thin lips pulled back into a cold smile when he noticed her staring at him. Cho Lin could not keep from shivering – never had she seen such emptiness. She could not set aside the feeling that he was just a husk of a man, and some terrible, ancient presence had come to inhabit his body.

Lask did not speak to her, sweeping past the silent man carrying the Sword of Cho and coming to crouch beside Jan's cell. One of his hands closed around an iron bar, but he showed no sign of discomfort from the searing cold.

"Sorcerer," he murmured in a soft voice shriven of emotion.

Jan did not stir.

The shaman waited. Looming beside him, the southerner was absolutely motionless. Cho Lin's panic started to rise as she watched them waiting so patiently. It was far more terrifying than if they had threatened or raged or mocked. Finally, she could take it no longer.

"He's dying," she said desperately. "Please. He needs a healer."

Lask did not turn to look at her. "All things die."

"But this doesn't have to be his time. He just needs warmth and food. His wounds cleaned. He knows many things . . . he knows secrets about this place. He claimed to be a sorcerer of Min-Ceruth."

The shaman reached into his robes and withdrew a wadded piece of cloth. "His death is not in this room today. He is strong, the strongest I have ever felt. A deep, deep well to drink from." Lask twisted around, and his unnatural eyes found hers again. *"Gen thrik a len, monek vash tenen a polvinach.* This is a saying of my people: all things die, and in the time of sweet decay the Worm feasts." He unwrapped the cloth in his hand, and she could see something small and dark nestled within its folds. "Existence is a circle. We live, we die, and our strength is passed to what consumes us."

Her blood was thundering in her ears. What was he talking about? What did he have in his hand? Cho Lin hadn't realized she'd been holding her breath until the shaman turned away from her, and then she drew in a shuddering sob.

"Attend to me, sorcerer," Lask said calmly. When Jan still did not respond, the shaman beckoned with a long, thin finger. An invisible force slid Jan's unmoving body across the prison floor, then raised him up so that his slumped head was nearly touching the iron bars. His slack face was only a few span from the shaman, who had leaned closer as his sorcery drew Jan near.

Cho Lin gasped when she saw how the demon had ravaged Jan's face. The Betrayer's claws had carved deep furrows from his temple to his lips, plucking out his right eye and narrowly avoiding taking his nose as well. The empty socket was shadowed, its edges scabbed and oozing pus. Around his neck was the metal collar he'd been wearing when she'd freed him from the tower of the Crimson Queen, the thing he claimed kept him from using his sorcery. In the chamber of blue ice, Lask had humbled Jan after removing it, and then shackled him again.

"Wake," Lask commanded, and a ripple went through Jan. His eye fluttered open, his head slowly lifting. Cho Lin could see in his face the fever that was consuming him, and she wondered if he thought he was still dreaming.

Jan swallowed and licked his lips. "What are you?" he whispered hoarsely, struggling to focus on the shaman crouched beside him.

Lask reached through the bars and cupped Jan's chin. "I am the end of your journey, sorcerer. You should be honored: it is a rare thing to meet the one who will inherit your strength." He let the cloth in his other hand flutter to the floor. Between his fingers he held a small, gnarled object.

Cho Lin moaned when she realized what it was. No. This was madness . . . no one would do such a thing.

Still holding Jan's chin, staring at him with a terrifying intensity, Lask brought the withered remnant of Jan's lost eye to his lips. He placed it in his mouth and began to chew slowly. Cho Lin could not stop herself from retching when he finally swallowed. Jan showed no sign that he understood what was happening, his gaze unfocusing as he slipped once more into his delirium.

Lask let go of Jan's chin and the sorcerer collapsed again. Then the shaman sat back on his haunches, raising his face to the ceiling. His breath plumed the frozen air, coiling in the trickle of wan light. It seemed to shimmer, like there was something more that he was expelling from deep within his body.

"Such power," he said softly, his voice thick. "It burns so hot."

With gasping, hitching sobs Cho Lin scrambled across the stone floor, as far away from this madman as she could get. The sound seemed to rouse the shaman, who turned to her once again. A bruise-colored blush now stained his sallow cheeks.

"The Worm creeps closer to you as well, spider-eater." Lask's lips twisted into a cruel smile. "But you should not worry, for it will not be I who feasts on you."

Cho Lin's gaze flickered to the man who held the sword of her ancestors. He had not moved in the slightest, and yet she could sense his desperate hunger straining towards her.

The shaman rasped a chuckle. "No. Not him, at least not yet. You have drawn the attention of a god, Lady Cho. You should prepare yourself – the Skin Thief once more walks upon this world, and he wishes to meet you."

Lask reached again into the folds of his robes. The object he drew forth this time was a black crescent that glittered in the pale light. The shaman's lips pursed, his brow furrowing, and a moment later a slice of the air seemed to shimmer and writhe. The image of another place formed beside the shaman, as if he had opened an invisible door to elsewhere.

Torchlight flickered. This other space was shadowed, but recessed nearby a flame burned. Red light crawled across dark stone and a wooden frame, from which hung the limp body of a man. His shirt was reduced to ragged strips, showing flesh laced with dark welts, and his gray beard looked to be damp, matted with what she suspected was blood. He did not move.

A dark shape occluded the view of the other place, and then a large man in black robes stepped through the portal. Even after he had passed into the prison the wavering vision of the tortured man remained hanging in the air like some gruesome painting.

Cho Lin gasped.

This new stranger was a Shan, and though hugely fat he moved daintily, with an effortless grace that reminded her of her old masters on Red Fang. She guessed he had trained as either a warrior or a dancer. What was he doing here?

Then it struck her, as bracing as a gust of frozen wind: the Raveling. This man must be sworn to that death-cult – a warlock who served the Betrayers. If there were traitors in the bone-shard towers then the threat to the empire was even greater than she had feared. Perhaps this was how the demons had first escaped.

"Who are you?" she called out in Shan, struggling to keep her voice from cracking. "How could you serve them?"

The fat man turned slowly, ignoring her outburst. His gaze slid over Lask and the southerner, lingering on the sprawled body of Jan.

The shaman had dropped to his knees before this stranger, lowering his head.

"Answer me, traitor!" Cho Lin cried. "You've sundered your vows. You've—"

The Shan's attention finally settled on her, and her words died in her throat. A cold grip had closed around her neck, and her hands scrabbled at her throat, attempting to pry away the invisible fingers.

"I do not speak your tongue, girl," the Shan said in Menekarian, dismissing her as he turned to where the shaman knelt. The choking force vanished, and she drew in a shuddering breath.

"Let me see the stone," the Shan said to Lask, holding out his hand. The shaman gently – reverently – laid the crescent in his palm.

"Remarkable," the stranger said, holding up a small, gleaming white circle in his other hand, then fitting the curve of black stone over it like it was the moon eclipsing a dark sun. "You carved this?"

Lask nodded, never taking his eyes from the huge Shan standing over him. "With the help of your servants. They showed me how."

The Shan chuckled. "My servants." He peered closer at the carvings, as if examining the workmanship. Then he shook his head. "Even the bitch who bound me could not fathom the depths of the riftstone. And yet here, on the edge of the world, a savage in rags and furs has done the impossible and paired a sundered stone again."

Lask blinked rapidly, as if he was trying to understand the meaning of what the Shan was saying.

"Leave," the Shan said, gesturing towards the door after handing back the crescent of black stone. "I would speak to them alone."

The shaman hesitated, ever so slightly, but then he nodded and stood. When he passed the motionless southerner he tugged on his arm, as if telling the man to accompany him.

"No. That thing stays here."

The shaman cast another curious glance at the Shan, but still he withdrew. When the door clanged shut behind him, the Shan sighed.

"The sorcerer is dangerous," he said, turning back to her. "But I suppose you've guessed this already."

His black eyes glittered as he stared at her, and Cho Lin's skin crawled under his scrutiny. There was something unnatural about this man. Something monstrous.

"You're not from the empire," she said in Menekarian.

"No."

"Your family was cast out?"

Another dry chuckle. The Shan wandered close to the southerner and reached out to pluck the Sword of Cho from where it lay across the silent man's arms. Anger flared in her to see his fingers around the dragonbone hilt.

With a flourish, he ripped away the scabbard, letting it fall and clatter upon the stone. He studied the rippling length of steel with the same interest he had shown the black and white carvings.

"This is the one thing they fear," he said softly, turning the sword slightly so that the pale light slid along the blade. "A magnificent artifact. I can feel the soul inside, recoiling under my touch. She had a great Talent, though it was never refined."

The Shan breathed in deep. "Oh, she can smell their taint on me. She despises what I am; she is familiar with my kind, but still she begs for me to wield her against the Chosen."

"The Betrayers." The words were out of Cho Lin's mouth before she could hold them back.

The Shan turned to her. "I know their story, girl. You should call them the Betrayed, for your ancestors did a terrible thing. At least with this one," he slashed the air with the sword, "she went to her death freely."

"How do you know about the sword?"

He set the point of the blade on the stone, resting his hands on the pommel. "I've seen it before, you know. I felt there was something . . . strange about it at the time, but I had no chance to investigate it more thoroughly."

"What are you talking about?" she whispered.

In reply, a ripple seemed to go through the fat man. It was not a spasm of the body, though at first she thought that's what it was. Instead, his flesh actually trembled like water. Black hair emerged from his bald head, twisting into a topknot. His body dwindled, becoming leaner, and even his clothes changed, the simple black fabric shifting to a glistening green robe, a red phoenix unfurling along its length.

Cho Lin moaned. Her father stood before her, holding the Sword of Cho again. Her brother's words floated through the numb horror that was rising up to overwhelm her.

'He was slain by a demon that wore the skin of a man like a cloak.'

This was the thing that had killed her father.

She scrabbled for the Nothing, trying to retreat within herself to keep the panic at bay. *The self my nothing the self my nothing the –*

The demon raised the Sword of Cho lengthwise, one hand upon the hilt and the other clutching the curving blade near where it started to taper. Blood welled up between its fingers. A single drop hung suspended for a long moment, and then it fell.

The demon brought the sword down across its knee.

Cho Lin screamed as the blade shattered. Gleaming shards spun away, ringing upon the stone. At the sound, the tortured man hanging on the other side of the portal raised his bloody head and began to keen like a dying animal. Her fragile hold on the Nothing vanished, and she was thrust again fully into her own mind, returning to the prison – the biting cold pierced her flesh, her fingers clutched helplessly at the dry rushes, and the hanging man's ragged, incessant shrieking cut through her like a knife.

The fragments of the ruptured soul swirl and eddy, untethered from the sword. They slide across its skin, a cold and tingling caress, and then dissipate. It should have shifted into its trueform before breaking the blade – it was difficult to drink souls that had once been bound, but not impossible. And what a rich vintage that would have been, aged a thousand years inside the spell-steel.

It gnashes its teeth, the thought of feeding sharpening the ache in its belly. For too long it has been forced to keep its mask in place in the empire of the burning men, with no chance to sate its needs. It glances at the dying Min-Ceruthan. No, there is still a use for him. What about the huddled girl? She would be sweet, it knew, a torrent of bright flashing life that would swell the blood surging in its veins. But the Chosen have other desires. They want her to be humiliated for the sins of her people, and then given to the empty creature standing here.

Its mind slithers out, questing to understand the nature of this thing the dark children have fashioned. But there is nothing. Just emptiness . . . emptiness, and a gnawing, endless hunger. It is unnerved by its presence. For all its ancient power, it is still a child of this world, and what inhabits this shell is not . . . this thing was summoned forth from some distant dark abyss.

What will the creature do when it finally is allowed to feed upon the one for which it hungers? Something worse than merely killing her, it suspects. The girl would suffer terribly.

2: ALYANNA

WINTER HAD FINALLY claimed these lands. Most of the blood-red leaves had sifted down from skeletal branches, laying a carpet upon the dirt road that crackled beneath the wagon's turning wheels. The trees were not bereft of color, though, here at the edge of the Blightwood: jewel-bright birds flickered between perches, peering down at the strange procession that had invaded their forest. Six covered wagons of white wood, their sides painted with golden sunbursts: the faithful of Ama, returning from a long pilgrimage to the holy city.

Alyanna wrapped the woolen shawl Mam Jerith had given her tighter around her shoulders, but despite the thick fabric she still felt the day's bite. She sat on a small ledge of wood at the back of the last wagon, her legs dangling over the side. Beneath her the ground flowed by in a river of brown and red, dry winter earth and withered crimson leaves. She squinted at the mountains receding into the distance, where the jagged peaks of the Spine gnawed at the white sky. Somewhere among those mountains was the sanctuary of the kith'ketan, but it had vanished from her sight long before she'd even descended into the foothills of the Shattered Kingdoms.

From behind her came the rapid clapping of hands and a tumble of bright laughter. Mam Jerith's girls, playing a variation of a children's game that Alyanna herself had enjoyed long, long ago. She leaned her head back against the wood, listening to the familiar verses being sung within the wagon. Strange how it was children's rhymes and games that survived across the ages, through war and famine and pestilence. Grown men and women had no qualms about reinterpreting scripture or changing traditions to suit their needs, but to children, what had been shared was immutable. If she ever wanted to pass a message to future generations she would hide it in the lyrics of a children's song.

Cloth rustled as a stout, matronly woman pushed through the wagon's curtain. She held two steaming mugs, and a cheroot was clamped between her teeth. After a deep sigh, she settled on the wooden ledge beside Alyanna, passing her one of the cups.

"A fine winter's day," Mam Jerith said, then removed her cheroot and blew out a stream of blue-tinged smoke.

"Too cold," Alyanna murmured, warming her fingers by holding the cup with both hands. She breathed deep of the rising vapors – the drink was scalding hot water poured over a gnarled root, and one of the most bitter tastes she had ever tried. After her first sip a few days ago she'd nearly gagged, and only the intense desire to put something hot in her body had compelled her to finish the cup. Now she wondered how she would ever be able to continue living without bitter root tea.

Mam Jerith squinted at the dwindling mountains. "Too cold, you say. Much colder up in them peaks. Only by the Radiant Father's grace did you make it out of there alive, blessed is His light."

Alyanna said nothing in reply and sipped from her cup. After fleeing the mountain of the kith'ketan she'd spent several days hiking through the narrows passes and across the high bluffs of the Spine. The way would have been impassable for her a fortnight ago, but now that she could again draw upon her sorcery the going had been easy enough. Wrapped by layers of warming spells, she'd barely felt the frozen winds, and no animal had dared bother her. Then, when she had emerged from the mountains, she had found herself on one of the tributary roads of the Wending Way, the great highway that linked the east and west. Not long after that, these pilgrims had appeared. She'd told them a tale of how her merchant father's caravan had been buried in a rockslide while crossing the Spine, and that she was the only survivor. Mam Jerith had immediately adopted her.

"You give any more thought to letting the Father's light into your heart?"

Alyanna quirked a smile and shook her head slightly. Mam Jerith had taken it as her personal holy mission to bring Alyanna into Ama's sheltering radiance. At another time the woman's proselytizing would have infuriated her, but not now. Perhaps it was because, despite her best efforts, she found herself drawn to Mam Jerith and her girls. From what Alyanna could piece together, her husband had been a tanner and master leatherworker in Theris. He'd died from some sickness, leaving her with four young children and a struggling shop. Instead of accepting her fate as a poor widow, she'd learned her husband's trade and become far more successful than he had ever been. Alyanna could tell she was a woman of considerable wealth, despite the vow of temporary poverty this pilgrimage demanded.

Mam Jerith took another deep draw on her cheroot and expelled a cloud of blue smoke. "Ah, well. If you're meant to come to the light, those walls within you will come down eventually." She grinned, showing teeth stained by the evonasia weed. "But perhaps I'm the stubborn one meant to knock 'em over. So I'll keep bothering you."

"I expect nothing less," Alyanna said softly.

"Mama! Mama!" cried a tow-haired little girl as she came crashing through the curtain.

Alyanna tensed, readying her sorcery to catch the girl if it seemed like she was going to tumble off the back of the wagon, but the girl arrested her hurtling momentum by wrapping her arms around her mother's neck.

"Careful, child!" Mam Jerith snapped as some of her tea slopped over the rim of her cup. "I'll paddle you so hard you won't be able to sit for a month!"

The girl giggled, and Alyanna released the strands of her sorcery. Good; this time she'd managed to grasp them immediately. Ever since her power had come rushing back she had found herself fumbling with simple spells, as if once again she was a newly-robed apprentice at the Arcanum. It was why she was hesitant to use her power to warm herself while traveling with the pilgrims – one of the Pure rode with them as an escort, and any small slip would reveal herself to the paladin.

The girl rested her head on her mother's shoulder, staring at Alyanna with guileless blue eyes. "Mama, can Ali come inside and play with us?"

Mam Jerith snorted. "Didn't I hear you playing with her all morning, Jessia? You shrieking demons have exhausted her. That's why she's snuck back here to rest."

"I'm not a demon," the girl said, tangling her fingers in her mother's hair.

"I suppose not," Mam Jerith grudgingly agreed, "because Lord Septimus would have banished you back to the abyss if you were."

"Mama, we need a queen to play Lords and Ladies!"

Mam Jerith spread her arms wide, holding her cheroot in one hand and her cup of bitter in the other. "And why can't *I* be your queen?"

Alyanna chuckled when she saw Jessia's eye-roll.

"You don't look like a queen, Mama. But Ali does." The small, shy smile the girl gave her plucked at something deep inside Alyanna. This disquieted her, and she turned away to watch the barren forest sliding past. What was this hollow feeling in her chest? Ever since her sorcery had returned she had felt different, like the flood had swept away other things as well. Barriers that had been constructed over many centuries. She would have to rebuild what had been breached – this was not a time for weakness. Especially considering where she was going now.

Mam Jerith crushed the remnants of her cheroot against the wood. "Perhaps tomorrow Mistress Alyanna will play with you and your sisters, Jessia. Leave the poor woman alone."

"I'm leaving in the morning after we break camp," Alyanna said suddenly, and Mam Jerith glanced at her in surprise.

"What? There's nothing here. Theris is still a few days away, and these woods aren't safe – there's always fighting in these parts, some lordlings settling grudges. Bandits and desperate farmers as well."

"Ali, stay," whispered the small girl, reaching out to clutch at her shawl. "Please don't go."

"I know these lands," Alyanna said, hardening herself against the sadness she heard in their voices. "My old home is near."

"Must be a town I don't know," Mam Jerith muttered, peering into the woods. "Didn't think there was much out here."

Alyanna did not reply to this, taking a sip of her bitter tea. Mam Jerith was wrong – she likely did know the name of the place where Alyanna was going. But if she shared her destination with Mam Jerith, the woman would think her mad.

Alyanna closed her eyes, sending out tendrils of sorcery, taking utmost care that none of her power leaked beyond the barriers she'd constructed to keep herself hidden from the paladin riding with the pilgrims. She found what she was looking for almost immediately. It chimed like an answering bell as her sorcery brushed against it, and the reverberations made her shiver. The sensation was so familiar, and yet decades had passed since last she'd felt it: the Black Road, the great avenue that had once linked all the mightiest cities of the Kalyuni Imperium, twisting through these forests like a sleeping serpent. It was only a few leagues away, waiting for her to stride its gleaming tiles once again. And if she followed the road it would lead her to the reason she had come into the kingdoms – to the only one of the Mosaic Cities that had survived the cataclysms.

Uthmala.

Alyanna felt the eyes watching her before she saw them through the trees.

They were embedded in a great pile of jumbled black rock – the ruin of the Unblinking Gate. Slitted reptile eyes, wide and staring fish eyes, the eyes of men and cats and crawling things, all sunk into dark stone riven by grasping vines. The entrance to every city in the Imperium had been the same, carved with these guardians, spells woven into the stone so that the sorcerers of the Star Tower would know if a threat was approaching. The strength of the warning would have been commensurate with the degree of danger; she could only imagine what a cacophony it must have been as the great tidal wave that had obliterated the Imperium swept over these lands.

But Uthmala had escaped that flood. It had been destroyed in the chaotic times that followed, when the armies of Menekar had surged over the Spine and put what sorcerers remained to the sword. Alyanna was surprised anything at all remained of this Unblinking Gate; surely the Pure must have sensed the spells infusing its stone, and the paladins of Ama were implacably thorough when it came to eradicating sorcery.

Likely the wizards of this city had fled the Star Tower here long before the legions had arrived, knowing that their cause was hopeless. The sorcerers of the Imperium had not been the sort to sacrifice themselves when all was lost, and perhaps the armies of Menekar had been too intent on sacking the helpless city and tearing down its tower to bother with what flickering remnants persisted in the abandoned gate.

The crumbling pile of stones swelled higher as she came to the end of the Black Road, blotting out the midday sun and casting her into shadow. Strange; her skin was tingling like she really *was* being watched, but the sensation did not seem to be coming from those empty eyes staring down at her—

Ah.

Creeping movement among the vines threading the stones. A spider the size of a small dog edged out of a gap above the gate's entrance, its carapace nearly invisible against the dark rock.

So her approach had not gone unnoticed.

For a long moment Alyanna and the spider were both motionless, each watching the other. A cold wind gusted, stirring her hair, and she tucked her hands into the long sleeves of her shawl. Then she sighed. *Enough of this hiding.* The paladin was far enough away that even if her control slipped, he would not be able to track her here. With a flicker of sorcery, she wrapped herself in a cocoon of pulsing warmth.

The moment she grasped the strands of her power the spider began to move again, scuttling down the stones and vanishing within the gate.

Perhaps it had been waiting to make sure she truly was who she appeared to be.

Ignoring a small tremor of apprehension, Alyanna threw back her shoulders and followed the spider into the darkness.

Uthmala had not changed much. Tumbled stone veined by roots, gnarled trees growing out of shattered buildings, blocks of black rock scattered in a shimmering field of milk-pale grass. She recognized some of the structures, as they were very similar to what had stood in the other Mosaic Cities. There was the foundation of the Temple of the Last Flame, where countless animals and human prisoners had been led to their fiery deaths. There were the cyclopean pillars that had always flanked the entrance to the various acorpias of the Imperium. Poets had declaimed on those raised stages, and depending on their performance had been rewarded with thrown flowers or rotten fruit. That would have been the local chapterhouse of the Tarnished, home to the mutilated warriors charged with protecting the gates of the city.

All just ruins now, bones bleaching in the sun.

The spider was picking its way across the broken tiles of the avenue that sliced through the heart of the city. It was strange to see a creature that usually skulked in shadows and hid in dark corners moving so brazenly in the light of day. Unnatural.

Alyanna followed.

The wind strengthened again, rippling the tall white grass growing between the fallen buildings, whispering as it slid across the stone; the voices of her vanished people, crying out into the emptiness. Beyond what was stirred by the wind there was only silence. Stillness.

But she knew Uthmala was not abandoned.

The spider led her to one of the few structures that had not collapsed in upon itself. At the arched entrance, which was decorated with an assortment of fanciful monsters carved into the stone, stairs led down into the gloom.

With surprising daintiness the spider navigated these steps, reaching out carefully with its front legs, not unlike an old man descending a steep staircase. Alyanna paused before following, her hand on the ancient, cracked portico, and glanced behind her to squint at the city. Bright sunlight splashed over white stone; wisps of clouds threaded a brilliantly blue sky. She turned back to the seamless black where the stairs vanished. It seemed like she was at the entrance to the underworld, poised to pass from the world of the living and into the realm of the dead.

It reminded her of how she had felt as she spiraled down into the depths of the mountain to meet the thing that coiled in the darkness. Demian had been at her side then, and she had drawn strength from his presence . . .

Alyanna shook her head, banishing those memories. With a thought, she summoned a pale sphere of wizardlight and sent it floating down the steps. Ghostly light skittered over the stone, revealing a large open space at the bottom of the stairs. Alyanna spent a moment hardening her wards. She would not be taken unprepared, she promised herself as she started to descend.

It had been a bathhouse. A dozen pools of varying sizes were sunk into the tiled floor; most were empty, but a few were still partially filled with stagnant water. The remnants of vast mosaics covered the walls and the ceiling; in places, large swathes of the stones had been gouged from the walls, but in others the images were still recognizable, unclothed men and women cavorting in the pools.

The spider had already reached the far side of the great room, and as Alyanna watched, it vanished inside a ragged hole cut into the base of one of the mosaics, its bulging abdomen nearly brushing the stone.

Of course the Mazespinner would make Alyanna approach on her hands and knees. A reminder of who was the empress in this domain.

Alyanna stalked across the decrepit bathhouse, trying to keep her annoyance in check. What if she enlarged the hole with her sorcery, ripping a larger tunnel from the rock? Perhaps if the Black Lady felt again the intensity of her power she wouldn't dare to play such games.

Alyanna breathed in deep, mastering herself. The one she had come to see had survived for so long by being exceedingly cautious – perhaps there were no larger entrances remaining to her labyrinth. Also, Alyanna had come to beg for favors, and was not so stubborn that she couldn't swallow her pride.

Darkness poured into the bathhouse once more as she sent her wizardlight drifting into the hole where the spider had vanished. Then she crouched and squeezed herself into the tunnel.

Her shoulders brushed the sides, her head bumping the ceiling, and she wanted to shudder at the thought of all the dust and grime that was getting into her hair. There were webs, too, as was to be expected. Her wizardlight had pushed through most of them as it preceded her down the tunnel, but gauzy scraps still clung to her face and hands as she moved forward.

To her relief, the way quickly grew larger, until she could walk only slightly bent over. The tunnel did not seem to have been hewn by human hands – the walls were too rough, as if some burrowing creature had carved it from the stone. Up ahead her wizardlight waited, suggesting that either the passage came to a dead end, or that there was more than one way to proceed.

It was the latter. Her wizardlight had paused just outside another small hole hacked from a wall of rock. Turning her body sideways she slipped through and found herself in a much larger corridor. The walls here were smooth and decorated with designs incised into the stone, geometric patterns that reminded her of something she had seen before in nature, strung between branches or recessed in the corners of unused chambers.

Webs, of course.

The spider waited for her, clinging to the ceiling, but as she emerged it turned and scuttled down the passage. Alyanna let it lead her on. They arrived at several branchings, and each time her guide chose the way with confidence. Almost always the passages slanted downwards, bringing her deeper and deeper below the city. Dust lay thick in these corridors, and it did not look like men or women had disturbed the silence of this place for countless years. There *were* markings in the dust, though clearly not made by human feet.

Alyanna came to a chamber's entrance – the spider did not hesitate as it crawled past, but she did, as this was the first room that she had seen within this twisting labyrinth. Strange reverberations were welling up from within, spilling out into the passage.

Her skin prickled, and it was almost like she could faintly hear a chorus of whispers. With a thought, she sent her wizardlight drifting into the chamber. The pale radiance slid across the surface of many inky-black shapes, failing to fully illuminate what was inside, but from what she could discern in the gloom it looked like a host of tall stone statues, unnaturally thin and elongated. All their heads were severed. Alyanna swallowed at the rolling waves that were emanating from these statues.

She noticed something small and dark hunkered among the looming stone things. It drank her wizardlight, but it certainly looked to her like the shadows clinging to it had suddenly rippled. Like it had moved . . .

A tapping came from above her, and she glanced up. The spider hung just above her head, its foreleg rapidly pattering against the stone. It seemed almost . . . frantic.

"You don't want me going in there," she said to the spider. "And I'm not sure I want to, either. So lead on."

As if it understood and agreed with her, the spider scuttled away. Alyanna peered one last time into the chamber, and she couldn't dismiss the feeling that whatever crouched there was watching her as well.

Enough. She was not here to find out what other relics of the old world were hiding within this forgotten sanctum.

The undercity of Uthmala twisted ever deeper, and at times the passages seemed to fold back upon themselves, as if the place had been designed by madmen. It was such a vast structure that she wondered – not for the first time – how Caryxes and her spawn had managed to hide for so long. Alyanna suspected the Mazespinner predated the founding of Uthmala – perhaps, even, that the city had grown up over this complex. She must have crouched down here in the dark for centuries, feeding on the mortals who dwelled above.

To avoid the attention of the Imperium's sorcerers was impressive, especially considering that these tunnels were almost directly below one of the Star Towers. And then she had also remained hidden when the Pure had come to destroy the city and Cleanse its sorcery. The Mazespinner was exactly the kind of creature the paladins of Ama hoped to uncover in their hunts, yet the city had fallen and she had remained forgotten.

Which was why Alyanna had entrusted the Black Lady with her most precious treasures.

The entrances to more chambers appeared. Alyanna did not glance within any of them; she could sense other things down here, refugees from ages past, but she did not want to be distracted. If her focus slipped, she might never see daylight again.

She knew she was getting closer to the heart of this labyrinth. Webs clotted the corridors, so thick in places that she had to brush them out of her way to slip past. More spiders hunched in the shadows, watching her. Some were as small as her fist; others were even larger than the one she followed. What did they eat? Surely they could not all survive feeding merely on rats and other vermin.

Alyanna turned a corner, and she found that the corridor suddenly ended, emptying into a vast space. The spider waited for her at the threshold, its mandibles clacking, as if it was trying to tell her that they had arrived.

"I can see," she told her guide, brushing past the creature. A long leg, bristling with hair, reached up to lightly touch her as she passed. Alyanna fought back the urge to shudder. Instead, she wrapped herself in sorcery, layers of defenses that should protect against whatever she found within. *If* there was danger; she and Caryxes had long been something resembling allies. Well, mutual admirers, at least. But these were uncertain times, and old alliances might have to be renegotiated.

Alyanna entered the lair of the Black Lady. It was a chamber so large that it almost felt like she was no longer beneath Uthmala. She stood upon a narrow stone path only a few paces wide, lacking a balustrade to protect her from the great pit in the center of the room. Warm air billowed up from the unseen depths, smelling faintly of sulfur and rot. The narrow way skirted the edge of this abyss, and though her wizardlight could not clearly see the far side of the chamber, she thought she glimpsed the entrances to other passages, pockets of deeper blackness within the gloom.

Webs festooned the space above the great pit, stretching from one side of the room to the other. The ceiling was lost behind these gauzy layers, so she could not tell how high the chamber actually soared. A body was trapped in a patch of webbing – it was a man, perhaps a farmer or woodsman, as the tattered rags he wore looked to have once been simple homespun. His face was pale and sunken, drained of blood, his eyes closed.

Alyanna stepped to the edge of the path, staring down into the darkness. The last time she had been to this chamber, Caryxes had emerged from the pit, clambering up out of the shadows with the corpse of a deer clutched in her jaws.

Something shifted above her. Alyanna peered into the thick lattice of webbing, trying to make out what lurked beyond the reach of her wizardlight. Another shiver of movement came, reverberating down through the strands of the great web. There, she saw it now: a black shape hunched in the dimness.

The Mazespinner. The Black Lady. The Night Huntress. Caryxes, worshipped in these depths for ages undreamt.

What was she? The last remnant of a lost race? A fallen god? A mad sorceress? Alyanna had never learned. Nor did she care very much, outside of simple curiosity. Caryxes was one of the elders of this world, though she had survived the upheavals because almost no one remained who remembered she existed. Alyanna had only discovered her lair by chance when she had been scouring the ruins of Uthmala a thousand years ago for any artifacts the Pure might have missed.

"Alyanna."

She jumped, her wards flaring around her.

The body hanging in the web turned its desiccated head towards her. Its eyes were open now, but she did not think it saw her, as a milky film covered its pupils.

Was this thing dead? The last time Alyanna had stood in audience to the Mazespinner, a shrouded child – very much alive – had spoken on behalf of the great spider.

"Caryxes."

"*The Weaver of wonders graces my abode, and the worldstrands tremble with joy.*"

The man's voice was a harsh, cracked whisper. It had not been used in a long, long time.

"Thank you for sending a guide. It is good to see that you are still safe here."

The body's half-rotted lips twitched, as if it was trying to smile. "*It is true it is not so safe for us old ones these days. Of your ancient cabal only two now remain, when but a few moons ago four still drew their stolen breaths.*"

Alyanna blinked. The Mazespinner knew about Demian, which did not surprise her, as the spider was devilishly sensitive. But . . . four? Another of the sorcerers who had drunk with her from the soul jewel had persisted down through the centuries? And had died only recently? The thought was alarming. But perhaps the spider lied – it was known to play such strange games.

"Do you know why I have come?"

"*There could be only one reason.*"

"And you still have it?"

"*Of course. I would not betray you, Weaver.*"

A thought occurred to her. "Do you feel them? The Chosen?"

"*The dead children?*"

"Yes."

"*I cannot unfeel them. They tear gashes in the great web wherever they go. They leak the poisons of the Void into this world with their passage.*"

"Do they hunt me? What do they desire?"

The great dark shape looming within the webbing shifted, dropping closer. Alyanna's wizardlight gleamed upon a vast, curving abdomen. It hung suspended above her like a moon carved of obsidian. She felt a trickle of fear, but then she burned that to ash in the blaze of her will.

Caryxes would not risk conflict with her.

"I do not know if they search for you. I find it likely, though, as you are one of the few who could threaten their plans."

"Their plans. You know what they want?"

"Revenge."

Alyanna sighed. "Yes, I gathered as much. Something terrible was done to them to make them what they are. They truly were children once, weren't they?"

"Yes."

"And what do they plan on doing?"

A scraping came from above, the same sound that had been made earlier when her spider-guide had clacked its mandibles together. Except many times louder.

"A boy came to my lair many moons ago. A rare Talent, like yourself. He found his way into a part of my maze and disturbed my children. When he grew close, I discovered to my great surprise that he smelled like one of the Ashenagi."

Ashenagi. Alyanna had come across that term before, in the writings of a lost people. It referred to the Ancients, the great god-like beasts that slumbered in the hidden places of the world.

"That must have been the boy, Keilan. I did not know he came here. He was the one who disturbed the Sleeper in the Deep – I'm sure you felt the tremors in the worldstrands."

"Yes. And now the strands tremble again."

"The Sleeper is waking?" A cold wash of fear accompanied that thought. If one of the Ancients truly woke, the age of man would end.

"Not the Sleeper. The one in the north."

The White Worm. The only Ancient she knew of that was not at the bottom of the ocean or buried beneath the black sands in the distant southern deserts. And also the only Ancient that could be reached with relative ease. If the spells the Min-Ceruthans had woven to keep it undisturbed were sundered . . .

She knew what the Chosen planned. And what she must do.

"I will stop them."

The milky eyes of the corpse in the web widened slightly. Some grotesque approximation of surprise, though she didn't understand why the puppeteer above was bothering with such theatrics.

"Truly, Weaver? I thought you cared only for yourself."

Alyanna shook her head. "Where could I hide if the White Worm thrashed awake? Would even you be safe here in your burrow if it slithered forth?"

The silence was answer enough.

"So give back to me what I came here for."

The body hanging in the web sagged, as if whatever force animating it had suddenly fled. More shifting came from above, the threads shivering violently. She waited, counting her heartbeats, until she saw a flash of black emerging from within the hanging layers.

It was a spider the size of a horse, slashes of red like tigers' stripes streaking its black carapace. One of Caryxes's larger spawn, but by no means the largest. With its front legs it was rolling a great ball of wadded silk. When it reached the edge of the web that overhung the stone path Alyanna stood upon, it gave its burden a final shove. The silken cocoon landed next to her with a fleshy thud.

Alyanna's throat was dry, and she swallowed. She could feel the tendrils of power leaking out from within.

"Your possessions are returned to you. Our old bargain is fulfilled."

"Yes, it is," Alyanna breathed softly. She raised her hand, and found that her fingers were trembling in anticipation. Centuries ago, she had entrusted her most prized treasures to Caryxes; there was no place in the world safer from thieves and the lingering danger of her old, vanished rivals. She had known at the time that she would only see these things again in the direst of circumstances. Even the threat of Cein d'Kara had not warranted reclaiming what she had set aside. *Though*, she silently admitted, *in retrospect, they* had *been needed.*

With a whisper of sorcery, she sheathed her fingers with flickering blue talons. Then with a swipe she parted the cocoon, the silk blackening and falling away, and her treasures were revealed once more.

Her hand found the ebony hilt of her flail, the living shadows twitching into existence.

"Yes," she murmured as the old, hoary presence slithered once more into her mind. "I've returned."

3: KEILAN

"WE'LL BE IN Chale by midday."

Blinking away his daydreams, Keilan returned to himself. He'd been staring at the riverbank as it flowed past, but hadn't even realized that the bare trees had given way to the high, yellowing grass of the salt marshes south of the town. His thoughts had been elsewhere.

He lifted his aching head from his folded arms and sat back from the ship's railing, turning towards Nel. She stood a few paces away, one hand clutching at a rope that climbed midway up the small merchant ship's stubby mast. The sail had already been taken down and stowed away; the contrary current of the Lenian meant that since leaving the sea they'd had to rely on the strong backs and arms of the rowers to travel up the river. In her other hand Nel held out a biscuit.

"Did you have breakfast?" she asked, brushing back a dark lock of her hair as the wind blew it across her face. When Keilan had met her a half-year ago she'd sported a boy's cut, but now her hair had grown out until it reached past her shoulders. If one didn't notice the travel-stained clothes – and the hilts of the daggers poking out from her belt – she could almost pass as a respectable young lady.

Keilan accepted the biscuit and nibbled its edge. Dry and tasteless. He forced himself to choke down a larger bite.

"You ate?" he asked her, and she grimaced.

"I'm waiting to stand on ground that doesn't move," she replied, releasing the rope and putting her hand over her stomach. "The river is smoother, but every time they pull hard on the oars my belly lurches along with the boat."

"Hm," he grunted back through a mouthful of stale biscuit. He wished he had a cup of water or the sailor's wine he'd had at dinner last night to help him swallow. For some reason alcohol seemed to quiet the pounding in his head, at least for a moment.

"Have you given any more thought about what we should do when we reach Chale?" Nel asked.

Keilan used his finger to scrape away some of the tasteless mash that had become mortared to his teeth. "You mean, have I changed my mind?"

Nel frowned. "Yes. We need him."

Keilan glanced at the prow of the boat, where Senacus stood like a shining figurehead, his silver hair gleaming and his white cloak rippling in the wind. "No. We return to Dymoria alone."

"We didn't have any trouble on the Iron Road when he rode with us," Nel said, her voice tinged with exasperation. "It won't be as safe without him."

"I don't care," Keilan said angrily, the throbbing behind his eyes sharpening. "We can hire guards to protect us. I know you took some treasures from the island." Keilan turned away from Nel, staring out again at the gray marsh, trying to avoid the bright sun. "He killed my grandmother, Nel."

"He was trying to protect us."

"He's a zealot," Keilan spat back, his fingers tightening on the wood of the railing. "He wanted a reason to murder Niara."

"She imprisoned us," Nel said, her own voice hardening.

"Because Sella took something. Her servants were mindless. They did only what they had been instructed to do when a *thief* stole something precious."

"So why not blame her?"

"She's a *child*," Keilan hissed. His gaze slid across the deck until he found Sella, hunched near the hatch with the captain's son, a boy of about her age. He looked like he was showing her how to tie a sailor's knot, wrapping a small bit of rope around a piece of wood. Sella had been avoiding Keilan ever since they'd left Niara's island, barely speaking more than a few words to him during the days they'd waited in Ven Ibras for a ship to appear that would take them back to Chale. Keilan knew she felt terrible about what had happened – he recognized it in her eyes, that look of guilt and self-loathing he had last seen when she had tricked him into the ambush set by his cousin Malik. A lifetime ago, it seemed. He hadn't yet found the strength to forgive Sella for her foolishness, but his anger towards her was a shadow of what he felt when he looked at Senacus.

The paladin must have been extremely pleased with what had unfolded on the island – a great sorceress had perished, and they'd found a weapon to use against the dark children. That thought made Keilan's jaw clench, and his fingers gripped the railing so tightly that pain prickled his skin, a splinter working its way into his flesh. He let go as a wave of dizziness washed over him.

"Keilan, are you all right?" Nel asked, her hand touching his shoulder.

He shrugged her away, and then felt a pang of guilt when he saw her face. "I'm fine, really. I'm sorry." He was just tired. He hadn't been sleeping well. At first it had been the infection in his arm from when Niara had cut him, but even after the blackness in his veins had faded away his sleep had remained troubled. Terrible dreams that brought him awake gasping. And this incessant headache, making him feel like his head was stuffed with straw and shards of broken glass. The horror of what had happened on the island wouldn't let him go.

Because despite what he'd said to Nel, and what he had tried to convince himself, it hadn't been Senacus who had murdered Niara. No matter how much he tried he could not forget the memory of her wrapped in blue flames, screaming as she ran towards the balcony and the sea below.

He had killed his grandmother.

The docks of Chale were busy that morning. Along with the small trading ship they had sailed on, two other merchant carracks had arrived with the dawn, and burly men were helping to unload crates of Shan winter fruit and bales of undyed cloth from the Whispering Isles. Keilan had been curious as to why they'd bring the goods ashore here, instead of Theris, which was just a day's travel up the river. When he'd asked one of the sailors he'd been told the Iron Duke had recently put a substantial tax on the river trade, large enough that it made sense to make the last leg of the journey overland.

After disembarking, Keilan guided Sella away from the frantic commotion down by the water's edge. He clutched the rosewood box to his chest, his arms already starting to ache. The lacquered red wood was surprisingly heavy, but still he did not want to remove the black dagger from its container and carry it separately. The coldness seeping from the blade unsettled him, though at least he felt no sorcerous reverberations. Carefully, he slipped the box into his pack, nestling it among his clothes and the books he'd taken from Niara's library.

Sella carried the doll she had found on the island. It was a lumpy bit of cloth with straw for hair and a frilled green dress, button eyes and a line of stitches for its mouth. The sight of it annoyed Keilan – if she had not snuck off and stolen the doll then they'd likely still be on the island. Niara would be alive, instructing Keilan on how to harness his sorcery, and he'd have the time to convince her to join with Cein d'Kara in stopping the demon children. Sella still insisted that the doll had spoken to her and had told her some ridiculous story, yet it hadn't said anything else since that morning. Clearly, the doll was just a toy, probably once played with by his mother. The thought that his grandmother had died because of Sella's overactive imagination was galling.

Nel was speaking with Senacus near the ship's gangplank. The paladin had donned the bone amulet that hid the light that usually spilled from his eyes, but still he was wearing the white-scale armor and cloak of the Pure, which was drawing some curious stares from the dockworkers. He looked somber, Keilan thought. Like he was sad that this was how their journey together would end. Keilan searched within himself for any sympathy and found maybe the barest trace, but it was greatly overshadowed by his anger. He knew the paladin didn't feel guilty about Niara's death – Senacus had devoted his life to killing sorcerers. No, his only regret was that it had driven a wedge between them, and this Keilan could not forgive.

Finally, Nel held out her arm, and after a moment's hesitation Senacus clasped it. Keilan was a little surprised, considering where Senacus and Nel had started out only a few months ago. She'd been ready to slip a dagger between his ribs for his role in bringing the shadowblades inside Saltstone, and yet here she was showing Senacus that she considered him to be a friend. Keilan shifted uncomfortably as he considered this. His feelings towards the paladin had also changed considerably, and now he regretted asking him to accompany them. Nel apparently felt the opposite.

"Where is he going?" Sella asked, tugging on Keilan's sleeve. She sounded worried.

"Home, like us."

Nel finished saying her goodbye, then turned away, shouldering her heavy pack. Keilan knew she'd stuffed it full of strange artifacts and trinkets she thought might interest Vhelan. Behind her, Senacus scanned the crowded docks until he found Keilan. He didn't smile, but he raised his hand and inclined his head.

"Why isn't the Pure coming with us?" Sella asked Nel when she reached them.

Nel glanced at Keilan. "He has . . . important things he must do in Menekar. And the Pure aren't welcome in Dymoria – the Crimson Queen would throw him in the dungeons."

Sella scrunched up her face. "But he's so strong. Who's going to protect us now?"

"No one is going to protect you," Keilan said, trying to sound stern, "because you're going back to your farm."

"Keilan," Sella pleaded, "let me go with you. Nel can teach me to be your knife. I can learn, I promise."

This was only the latest of many such pleas, and Keilan shook his head. "It's too dangerous. I'll come back for you in a few years, when you're older. Right now, you should be with your mother. Pelos will take you home."

Tears glimmered in her mismatched eyes. "You're going to leave me again."

"I'll return, I promise," he said, but she turned away angrily. He looked at Nel for help, but she only shrugged.

Sighing, Keilan glanced to where Senacus had been. Sella had always listened to the paladin, for some reason, and he in turn had shown great patience with her. He seemed to find amusement in her fierce spirit and the way in which she saw the world, so full of wide-eyed wonder.

But the Pure was already gone.

The day was gray and cold, a light drizzle prickling Keilan's skin as they walked through the town. The heavy rain the night before had turned the road to mud, and only a few customers were frequenting the vegetable and fish stalls hemming the way. Most of the townsfolk must have been hunkering in their homes, as smoke was trickling from the tops of many of the white stone and clay buildings they passed. The bleakness of the weather mirrored his mood, and he found he couldn't stop thinking about Senacus and Sella and what had happened on the island. Nel had been right – Sella *had* betrayed him. All she'd had to do was wait while Niara guided him towards an understanding of sorcery. Instead, she'd snuck away and *stolen* something of great value to the sorceress. If Sella hadn't come along – if he hadn't given in to her pleading to be allowed to come along – then nothing terrible would have happened.

Resentment churned in his stomach. He glanced at Sella, plodding along beside him, seemingly lacking any sense of the tragedy she had caused. Selfish, stupid little girl. He found his hands were balled into fists, and he had to fight back the urge to grab her and shake her and scream in her face.

The cut on his arm itched, and he scratched at it. His anger was not only intensifying the pain behind his eyes, but also making him feel lightheaded. The little light seeping through the layer of gray clouds hurt his eyes, and he had to raise his hand to try and shield his face.

The world lurched, a cart passing next to him tilting – though none of the vegetables piled on it shifted – and he stumbled. The ground rushed up, smashing him in the face; cold mud was on his lips, pressing against his cheek, and a tingling numbness was spreading down his limbs . . .

"Keilan!"

Nel's voice, from very far away. Ringing like a distant bell.

His fingers clutched at the dirt. The throbbing in his head was now a pounding, like something was trying to break out of his skull.

"Look at his arm!"

Sella's voice, floating on a distant wind. She sounded terrified.

"Help me."

Nel, calmer but still shaken. Hands gripped him under his arms and lifted. His head pulled away from the mud.

"Gods, he's heavy."

"Keilan, you need to walk. We can't carry you."

The edge of urgency in Nel's words cut through the haze. He found he was standing, and he took a staggering step forward. The world around him was blurry, but he sensed he was stumbling towards a building. Nel was under one of his arms, Sella the other. He heard the girl whimper, and Keilan tried his best to take more of his weight.

"That's right, that's good," said Nel soothingly. "Just a little farther."

Wooden steps. A door swinging open, and the brightness of the day gave way to gloom. The smell of animal dung and roasting corn was replaced by bitter smoke and a simmering stew.

"He can't come in here so deep in his cups," growled a man.

"He's not drunk; he's just not feeling well. We just need to sit for a moment, get something in his stomach."

"He got a sickness?" This was a woman's voice, laced with caution.

"He's lightheaded. Too long on a boat. Please, we'll take a bowl of whatever is cooking. And a flagon of water."

Keilan's knees bumped against something, and then small hands were helping him step over a bench and sit. His elbows rested on wood, and the desire to pillow his head in his arms and let the darkness carry him off was nearly overwhelming.

"No," Nel said harshly, pinching his cheek hard. He flinched, the fog that had been settling over him lifting slightly.

"Stay awake, Keilan."

"Do you see his arm?" That was Sella's voice.

"I see it," Nel replied grimly.

What was wrong? Blinking through the shadows, he focused on his arm. The veins near his wrist were etched black and swollen, like worms burrowed just beneath the surface of his skin.

Keilan breathed out slowly. The shadows pressing down on him lightened, and the ground beneath his feet – which had been moving up and down like he was still on the boat – finally settled.

He sat at a trestle table of pitted wood. A fire burned in a hearth, an iron cookpot suspended over the flames. He weakly turned his head. Nel was beside him, concern in her face. Beyond her were another few tables and a scattering of men with long beards and rumpled work clothes. Bowls of stew steamed in front of them, but most of the men were staring at him instead of eating.

Keilan swallowed. They were in some kind of tavern. Nel was on his left, Sella his right.

"Look!" Sella hissed, pointing at his arm. The blackness was fading from his veins, as if being drawn out as they watched. What remained was inflamed and swollen, but only a little darker than usual.

"I'm . . . I feel better," Keilan murmured, licking his dry lips.

"What happened?" Nel asked, clutching at his arm.

"I don't know, it was like—"

His words trailed away as a dark shape appeared on the other side of the table, blocking the fire-light. He looked up, blinking.

A woman nearly as wide as she was tall loomed over him, her ruddy face showing both concern and a healthy dash of wariness. She held a bowl in one hand and a dented tin flagon in the other.

"You all right, lad?" she said, setting down the bowl and flagon with a clatter.

Keilan nodded, running a shaking hand through his hair. "Aye. I think I ate something that didn't agree with me."

"You won't find anything more agreeable here!" someone shouted from a nearby table, to loud guffaws. The stout matron scowled and stomped off in the direction the voice had come from.

"Funny, are ya? How funny are ya gonna be, Terrin, if I throw ya out on your arse and you have to slink home to spend time with yer missus?" Laughter rippled around the room, Keilan's fainting spell forgotten.

"Here, eat," Nel said, pulling the bowl in front of Keilan. He dipped his spoon and brought it to his mouth – the stew inside was a bit watery, and the amount of salt might have been masking some very questionable fish, but it was hot, and as it pooled in his belly he found the weakness that had overcome him fading further. Loud banging from elsewhere was followed by a sullen-sounding apology, and then the stout matron stomped past their table again muttering angrily to herself.

"Your arm," Nel said, lightly brushing his inflamed veins with the tip of her finger. "I thought you said the infection had gone away."

"It had," Keilan replied, wincing. The area was tender, even when touched so gently. "I thought I was getting better. I guess I hoped the sickness was breaking."

"And now?"

"I don't know."

Nel drummed her fingers on the table. "We need to get you to an apothecary. Clearly you need something to cleanse this infection. Pelos will know who to go to in Chale. Do you think you can make it to his house?"

Keilan nodded, then took another slurp of stew. Nel watched him carefully, chewing on her lip.

"Well, I don't think you're going to die right now. And the food might be doing you some good." She raised her hand, catching the eye of the still-fuming woman. "Another bowl of this stew!"

Keilan felt better than he had in many days after finishing a second bowl of the stew while soaking up the fire's heat. His skin was no longer clammy, and the headache that had been muddling his thoughts had finally vanished. There was still a shadow to his veins, though, and the quickness with which the sickness had overwhelmed him and then receded again was frightening.

When they had all cleaned their bowls and their clothes were pleasantly dry and warm, Nel paid the woman a couple of Lyrish coppers from the diminished purse given to them by the Lady Numil almost two months before. Then they clattered down the rickety steps spilling onto the town's main thoroughfare, Keilan waving away Sella as she offered him a shoulder.

"This way," Keilan said, remembering that they had once walked along this very road after spending the night at Pelos's house.

Sella dashed ahead, pausing here and there to inspect the various stalls that lined the street. The wares of an older man with a drooping mustache in particular caught her interest, and as Keilan drew close he saw painted dolls and various monsters carved from red wood.

"Look, Kay!" she cried excitedly, pulling out from her pack the doll she had taken from Niara's island, and then holding it up to compare it with the workmanship of the dolls that were laid out for sale.

"Come along," Nel said sternly, dragging Sella away from the toymaker's stall. She went with the knife reluctantly, still clutching the doll to her chest.

Keilan's chest ached watching this. She was still a child in so many ways. And yet she was only a few years younger than him. Was this gulf that had opened between them just from their age difference, or had everything that had happened to him wiped away all that remained of his childhood?

He was surprised that he remembered the way back to where Pelos lived, as he'd been nursing a terrible hangover the morning they had departed for Ven Ibras. But he recognized an old pear tree that looked to have been scarred by wormrot, and turned onto the side street that passed beneath its branches. Tidy cottages hemmed the way, their doors and shutters painted bright colors. Wisps of smoke curled from chimneys. His heart lightened at the thought of seeing Pelos and Amela again – he desperately needed the fishmonger's calm wisdom right now. Perhaps Pelos could help quiet whatever demons were loose in his head.

That was it, wasn't it? The small white house with a roof of red slate, a carved wooden fish hanging down from the eaves. Its door was cracked open – perhaps Amela was letting in some fresh air while she worked. Pelos was likely down at the market selling yesterday's catch, but Keilan knew the fishmonger's wife would welcome them warmly.

"Amela!" he cried, running up the path to the house. He caught a flash of movement from inside and pushed wide the door, a smile already on his face.

Keilan gasped. Two men sat at the fishmonger's table, and they returned his surprised look. Both wore armor of the same make: leather cuirasses over red tunics, their arms protected by bronze vambraces. One wore an open-faced helmet, while the other had taken his off and placed it beside a pile of small bones on the table.

For a moment no one moved. Then the men leaped to their feet, overturning the chairs they'd been sitting in, hands going to the hilts of their short swords.

"Commander!"

Soldiers. Keilan stumbled back, nearly falling as he turned to run. There had been a small tattoo beneath their left eyes, like a falling tear, and he knew what it must be even though he was too far away to see it clearly: a sunburst, the mark of the god Ama. These men were from the legions of Menekar.

"Nel!" he cried, but then skidded to a halt again.

Three more soldiers had appeared, emerging from hidden places with stubby swords drawn. Nel pushed Sella behind her as the men fanned out to cut off their escape.

Keilan fumbled with his sword as he rushed over to his friends, the hilt nearly slipping from his fingers when he pulled it awkwardly from its sheath.

Sella clutched at him, her eyes wide and panicked. "Who are they, Kay?"

"Menekarians," Nel answered, her voice cold.

Keilan tried to adopt the stance Xin had taught him, the second form of the One Who Waits, but it was like he suddenly had two left feet. His heart skittered, and he fought to keep his arm from shaking.

"If they charge us," Nel said calmly, "I'll put my dagger in the one with the scar. You see him, Sella? I want you to run in his direction when he falls and not look back. Keep running until you're far away and you can't hear anything anymore. Do you understand?"

Sella only whimpered, and Nel let out a little hiss of frustration.

"Do you understand?" she repeated harshly, daggers materializing in her hands.

"Yes," Sella whispered.

But they did not charge. Instead, the soldiers stopped their slow advancement and turned towards the fishmonger's house. Nel tensed, as if readying herself to seize upon their distraction, but then she stiffened.

"No," she breathed, and the despair in her voice sent a chill through Keilan.

He turned slowly, the fighting forms forgotten.

A paladin of Ama stood framed in the doorway, sunlight burning on his white-scale cuirass. He was as tall as Senacus, but leaner, and though he had a trimmed silver beard his head had been shorn, a spiderweb of copper tattoos covering his gleaming scalp.

The Pure was staring at Keilan intently, his arms folded across his chest.

"Tell your men to stand down, Menchai," he said. "The boy is the sorcerer."

The soldiers shifted and muttered, and Keilan thought they might have drawn back a pace, but he couldn't be sure as he was having trouble tearing his gaze away from the Pure's burning eyes.

"Where is Senacus?" asked the paladin.

Nel answered first. "He's dead. Swept into the sea during a storm."

The Pure's jaw tightened. "A pity. The High Mendicant demanded the apostate be brought before him. I suppose you three will have to suffice."

What were they doing here? "What about Pelos?" Keilan shouted, the sword hilt slick in his grip.

The paladin frowned. "Who?"

"The one who lived here with his wife. What have you done with him?"

"The old man?" The Pure shrugged, as if this were of no importance. "He was taken by the inquisitors for questioning. He's beneath the temple in Theris by now, I would assume, no doubt praying to whatever heathen gods he worships to let him die."

They were torturing Pelos. Anger flared in Keilan, and he took a step towards the paladin.

"Keilan, wait," Nel hissed in near panic as the Pure arched a pale brow.

Searing radiance consumed him, and he was falling.

His cheek.

His cheek throbbed, pressed against dirt. Points of light flared, then faded just as suddenly, leaving his vision full of strange dancing shadows. He tasted vomit, his arms and legs moving feebly as he tried to push himself to his hands and knees. For the second time that day he had fainted, but while earlier he had been overwhelmed by something welling up inside him, now a great force was pressing down from elsewhere.

"Keilan!" Small hands clutched at his shirt, trying to pull him up.

"Embrace the light, sorcerer," he heard the Pure say from far away as waves of scalding power pummeled Keilan. He was caught in a riptide, being pulled farther and farther away from shore. It was all he could do to keep his head above the churning water.

And then it was gone.

He drew in a shuddering breath, coughing into the ground, tasting dirt.

Something was happening. Raised voices were arguing. He concentrated, trying to understand what was being said.

"You have betrayed your oaths... the Radiant Father weeps..."

It was the paladin, spitting his words angrily. Who was he talking to?

"Ama has spoken to me, brother. The faith has become tainted."

Senacus! Keilan groaned and rolled onto his side, squinting into the day's brightness. Relief roiled in his chest. "Save us," he tried to say, but what emerged was nothing more than slurred nonsense.

Nel and Sella were crouched beside him, watching the two paladins as they faced each other. The soldiers that he could see were likewise frozen, apparently struck dumb by the sight of two warriors infused with their god's power on the verge of fighting.

And they were: both Senacus and the other paladin had their hands on the copper hilts of their white-metal swords, though neither had yet started to draw their blade.

The Pure with the tattoos sneered. "You still call me brother? You are no longer part of our order. The High Mendicant has named you apostate."

Something passed across Senacus's face, a momentary sadness. Then his expression hardened. "You do not understand. Sorcerers have infiltrated the temple. You must believe me, brother. Give me a chance to prove it to you!" His voice was pleading, but the other Pure was unmoved.

"I reject your lies, traitor!" cried the paladin, lunging forward as he ripped his sword free of its sheath. "For Ama and the emperor!"

A shuddering crack and a flash of light as Senacus's own white-metal blade met and turned away the blow. The tattooed Pure recovered instantly, his sword a blinding crescent as he hammered at Senacus's guard again and again, driving him backwards. With each ringing clash Keilan feared that Senacus would falter, but he managed to ward away each attack as he gave ground. For a moment none of the soldiers moved, seemingly awed by the speed and power of the paladins as they came crashing together, but then one of the Menekarians pointed at Senacus and screamed, though whatever he said was lost beneath the clanging of the white-metal swords.

His meaning was clear enough, though, and one of the soldiers charged towards Senacus while he was busy fending off the paladin. Fear rose in Keilan, and he grasped desperately for the power that Niara had taught him how to seize. He imagined twisting it into blue fire, but before he could unleash his sorcery the memory of his grandmother enveloped in flames rose in his thoughts, and the tendrils of the spell slipped through his fingers like water.

"No!" he sobbed as the soldier hurtled towards Senacus.

Then the Menekarian toppled over, a knife hilt jutting from his back.

"Run!" Nel screamed as the other soldiers turned towards her with murder in their faces. With blinding quickness she reached beneath one of her leather bracers and sent a smaller dagger spinning at another of the Menekarians, but this time her aim was not true, and it skittered off his armor harmlessly.

"Get out of here!" she cried again, putting herself in the way of the advancing soldiers, yet more daggers appearing in her hand. The blades of these ones were slightly longer, and Keilan recognized them – Chance and Fate. She meant to fight dagger to sword – *four* swords – exactly what she had once told him never to do if he wanted to live. Better to run away and fight another day, she had said. But if she fled, she'd leave Sella and him behind.

Keilan staggered to his feet. The suffocating pressure had vanished, though he still felt lightheaded. He picked up his sword from where it had fallen in the dirt and set his feet in the second of the forms. Nel saw what he was doing and growled something about him being a stubborn fool. Then she ran straight at the soldiers, screaming and brandishing her daggers.

She's trying to draw them away, Keilan thought, and for a moment it looked like they all would pursue her as she suddenly swerved from her headlong charge and dashed towards another of the small houses. But one of the soldiers hesitated, then turned back to Keilan as his three fellows followed Nel.

Keilan swallowed back the lump of fear in his throat, trying to find that clarity, the perfect battle-calm that Xin had always claimed was what a warrior must embrace if he wished to fight at the peak of his training.

It wasn't there.

But the soldier cautiously approaching him looked as nervous as he felt – the paladin had named Keilan a sorcerer, and Menekarians were taught to fear and loathe sorcery above all things in this world.

"Lay your sword down, boy," the soldier rasped, raising his stubby sword as he adopted some fighting stance Keilan had never seen before.

"I can't," Keilan replied, shifting his weight to the balls of his feet. As he lifted his own blade it caught the sun, light skittering along its silvery length and blazing in the rubies set in the hilt.

The soldier cursed and spat, then lunged forward. For a brief moment Keilan felt fear, but it vanished as his own sword leapt to meet the soldier's and they came together with a clash of steel. Surprise flickered in the Menekarian's face, and then he swung again. Keilan shifted to the third form of the One Who Waits, turning aside that blow as well. The soldier thrust out and Keilan danced back, the sword's tip nowhere close to catching him.

Keilan tried to tamp down his excitement. Maybe the soldier was just testing him, trying to take his measure, and he'd suddenly close with a barrage of blows that Keilan couldn't parry. But he suspected that the soldier was not holding back. Perhaps he had been trained in formation fighting, mechanical sword blows that perfectly meshed with those of the legionaries pressed to either side, and he was entirely unprepared for this sort of single combat. Or perhaps the long lessons with Xin and Senacus had taught Keilan to fight better than he had thought, because in comparison to the Pure or the Fist warrior this man seemed to be wading in mud.

The soldier came at him again, faster than before. Still Keilan deflected each blow with variations of the One Who Waits, and then instinctually he followed his defense with a quick thrust, something Xin had taught the apprentices of the Scholia as they trained atop Saltstone. He felt brief resistance as the point of his sword pierced the leather cuirass of the soldier and slid into his belly.

"Oh," Keilan could only murmur, shocked, as the soldier staggered back a step and dropped his sword. The Menekarian looked confused, like he couldn't understand what had just happened. Keilan's blade slipped out, streaked with red, and then the soldier sank to his knees, clutching at his stomach as blood poured from between his fingers.

"I'm sorry," Keilan whispered, and he had to fight back the urge to kneel beside the soldier and try to find something to staunch the wound. The soldier toppled over, groaning.

He'd killed a man. He'd killed again.

The soldier squirmed in the dirt, panting, trying feebly to keep his lifeblood from leaking out. Keilan desperately wanted to look away, but he could not.

Then Nel was beside him. "Wake up!" she yelled, striking him in the shoulder with the pommel of a dagger.

"I killed him," Keilan said numbly, gesturing with his bloodied blade at the moaning soldier.

"No, you didn't," Nel said, stepping over to the soldier and taking a fistful of his hair. In one quick motion she lifted his head and sliced his throat with her dagger. "I did," she told Keilan, letting the soldier's limp body flop forward.

"Shael's mercy," he breathed softly.

"This is not a time for mercy," Nel replied as she turned back to where the Pure were locked in combat.

"The other soldiers . . ." Keilan began, but then he saw them splayed out unmoving on the ground. Three of them, incredibly. And there was Sella, cowering behind the trunk of a gnarled little fruit tree, her face ashen and her eyes wide. She was staring at the dead soldiers like she feared they might rise again.

A quick flurry of clashing swords brought Keilan's attention back to the paladins. Senacus was being pushed backwards by the Pure with the copper tattoos, desperately fending away his flickering blade. Every time the white metal came together there was a hollow chiming, more like a bell being struck than the ringing of steel. That sound, coupled with the grace with which they were moving, almost made it seem like this was a performance and not a lethal duel where the smallest mistake would mean death.

Nel stalked closer, looking for an opening, but given the quickness with which the paladins were moving Keilan couldn't imagine how she could throw a dagger without risking accidentally striking Senacus. She must have agreed, as he saw her raise and then lower her arm several times.

A white-metal blade lashed out, and Senacus reeled away, the long sleeve on his left arm torn. For a moment Keilan thought it must have struck his vambrace, but as he turned away another thrust he saw darkness welling up from beneath the rent in the white cloth. Fear seized Keilan at the sight. It was not his sword arm, but certainly such a cut would bother him. And yet it did not appear to. If anything, Senacus seemed to gain strength from the wound, and then suddenly it was the other paladin warding away blows that seemed on the verge of slipping past his defenses.

It happened so suddenly that Keilan couldn't hold back a gasp of surprise. After a ringing series of parries, the white-metal swords little more than pale blurs, one of the Pure was a moment late in raising his guard, and his opponent's blade slipped through, plunging into his chest. It happened so fast that for a terrifying instant Keilan wasn't sure who had been struck, but then the paladin with the copper tattoos crumpled with a pained cry. After sparing a glance at his companions – making sure no aid was needed, Keilan assumed – Senacus knelt beside the dying paladin, dropping his own sword and cradling the Pure's head in his hands.

As Keilan approached with Nel he saw Senacus's lips moving as he intoned what sounded like a prayer. The wounded paladin's chest heaved and he coughed raggedly, spattering Senacus's white-enameled gauntlets with blood. As Keilan watched, the light leaking from the Pure's eyes gradually faded, revealing dark irises that stared sightlessly up at Senacus as he finished ushering the dead paladin's soul along on its way to the Golden City. Then he gently brushed the Pure's eyes closed and placed the paladin's sword lengthwise on his body, arranging his hands so that he could hold the copper hilt of his holy blade one last time.

"Are you hurt?" Nel asked, crouching beside Senacus.

The Pure glanced at the stain on his tunic's sleeve, as if he'd forgotten the wound he'd taken. "It's a scratch," he said dismissively.

"Scratch or not, let's clean that and get it bound up." She looked at the open doorway to Pelos's house. "The fishmonger had ale, I remember, and I'd wager probably something harder as well. A splash for your arm, and then I think I need more than a splash for myself."

Senacus's burning gaze wandered for a moment before settling on Keilan. Lines of sorrow were etched in the paladin's face.

Keilan swallowed away the dryness in his mouth. "Senacus, I—"

A door clattered open behind him. "Keilan!"

He whirled around as a plump, gray-haired woman emerged from one of the neighboring houses.

"Amela!" he cried as Pelos's wife rushed towards him, and then a moment later he was being crushed to her bosom.

"Oh, lad," she said, her voice cracking. "You're alive."

He pushed himself away, putting his hands on her shoulders. "Where's Pelos?"

Amela was gazing around at the bodies sprawled outside her house, her eyes wide. Her face had gone deathly pale.

Keilan gave her shoulders a squeeze, and she seemed to come to herself. "They took him. They wanted to know where you'd gone, but he wouldn't say. He wouldn't betray you, Keilan. He's a good man, my Pelos." When she said her husband's name a tremor went through her, and then she gave a hitching sob as tears streaked her face.

"Come inside," Nel said, pulling on Amela's arm. The tone in her voice brooked no argument.

As Nel led the fishmonger's wife inside her house, Keilan went over to meet Sella as she tentatively crept out from behind the tree she'd been hiding behind.

"They're all dead," she said numbly, skirting around the outstretched arm of one of the soldiers Nel had slain.

"They would have killed us," he assured her as he gathered her in a quick embrace. "Or done other terrible things."

"Why do they hate you?" she whispered, her fingers clutching at his back.

"They hate what I am," he replied. "A sorcerer."

"But you never did anything bad," Sella said.

I have, Keilan thought, his gaze straying to the soldier he'd stabbed. The man's empty eyes stared at him accusingly. *But I just wanted to protect my friends.*

Keilan guided Sella inside the fishmonger's house, where they found Nel and Senacus seated around the table where they'd feasted and celebrated before leaving for Ven Ibras. It felt like a lifetime ago, even though barely more than a month had passed. Amela was fluttering around the room, talking to herself as she bemoaned the mess the soldiers had made.

"We need something to wash this wound," Nel told Amela as she examined the cut in Senacus's arm.

The fishmonger's wife paused, clenching fistfuls of her stained dress. "Yes, yes. And then some honey to dress it. Old fisherman's trick, keeps away the infection." She started rummaging through a shelf full of glazed clay pots, eventually pulling one down.

Nel twisted off the lid and then took a quick smell of what was inside. "This will do," she said, and then tipped the jug so that some of the clear liquid inside splashed over the cut. Senacus's jaw tightened, but he did not make a sound.

"What happened?" Keilan asked as Amela set another container on the table.

She paused, her hands shaking so hard that she had to grip the back of one of the chairs. "They arrived a few days ago. Many soldiers, and three of the Pure. Mendicants, too, some with gold on their robes . . . but the one they took orders from had white robes banded with black."

"An inquisitor," Senacus said softly as Nel began to spread honey on his wound. "They are trained to find the truth by any means necessary."

"They took my Pelos," Amela finished with a wrenching sob, fresh tears trickling down her cheeks.

"To the temple in Theris," Nel said. "That's what the paladin said."

"We have to save him. We have to go to Theris." Keilan saw Nel's mouth thin as he said this.

"Remember what we have, Keilan," the knife admonished him, glancing pointedly at the rosewood box Sella was still clutching to her chest. "A single life cannot be weighed against what we saw in the Oracle's vision."

"He's there because of us," Keilan insisted, his voice rising. "Because of *me*."

Nel muttered something under her breath as she began to cut a piece of cloth on the table into strips.

"I have lived for many months at the temple in Theris," Senacus said slowly, not looking at Nel. "And there's a way inside known only to the Pure."

Amela's breathing quickened, hope rising in her face. "Oh, by the Ten, please save my Pelos. Please, Keilan."

There had been a thousand afternoons he'd sat beside the old fishmonger as Pelos drove his wagon from the beach back to his village. He remembered the old man tickling his ear as he pulled forth a copper coin with a sly wink. Keilan had clutched at his mother's dress as she stood beside Pelos, her laughter high and pure from something the fishmonger had said, as his father pulled his fishing boat out of the surf. He knew what Nel was saying was true, but he could not simply abandon Pelos to whatever horrors the inquisitors of Ama would inflict.

"We will find him," he said to Amela. "But there's something you must do as well."

"Anything," she murmured, her eyes shining.

"You have to leave here. It's not safe. Take Sella back to her family and stay at her farm until you get word about Pelos."

He turned to Sella, who was staring at him with her wide, mismatched eyes. For once she wasn't arguing. "I will return one day for you, and bring you back to the Scholia. But it's too dangerous for you to come with us – you see that now, don't you?"

Sella gave a shaky nod, and then she slid the box she'd been holding onto the table and put her arms around him again, resting her cheek on his shoulder. She didn't make any noise, but he could feel her sobs as her thin body shuddered against him.

4: THE CRONE

IT HAD TAKEN less than two days for the armies of Dymoria to slay the mighty Serpent.

"Clever bastards."

Willa ri Numil grunted her agreement, leaning heavily on the ebony sphere that topped her walking cane. She shivered as the wind swirling down from the Bones wriggled through her layers of furs and brushed skeletal fingers against her skin.

"You want to get inside?" Telion asked, eyeing her with concern.

"Not yet," she said, then coughed discreetly into her glove. Telion had turned away from her, gazing down again at the river below them, and so she stole a quick glance at her palm. Good, no blood this time. Maybe whatever sickness had settled in her lungs during the march had run its course.

"Do you think they'll keep the bridge up until we return?"

Willa stepped forward to the edge of the knoll they'd climbed after crossing the Serpent. Below them, a hundred boats bobbed in the swift-rushing waters of the river, lashed together to form a chain stretching from one frozen bank to the other. Planks had been laid down, making a wooden road that the last of the supply wagons were now trundling across.

Willa shrugged. "I do not think so. Already I think the bonds holding together the bridge are fraying. Or at least I don't remember the boats shifting so much when we crossed. I imagine they'll haul them in and keep them here for when we return."

If we return.

She swayed, suddenly unsteady as a tingling numbness swept through her, her head growing light. Before she could fall, though, Telion was beside her, his strong hands holding her up.

"Lady Numil, we should find a fire."

"Very well," she said with a sigh. "A cup of hot soup would be welcome."

Together they began to descend the grassy hillock, her cane thumping on the frozen ground. Telion kept his hand on her arm, and for once she did not pretend she didn't need his support. Below them, the Dymorians had begun to set up camp, tents and the glimmer of kindling fires appearing in the sere gray field. Brooding over everything were the Bones, vast unknowable presences like squatting gods. Deep pools of shadow had spread across their upper reaches as the sun sank towards the horizon. Soon the mountains would merge seamlessly with the night, visible only by the absence of stars.

"You feel the change in the air?" Telion asked, then exhaled hard, as if he could see something in the curling plume of his breath.

"A change?" Willa asked, forcing a faintly mocking edge into her words. "It's the same air here as across the river."

Telion sniffed, the sound he made when he disagreed with her. "Don't seem like it. Feels colder."

"We are farther north by the width of one very large river."

"It's something else."

"Are you scared?" she asked, keeping her voice light and mocking, though she was worried how he would answer. Telion had never admitted fear to her before.

"I suppose I am. Haven't felt like this in a long time."

"Since before you entered my service?"

They had reached the base of the small hill, and the clangor of the unfolding camp swirled around them. Grim-faced soldiers hunched beside the fires, sharpening swords or stirring the contents of iron cookpots. Others pounded stakes into the hard ground or worked at digging out latrines. A Scarlet Guardsman, his red cloak stained and muddied from the river crossing, led his snorting mount through the confusion. Rising above the tents was a great red pavilion, sinuous golden dragons coiling down its sides.

"A long time ago," Telion finally replied, his voice distant. "My family lived on the western side of the Spine. We were Myrasani, I suppose, though we didn't think of ourselves as anything but hill-people. We'd been there for generations, in this rambling old hovel. It was huge – maybe it had been built by some earlier folk. There was this one room that my cousins and I always kept out of. My grandfather had been stabbed to death there by his brother years ago, some foolish blood feud. Holding grudges – that's about the only thing my people did well." Telion guided her around where a handful of soldiers were hard at work hacking a trench out of the earth. "This room . . . you could feel something when you went inside. Not a spirit, though. It was like the evil that had been done there had seeped into the very stones." A small shiver went through Telion, and it passed to her from where he still held onto her arm. "I haven't felt that since I left the hills." He squinted up at the Bones. "I feel it again now. Like the land itself carries a great sorrow."

Willa kept her silence as they continued through the camp. She also felt this creeping unease, here on the fringes of the Frostlands, but she had learned long ago that a leader must always show a strong facade, or those that followed would falter.

"Perhaps it's just me," Telion admitted grudgingly. "The Dymorians seem untroubled by this place."

"Many of them must have been here before," Willa reminded him. Five years ago, not long after the coronation of Cein d'Kara, the new queen had led her army across the Serpent to confront the Skein king who had raided Dymoria for years while her father lay dying. The crushing defeat of the northern barbarians had solidified her hold on the dragon throne, and served notice in all the other courts of Araen that the bastard daughter of the old king was not to be dismissed. Since then, she had gone from triumph to triumph, transforming her northern kingdom into the greatest power in the west. And it was an open secret that she had ushered in a new era of sorcery, which had been suppressed since the days of the ancient cataclysms – the very disasters that had cursed the Frostlands and the lost holdfasts of Min-Ceruth.

"Lady Numil! Lady Numil!"

A young man in the livery of House d'Kara was making his way through the chaos of the camp, waving to get her attention.

Willa shook herself free of Telion's grip and drew herself up when the boy finally reached them. "Yes?"

The servant bowed deeply, breathing heavily, then straightened and held out a slim ivory message case. "My lady, the queen has requested that you join her in the royal tent immediately. Also, a rider from Herath arrived not long ago bearing a letter meant for you."

Willa plucked the case from the boy's hands, turning it over to inspect the red wax seals. They appeared intact, but as a spymaster herself she knew the ease with which a broken seal could be repaired.

"Tell Queen Cein I will join her shortly," she said to the boy, then dismissed him with a flick of her wrist. He sketched another bow and dashed away, weaving among the soldiers as he hurried in the direction of the great red pavilion.

With a last look around to make sure there were no wandering eyes watching her, Willa broke the seal and withdrew the rolled bit of vellum within. She quickly scanned the contents of the letter.

Dearest Auntie,

I hope you are enjoying your sabbatical in Dymoria, and that you are finding the northern air as agreeable as you'd expected. We miss you, but of course you must do what's best for your health. The family has begun to squabble without you here to settle them down, I'm afraid. Uncle has become particularly unruly, and several of the cousins agree with his point of view. You will be happy to know that your hound that had fallen sick has made a good recovery. She and the rest of us eagerly await your return.

With great affection,
Lessian

When she looked up, she found Telion watching her anxiously. "What news?" he asked.

Willa slipped the message into her pocket, wondering if she could take the risk of consigning the paper to one of the campfires. She didn't want to linger long enough to make sure that every scrap had been burned to ash.

"The archons are in disarray. Ghalan has his faction riled up, it seems, and they disagree with my decision to pledge Lyr's strength behind the queen's actions. But he lacks the support to throw a formal challenge. Lessian will keep him tied up for a few months, and by then I'll have returned and can deal with the archon council directly."

"And anything about her?"

Willa tried to draw out the moment, but couldn't hold back her smile. "She will live. Lessian even noted that her recovery was going well."

Telion let out a long, slow breath. He removed the ridiculous fur hat he'd acquired in Herath and ran a hand over his bald head. "Good news, that."

Willa nodded, noticing that Telion's fingers lingered on the scars pockmarking his cheek. "Philias is strong. I knew she would survive." The light inside the woman who had once been a nun of Ama made her as hard to kill as a true paladin. But still, the wounds inflicted by the demon's claws had been severe. Willa pushed away the memory of strips of flesh hanging from Philias's face, bone shining beneath a mask of blood.

"Any word on reinforcements?"

"Lessian makes no mention. We are on our own, it seems." They had ridden north with only a fifty-strong honor guard, but Willa could not really blame herself for taking too few soldiers; even in her wildest imaginings she never thought they'd march into the Frostlands with the Dymorian army.

Telion slipped on his bristly fur hat again. It really did look like there was a weasel curled atop his head. "I suppose it doesn't matter, anyway. Our fight with the Skein would be long over by the time they reached us."

Willa sighed. "Still, it would have been a useful show of support from the council. I have no doubt the queen will notice that we've been abandoned."

Telion stopped as a column of horsemen clopped past, the silver barding of their mounts gleaming in the fading light of day. They had nearly arrived at the center of the camp, the great pavilion rising above the swirling chaos. "At least the Lyrishmen likely won't be needed. No ragged barbarian horde is going to stand against this army, I'd bet my last copper on it."

"The Dymorians triumphed once before," Willa admitted, navigating carefully the churned earth the cavalry had left in their wake. "But that was a different time. The tribes have changed, I've heard. Harsher men from farther north have usurped the Skein who used to squat in the old holdfasts." *And they have dangerous allies*, Willa thought. The demons she had glimpsed in the Oracle's vision, the ones that had lurked in the ruins of Menekar beneath a sundered sky.

"Perhaps," Telion said as they arrived at the entrance to the pavilion. "But I trust in this Crimson Queen." A dozen warriors wearing scarlet cloaks were arrayed around the tent flap, their hands on the hilts of their longswords. One of the guards stepped forward as they approached, then bowed stiffly.

"Lady Numil. Please enter. The queen is expecting you. And if your manservant will accompany you inside he must—"

"I know what I must do, lad," Telion said, shrugging off the sheathed swords strapped across his back. As the Scarlet Guardsman accepted the swords, Willa noticed his gaze lingering on the twining silver serpents that had been artfully fashioned into hilts. In Lyr, these blades would have been recognized at once, but she wasn't sure if the same stories had made their way to Dymoria. Perhaps they had, considering the almost reverential manner in which the Dymorian soldier handed the swords to a waiting servant.

The guardsman gave a curt command and the flaps to the great pavilion were drawn aside. Despite the impressive size of the queen's tent the interior did not seem suitable for royalty. There were wooden screens erected to keep the sleeping compartment and personal quarters hidden away, but what furniture Willa could see was more utilitarian than decadent. No divans mounded with cushions or ornate crystal decorations – just a table of gleaming ebonwood surrounded by chairs that would not have been out of place in a respectable tavern, a simple writing desk recessed in the corner, benches of unadorned wood, and a few low side-tables laden with silver decanters and platters heaped with fruit. It looked more like the command tent of a general who had risen from obscurity and still clung to the old habits forged when he was merely a common soldier.

Most of the chairs were filled, and their occupants turned to regard Willa as she entered. The youthful magister that seemed to have the queen's ear flashed her a friendly grin, his fingers curled around the stem of a wine glass. The two older magisters on his right and left – a thin woman with dark red hair threaded with gray, and a fat man wearing several golden chains beneath his nested chins – watched her with more guarded expressions. There was also the Shan captain of the Scarlet Guard, Kwan Lo-Ren, his arm still in a sling from when it had been injured during the attack by the shadowblades on Saltstone. He offered Willa a curt nod in greeting. Across from him was a lanky Dymorian clad in the simple gray garb of the rangers, his cloak clasped by a brooch fashioned into a golden dragon biting its own tail. Several other soldiers were present as well, and Willa recognized Lord d'Chorn, the canny old field marshal of the Dymorian legions, and Lord d'Fershing, his rival and the commander of the cavalry. D'Chorn wore a scarred, ancient cuirass that appeared identical to the armor of the foot soldiers outside, his only affectation the plume of bright red horsehair that tumbled from the top of the helmet he had placed on the table in front of him, while d'Fershing glittered like a fresh-made sword, every plate of his elaborate armor polished to a mirror sheen.

Cein d'Kara rose from her seat at the head of the table, and with a scraping of chairs all the others hurried to join her. The Crimson Queen of Dymoria had altered her appearance while on the march – no longer did she paint her skin white, nor did she adorn herself with jewels and gold. Her long red hair had been bound back into a plaited braid, and over a simple red tunic and skirt she was armored in a corset of white leather. She also wore matching pauldrons and bracers, all finely tooled with the sinuous dragon that was the emblem of House d'Kara, and a large fire opal flashed on the hilt of the sword at her waist. Cein looked very much like a warrior queen from one of the old stories.

"Lady Numil," she said, gesturing towards the only empty chair at the table. "Join us, please."

"Thank you, Your Highness," Willa replied. After the queen was seated once more, Telion helped Willa to her seat and then retreated to the benches pushed against the walls of the pavilion, which were occupied by several lower-ranked magisters and soldiers trying their best not to draw undue attention to themselves.

A servant hurried up to her bearing a tray of drinks, but Willa waved him away. She wanted a clear head when dealing with the queen.

"Let us continue," the queen said, steepling her hands on the table. "Lord d'Chorn, you were about to describe your battle plan?"

"Aye, my queen," the old soldier replied, his voice as rough as his pockmarked armor. He crooked his finger towards the benches, and an adjunct in much finer garb than his commander leaped up, a large roll of parchment cradled in his arms. With quick, jerky movements that betrayed his nervousness, the young soldier spread the paper upon the table, revealing a map. Forests and hills and rivers were rendered in exquisite detail, with numbers scattered about to denote various degrees of elevation.

"This is where we should make our stand," d'Chorn said, sweeping out his arm to indicate the map. "Three days' march from here, just on the other side of the Gulgetha Pass. Our scouts say that the Skein will march out from Nes Vaneth soon, but it will be nearly a week before they can get that far south. We'll have plenty of time to prepare the ground and set our fortifications."

"And why did you choose here?" the queen asked, leaning forward to study the map.

The old soldier stabbed a finger at a wide empty space between two small hills. "This is easily defensible, and our archers can take the high ground. The slopes are covered in scree and difficult to climb – if the Skein try to dislodge our bowmen they'll be met with volleys of arrows as they struggle up. We can array our pike-men here" – d'Chorn indicated the field again – "with the cavalry held in reserve to meet any attempts to flank our position."

D'Fershing cleared his throat, eliciting a scowl from the old general.

"My queen," the commander of the cavalry interjected before d'Chorn could continue. "Our heavy horse is our greatest advantage against the barbarians. Their stunted little ponies will be swept away in a charge. Why hold our cavalry back? Let us scatter them first and then bring forward our pike to mop up the remnants."

"I agree with the esteemed lord," d'Chorn said through gritted teeth, "that the Skein have no answer for our cavalry. We saw that five years ago. But we should hold them in reserve until we need to strike the decisive blow."

"The gods favor the bold, not the cautious," retorted d'Fershing with a sneer.

The old general flushed, but he ignored his rival to address the queen directly. "We know they will attack us, Your Highness. We must use their impetuousness against them, and let them bleed against our entrenchments."

"How do we know they will attack us?" interrupted the young magister, the one with the streak of silver in his hair.

D'Chorn turned to him with raised eyebrows, as if surprised that the young sorcerer would challenge him in matters of war. "The Skein are proud savages. They fight with little discipline or tactics, and they will be incensed that we've dared sully the sacred earth of their homeland."

"Five years past, that was what happened," the queen began slowly. "But surely they will have drawn their own lessons from that defeat."

The old general tugged on his drooping gray mustache. "The Skein have been the same for a thousand years. Their entire culture is obsessed with finding glory on the battlefield, and we can use this to our advantage once again." D'Chorn glanced smugly at the cavalry commander, who had folded his arms tightly across his chest in disagreement. "So long as we do not try and fight in their manner."

The queen's gaze drifted between her two commanders for a long moment. Then to Willa's surprise she turned to her.

"Lady Numil. What is your advice?"

All eyes in the pavilion settled on her. For almost anyone else, such attention would prove unnerving, but Willa had spent decades dealing with the archons of Lyr, and more than once she had stood before the Council of Black and White to defend her actions. She laced her fingers in front of her and offered up her most conciliating smile.

"Your Highness, esteemed lords and generals. I have little experience planning for battles, but it seems to me that one must assume an old enemy will not make the same mistake twice. I have heard that a new Skein king rules in Nes Vaneth, and he may be a more wily foe than the last."

D'Chorn's face darkened at her words, but before he could respond the queen spoke.

"And I agree with you, Lady Numil. We must not underestimate our enemies." She looked pointedly at d'Chorn before continuing. "But we must also be cautious, and be sure our strategy favors our strengths." This she directed at d'Fershing. There was no censure in her tone, but both generals looked suitably chastened. "We will hold our horse back at first, but I want contingency plans devised for if the Skein do not behave as we expect. Tomorrow evening I want to know what we will do if they show uncharacteristic restraint and will not attack us first. We only have a few weeks' worth of food, and with the Serpent behind us and little enough forage here we cannot wait the Skein out. That is something we must avoid at all costs. How will we draw them out in that scenario, or bring the fight to them, if we must?" She swept those assembled around the table with her gaze. "We will be encamped here for another day, so you have time to prepare. Now go." She stood, splaying her white fingers on the gleaming black ebonwood. Willa pushed herself to her feet as everyone rose with the queen, wincing as a shard of pain jabbed into her spine. The cold of these lands seemed to inflame her old aches.

"Lady Numil. Vhelan. Lo-Ren. Stay with me for a moment longer."

"Of course, Your Highness," Willa said, ducking her head respectfully as the soldiers and magisters filed from the pavilion. Telion caught her eye, clearly unsure what he should do, and she motioned for him to go. The queen hadn't explicitly said he should remain.

When it was just the four of them in the pavilion, save for the servants and guards, Cein closed her eyes and let out a long sigh. It was barely perceptible, but Willa thought she saw a softening in the queen's mien, like she had unclenched the strands of authority gathered in her fist.

"That was well done," the young magister – Vhelan – said lightly, taking a quick sip from his wine glass. "A subtle remonstration to both generals, so neither feels favored."

The queen began to knead her temple, as if she was suffering from a headache. "They are both good men, and capable. But Lord d'Chorn still sees me as the girl that used to dash around Saltstone in a grass-stained dress, and Lord d'Fershing finds the idea of a young woman questioning his tactics outrageous." She opened her eyes, meeting Willa's gaze. "Thank you, Lady Numil. Your support was appreciated."

Willa inclined her head at the queen's words. "The pleasure is mine, Your Highness. Though if they do not value the advice of a young woman, I'm not certain they'll put any more weight in what an old lady says."

The queen gestured, and one of the servants scurried from the shadows bearing a crystal decanter and half-filled the empty cup in front of the queen with firewine. Cein stared for a long moment at the amber liquid as it roiled like the sky during a storm.

"They know you to be canny, Lady Numil. Since my grandfather's reign you have outfoxed the ministers and spymasters of Dymoria. They respect your words, of that I am certain."

Again, Willa ducked her head in appreciation, hoping that the warmth she felt at the queen's praise wasn't showing in her face.

"How are you faring?" the queen asked, picking up her glass but not yet taking a drink.

"Well enough, Your Highness. My old bones ache, but they ached in Lyr as well. At my age there are only degrees of discomfort, and this is not the worst I've felt."

"Good," the queen said, finally tasting the firewine. "I know an army on the march is not where you should be. But I value your advice. And you are the only other person I know who has seen them."

Them. There was no doubt who she meant: the demon children that would bring about the end of the world, if what the Oracle had shown her was true. They were the reason Cein had brought her army into the Frostlands. The queen had glimpsed them here, in Nes Vaneth, through the scrying pool she had used to track the sorcerer who had escaped Saltstone.

The queen waved her hand to encompass the now-empty chairs. "We speak here of pikes and swords and horses, but the coming battle will likely be very different than what happened the last time I was in the north."

"Do you think those demons will join the fight?"

The queen shrugged. "I do not know. My lack of understanding of what these things are and what they want concerns me greatly. Also, I do not know the extent of their powers. It is why I have brought almost my entire Scholia north. Only the apprentices and a handful of magisters remained in Herath. If those demons bring sorcery to the battlefield, they will be met with fire and fury unlike anything that has been seen since the cataclysms."

The memory of black lightning scything from the child demons to fracture against the wards of the silver-haired sorceress came unbidden to Willa. She hoped these things would not accompany the Skein horde south.

"What are they doing in Nes Vaneth? Why have they allied with the northern barbarians?"

The queen tapped her fingers on the rim of her glass. For a long moment she was quiet, as if considering carefully what she should say. Then she half-rose from her chair, her hand going to the silver sword-hilt at her side, and with a single smooth movement she drew the sword from its sheath and laid it upon the ebonwood table.

Willa found that she was holding her breath. The sword was beautiful; she'd never seen its equal before. In the light of the hanging lanterns the steel seemed to have a faintly blueish cast, and runes were incised along its rippling length. The burning fire opal set in its exquisitely-wrought silver hilt looked like it could ransom an archon. Beyond simply the craftsmanship of the sword there seemed to be a weight to it, as if it was forged of some substance greater than merely metal.

"This was made in the holdfasts, perhaps even in Nes Vaneth." The queen's fingers traced the runes carved into the blade. She was gazing at the sword in something like awe. "There is more here than you can see, Lady Numil. Great sorcery is bound within this sword. Nothing like it has been fashioned in a thousand years."

"Where did you get it?" Willa asked, having trouble looking away from the gleaming sword.

"It belonged to the sorcerer I imprisoned. The same one whose blood infused my scrying. He was Min-Ceruthan, an immortal from before the black ice swallowed the holdfasts."

"You said he encountered the Shan demons in Nes Vaneth?"

The queen grimaced. "It was the last thing I saw before the link was severed. Jan had descended beneath the city and found a great chamber swirling with sorcery. Even through the scrying bowl I could feel the power."

"So that was why he traveled north?"

"I believe so. When I first met him, he could not remember his past. But I helped bring his memories back."

"And you think he was seeking out this lost sorcery of his people?"

The queen nodded, her slim white fingers tightening around the sword's hilt. "But the demons were there first, and he was captured or killed. Perhaps whatever lurks in the ruins of Nes Vaneth is what these creatures will use to bring down the devastation the Oracle showed you in her temple."

Willa kept her face carefully blank, but her thoughts raced down twisting corridors. When the queen had first told her she was going to bring her armies into the Frostlands, she had explained to Willa that she had discovered the whereabouts of the Shan demons that threatened the world. But now a worm of doubt was squirming in Willa's mind.

Had Cein d'Kara marched into the Frostlands to destroy the unholy children . . . or to claim whatever great sorcery persisted in the ruins of Nes Vaneth? What were the limits of the Crimson Queen's ambition? Would her meddling in the magic of the ancients unleash the same doom the demons wished to bring about? A cold fist clenched her gut as she gazed across the table at Cein d'Kara. How far would she go to reclaim the lost sorceries? Would she risk the world itself?

Willa sought to change the subject before her concerns showed in her face. She shifted in her chair, reaching for something to ask the queen.

"I was curious, Your Highness. This, ah, this sorcerer. You said he was your prisoner, and he was freed by that Shan we saw in your scrying bowl. How did she do that? Was he not well guarded?"

Cein's mouth twisted ruefully, and she shot a quick glance at Kwan Lo-Ren. "It was my mistake."

"The Cho girl snuck past my Scarlet Guardsmen, my queen."

Cein made a cutting motion with her hand, dismissing her captain's words. "I was the one who decided to imprison Jan in the ruins of Ravenroost and not the bowels of Saltstone. I was . . .

dangling him, like a lure on a hook. I hoped the sorceress who had led the shadowblades – the one who had challenged me that night – I hoped that she would come for him. I wove powerful sorceries into the stone of that tower to trap her . . . but in the end, it was not the sorceress who freed him." She shook her head. "I erred, obsessing over these immortals and ignoring the fact that the ripples caused by the assault would attract the interest of others, not all of whom draw their strength from sorcery."

"It was not what you foresaw, but he did lead you to the demons," Willa reminded her. "And they are the true threat." *You do believe that, don't you? We are not here to plunder the holdfasts, are we?*

The queen smiled at her, but it did not seem to touch her eyes. "Of course."

5: CHO LIN

SHE HAD LIVED her life alone, and now she would die alone.

The Skein had dragged Jan from his cell two days ago. Cho Lin thought he had still been alive at that time, but since he had never returned, she had now given him up for dead. She should have felt some sadness about this, she knew, but it was as if the cold had leached all her emotions away. The despair and sorrow and anger that had once filled her had been replaced by an aching numbness.

When the prison's door grated open, she was not flooded with fear or hope. She could not even bring herself to raise her head to see who had come. If it was Jan being brought back, it only meant his suffering had not yet ended. If it was her own death that had arrived, at least she would escape this place. And if it was the gaoler, she would have fresh bones to gnaw and water to drink.

Many boots scuffed the stone, and harsh Skein voices she did not recognize filled the chamber. With some effort she finally drew herself back from the darkness, struggling to focus on the figures clustered outside her cell. A key squealed in the lock, and for the first time in what seemed like forever the barred door swung wide.

Once, she would have leapt towards freedom, tearing at her captors like a wild tiger. But there was no strength left in her limbs. Even the Nothing had abandoned her, and she had proven herself unworthy of her family name. The Cho ancestors must be peering at her contemptuously from beyond the veil, ashamed of what she had become.

Rough hands grabbed beneath her arms and hauled her to her feet. Massive Skein warriors loomed on either side of her, keeping her upright. Another stood in front of her, smaller and slightly stooped, dressed in tattered black robes. The hands curled around the staff he leaned against were ancient and spotted, threaded with veins, but Cho Lin could not see the man's face; he wore a mask stitched of many scraps of skin: some of the swatches were dark as pitch, others pale and cracked like marble. Ragged holes had been cut for his mouth and eyes, though she saw only shadows pooled beneath the mask.

A priest of the Skin Thief, the blackest of the Skein gods. Cho Lin had seen men like him before, when she had dwelt in the Bhalavan as a guest of the Stag thane. Only the White Worm welcomed the chosen of the Skin Thief, though even then the priests had not mingled on the benches or in the great hall.

The priest regarded her for a long moment; then he barked a command, and she was dragged stumbling from the cell. She tensed, trying to muster the strength to resist, but the hands clamped on her arms were like bands of iron.

Flickering torchlight illuminated ancient stone and broken statues looming from the darkness. Twisting passages weathered by the turning of countless ages flowed past as they forced her along. Then the ceiling opened up above her and she was once more in the great hall of the Bhalavan, the vast space filled with long tables and the tiered dais where the king and his entourage feasted. The benches were empty, the fire pits cold. She glimpsed huddled thralls recessed in the shadows, watching her fearfully as the Skein carried her through the silent hall.

Where was everyone? Even on the morning the king had returned from his great hunt, when nearly all the Skein had waited for him on the great avenue that cut through Nes Vaneth, the Bhalavan had not seemed so abandoned.

The priest stumped across the hall, leaning heavily on his staff, and the warriors holding Cho Lin followed. They slipped through the massive bronze doors, and the brightness of the day struck Cho Lin like a slap across the face. She blinked, her eyes burning after so many weeks in her cell with only a thin shaft of light trickling from a single narrow window. Her head reeled, her gorge rose, and if there was anything in her stomach she probably would have been sick. Around her sprawled the shattered white-stone ruins of Nes Vaneth, here and there pocked with gleaming chunks of the black ice that had swallowed the city. A winter storm must have raged while she'd been imprisoned, as fresh snow lay heavy over the city.

"Where are you taking me?" she rasped, her throat feeling like it was coated with crushed glass.

She hadn't expected an answer – not many of these barbarians even spoke a southern tongue – but the priest in his tattered robes suddenly halted, turning back to her.

"He demands you," the old Skein said in rough Menekarian, his frozen breath trickling from his mask's mouth-slit.

"Who?"

"The servant of the Skin Thief. He spoke to me." The fervor with which the priest said this chilled Cho Lin. "Soon he will wriggle inside your flesh and eat your soul, and I will be favored above all others for bringing him to you."

The Betrayers. They must have decided to finally punish her for what her ancestor had done to them. The Sword of Cho was broken, and now the last daughter of Cho Xin would spill her life-blood in the snow.

They turned from the central artery that linked the distant collapsed gates to the Bhalavan, starting on a smaller road that wended between sundered pillars and the remnants of once-mighty buildings. This surprised her – she had been told several times that the Skein avoided going into the ruins of Nes Vaneth, believing the city haunted by the ghosts of the cursed people that had perished here long ago. Most of the barbarians instead dwelt in longhouses outside the tumbled walls, save for the king and his favored warriors, who ruled the Frostlands from the Bhalavan in the manner of the Min-Ceruthan sorceress queens of old.

Yet the priest was leading them deeper and deeper into the corpse of this dead city, wading through knee-deep drifts, muttering to himself in his twisted northern language.

A low roar came from further ahead, many voices speaking at once. The snow here was churned, as if a great number of people had passed this way recently. The footsteps funneled through a large doorway set into a high wall, still standing among the devastation. On the other side of this entrance Cho Lin saw movement, dark furs, and the glint of metal.

Again she strained to escape the warriors, but she was too weak. She controlled her breathing, reaching for the Nothing within the Self, praying to her ancestors to feel that flood of strength. She scrabbled helplessly, unable to find the calm and focus she needed.

Without hesitating, the priest of the Skin Thief preceded her through the entrance, and she was forced to follow.

They stood high up on the lip of a great half-bowl sunk into the side of a slope. Tiered white-stone benches rippled down the side of the hill before dropping abruptly into a snowy pit bounded by stone walls. Dozens of Skein were clustered upon the benches, and a roar went up when those closest to the doorway saw her standing there. It looked like a place for the spring-blossom theater or the acrobatics that wandering troupes performed in Shan during the solstices. Though that sunken pit did not so much resemble a stage as . . .

An arena.

A lone figure stood in the center of the snow, and even from this distance Cho Lin could see who it was. The knot in her stomach tightened. The southerner's head was tilted up, watching her, and though she couldn't see his face she was sure he wore the same blank expression as when she had seen him before. There was no tension in the way he waited, as if whatever was to come this day was of no real consequence. But Cho Lin remembered the yearning hunger she had felt in the presence of this man; she knew he waited down there for her. And he meant to kill her.

"No, no," she murmured, redoubling her efforts to tear herself from the Skein. Terror sluiced through her. This thing, this creature . . . it was not a man, of that she was certain. It was a servant of the Betrayers, enticed from whatever dark place they drew their power.

Laughter erupted from the watching Skein when they saw her feeble struggles. Cho Lin dug in her heels on the stone, but the warriors easily lifted her as they started to descend. She thrashed in their grip, trying to look anywhere but the demon in the pit, her eyes sliding over the jeering Skein as she desperately searched for any who would help her.

There! A familiar face within the crowd.

"Verrigan!" she cried when she caught sight of the Stag captain. He had saved her from the wraiths in the Frostlands, then brought her to Nes Vaneth and vouched for her before his thane. They had ridden together over those endless frozen leagues, sharing stories of life in the north and the south. He had been kind to her. A friend.

"Help me!" she screamed, reaching towards him. But in reply he only ducked his head and looked away, as if embarrassed to meet her eyes.

"Verrigan! I am your guest here! A guest of the Stag!" she persisted, her voice raw from screaming. Yet she knew there was no hope. What could he do, with so many of his countrymen baying for her blood? She sagged in the grip of the Skein warriors, feigning defeat as they carried her down the stairs.

They were nearly at the edge of the pit now. It was a circular space a hundred paces or so wide, empty save for the man waiting for her in its center. A curving stone wall rose up along the pit's far side, and there was a large archway that once would have emptied into the ruins, but it was now filled with a seamless chunk of the black ice. She could see no way in or out of the pit . . . except by being tossed down.

Which was what the Skein clearly intended to do to her. The masked priest had stopped at the cracked stone balustrade that encircled the edge of the pit, watching her as she was carried closer.

Cho Lin threw her head violently to the left, smashing into the face of one of the warriors. He gave a pained cry as something popped in his cheek, and his grip on her arm slackened just enough for her to wrench it free. With all her faded strength she slammed her open palm into the nose of the other Skein, driving the bone upward; she'd hoped to push it into his brain and kill him instantly, but either she hadn't struck with enough force, or his face was as hard as stone. Blood splattered her hand and he reeled backwards, but he did not fully let go of her arm. She kicked the inside of his leg hard and he went to one knee, but still he did not unclench his grip. Cho Lin shrieked in frustration, prying desperately at his fingers.

But he'd held on long enough, and she'd missed her chance. The Skein around her surged, and a dozen more pairs of hands grabbed at her arms and body and legs. Cho Lin thrashed as she was lifted and carried forward; above her, the gray sky spun, and then she was tumbling through the air.

The force of hitting the snow drove the breath from her lungs. Her side ached where she'd landed, but luckily because of the recent storm the snow was not hard-packed – she could easily have broken a limb falling from this height. She wiped snow from her eyes and glanced up at the Skein who were leaning over the balustrade, laughing and pointing down at her. Cho Lin spat a Shan curse at them and then pushed herself unsteadily to her feet, her boots disappearing into the powdery snow.

The southerner had not moved. He was dressed in the same frilled linen doublet, though it had grown more tattered since she'd last seen him in her cell. His breeches belonged on a southern dandy, loose and billowy. With a creeping dread she realized that he had lost his shoes and now stood barefoot in the snow, unconcerned by the cold that would have quickly claimed the toes of any normal man.

"What are you?" Cho Lin murmured as the southerner began to stride towards her. His face was frozen in a grin, and his pale blue eyes were locked on her. There was no blade in his hand that she could see.

Cho Lin calmed herself, reaching for the Nothing. She focused on the pounding of her heart and the deepness of her breathing, and the world around her seemed to fade away. The jeers of the watching Skein dwindled to a distant whisper. For many days she'd struggled to grasp the emptiness inside her, but here and now, as this thing stalked closer, she found herself falling deeper and deeper within herself. This was what she was born to do. She was a weapon, honed to perfection. Let this thing come.

She barely saw the first blow. One moment the southerner had been calmly approaching her, his long arms swinging at his side, and then her head had snapped back and she'd been tossed in the air, the side of her face burning. She sprawled in the snow, gasping. He'd struck her, a casual backhand like he was punishing an insolent child. Cho Lin scrambled to her feet, desperately holding fast to the Nothing as her surprise threatened to sever her connection.

The man had not pressed his advantage. He continued to stroll towards her, the same empty smile curving the edges of his lips.

Cho Lin snarled, wiping blood from the corner of her mouth, and brought up her hands as she set her feet in the Leaping Tiger stance. Another blindingly fast strike, and she just managed to jerk herself backwards, his fingers nearly brushing her neck. She lashed out with her own blow, driving her fist into his jaw.

It was like punching iron.

His counter caught her in the stomach and for a moment she was airborne again, her boots lifting from the snow. She managed to keep from collapsing, though, landing on her feet and backpedaling frantically to put some distance between her and this thing.

It wasn't human. It couldn't be. The blow she had just landed should have shattered its jaw, and she hadn't even managed to dislodge its grin.

Tears were streaming down its face, but otherwise its expression remained unchanged. Tears of joy, Cho Lin realized with a shudder as she stepped backwards, gathering herself again. The thing looked to be in the throes of ecstasy.

Her ribs were cracked, if not broken. She struggled to ignore the grating pain in her side as the creature sauntered closer. The thing was faster than any man, yet it had showed little actual fighting skill. Every blow had been delivered with unnatural speed and strength but nothing else. She could use that. Anticipate its actions.

As soon as the creature drew within striking distance Cho Lin twisted away from the blow she hadn't even seen coming yet. But it did come; she felt its passage as a rush of air on her cheek, and then she used her preemptive dodge to spin closer to the thing, slamming her elbow as hard as she could into its throat.

The thing that looked like a man stumbled back, clutching at its neck. Cho Lin didn't give it time to recover, surging forward, channeling the Nothing through the strikes she rained down on its head. She drove it to its knees, unleashing all the helpless rage that had consumed her during her weeks of imprisonment. In her desperation, Cho Lin found a reservoir of strength she never imagined was inside her.

She bludgeoned its face, skinning her knuckles raw as she struck it again and again and again. There was blood on her hand, some of it hers, but most coming from the gashes she had opened on its brow and cheeks. Cho Lin screamed as the creature went to its hands and knees, slamming her fist into the base of its skull.

Then she was retreating, clutching at her side in shock. Her furs had been shredded, and she could feel hot blood pulsing from wounds that had appeared just above her hip. She struggled to understand what she was seeing.

The creature was climbing to its feet again. Its face was hidden behind a mask of blood and bruises – one of its eye sockets had been crushed, the eye reduced to nothing more than white jelly, but if anything its smile had widened, showing teeth stained red.

Its hands. Cho Lin moaned, her head spinning, and nearly collapsed in the snow. The fingers of the creature had changed, lengthening into glistening, tapered claws, wet from having ripped her open moments ago.

Cho Lin's tenuous grasp on the Nothing slipped through her fingers like water. She was thrust back into the moment, the thud of her heart and her ragged breathing swallowed by the avalanche of noises from the outside world: her boots, crunching in the snow as she scrambled away from this thing; the piercing cry of an eagle circling far overhead; the muted rumblings of the Skein. They were not jeering anymore, she realized. They seemed stunned by what was happening in the pit.

The creature stalked after her, unconcerned with the reactions from those watching above. Cho Lin saw droplets of her blood fall from the thing's claws, a trail of red appearing behind it in the snow.

"Your heart I will carve from your chest," the thing said in a cracked and broken voice. "And I will make a gift of it."

Cho Lin threw herself to the side, barely keeping her feet as the talons flickered out to carve the air. Lines of fire opened in her left shoulder, and it felt like a chunk of her flesh had been gouged away. She stumbled back, unable to stop the hitching sobs rising up inside her. Beneath her furs, warmth slid down her arm.

Out of the corner of her eye she saw something glitter, a silvery shape, arcing across the bleak gray sky. It landed a few dozen paces from her, raising a spray of snow.

What was this? Even the creature had paused, as if confused.

She turned towards the tiers of benches sunk into the side of the slope. A man with yellow braids stood at the balustrade above the pit, and as she watched he heaved something else with great force, nearly tumbling over the edge.

Verrigan.

Whatever it was he had thrown flashed as it tumbled end over end. Then it sank quivering into the snow, nearly touching the first object: a length of gleaming steel with a carved ivory handle.

Her swords. Without pausing to consider the how or the why of it, Cho Lin lunged towards the blades, her boots churning the snow. Time seemed to grind slower as she approached where her butterfly swords waited, and she feared that the thing's talons would plunge into her back before she could reach where they lay.

But with a wordless cry of triumph she arrived first and scooped her swords from the snow, her fingers sliding into their accustomed grooves. She whirled around, bringing up both blades, the Nothing flowering within her as if a key had been fitted into a locked door. Her arm and side pulsed with pain, her ribs ached, but she was whole again. Now she was the one stalking forward, her butterfly swords dancing.

The creature's bland smile faltered, a flicker of something like uncertainty shivering its ruined face. Then it hissed like a serpent and leaped at her; its claws had continued to grow, and now were longer than daggers, curved like the talons of a raptor.

Cho Lin twisted to avoid the strike and lashed out with her sword. She felt the briefest of resistance and two of the claws tumbled to the snow. No gore leaked from the talons – instead, thin lines of blackness dribbled from the stumps, unspooling in the air like blood spilled in water. The creature raised its hand, its brow knitted in confusion as it examined its mutilated fingers.

Cho Lin didn't give it time to recover. She rushed forward, swords flashing. The creature brought its hands up as if its talons could ward away her steel, and she sliced through them, chunks of bone and flesh falling away.

The thing screeched. It sounded like nothing human, like nothing of this world. Cho Lin gritted her teeth and pressed forward even as the curling black smoke from the creature's ravaged hands slid across her own wounds, sending fresh waves of pain coursing through her. She thrust one of her swords into the thing's chest, searching for its heart, but despite piercing whatever was beneath its ribs the demon did not die, and it swiped at her with its shattered claws. Cho Lin leaped back, ripping her sword free as the jagged stumps of its fingers passed in front of her eyes.

The thing seemed to flicker for the briefest of moments. It came and went so fast Cho Lin wasn't sure what she had seen, but the blood-drenched man in front of her had vanished and been replaced by . . . something else. Twisting black flesh, a distended jaw bristling with fangs, and huge, slitted yellow eyes as blank as the moon and as fathomless as the Nothing. Then it was only a wounded man once more with claws for hands, swaying as it struggled to stay upright.

Gathering all her remaining strength, Cho Lin stepped closer and slashed at the thing's neck. Its head tumbled to the snow, followed a heartbeat later by its limp body.

Cho Lin nearly collapsed as well, and she had to brace herself by thrusting her blades into the snow and leaning on the hilts.

She took great gulping swallows of the frozen air, her breath steaming around her. Her legs trembled, and the day seemed to darken.

Screams came from behind her. With some effort she twisted around and tried to focus on the benches ascending the slope; they were swarming now as the Skein surged from their seats. The black-robed priest of the Skin Thief was the one yelling the loudest. He stood on the lip of the pit, leaning out over the balustrade and pointing at her. A few of the Skein were rushing to join him, and Cho Lin knew it would only be a short while before they dropped down into the pit and came for her.

Fighting back the shadows that were trying to creep across her vision she glanced around frantically, hoping for some crack in the wall that she could squeeze through. Nothing – this seemed like the only building in all of Nes Vaneth that wasn't at least partially collapsed. There was only the arched entrance to the pit, and it was sealed by a wall of black ice. At least that was as far away from the Skein as possible, and she could put her back to something and keep them from encircling her. With stumbling steps she began running towards the ice.

Wait. Cho Lin squinted, unsure if what she saw was a trick conjured up by her pain and exhaustion. But as she neared the wall, she realized it was real. A woman was encased within like a fly in amber, her mouth slightly parted and her palms pressed against the ice. She wore a flowing dress, and a thin diadem made of twisting silver threads encircled her brow. Her eyes were wide and glassy in death.

Another barked command floated across the pit, and Cho Lin turned to see several Skein warriors being lowered over the balustrade by their brethren. Soon they would be charging across the snow towards her, far too many for her to fight. She tightened her blood-slicked grip on the handles of her swords. Let them come. She would die, but she'd send as many as she could screaming down into whatever abyss welcomed their heathen souls.

A crack sounded from behind her like a frozen lake fracturing. She twisted around, staring in confusion at the black ice and the corpse trapped within.

Except there was no corpse; nothing was inside the ice now. Cho Lin swallowed, trying to make sense of this. A fissure had appeared that hadn't been there a moment ago. It started from where the ice merged with the stone archway and split right down the center until it reached the base. As Cho Lin watched in mute astonishment, the crack widened, chunks of ice sloughing away.

Then the ice shattered, breaking apart like a mirror smashed against stone.

Battle cries reached her through the haze of her surprise. A handful of Skein were rushing across the pit, swords and axes upraised. They would reach her soon, and more were clambering down the wall. Death was here for her if she stayed and fought.

She glanced back at where the ice had been. Beyond the stone archway the tumbled white-stone ruins of Nes Vaneth stretched away, desolate and empty.

Not empty. A shiver went through her as she glimpsed a slim white arm disappearing around a cracked pillar. Someone was out there.

"Wait!" Cho Lin cried, moving as fast as her aching body would let her, the shards of the black ice crunching beneath her boots.

Gritting her teeth against the pain, Cho Lin hobbled to where she'd seen the stranger. Nothing. Just more snow-covered chunks of stone and the husks of collapsing buildings.

Cries of alarm from the arena. The Skein warriors had reached the stone archway, and were gesturing at something among the ruins that from her vantage she couldn't see. None of them were looking at her, or seemed willing to enter the ruins. After a few moments they began to back away, and a few even turned and ran, slipping and stumbling in the snow. Fear was evident in the faces still turned towards the ruined city.

They were not pursuing her. At least not yet, though surely they would find their courage soon enough. Cho Lin pushed deeper into Nes Vaneth, her hand pressed to her side to stop as much of the bleeding as she could. Still, she felt it soaking her furs and crawling down her legs, pooling in her boot. She had to keep one hand on the ancient stone walls to keep herself from falling.

She was going to die.

Movement ahead of her. A pale woman in a flowing dress walked across the gap between two buildings. She did not notice Cho Lin, staring straight ahead.

"Help!" Cho Lin croaked, stumbling after her. If the woman lived among the ruins she might have cloth to bind wounds, or some other means to staunch her bleeding.

Cho Lin emerged from the alleyway and found herself in a tangle of narrow streets, listing ruins rising up around her. There was no sign of the woman.

"Where are you?" Cho Lin yelled, looking around frantically. A numbness was creeping through her now that was even more terrifying than the pain it replaced.

She gasped in relief when she saw the woman drifting inside a half-collapsed doorway a hundred paces deeper within this warren. Real or not, a ghost or a refugee from the recent Skein civil war, Cho Lin did not care. This was her only hope.

Half her lower body was now tingling, and she was forced to drag one of her legs in the snow as she struggled towards where she'd seen the woman disappear. Had she been wearing the same dress as the woman in the ice? Perhaps she'd been on the other side of the black ice, looking in, and it had only been some trick of Cho Lin's addled mind that she had appeared to be trapped within.

Cho Lin did not hesitate when she arrived at the entrance. Its lintel was cracked, buckling under the weight of the stone above, but the building had stood for a thousand years, so it wasn't likely to collapse today. Cho Lin plunged into the gloom and found herself in a large circular chamber, empty except for a block of white stone in the center.

No woman. But there was a crack in one of the walls, just large enough that Cho Lin thought she could squeeze through. Perhaps that was where she'd gone.

Her breathing rasped loud and wet as she crossed to the fractured wall and peered into the darkness within.

"Hello?" she cried, but there was no answer.

Biting her lip to keep from crying out in pain, Cho Lin wormed her way inside the crack. There was a passage here, so low-ceilinged that she had to crouch. With her hands braced on either side of the cold passage she began to move forward in a crouch. She'd thrust her butterfly swords into her belt, and the only sounds she heard were their tips scraping against the stone floor.

The corridor twisted, and for a few long moments she crept along in absolute blackness. Panic rose up inside her, but before it seized her completely she saw a glow spilling from somewhere up ahead.

It was another chamber, illuminated by shafts of sunlight falling through holes in the domed roof. There were no other entrances to the chamber, but the woman was not here. Where could she have gone?

The statue of a robed girl stood in the center of the room, its arms held out with its palms upraised, as if it had once carried some burden. At its feet was a stone basin overflowing with water. Cho Lin was suddenly painfully aware of her thirst, and she pushed herself through the rift in the wall and limped across the chamber to the looming statue. Her body burning in agony, she lowered her face to the basin and scooped water into her mouth. It was sweet and surprisingly warm.

She drank deeply, and then with her head whirling she laid herself down between the statue's bare stone feet. The darkness she'd been fighting so hard to keep from swallowing her crashed over Cho Lin like a wave, and she knew no more.

6: KEILAN

THE BRIGHT YELLOW moon hung heavy and swollen in the cloudless sky, gilding the tombs and graves of Ama's lichyard. Unlike in life, the poor and the rich existed here side by side: many of the resting places were marked simply by unadorned stones chiseled with the names of the faithful, while above other graves loomed elaborate statues, representations of the Aspect of Ama which the dead had once embraced. There were even a few stone houses set into the side of the hill, the names of rich Theris families carved above the locked entrances.

Keilan hunkered in the shadow of one of these tombs, his eyes on the temple of Ama below. It was a sprawling edifice, so large that it blocked much of the view of the city beyond. Thin minarets pierced the night sky, rising up around a great copper dome that glowed with a spectral radiance in the light of the moon. Most of the windows of the temple were dark, though a few small flickerings suggested that some mendicants were up late, perhaps studying the Tractate, or with a candle beside their bed to keep the night-terrors at bay.

Was Pelos sleeping somewhere inside? Senacus had said there were underground cells where the inquisitors of Ama plied those who had knowledge they desired. Would they be allowed to rest at night, or did their tortures continue unabated?

Keilan swallowed back a sudden ache in his throat. This had happened because of him. And Pelos must not have told them where Keilan had gone, otherwise the fish monger would have returned to Chale. He had stayed strong. Somewhere, Nel was creeping through the darkened corridors of the temple, following the route Senacus had mapped for her. Keilan desperately hoped that the Pelos she found was still whole in mind and body, and that whatever scars he bore were not too deep.

Thinking of Senacus made him cast about for the paladin. Keilan found him quickly, even though he had donned the bone amulet that hid his radiance. The Pure had not moved very far since Nel had slipped away into the darkness. He was a shadow kneeling before a shrouded statue, some Aspect of Ama, and from the way his head was bowed, Keilan thought he must be lost in prayer.

Or perhaps he begged for forgiveness. Killing another of the Pure had taken a terrible toll on the paladin – Senacus had not spoken of it on the road to Theris, but his haunted eyes and haggard face told Keilan that he suffered terribly. Keilan still felt some lingering resentment for what Senacus had done on Niara's island, but it pained him to see the paladin so distraught. And again, his grandmother's death was truly his fault. Tragedy clung to him like a funeral shroud, destroying the lives of those around him. Xin would still be alive if they had never met along the Wending Way. Keilan scratched absently at the scar on his arm as a wave of guilt and self-loathing swelled within him.

Maybe he could save Pelos. Or at least Nel could. If anyone was capable of sneaking inside a temple of Ama and freeing a prisoner of the inquisitors, it was the knife from Lyr. Muttering a prayer to the sea gods of his father, Keilan drew his cloak tighter and waited.

"Keilan."

He came groggily awake, for a moment confused as to why he was huddled against a stone slab, his head pillowed on his pack. Then it all returned in a rush. Pelos. Nel. The inquisitors. Senacus crouched over him, his face shadowed.

The sky was just beginning to lighten, and the copper dome of the temple was infused with a pale pink. Shreds of dawn were creeping over the distant horizon, revealing the red-tiled roofs of Theris and the mighty keep of the ruling duke. Keilan's clothes were damp from the morning dew, his exposed skin cold and slick. He shivered, uncoiling from the uncomfortable position in which he'd fallen asleep.

"Nel's back?" Keilan murmured, blinking away the gumminess in his eyes as he peered down the gravestone-littered slope of the lichyard.

"There," Senacus replied.

Keilan followed his outstretched hand to where two figures were laboring up the hill. Relief washed through Keilan when he recognized the spindly-legged and barrel-chested shape of Pelos. Nel was holding tight to the fishmonger's arm, and from the way he was struggling, that might have been the only reason he was still upright.

"Pelos!" Keilan cried, coming to his feet.

"Quiet," Senacus hissed, but Keilan ignored the paladin, nearly slipping in the wet grass as he rushed towards his old friend.

The fishmonger paused, swaying, then raised a shaking hand when he noticed Keilan approaching.

Keilan couldn't hold back his tears. Pelos looked like he had aged a dozen years since he'd seen him last. His once-dark hair and beard, which had always been threaded with gray for as long as Keilan could remember, were now bone-white. Lines creased his face, and purple blotches shadowed his red-rimmed eyes.

Careful not to knock over his friend, Keilan embraced Pelos. Beneath his filthy clothes he was shockingly thin, and Keilan could feel the bones of the fishmonger's back through his shirt.

"I'm so sorry," Keilan whispered into the old man's shoulder.

"It's all right, boy," Pelos replied hoarsely. "I'm still here."

"Just barely," Nel said, stepping away from Pelos. She folded her arms across her chest, leaning against a cracked grave marker. "I thought he was gone when I found him hanging there in the catacombs. But the old man is stronger than he looks." She ran a hand through her hair, and Keilan saw how exhausted she was as well.

"We can't stay here," Senacus said, staring down at the awakening city. "Perhaps we can find a room in an inn for the day." Abruptly, he turned towards Nel. "Did you kill anyone?"

She shook her head, and at least some of the burden the paladin was carrying around seemed to lift.

"Thank you," he said, the relief plain in his voice. "There are many good men in the temple."

"More of your brothers," Nel said. "I saw two of the Pure, and there may be others." She glanced at Keilan. "I wouldn't use any of your sorcery until we're well outside the city."

"Let me sit for a moment, boy," Pelos said, clutching at Keilan's arm as he stiffly lowered himself onto a stone slab, the base for one of the Aspects.

"Rest," Keilan murmured, peering at the sprawling temple below. He couldn't see any activity – no lightbearers or mendicants were boiling from the doors searching for Pelos, so it seemed his escape had so far gone unnoticed.

When he looked again at the fishmonger, he saw that Pelos had placed his elbows on his knees and was leaning forward, his head hanging down. For a moment he was so still that Keilan thought his exhaustion might have overwhelmed him and he'd somehow fallen asleep while sitting, but then the old man spoke.

"So did you discover where your mother came from?"

Keilan rubbed at the back of his neck, where there was a knot of pain from how he had slept. "I did. I met my grandmother, Pelos. She was a sorcerer, too."

"Was?"

"She . . . she died. Her name was Niara."

Pelos fell quiet again, but to Keilan's surprise his shoulders were moving up and down. Was he sobbing? Keilan stepped closer, concerned, and laid his hand lightly on his old friend's head.

"Are you all right?" he asked.

Pelos reached up to grip Keilan's arm. Slowly he turned his face, and Keilan saw that his cheeks were indeed glistening with tears. But there was no sadness in his expression – rather, his smile was broad and his eyes danced with humor. Unease filled Keilan. Had his ordeal broken him?

"Niara," Pelos said, rising. His hold on Keilan's arm tightened. "I always wondered what happened to that strange witch."

"What?" Keilan managed, and then his shoulder was wrenched from its socket and he was tumbling through the air.

Blinding pain overwhelmed him as he struck a grave marker, the bones in his side crunching. Keilan gasped, points of light exploding in his vision, his fingers clawing weakly in the wet grass. He tried to push himself to his hands and knees, but the arm that Pelos had ripped loose betrayed him and he sprawled face-first, tasting dirt.

No. Not Pelos.

His old friend was gone, and in his place loomed the creature from Keilan's nightmares. The genthyaki, Seeker Garmond had named it. Leathery wings unfolded behind a gaunt, scaled body pocked with curling thorns. The thing was still smiling, but now its leer was filled with sharp, yellowed teeth. A long arm roped with muscle lashed out at Nel; the knife ducked, and the genthyaki's talons shredded the face of an Aspect statue like it was truly flesh and blood, chunks of stone falling away. Before Nel could recover, the monster's stunted tail whipped around and caught her, tossing her aside like she was a cloth doll. Keilan moaned when she smashed into one of the tombs, the back of her head bouncing off stone. She slumped to the ground, unmoving, the daggers she had somehow managed to draw sliding from her limp fingers.

"Nel," Keilan whispered, scrabbling for his sorcery, but the throbbing pain in his shoulder made the magic run through his fingers like water.

Senacus and the genthyaki circled each other among the gravestones. Dawn light slid along the length of the paladin's white-metal sword, and the radiance of Ama spilled once more from his eyes.

"I will drink you, burning man," said the creature in its ragged voice. "Your soul will never walk through the gates of the Golden City."

Senacus lunged, his sword flickering, but the genthyaki seemed to flow out of the way of the blade. It gave a croaking chortle, the spines on its back flaring.

"You are just a sad, crippled thing. They cut away your power and turned you into this abomination. A shadow of what you could have been."

Senacus lashed out again, and the genthyaki twisted away. Keilan's breath caught in his throat as the monster swiped with its talons, almost too fast to see, but somehow the white-metal sword was there and with a rending shriek deflected the blow.

The genthyaki hissed in what sounded like frustration, then came again at the paladin in a flurry of arcing claws. Senacus gave ground, catching one swipe with his sword as he dodged behind the same shrouded stone Aspect he had been praying to the night before. With contemptuous ease the genthyaki curled its talons against the statue and shoved it hard to the side; a crack sounded as the Aspect slid from its base, toppling, and before Senacus could react the monster surged forward.

Blood sprayed as claws as long as daggers sliced through the Pure's armor, and Senacus reeled away, just barely avoiding being disemboweled by the following strike. The genthyaki followed, scenting weakness, but the pale crescent of the paladin's white-metal sword flashed and then it was the genthyaki stumbling back, its black blood steaming in the cold morning air. Roaring in pain and rage, the monster leaped forward, batting aside the Pure's sword and sending it spinning from his hand to clatter among the stones. Senacus cried out as the genthyaki's claws sank into his chest, shredding his white-scale cuirass and piercing the flesh beneath. Weakly, he raised his blood-stained arms, as if this could ward away the demon swelling above him.

Bracing himself on a grave marker with his one good arm, Keilan hauled himself to his feet and screamed, desperately attempting to distract the genthyaki before it killed Senacus. The shapechanger ignored him, wings flaring as it reared back with its claws upraised.

Strands of squirming darkness slithered from elsewhere, sinking into the genthyaki's back and wrapping around its arm and neck. The beast keened as flowers of black blood bloomed across its body, shaking itself violently to try and dislodge where the shadowy ropes had plunged into its flesh. A few came loose, but like serpents they struck again and again.

"Mistressss!" the genthyaki screamed as the strands pulled hard in unison, hurling the monster backwards to crash amongst the graves.

Keilan stumbled towards Senacus, cradling his dislocated arm. He searched frantically for what had attacked the genthyaki.

A slight woman with dark hair and dusky skin was calmly threading her way between the stones of the lichyard. She was dressed in a simple brown tunic and dress, like a peasant of the Kingdoms might wear, but there was nothing common in her looks or bearing. She was beautiful, and she held her head high with her shoulders thrown back as she approached the genthyaki. The writhing whips of darkness all emanated from a gleaming black rod she held. Over her other shoulder was slung a bulging sack.

"Do you remember that sting?" she called out, tossing the sack into the grass as she halted a dozen paces from where the genthyaki huddled behind a partially collapsed monument.

"You were Cleansed!" shrieked the monster as Keilan reached Senacus and knelt beside the paladin. The Pure's armor was in tatters, riven by great bloody gashes. His chest rose and fell weakly, though, and the light still trickled from his eyes.

An explosion sounded, and Keilan was nearly knocked over by a rolling wave of force. Slivers of stone pelted him, opening tiny gashes where his skin was uncovered. His head ringing, he tried to focus on what had just happened.

The monument that had momentarily shielded the genthyaki was gone. The young woman – the sorceress; Keilan could feel her surging power – stood with her arm outstretched, her dark hair coiling in the air like the strands of her strange weapon.

And he knew her. This was the same sorceress he had seen in the memories of the immortal Jan. She had brought down the cataclysms that had destroyed the old world, and then emerged a thousand years later to challenge the Crimson Queen.

Alyanna.

Blue lightning arced from the genthyaki's talons, shattering against a shimmering barrier that flared into existence around the sorceress. It crawled briefly along the edges of the ward, as if looking for a way inside, and then dissipated.

Searing lances of red power erupted from Alyanna, pummeling the suddenly visible shields protecting the genthyaki. The monster staggered as cracks spread across its wards, but Keilan did not know whether its weakness was from the sorcerous assault or the wounds pockmarking its flesh.

"You thought I did not have the will to recover what is mine?" cried Alyanna as a hot wind rushed over the lichyard. "What is my *birthright*?"

She was swollen with crackling power, an enraged goddess. Awed, Keilan at first did not feel the tugging on his hurt arm. Finally, the pain squirmed into his consciousness, and he turned to find Nel crouched beside him, her eyes wild.

"We have to find cover!" she screamed at him over the rising wind.

"Senacus!" Keilan shouted back, but Nel shook her head fiercely.

"The sorcery can't hurt him! But it will tear us to pieces! Come!"

She pulled him away from the paladin, and together they stumbled towards one of the tombs. They collapsed behind a stone wall just as a fresh barrage of spells shook the lichyard, bright colors flaring in the sky above them.

Keilan winced as Nel's grip on his arm tightened, and she finally noticed something was wrong.

"You're hurt."

He nodded, his thoughts scattered from the intense pain in his shoulder and the overwhelming rush of the sorcerous battle raging nearby.

Nel gripped his dangling arm and then gave it a hard shove, and Keilan felt a click as it slipped back into place. The rolling waves of intense pain lessened immediately, and he gasped in relief.

"Thank you," he managed.

"Not the first shoulder I've fixed," Nel replied.

Keilan realized that they were no longer shouting. The thunder and wailing of the sorcery crashing together had suddenly and eerily stopped. He peeked around the edge of the tomb's wall, afraid of what he might find.

The lichyard had been devastated. Only rubble remained of the gravestones and statues, and the ground was churned as if it had been plowed by teams of oxen. Alyanna stood among the ruin, blazing with sorcery, the strands of her dark flail writhing in the air around her. The genthyaki crouched amid the shattered stone, its huge body folded into an impossible tangle of thorns and scales. It looked beaten. Whipped.

"Beg for mercy," Alyanna commanded.

The genthyaki whined and shifted. Gleaming black ichor pulsed from the wounds lacing the monster, and Keilan wondered how it still clung to life.

"Mercy, Mistress," it hissed, edging closer with its twisted arms outstretched in supplication. "Enslave me once more. Grant me existence and I will be your servant again, your most valued servant. As it was before."

Alyanna sneered. "Some deeds cannot be forgiven. You tortured me. Cut away my sorcery, and to reclaim it I was forced to sacrifice the only one who had always been loyal. Who needed *nothing* from me and gave of himself whatever was asked."

The genthyaki tilted its monstrous head to one side in a surprisingly human-like motion. "The swordsinger," it rasped.

"Yes," Alyanna said, stepping forward. Keilan saw the sorcery swelling in her like a cresting wave.

The genthyaki must have seen it as well. The monster uncoiled with blinding speed, thrusting its claws out towards her. Glistening black energy englobed its talons, a terrible emptiness that plucked at some primal fear deep within Keilan. This was a sorcery unlike any he had seen before.

Green light leaped from Alyanna's hand, carving the air. The genthyaki's claws and the congealing darkness vanished, and when the beam faded the creature's arm ended in a steaming stump. It threw back its head and howled, pressing its mutilated limb to its sunken chest. Alyanna gestured and a swarm of glittering silver blades flashed towards the reeling monster, tumbling end over end. But just before the first of the summoned knives pierced the genthyaki, it fell backward . . . and vanished through a rippling patch of air.

Alyanna screamed in rage, the knives winking out of existence. She threw out her arm, and a line of monuments farther up the hillside tore loose from the earth and went crashing down the slope.

For a long moment she stood there, head down, breathing heavily. Then she turned, looking directly at where Keilan was watching from around the edge of the tomb.

"Come out," she said. "I won't hurt you." She sounded exhausted.

Keilan glanced at Nel. Should they trust her?

"The paladin is dying," Alyanna said, waving her hand dismissively towards where Senacus was crumpled.

She was right. Taking a deep breath, Keilan came out from behind the tomb and hurried over to the Pure. Despite the razed lichyard, the paladin had been untouched by the sorcery, though his face was pale and blood trickled from the corner of his mouth. His shining eyes were only slightly open and seemed duller than just a few moments ago; Keilan thought he was unconscious, but it was hard to tell with the Pure. As Alyanna had claimed, he was clearly slipping away.

"Can you help him?" Keilan asked, his concern for the paladin overwhelming the fear he felt towards this ancient sorceress.

Alyanna snorted. "He is one of the Pure. Healing magic would do nothing for him. And anyway, I am no healer."

Nel appeared beside Keilan holding strips of cloth and a flask. "Help me get his armor off," she told Keilan. "We need to clean the wounds and stop the bleeding."

"Leave him," Alyanna said, bending over to rummage through the sack she'd dropped earlier. "More of the light-blinded fools are coming. They will save him, if he can be saved."

"He killed one of his brothers," Nel hissed through gritted teeth, struggling with Keilan to pull off the paladin's white-scale cuirass. Finally, with a grunt she slipped it over his head and tossed it aside. Beneath the armor his tunic was soaked with blood.

"I'm sure he had a good reason," Alyanna said. "Perhaps he can explain himself to them."

There was something in the sorceress's voice that indicated they were not alone. Keilan looked towards the temple as Nel began to slice away the stained cloth. At the foot of the hill, a crowd had gathered around the wrought-iron entrance to the lichyard. Mendicants in their white robes, lightbearers carrying swords and axes . . . and a pair of tall warriors in gleaming white armor, their eyes burning like embers in the early morning light.

"Oh, no," Keilan whispered. The Pure would be arriving soon, and there would be little mercy shown with the reek of sorcery in the air and a dying paladin leaking his lifeblood into the soil.

A shiver passed through Keilan as Alyanna formed a spell. He turned his eyes to her and found that the sorceress had pulled a silver sphere from the sack she'd brought. She let it go and it hovered in front of her, and with another tendril of sorcery she made its surface ripple like water. She placed one hand above and one hand below the orb, and then began to compress it so that it bulged outwards, becoming flatter.

"Keilan!" Nel said sharply, and he pulled his gaze away from what Alyanna was doing. "I'll need you to lift him soon."

The knife splashed the contents of her flask on Senacus's wounds, and the paladin groaned and shifted weakly. "Up," she commanded, and grabbing hold of the Pure's shoulders Keilan raised him slightly so that Nel could wrap the strips of cloth around his body. She managed to cover most of the cuts, but the cloth instantly darkened as the blood continued to flow.

"We have no time," Alyanna said. "Keilan, you must come with me. If the woman wants to stay with the paladin, so be it. But you are needed elsewhere."

A thin disc now floated beside the sorceress, wide enough for a horse to stand on. It dipped slightly and then rose again as she climbed atop it and settled herself cross-legged, placing the sack beside her. Alyanna beckoned at him impatiently, sparing a quick glance towards the faithful of Ama laboring up the slope. They would be here in moments.

"We have to bring him!" Keilan cried.

The sorceress muttered something, and for a moment Keilan thought she would abandon them, but then she sighed. "Very well. But be quick."

Keilan hurried to where they had stowed their travel packs on the other side of the tomb they'd sheltered behind and slipped the straps over his shoulders. There was no way he was leaving the black knife behind, not after all it had cost him. Then he returned to where Nel squatted behind Senacus's head. "Take his legs," she commanded, and together they lifted the limp paladin. Straining under the big man's weight, they carried him over to the hovering disc and slid him onto its shimmering silver surface.

Keilan clambered up beside Senacus. Instead of joining them, though, Nel dashed away.

"Where are you going?" he cried after her.

"Fool," Alyanna hissed, and Keilan felt the sorceress send a flicker of sorcery into the disc, compelling it to rise. Without considering how he knew what to do, Keilan sent his own pulse of magic flowing through the disc, holding it down. Alyanna glanced at him in surprise, her large dark eyes wide.

With the Pure and the other warriors of Ama less than a hundred paces away, Nel scooped the paladin's fallen white-metal sword from the churned earth. Something else small was on the ground near the blade, and she picked that up as well, and then she was running back towards the disc.

A great wave surged from the onrushing paladins, and for a moment Keilan feared he would drown again in the power of Ama's chosen, but it broke harmlessly against an invisible barrier. He looked in surprise at Alyanna as Nel leaped onto the disc, making it rock dangerously.

"They cannot touch ones such as us," the sorceress said, holding his gaze, "if we do not let them. Now release your hold on the chavenix."

Keilan assumed she was referring to the disc, and he unclenched his sorcery.

The disc rose smoothly into the lightening sky, the upturned faces of Ama's faithful dwindling beneath them.

7: CHO LIN

SHE SHOULD BE dead.

That was her first thought as she came awake. Cho Lin lay there, stiff from sleeping on the cold stone, and considered her slow, even breathing and the dull thudding of her heart, trying to make sense of things. Around her, moonlight trickled through the rents in the ceiling, illuminating the small chamber with a pale radiance.

Her hand drifted to where the demon had cut open her side, fingers pushing through furs stiff with blood. She brushed her skin, tracing the ridges of a scar that felt like it had healed some months ago. To her surprise, the wound barely ached as she prodded it. She touched her ribs, the ones she'd feared had been broken. Again, only the slightest discomfort. It was like she'd spent months recuperating from her ordeal in the arena.

Fragments of her dreams floated up. She had been in Nes Vaneth, walking among the white stone buildings. But instead of tumbled ruins the city had been whole, though a thick mist had clotted the streets, coiling around columns and making it impossible to see more than a few span in front of her face. That had made it hard for her to follow the woman in white as she drifted down the streets – no matter how fast Cho Lin ran she never managed to catch her, and the intense frustration she'd felt still lingered, even now that she was awake.

The Pale Lady. When she'd stumbled from the arena Cho Lin had been half-dead, her thoughts addled. Now, as she lay in the ruin where she'd found solace, she remembered the story Verrigan had told her when they first approached the Bhalavan, about the Min-Ceruthan ghost that haunted Nes Vaneth. A harbinger of bad luck, he'd claimed. Is that why the Skein had turned back rather than follow her into the ruins? Had they also seen her?

Cho Lin shivered. In Shan, the spirits of the dead did not slip across the veil unless they wished to inflict harm. Usually they raged against some injustice that had been done to them, taking vengeance by leading men to their doom, then drawing the warm breath from their mouths so that for a brief moment they could feel what it was like to live again. Had the Pale Lady led her into Nes Vaneth to die? And if so, why was she not only alive, but unnaturally healed?

Cho Lin climbed slowly to her feet. The small chamber looked different in the falling moonlight. The water in the basin at the statue's feet had a silvery hue, and as she watched, a ripple spread across its surface. She looked up, squinting at the holes in the ceiling, wondering how it could rain in these cold wastes. For that matter, why was the water in the basin not frozen? What was keeping it warmed?

That was when she saw it. The statue's cheeks were veined with dampness, as if it had been crying, and the tear-tracks glistened the same silver color as the water in the basin below. Against her better judgement, she stepped forward and pressed her thumb to the face of the stone girl. It came away wet.

And that wasn't all. A long and thin piece of metal had been placed in the outstretched arms of the girl, and Cho Lin was certain it had not been there when she first entered the chamber.

Tentatively, her heart beating fast, she lifted the metal shard from where it rested and carried it to where she could see it more clearly in the moonlight.

It was a piece of a blade about the length of her forearm. The end tapered to a curving point—she knew what sword this had once been a part of, and she barely held back a choking sob, her hands shaking. It was the Sword of Cho, the ancient weapon of her ancestors. She glanced around wildly, peering into the chamber's shadowed recesses. Who had brought it here? And why?

The sword seemed to shiver in her hands, and she looked at it again in surprise. Was she going mad? Moonlight slid along the blade, and she saw her reflection staring back at her.

No. That wasn't her. The girl in the metal had the same glistening black hair, but her skin was darker, her face broader. Cho Lin brought her fingers to her thin lips, and the image in the sword did the same, except the girl trapped in the sword brushed lips that were much fuller. There was a humming in her head, faint but growing louder. Cho Lin fell to her knees, swaying, unable to look away from those piercing eyes . . .

The screams were terrible.

They came clawing up from Consort Wei's swollen belly, ragged with pain and fear. Jhenna crouched in the corner, hugging her knees to her chest, watching in cold dread as midwives in olive robes scurried back and forth. Some held silken sheets stained bloody, while others carried silver bowls slopping over with pink water.

Something was very wrong. Jhenna had witnessed a dozen births out on the steppes, beneath the Great Sky, but never had any lasted this long. It had seemed like an eternity since she'd watched fingers of pink dawnlight crawl across the floor. Now that same stone was bruised purple by twilight, and servants had hung lanterns from the ceiling, though they had not yet lit the candles within.

Then it was finished. As terrible as the screams had been, the silence that followed was worse. It clotted in the room like milk gone sour. Finally, when Jhenna thought she couldn't bear it any longer, a trembling, age-spotted hand pulled back the moon bed's gauzy red curtain. The Autumn Warlock of Shan emerged, blinking, his face slack, his arms stained red up to his elbows.

The head midwife approached respectfully, her face lowered. "The child, my lord?"

"Dead," the warlock murmured, shaking his head slightly, as if having trouble focusing on the matronly woman standing before him. "And the mother as well."

Scattered gasps came from among the gathered midwives. Jhenna had to bite down on her knuckles to stifle a sob.

The midwife bowed her head. "It was Heaven's will, my lord," she said, but the strength in her voice faltered. Jhenna saw a tear fall, and she rubbed at the wetness on her own cheeks.

A curt gesture from the midwife brought several of the servants who had been standing in the shadows forward. They held a long bolt of gleaming black cloth; behind them, other servants bearing cloth the color of the morning sky clutched their burden to their chests and remained motionless. They would not be needed this day.

Their movements slow and solemn, the servants unhooked the red curtain and replaced it with the black. Jhenna glimpsed what lay upon the bed: a tangle of soiled silks, smeared with blood. Black hair spread over velvet cushions. She couldn't tear her eyes from Consort Wei's pale arm, dangling over the edge of the bed, and her plum-colored nails – it was only yesterday that Jhenna had applied that lacquer while they gossiped about the other women in the palace. Now she was gone.

The head midwife cast a fearful glance behind her, at the chamber's entrance. "My lord . . ."

"Go," the warlock said tiredly. "He may be wroth."

The midwives and the servants hurriedly retreated from the room, their eyes downcast. The head midwife was the last to leave, briefly slipping within the black curtains, then emerging a moment later cradling a small bundle. She bowed again to the old warlock and followed the others from the chamber.

Only Jhenna and the sorcerer remained. He did not seem to notice her, huddled as she was in the corner. This did not surprise her. She had grown very skilled at not being seen in the months since arriving at the Jade Court.

A shudder passed through the old warlock, and before her eyes he seemed to grow more gnarled and stooped, as if finally allowing the weight of what had happened to fall fully upon his shoulders. He raised his hand to run it through his gray-threaded hair, but then stopped himself, staring at his blood-drenched arm.

Footsteps. Not the whisper of a servant's slippers as they hurried to their tasks, or the heavy clump of a soldier's boots, but confident, measured strides. Jhenna turned to the archway that led deeper into the women's quarters and caught a flash of yellow robes as someone entered the room.

Her breath seized in her throat and she threw herself to the floor, pressing her forehead to the cold stone.

He was here. The Beloved of Heaven had come. *He may be wroth.*

"Excellence."

"Bae Fan," the emperor said softly, "what has happened?" He didn't sound angry, Jhenna thought. Weary, perhaps.

There was a long pause. Jhenna could imagine some of the various explanations and excuses the old sorcerer was considering. In the end, he told the truth, as Jhenna had witnessed it.

"Consort Wei went into labor soon after breaking her fast this morning. I hurried here, and immediately could tell that something was very wrong. The child . . . your son had wrapped his birth cord around his neck. He was strangling himself, and he could not finish pushing his way out. I tried to save him and the mother by cutting . . ."

Again, a terrible silence filled the birthing chamber. Jhenna wanted to glance up and see the expression on the emperor's face, but if he glimpsed her doing so, such impertinence would result in a beating, or worse. So instead she ground her forehead into the stone and breathed as quietly as she could.

"Give the prince and his mother a proper funeral. Let them lie for three days and three nights in my family shrine, then inter them in the tomb of my ancestors."

"As you wish, Excellence."

The footsteps began again, this time receding. Jhenna stayed in obeisance for another dozen heartbeats to make sure the emperor was truly gone. When she finally raised her head, she found that the Autumn Warlock had vanished as well. She hadn't heard him leave.

She took a deep, shuddering breath. Not long ago the birthing chamber had been a riot of activity as a dozen people had endeavored to bring new life into this world. Now she was the only one here that drew breath.

Jhenna rose and slowly approached the bed. Hesitating only for the briefest of moments, she pulled back the curtain.

Consort Wei lay as if asleep. Her eyes were closed and her striking face was untroubled, her thin lips slightly parted. She had always been unusually pale, but now she looked like one of the noble children's ceramic dolls. The color that had drained from her cheeks stained the sheets. Jhenna reached down and laced her fingers with Wei's, brushing her thumb against the consort's still-warm skin.

She brought her lips to her ear. "May the Mother of Mares carry you past the Great Black Grass, my heart sister."

A tear escaped as she gently kissed her friend's brow. It fell upon Wei's cheek and trickled away, leaving a glistening path.

Jhenna straightened. With a last, lingering look at the one friend she had made in Shan, she drew back the black curtain—and gasped.

She was no longer alone.

A young man stood in the chamber, his hands clasped behind his back. His dark blue robes were decorated with twining dragons picked out in shimmering red thread, and the hilt of a jeweled sword was thrust through his black sash. He watched her without expression. Her heart thundering, Jhenna stepped from within the curtains and fell to her knees.

She knew who this was – she had seen him in court, standing high up on the Heavenly Steps. Ma Qin, first son of emperor Ling Qin.

Jhenna dared to look at him. He had his father's strong jaw and fierce black eyes, but there was also something different. While the emperor's gaze reminded her of the golden eagle that her father, the Yari of her people, had kept as a hunting bird, the prince's did not. There was less of a predator about him, more softness in the corners of his eyes and the cant of his mouth. She swallowed as they stared at each other for a long moment, and then some emotion she could not place shivered the prince's face.

"She died," Jhenna said, surprising herself. One of the first rules that had been drilled into her when she had arrived at the Jade Court was that she should never speak first.

But the prince only continued to watch her. "I know," he finally said. His voice was quiet, and she heard the sadness. "I came to show my respect to my brother and his mother."

He bowed his head in silence, closing his eyes. When he opened them again, he nodded to her, and then with a mourner's solemn steps he turned and withdrew from the chamber.

When the scrape of his slippers had faded away and she was alone again, Jhenna gave herself over to the grief that had been swelling inside her. With a wrenching sob, she fell to the floor and let the tears come.

He found her the next morning in the Labyrinth of Ten Thousand Blossoms.

She had woken early and entered the imperial gardens, following the twisting copper paths through shadowy grottos and beneath the limbs of monstrous banyans, until she had come to the tree her people called *tsenalish*. It was barely more than a shrub compared to the ancient sentinels standing vigilant beside the shrines and koi ponds, a tangle of spidery branches speckled with leaves red as heartsblood. She had wondered why the imperial gardeners had decided to include such an unimpressive tree in the Labyrinth, but when she'd voiced this question to Consort Wei, the answer she'd given had seemed so obvious. The *tsenalish* was the only tree that grew on the steppes, over which the Empire of Silk and Celadon claimed dominion. Just like her own presence here, its inclusion symbolized that it belonged to Shan.

She came to this tree when she needed to commune with the gods of her people. Watching the yellow and blue birds hop among the branches, hunting the tree's small bitter fruit, she could almost imagine that she stood once more upon the steppes. If she closed her eyes, she could hear the wind slithering among the long grass and the distant shriek of a hawk as it turned circles in the sky . . .

"Good morning."

Jhenna whirled around, the sounds of the steppe vanishing. He stood upon the gleaming path only a few paces behind her, resplendent in a green robe trimmed with gold.

"Prince Ma," she murmured, dropping to her knees.

"Please, stand," he said, motioning for her to rise. "Jhenna nas Kalan. You are my father's consort. You do not need to abase yourself before me."

She felt her face flush. "I . . . forgive me, Prince. I do not know all the court's—" She searched for the proper word, but her limited Shan failed her.

"Customs. Intricacies. Rules."

She smiled weakly. "Yes. Those things."

His lips quirked, and she felt a small flutter in her chest. There was something pure about him. Without guile. Almost everyone she had met in the Jade Court – even Consort Wei – seemed to always be wearing masks that hid their thoughts and feelings. To show your true self was a weakness that could be exploited.

But not him . . . unless he played the game better than all the others.

"How long have you been here?" he asked.

"In the gardens?"

Again, the soft smile. "No. In my father's court."

"Three . . . no, four months. I arrived just before the earth shook and the eastern wall collapsed."

"You are the Mak Yari's daughter?"

"No . . . no. My father was one of the last Yari to fight him. When my tribe was defeated, I was taken as a prize."

Jhenna pushed down the terrible memories that threatened to rise up as she said this. Fire and smoke and her brother's screams . . .

"The Mak Yari sent me east as a gift for your father."

"Tribute."

Jhenna remembered the scarred giant astride his great horse, thundering towards her tribe's yurts as ten thousand screaming, white-painted warriors followed. She had only known the Mak Yari for a few terrible days, but she was sure he thought of his dealings with the emperor of Shan as an exchange between equals, and not the offerings of a vassal king.

"If you say so, Prince."

She started as the prince suddenly laughed. "I know what you're thinking, Consort Jhenna. You barbarians are a proud people."

"If you say so, Prince," she repeated.

More laughter. "You remind me of the stallions from the steppes that sometimes come before the court – the insolent glint in their eyes persists, even when saddled."

Jhenna had also known horses like that on the steppes. If their will didn't eventually break, then they would be broken in other ways. She kept this to herself, though – it was not wise to contradict a prince.

His face suddenly grew more serious. "You were in the birthing chamber . . . you knew Consort Wei?"

Jhenna swallowed. For a moment she'd forgotten about what had happened yesterday. She nodded curtly.

"You were friends?"

"Yes."

"It is not easy for consorts to make friends in the palace, especially with other consorts."

She knew this. True friends, at least. False friends were as common as worms after the rain.

"Wei was kind to me. She had a pure soul."

A distant look stole across the prince's face. "I thought the same. Perhaps it was why she could not persist in this place."

"My prince?"

He waved his hand, as if dismissing his thoughts. "Never mind." He squinted up at the sun and pursed his lips. "I must go, Consort Jhenna. But I will speak to you again soon. Do not let the falseness in this place taint you – there is still nobility in the empire, I promise."

The wagon lurched sickeningly, and something twisted inside Jhenna. She covered her mouth with her hand, willing her stomach to settle. The thought of being sick here, in this nest of pillows and silks that smelled of lavender and jasmine, was too terrible to contemplate.

One of the other consorts inside the wagon with her, an amber-skinned girl named Puli from the southern coast, noticed her queasiness and giggled. "You look terrible. Never traveled in a wagon before?"

Jhenna shook her head, struggling to even speak. "Horses," she finally managed, swallowing away bile that had crept up into her throat. "I always rode horses."

Puli made a face. "Horses, ugh. Big smelly brutes. Dangerous, too. My uncle was kicked in the head by one."

"You traveled by wagons everywhere in your homeland?"

"Boats. We lived on the southern ocean and only came to land to trade. This wagon ride would have to get a lot rougher to be worse than the sea during a storm." As if to prove her words false, the wheels bounced again, hard enough that Jhenna felt herself briefly lift from the pile of cushions she was sitting on. But Puli kept on grinning, as if nothing had happened.

The last consort in the wagon, Tan Pei, made a disgusted noise and stuck her hand out the small window beside her. A moment later a young soldier's face filled the frame.

"Yes, Honored Ladies?"

"Is the driver trying to hit every rock in the road?"

The soldier flinched at the anger in Tan Pei's tone. In the palace, she was known for having a wild temper, and it seemed that reputation extended into the barracks.

"No, Consort. I'm sorry for your discomfort. There is no road. We turned from it some *li* past. The ground here is very rough – but it seems to get smoother up ahead. We are almost to Sleeping Dragon Valley, I believe."

Tan Pei dismissed the soldier with a wave of her hand and sank back into her mound of pillows.

His gaze lingered for a moment on Jhenna and Puli, and then he bowed his head and vanished.

"Oh, he was handsome," Puli said after he had gone. "Let's find another reason to bring him back."

Tan Pei sighed and closed her eyes, ignoring Puli. Jhenna wanted to ask if she knew what this mysterious journey was about, but didn't care to risk Tan Pei's anger. The Shan consort had the milk-pale skin, glistening black hair, and wide eyes which marked her as a paradigm of beauty in the empire. But like most of the Shan beauties Jhenna had met, she married her flawless looks with a disagreeable temperament. In the empire, it seemed that beautiful girls were expected to be spoiled brats – on the steppes, the older women would have sent her to gather horse dung for the fire if she'd dared the same antics Jhenna had witnessed daily in the women's quarters.

Jhenna was curious why they had been chosen from among the emperor's hundred consorts to accompany the imperial retinue today. The selection of Tan Pei and Puli made sense – rumors in the palace claimed they were the current favorites of the Beloved of Heaven, and both had recently begun sharing his bed. Jhenna, though, had never been invited to the imperial quarters, and only twice had she even stood in the same room as the emperor: yesterday, when she had huddled in the corner of the birthing chamber while he had spoken with the warlock, and months ago when the Mak Yari's envoy had formally presented her to him in the palace's audience hall. She wondered if Prince Ma was the reason she had been invited to come and witness this ceremony in the northern wilderness. The thought made her feel strangely warm.

Lost in daydreams that featured the prince's soft voice and exquisite eyes, she didn't notice that the wagon had stopped until the sliding door was drawn back.

"At last!" Tan Pei cried, lunging for the doorway with a quickness Jhenna had never seen her display before; most of the time in the palace she lounged about with the regal indolence of a housecat.

Puli followed, and then Jhenna emerged blinking into the harsh light.

"Sleeping Dragon Valley," said the soldier, sweeping out his arm to encompass the vista before them.

Their wagon had halted on the lip of a rocky escarpment, and spread below was a deep and wide forested valley ringed by stunted mountains that looked to be in the process of collapsing back into the earth. A half-year ago even these stony hills would have awed Jhenna, but she had seen far larger peaks on the edge of the steppes where they'd crossed into the Shan heartland. The shadows of clouds crawled across the great green expanse, mapping strange continents upon the rolling woods. And they were rolling – the ground rippled strangely, like it was a rumpled blanket kicked from a bed during the night. If she squinted, it almost looked to her like there was a great serpent slumbering beneath the forest. That must be where the valley had gotten its name.

"Where is my palanquin?" Tan Pei shrieked, her long-nailed hands opening and closing like she wanted to throttle the gray-bearded functionary standing before her.

He regarded her calmly, even as the soldiers milling about shrank away. Clearly, he'd had some experience dealing with her in the past. "There is none, Consort Tan. Only the emperor and the empress will ride in palanquins today."

"By whose orders?" she seethed through gritted teeth.

"The empress."

"That insufferable bitch! It's just like her to . . ."

Jhenna turned away from the raging Tan Pei, lifting her robes as she picked her way across the stony ground to get a better view of their procession. Several dozen wagons had halted in front of their own, and it seemed like many of the most influential members of the Jade Court were disembarking. Though she'd only been in the palace for a short while, she recognized several of the mandarins and their wives: there was Lord Cai, warden of the western reaches, and there was Lord Cho, who owned half the silk plantations in the empire.

They did not seem upset by the lack of palanquins.

She noticed with some surprise that even though they had ventured deep into the wilderness, most of them had still worn fine ceremonial dress. Strange.

The glint of gold drew Jhenna's eye; two ornate palanquins had started on a path leading down into the valley. A tall man she suspected was Prince Ma walked beside them, his hand casually resting on the hilt of the sword at his side. The other mandarins and nobles were falling in behind the emperor and his empress.

Jhenna turned back to their wagon. Tan Pei was now stamping her feet, while Puli had sidled closer to the handsome soldier who had looked into their wagon earlier.

Leaving them behind, she hurried to join the procession.

They descended into the forest, passing from bright sunlight into a twilit gloaming. There was little underbrush, as trees with bark the color of mottled bone wove a dense canopy high above. The ground was covered by a thick carpet of moss; several times Jhenna's slippered feet sank almost to her ankles.

The silence surprised her. She had expected the air to be filled with birdsong and the buzz of insects, but the forest was as quiet as a temple . . . or a tomb. It was almost oppressive. She must not have been the only one who felt this way, as the babble of conversation ceased soon after entering the woods, replaced by whispers.

She gasped when she felt a presence appear beside her, and then gasped again when she turned and saw who it was.

"My prince," she murmured, ducking her head.

"Consort Jhenna," the emperor's son replied.

He didn't seem surprised to see her, so that explained who had invited her. Jhenna's heart quickened as she considered what this could mean.

"You don't mind traipsing through the woods like this?" Prince Ma asked, kicking at a fallen tree and sending chunks of rotten wood flying. A centipede the length of her forearm slithered deeper into the log.

Jhenna shrugged. "I've never been in a forest before, but I've lived my life on the steppes, under the sun and stars. I don't need silks and cushions to feel comfortable."

Prince Ma eyed her appraisingly. "That must make you unique among my father's consorts. Most of them seem to believe that waking up too late to be served breakfast is the greatest hardship anyone could endure."

Jhenna glanced at the prince, in his fine clothes and bearing a jeweled sword. He seemed to hear her thoughts, because he chuckled. "Ah, you think I'm just like them." He gestured at the Shan nobles stumbling through the forest. "Coddled and soft. But I've actually had my share of hardship."

She tried to better mask what she was truly thinking, but he saw her skepticism.

"You don't believe me. That's understandable." He looked away from her. "My father believes in strength, Consort Jhenna. He's a student of history, you see, and the history of my people – the Shan – is riddled with stories of fallen dynasties. Strong emperors whose sons were raised in luxury and became weak, inviting disaster. So, when I was ten years old, my father sent me to live in a garrison bordering your home. I was to accompany the soldiers when they ventured out onto the steppes – dine with them, care for my horse, suffer those scouring winds that bend the long grass, that sort of thing.

"But a few days into our first patrol we were ambushed by the Mak Yari's warriors. They butchered the Shan soldiers, sliced off swatches of skin to stretch across their shields, and took me prisoner. For five days I stumbled naked behind their horses with a rope around my neck. They joked about killing me, about cutting off my thumbs and nose and . . . other parts. I was sure I was going to die. I was tempted more than once to just stay sprawled on the grass when they kicked me awake in the morning and embrace the darkness that they would surely deliver. But in the end I found my will to live, and I reached the Mak Yari's encampment. What do you think was waiting for me there?"

Jhenna shook her head.

The prince grimaced. "Lord Ban, one of my father's foremost advisors, and a regiment of elite dragonhelms."

"They came to rescue you?"

"Not really. The ambush had been planned, orchestrated by my father with the help of the Mak Yari. It was done to temper my will and show me hardship. Lord Ban was there to collect me and bring me back, if I survived the steppes."

"Your father did it . . ."

"Yes. But my father is subtle – the lesson was not just for me. Do you know who else?"

Jhenna thought for a moment, and then it dawned on her. "The Mak Yari."

He smiled grimly. "Yes. You're quick. The steppe tribes are always a threat to the empire, and the Mak Yari has united them for the first time in a century. By enlisting the Mak Yari's aid in this scheme, my father also demonstrated to the steppe warlord that he was a hard, brutal man who would sacrifice anything to strengthen Shan. Not an emperor to trifle with."

They walked on together in silence for a ways, both lost in their thoughts. "Is that why you sought me out in the gardens?" she finally asked.

She could feel him glance at her. "Yes. I . . . wanted to know more about your people. The only other Nasii I'd ever met were horribly cruel and vicious." A small pause. "Though I now know they were acting on my father's orders."

"And what does that say about us barbarians?"

"Perhaps that we Shan are not so much more civilized," he admitted grudgingly.

Jhenna could feel something between them. She didn't want to touch it, lest it collapse.

"Where are we going?" she asked, changing the topic.

Prince Ma shrugged. "A temple of some kind, I think. My father has been very close-lipped about this trip." He gestured, encompassing the rest of the nobles trudging through the forest. "I had no idea half the Jade Court would come along."

"You truly don't know what this is about?"

"Some ceremony that's done every few decades. It's important, or else it wouldn't be so well attended. I see the head of every great house, the four warlocks of Shan, even one of their apprentices, and those boys almost never leave the towers." Prince Ma squinted, peering into the distance. "Wait, can you see that?"

She could. There was a fold ahead of them in the forest, a great hummock of earth covered with scraggly trees and waist-high red grass. A stone door was set into this hill, and long spidery roots had crawled down from the trees above to vein its surface, suggesting that it had not been opened in many, many years. A nervous muttering rippled through the gathered nobles as they finished emerging from the forest and formed a crescent around the imperial palanquins.

Gradually it subsided into an expectant hush. Jhenna thought the seated emperor might stand or announce something, but instead the ancient Winter Warlock in his snow-white robes stepped from the crowd and shuffled towards the huge door, leaning heavily on a staff of gnarled black wood.

"Lo Jin is a hundred years old, at least," whispered Prince Ma. "I'm surprised he chose to make this journey. He rarely emerges from the red tower."

The hunchbacked old sorcerer glared up at the vast door. Then he extended his staff and rapped harshly on the stone.

A deep grinding followed, and dust sifted down as the great portal swung slowly open. From the gathered nobles came a few cries, as if some feared what might be revealed.

But it was only blackness, utter and total. Jhenna realized she'd been gripping Prince Ma's arm fiercely, and she let go, hoping he wouldn't see her flush of shame.

Now the emperor did climb down from his palanquin. He slowly turned, his stern gaze passing over the great men and women of Shan.

"Some of you know why we are here," he began, his voice loud and clear. "You remember the last time we came to these doors, thirty winters ago. You know what will happen inside. But most of you do not. This is because it is forbidden to speak of what occurs here today. The punishment is death, for you and whoever you tell." The emperor paused, letting that sink in. "This is no simple thing we do. We did not come to make an offering to Heaven, or Mother Earth, or the Immortals. We did not come to pray for rain or victory in battle. We came to ensure that our children will live to greet the dawn tomorrow. That the empire – that the Shan – will persist."

Silence. Most of the nobles must have been ignorant of what would happen, as Jhenna saw surprise in their faces. Only a few of the oldest watched the emperor without expression.

At a signal from the emperor, soldiers who had accompanied their wagons entered the darkness carrying torches and a great rosewood box. Moments later, larger flames appeared within three massive iron braziers, illuminating the depths. Jhenna craned her neck, trying to see what was inside. The cave seemed to have been hewn by hand; the floor had been leveled, and its sides curved up into darkness. At the cave's far wall another door had been set into the rock. This one was much smaller than the entrance, yet still it towered taller than any man. Aside from the braziers, the only things Jhenna could see within were a chunk of pale white stone and the rosewood box beside it.

Jhenna shivered. Coldness was seeping from the cavern's mouth.

"You have all felt the earth shake these past few months," the emperor said. "A chasm appeared in the market square of Tianping town. The eastern walls of Lianjing collapsed. The priests say Heaven is displeased. The scholars say the fires deep under the ground are being stoked by demons. But neither is true." The emperor pointed inside the cave. "Within there, something sleeps. And it is stirring."

The three other great sorcerers of Shan came forward to stand beside the Winter Warlock, each wearing the robes of their office. The Autumn Warlock was dressed in the red of fall leaves; the Summer Warlock in the green of fresh grass; and the Spring Warlock wore the blue of swollen rivers. Their ages corresponded with their seasons: while the Winter Warlock appeared to be on death's door, the Spring Warlock looked only a few years older than Prince Ma. Jhenna had been told that when the Winter Warlock finally passed beyond the veil, the Autumn Warlock would take his place, each of the sorcerers changing their robes, and a new Spring Warlock would be chosen from the ranks of their disciples.

The four sorcerers of Shan stepped inside the cavern. Jhenna saw that the Winter Warlock's young apprentice accompanied them, supporting the old man by holding tight to his arm. No; that wasn't right. It looked to her like the Winter Warlock was actually helping his apprentice to stand, since the boy – who couldn't have seen more than eight summers – was walking unsteadily.

The Summer Warlock bent down to whisper something in the young boy's ear, then helped him to lie down on the rock. His arm hung limp, his fingers touching the stone floor. He looked to have been drugged.

"No," she whispered. "No, they can't do this."

"What do you think—" Prince Ma began.

The Winter Warlock withdrew a serpentine dagger from the folds of his robes.

"Heaven's Grace," murmured the prince.

The Summer Warlock crouched down beside the boy, speaking to him softly. The child's head was turned toward him, and the sorcerer tenderly smoothed down his long black hair.

The Winter Warlock moved across from the Summer Warlock, where the boy could not see him, and cut the child's throat in one smooth motion.

Startled cries from the Shan nobles. Jhenna wanted to scream, but she could not find her voice.

A wash of dark blood. The Spring Warlock positioned a container beneath the wound so that much of the blood flowed inside. It also dripped down the white stone, red fingers reaching for the cavern's floor. For the first time, Jhenna noticed the faded russet streaks staining the altar.

The boy had barely moved, and now he was still.

Shadows pressed at the edges of Jhenna's vision. She stumbled slightly, and Prince Ma grabbed her arm to steady her.

The four warlocks positioned themselves around the stone, linking hands as they bowed their heads. A hot wind came rushing from the cavern, stinging Jhenna's eyes and filling her mouth with the taste of ash. The sorcerers let their arms fall, and then the Summer Warlock bent over the boy. Steel flashed. When he straightened, one hand clutched a dagger, and in his other hand he held something that he had taken from the boy with a cut of the blade.

The Autumn Warlock scooped the dead child into his arms, and Jhenna moaned when the boy's head fell back limply, turned toward the watchers outside the cave. He seemed to be staring right at her, but where his eyes should be there were just dark holes. The sorcerer laid the boy down in the rosewood box, and then the Spring and Summer warlocks each took one of the box's ends and lifted it up. Jhenna hadn't seen who opened the far door, but now it gaped wide like the maw of some beast, ready to swallow the sacrifice that had been made.

The horror of this moment was overwhelming. Jhenna's head whirled, and she felt herself falling, spiraling down. And then nothing.

What happened after, she later remembered as fragments. Stumbling back through the forest, Prince Ma keeping her from collapsing among the moss and leaves. The long wagon ride back to the palace, drowsing fitfully on scented cushions while Tan Pei and Puli curled up across from her, lost in their own memories of what had happened. A servant leading her back to her chambers, and then a deeper, dream-plagued sleep.

When she finally awoke, moonlight drenched the room, burnishing her clothing cabinet and tea table in shades of bone and tarnished silver. She lay motionless, trying to ignore the fading echo of her dreams. But she could not. She had dreamed of a child with a birth cord wrapped around its neck placed upon an altar of white stone. Something had loomed beyond it, a hole cut out of the dark wall – no, not a hole—Jhenna had felt hot exhalations and heard ragged breathing, and the jagged fringe around its edge had not been stone but teeth. The smell of rotten meat and dead things had washed over her and Jhenna had wanted to snatch up the tiny corpse, but when she'd stepped forward the child's eyes had flicked open and she'd screamed and turned away and fled into the black.

Jhenna pulled her blanket up over her head and shivered. In the warm, close darkness she sobbed for Wei and her baby, for the poor boy in the cave, for herself in this strange and terrible place.

She even sobbed for Prince Ma, imagining him as a young boy tethered to a Nasii warrior's horse, stumbling through the grass.

With some effort she mastered herself, her gulping cries subsiding into whimpers. Then, reminding herself that she was the daughter of a Yari, Jhenna drew in a deep breath and let it out slowly.

The sobbing continued.

Quiet, but anguished. The back of her neck prickled.

It wasn't her. It was coming from somewhere else in her chamber.

Slowly, she drew back the blanket. After being in the darkness under the covers, everything seemed brighter, her few small pieces of furniture etched stark in the moonlight. Her breathing thundered in her ears, but still she could hear those tiny wrenching cries. Clouds slid past the window, making the moonlight run like water. Jhenna eased herself up into a sitting position, peering into where the blackness pooled in her chamber: beneath the tea table, next to her bed, beside her clothing cabinet—

Panic clutched at her throat, and suddenly she couldn't breathe. There was something there, in the shadow of her cabinet. A small, shivering shape.

Please let it be another consort, or a servant fleeing a beating. Reaching within herself for all the courage she could muster, Jhenna swung her legs over the edge of the bed.

"Who's there?"

No answer. But now there was silence, and the patch of deeper blackness within the shadows had vanished. Jhenna's feet touched the cool stone, and she took a few tentative steps towards her cabinet.

Nothing. She couldn't hold back a little cry as relief flooded her. *Just a dream.* Jhenna climbed back into her bed, forcing herself not to stare where she'd thought she had seen the huddled thing.

She did not fall asleep again until dawn lightened the sky outside her window.

A servant in imperial livery sought her out the next day in the great hall of the women's quarters, where consorts reclined on velvet couches chatting or doing needlepoint. Jhenna was surprised to see him here, and she noticed every eye in the room following him as he approached her across the inlaid tiles.

"Consort Jhenna," he said, bowing formally.

"Yes," she murmured, hurriedly sliding from where she perched on the edge of a divan and standing.

"Walk with me, please," he commanded. She fell in behind him dutifully as he turned and strode back the way he had come. She saw many heads among the lounging consorts coming together to whisper. More than a few rumors would be born today, she guessed.

They passed out of the women's quarters and entered the Labyrinth of Ten Thousand Blossoms. He led her along the twisting copper paths until they came to the blood-leafed steppe tree. Prince Ma was sitting under its boughs on a rosewood bench that had not been there previously. He dismissed the servant with a wave, and motioned for her to approach.

"Good morning, Consort Jhenna."

"Prince Ma."

They stared at each other for a long moment. The events that had transpired in Sleeping Dragon Valley seemed to hang heavy between them.

Finally, the prince cleared his throat. "I must . . . apologize to you. I did not know what would happen yesterday. If I had had even the slightest premonition, I never would have asked you to be included. Do you understand?"

"Yes." Tears prickled the corner of her eyes.

"And you trust my words?"

"I do."

He looked relieved. "Good. What occurred in that cave . . . that is the old Shan. My father's Shan, an empire built on blood and superstition. When I wear the yellow robes, such barbarism will end, I promise you."

"Then you do not believe what he said? About something in the cave?"

Prince Ma's mouth twisted. "No. It is a farce by the warlocks to show their worth to the court. I'm certain my father realizes that. And I'm also sure he's heard the rumblings from the temples that these earth tremors signify Heaven's displeasure. There were several ranked lamas among those watching yesterday – now he's given them a new narrative, and one where my father can claim responsibility if there are no more quakes."

Jhenna considered telling him about the terrible dream she'd had the night before, but finally decided that she should not, given the guilt he was clearly already carrying for bringing her to the cave yesterday.

Prince Ma rose and put his hands on her shoulders. The intensity in his dark gaze made her shiver. "No more children will die like that when I am emperor, I promise you."

She lay in bed and listened to the thing sob.

Her chamber was cold, as if the wooden shutters had been left open, but she remembered the servant pulling them closed while Jhenna had sat on the edge of her bed brushing her hair. It was also darker than the night before, although some moonlight still silvered the chamber. She wished desperately that she'd left a candle burning on the table when she'd gone to bed; she had wanted to, but in the end had chided herself for her foolishness.

She did indeed feel like quite the fool now, but for the wrong reason.

Was it a ghost? The spirit of the child who had been sacrificed in the cave? If so, why would it haunt her? Could it be Consort Wei? For some reason, she found that thought even more terrifying.

No, it sounded like a child. Small, wracking sobs, like it was trying to be quiet but failing.

Slowly, the paralyzing fear bled away. Jhenna was still afraid, but her terror had lessened to where she could consider what she should do.

If she threw off her blanket and lunged for the door, she could be outside her chamber in just a few moments. Or she could scream for a servant – one would come running soon enough.

A shuddering cry from the shadows. Jhenna felt a flush of shame. She was the daughter of a Yari, and she feared a child's ghost?

Gathering her courage, she slipped from her bed and approached her cabinet. The sobbing quieted but did not vanish.

"Don't worry," she said, willing herself closer to whatever was huddled in the darkness. "I am not going to harm you."

A stupid thing to say. How could she harm a ghost?

The thing fell silent, but Jhenna could tell it was still there.

Mastering her fear, she crouched beside the shadow. Her skin goosepimpled, as if the legs of countless spiders were crawling up and down her arms.

"It's so cold there," the ghost whispered. It was a child's voice, laced with fear and pain.

"There? Where is 'there'?"

"In the darkness. We're so cold under the ground."

Jhenna swallowed. "Is that why . . . is that why you've come here?"

"It's warmer here. You are so bright and hot."

The ghost moved out of the shadows. Moonlight fell on pale skin, and Jhenna saw the ragged gash in the boy's throat.

"Oh," she murmured. "I'm so sorry."

The ghost crept closer. "May I touch you?"

Every instinct was telling Jhenna to dash for the chamber's door, but she steeled herself. This poor, pitiful boy needed her. "You may," she heard herself say, as if from far away.

Tentatively, the ghost approached her. Its arms went around her neck, and she felt its tiny fingers clutch at her back . . . the same way her brother had once hugged her, before he'd disappeared beneath the hooves of the Mak Yari's horse. She fought the urge to scream as the ghost's small head rested on her shoulder. Where the spirit's skin touched her own, it burned like ice. Jhenna smelled nothing, except perhaps for the faint scent of earth and loam.

"Please," the spirit said. "Help us get out."

"Us?"

"The others. We are all scared and cold and want to go home."

Pity swelled in her chest. "I would help you if I could. But I cannot."

"Who can? Is there anyone?"

The name tumbled from Jhenna's lips before she could consider the wisdom of what she said. "Prince Ma. He has a kind heart. He would help you."

The cold fingers slipped from her back as the ghost pulled away from her. It receded into the shadows from where it had emerged, becoming more insubstantial, like smoke uncoiling in the sky.

Then it was gone.

Jhenna spent the next morning searching for the servant who had brought her to see Prince Ma the day before. She finally found him in a reception hall, directing two workers in the restoration of a statue of the Enlightened One, which must have been damaged during the recent quake that had shaken the city. A jagged crack had split the serene face of Sagewa Tain, an unsettling reminder of the wound in the ghost child's throat. She begged the servant to ask Prince Ma to meet her later in the Labyrinth, and without asking her why, he bowed smoothly and left.

She waited on the rosewood bench beside the *tsenalish* tree until the late afternoon light faded and the shadows gathered beneath the gnarled boles and branches. Jhenna was just about to leave when she heard the ring of footsteps approaching on the copper paths. She quickly stood, smoothing her hair and robes.

Prince Ma entered the small clearing. Something had happened to him: his face was haggard and drawn, and he gripped the hilt of his sword as if he meant to draw it. He saw where she was staring, and let his hand fall from the jeweled pommel.

"My prince," she asked, stepping forward in concern, "what has happened?"

His eyes were troubled. "Consort, I . . ." His voice trailed away, as if he could not find the words to continue.

"You saw it," she said.

He glanced at her sharply. "You . . . you saw it, too."

I sent it to you. Jhenna bit down on this admission. Dispatching a ghost to haunt someone was not something to claim lightly. "I did. It has come to me the last two nights, crying in my room."

Prince Ma rubbed unconsciously at his neck. "Last night was the first time for me. It's the child from the cave."

"I know."

"It asked . . . it asked that I let it out. It said it is cold. And that there are other children in there. But nothing else. No monster. No demon. Just the spirits of small children, suffering in the darkness."

Jhenna could barely breathe. "What will you do, my prince?"

"I must do something!" he cried, his voice cracking. "What kind of emperor would allow this to happen to those he has sworn under Heaven to protect?" He ran a shaking hand through his hair. "Today I went to the red tower. I have known the Autumn Warlock for my entire life. He pulled me from my mother. He has tutored me on how to be a just ruler, teaching me of the Seven Virtues, the Path, the Precepts of the Enlightened. I asked him how the Shan can allow such evil."

"What did he say?" Jhenna whispered.

"He said that this was one of the oldest traditions in our people's history. The sacrifices have occurred for a thousand years. But then he admitted something else." Anger twisted the prince's face. "He admitted that before, it was not children who were killed. He said that once it was the Winter Warlock whose lifeblood was drained upon that rock. That had always been the way. But Lo Jin changed that when he donned the white robes seventy years ago. He was a young man – the other three warlocks had died during the wars when the hordes boiled out of the Burning Lands. He did not want to be slain when next the earth shook or the sky wept blood, so he convinced the three new warlocks to accept a change to the ancient tradition. Now a child of great sorcerous ability would be murdered and placed beyond the door as an offering."

"So it should have been him," she said softly. The evil of it all – to change places with an innocent child – chilled her. "Will you ask your father to reinstate the old way?"

Prince Ma nodded. "Yes. But first I must make good on a promise I made last night."

"What was that?" Jhenna asked, though she knew already.

"I am going to open the door."

Her horse tossed its head and whickered, its breath pluming in the early morning chill. Jhenna leaned forward and patted Windrunner's side, murmuring nonsense words to try and soothe her stallion. Usually when she slipped from the stables before the sun had fully risen, it meant a fierce ride on the fields reserved for the imperial family, as if she and Windrunner were back on the steppes racing her cousins in the long grass.

But today was different. They had leaped the low fence that fringed the paddock and made their way to the great arrow-straight northern road. She'd brought a simple gray cloak to hide her rich vestments, and had pulled up the cowl so that none of the farmers driving their animals toward the city would notice that she was not Shan. Now she waited on a knoll overlooking the road, Windrunner stamping his hooves impatiently, no doubt feeling cheated of his morning run.

She recognized the prince from a distance, galloping along the road as if a pack of bloodwolves were nipping at his heels. He turned his horse from the road as he came closer and reined up beside her.

"You should return to the palace."

Jhenna stuck her chin out and met his eyes brazenly. Mounted on her horse, she felt like the old Jhenna, the girl who had challenged the boys to archery contests and snuck away to hunt the white antelope during the Whelming Time. Not the meek imperial consort who bowed and scraped and tried her best to avoid being noticed. "I saw the ghost as well. I want to help him."

He tried to match her gaze, but finally looked away, sighing. "Very well. Just know that even *my* life may be forfeit for doing this."

"If you think that, we'll keep on riding after we open the door. We'll ride to the shore of the bitter sea, or to the great white waste, or to the Burning Lands. Shan is the greatest empire in the world, but it is not endless."

The prince reached out and gently touched her hand. "Exile would not be so terrible if you were by my side."

Jhenna wanted to tug down her cowl to hide her blush. "How will you open the door?"

Prince Ma pulled his saddlebag up into his lap and untied the drawstring. "There are two doors, remember? I visited the red tower this morning and took this" – he gestured at something lashed to the side of his horse, the same twisted black staff the Winter Warlock had used to open the first stone door – "and this." He withdrew from the bag a key of heavy black iron. "This is for the inner sanctum. I saw it hanging in the tower before in a place of honor, and never knew what it was until the sorcerers used it in the cave."

"The staff will work for you?"

The prince nodded. "Bae Fan told me when I spoke with him yesterday that the door will open for anyone, so long as they strike the stone with the staff of the Winter Warlock. I suppose that harkens back to the days when the warlocks themselves were sacrificed." He cast a quick glance over his shoulder, at the distant peaked roofs of Lianjing and the red towers of the Shan sorcerers rising behind them. "Come, Consort Jhenna. We should hurry."

They rode north along the imperial road, keeping a good pace, though not one that would exhaust their horses. The last time, this journey had taken more than half a day, but since they were mounted and without those trundling wagons, Jhenna expected to reach Sleeping Dragon Valley soon after noon. They traded stories as they rode, tales of growing up on the steppes and in the court: Jhenna told the prince of the trials of strength that the tribes conducted every summer solstice, and how she had disguised herself as a boy one year and won a tiger claw necklace in the archery competition. In return, he spoke of his proudest moments as a child, most of which involved reciting poetry and the wisdom of ancient sages flawlessly.

When the sun had climbed high overhead, Prince Ma paused as they crested a hill and surveyed the road they had taken. His face tightened, and with a sinking feeling in her stomach, Jhenna followed his gaze. A thread of horsemen could just be glimpsed in the distance, and her suspicions were confirmed when something they were wearing glinted.

"Who are they?" she asked the prince.

He frowned. "Dragonhelms, almost certainly. My father wouldn't entrust this task to regular soldiers."

"Do you think the warlocks are with them?"

"Yes."

"What should we do?"

The prince wheeled his horse around and kicked it into a canter. "We ride!"

By the time they reached the edge of the valley the horsemen had closed the gap, but were not yet within arrow range. Jhenna could see them more clearly – her mother had always said she had eyes like a hawk – and the prince's guess had been correct: their pursuers wore scale armor that rippled in the light, and their plumed helms were wrought into the shape of roaring dragons, their faces recessed within the open jaws.

Prince Ma and Jhenna slid from their horses and led them carefully down the steep descent into the forest. Her heart seized in her chest several times when a hoof skittered on the loose scree, but the Great Sky had blessed them this day, and they reached the bottom safely. The forest's ground was equally treacherous, with the thick moss hiding deep divots that could easily break a horse's leg, but Prince Ma insisted that they push on quickly, so Jhenna clung to her stallion's back as they hurtled through the woods, praying that their luck would continue.

"How do you know which way to go?"

The prince paused their headlong flight, searching the ground for something. "Look!" he said, pointing at what seemed to her to be just more moss. "I've been on enough hunts to know how to track a fawn in the forest. Forty city-Shan bumbling about is easy enough."

Yet despite this claim, it took the prince several long moments to decide which way they should go. He leaned forward in his saddle, his brow furrowed and his hands clutching at the reins. "There's almost too many of them," he said softly. "And they don't move as one. It's like trying to follow a herd of cats."

Distant noises drifted through the woods. "We have to hurry," she said, glancing behind her and peering through the endless rows of white trunks for their pursuers.

"This way," the prince said with what sounded like forced confidence, and he kicked his horse ahead. She plunged after him, branches clawing at her face.

A slab of gray appeared through the bracken. It swelled larger, becoming the huge stone door set into the side of the hill. Jhenna hadn't noticed it before, but the trees seemed to be shying away from the cave; several serpentine roots extended towards the clearing and then veered abruptly away, as if afraid to creep too close. That thought made her skin prickle.

They dismounted and approached the great door. Prince Ma brandished the warlock's staff as if it were a sword, holding it by its end. He and Jhenna shared a long look, and then he reached out tentatively and touched it against the stone.

From the look of surprise on the prince's face, he at least partly hadn't expected anything to happen. But just as when the Winter Warlock had struck the door, a grinding began deep within the hill, and it swung open. Fetid, stale air washed over Jhenna, and she struggled to keep from coughing.

Shouting and the sounds of horses blundering through the forest came from behind them. Prince Ma grabbed her arm and pulled her inside the cave just as a warhorse caparisoned in gleaming armor burst from among the trees and charged into the clearing. It reared back, hooves churning, as the warrior in the black-enameled plate of the empire's elite dragonhelms drew his sword and cried out in triumph.

"I have them!"

Prince Ma hauled her across the cave, towards the smaller door set in the far wall. He fumbled with the iron key, and it fell clattering to the floor, skittering until it came to a rest beside the white stone where the child had died. Growling a Shan curse Jhenna did not know, the prince lunged forward and scooped it from the ground, then turned back to her.

"Wait, my prince!" implored the soldier, who had swung down from his horse and now stood silhouetted in the light of the entrance. "Speak with the warlock before you do anything, I beg you!"

Prince Ma pressed the heavy iron key into her hand, his fingers lingering where they brushed hers. His face was shadowed in the cave's darkness, but she could feel the intensity with which he was staring at her.

"Jhenna," he said, "open the door. I will keep them back. Let us bring peace to these poor children."

Then he turned away from her, steel rasping as he drew his sword.

Pushing aside her rising panic, Jhenna shoved the key as far as it would go inside the rusted iron lock, and then using all her strength, she tried to twist it.

Nothing happened.

Swords clashed behind her. Jhenna spared a glance over her shoulder, even as she strained to turn the key. Prince Ma was warding away three dragonhelms, sweeping his blade in broad arcs as more of the soldiers streamed into the cave. Jhenna had watched enough duels out on the steppes that she knew he was no great warrior – the dragonhelms seemed hesitant to attack their prince, and metal only rang when they deflected his awkward swings away.

"Stop this foolishness!"

The soldiers stepped back and sheathed their swords as those words echoed in the cave. The voice was cracked by great age. Jhenna knew who it must be.

The stooped Winter Warlock shuffled inside the cave, followed a step behind by the Autumn Warlock. They seemed not to be of the same mind: anger twisted the older sorcerer's lined face, but the taller sorcerer in his red robes looked fearful, staring at the imperial heir.

"Prince Ma, put down your sword and come away from the door," the Winter Warlock commanded. "This is madness."

"The only madness here is the killing of Shan children!" shouted the prince, pointing his blade at the wizened sorcerer.

"And they are dead!" Lo Jin said. "Nothing can bring them back!"

"Please, my prince," entreated the Autumn Warlock, "you know not what you do. You endanger us all—"

"I saw that child again!" interrupted the prince, his tone softening as he addressed his old tutor. "The one he killed. Its ghost came to me and begged me to let its soul free."

The two sorcerers glanced at each other. "Impossible," said the Winter Warlock. "A dream or a touch of madness—"

"I am not mad!"

The key screeched as it finally turned in the lock, and Jhenna nearly fell over.

"No!" cried the Winter Warlock. The sunlight pouring through the open portal seemed to shimmer and twist, hardening into glowing tendrils that gathered around the sorcerer's hands.

Jhenna pulled on the stone door, though she knew it would be too heavy for her to open by herself.

But it moved, almost as if something was pushing from the other side.

The Winter Warlock snarled and raised his hand, and the gleaming snakes twining around his arms erupted outward, slithering toward her and the prince. Prince Ma was struck first, the sorcery plunging into his chest and passing through him like his flesh was paper held over a candle flame.

Jhenna screamed.

The golden serpents squirmed towards her next, and she raised her arms even though she knew it was futile.

Yet she did not die. The sorcery had halted a few handspans from her, writhing, sparks falling away to glitter in the darkness.

Why had he spared her? But when she looked past the shimmering ropes, she saw surprise in the old warlock's face.

A sound made her glance to her side, at the thin slice of darkness where the door had cracked open.

Tiny fingers curled around the door's edge. Then it slid open wider.

Jhenna stumbled back a step as a shape emerged from the black beyond the door. It was the child, but it did not look like the ghost she had seen in her room. Something had changed. It was pale, but not the pure white she remembered from her chamber; rather, it was sickly and mottled, and black veins were etched beneath its almost translucent skin. Its hair was a tangled mess that hid its features, but Jhenna could see the line the dagger had made across its throat. The child lifted its face toward her.

midwife to us, we thank you. Its voice was terrible, many hoarse whisperings spoken as one.

"No!" cried the Winter Warlock, gesturing at the ghost like he could banish it back behind the door. "You are dead!"

we are, the thing said, stepping forward. It raised its hand and brushed its fingers against the sorcery that still hovered, crackling, in the chamber. Like ink dropped in water, a darkness unspooled within the golden serpent, and where it bled the warlock's magic melted into shadow.

"Go back, demon!" screamed the Winter Warlock, a bubble of shimmering power flaring around him.

but father, the ghost said, walking calmly toward the sorcerers, *we've wanted to meet you for so long.*

More children were emerging from behind the door. Their clothes were rotted and torn, their white flesh webbed with black lines. All their faces were hidden behind long, ragged black hair.

The ground buckled, and Jhenna fell to one knee. Stones and dust rained down from the ceiling. The dragonhelms glanced above, then at the approaching children. Some unspoken agreement passed between the soldiers, and they turned and ran.

Jhenna rushed over to Prince Ma and crouched beside him. His eyes were open. A black hole had been burned into his chest, and beyond the charred fringes of his robes she could see his blistered flesh. She cradled him, the horror of it all threatening to overwhelm her.

Again the ground shook, and a great chunk of the ceiling tore loose and plummeted toward the sorcerers. The rock struck the shimmering bubble they had summoned and bounced away with a ringing clang.

The first of the children reached the edge of the ward and stepped through it unhindered.

Another quake. Jhenna climbed unsteadily to her feet and ran toward the smear of green she could see through the shuddering doorway.

A rending crash and an old man's screams followed her as she fled the cavern.

Her hands cracked and bleeding, Jhenna pulled herself up onto the ledge where she had first beheld the valley.

She lay on her side, panting, her ribs aching and her legs numb. Waves of pain were coming from her right knee; she had smashed it against a rock one of the countless times the ground had spasmed and sent her sprawling.

The earthquakes had worsened as she'd fled through the forest and scrambled up the stony hillside. She had feared that she would be swept back down in an avalanche of gravel and rock, but somehow that had not occurred, and now from this higher vantage she could see what was happening in the valley below.

But she couldn't understand what she was seeing.

The forest was rippling. Swells like waves on the ocean seemed to be passing beneath the valley, sending great swathes of trees crashing down. Pillars of stone were exploding through the canopy, as if something were thrashing deep below the surface.

What was this?

Far away from her, a great patch of forest many *li* wide shuddered and lifted toward the sky. Earth and forest debris fell away from whatever it was that was pressing upward; Jhenna couldn't see it clearly, but what was emerging from the ground reminded her of a newborn serpent pushing through the shell of its egg. Scales flashed in the sunlight as a living river emerged from beneath the valley.

Jhenna watched in horror as the world began to unravel.

Cho Lin drew in a shuddering breath as she returned to herself. The shard of the Sword of Cho slipped from her numb fingers and clattered to the stone floor. Around her, the chamber was as she remembered, painted with moonlight. It seemed like it had only been moments since she'd gazed into the rippling steel . . . but it felt like the soul inhabiting the blade had shared with her a lifetime's worth of memories.

She sank to her knees, gently lifting the jagged metal and holding it up to the light. No face stared back at her, nothing to suggest this was anything more than a sliver of a broken sword. It felt empty, like whatever fragment of the soul that had clung to the shattered blade had finally let go and sank into oblivion. If that was true, Cho Lin hoped she had found peace.

Jhenna. In the annals of the Shan it was a cursed name, for according to the histories it was the name of the concubine who had tricked the emperor's son into releasing the Betrayers and ushering in the Raveling. But what Cho Lin had just experienced was very different from the vague stories she had heard from her teachers. Jhenna had been trying to stop the suffering of these children who had been sacrificed to the thing that had torn itself free from the earth. It was the emperor and the warlocks of Shan who had created the Betrayers and birthed their hate and rage.

What had the shapeshifting demon said before he'd broken the Sword of Cho? *She went to her death freely.* At the time, she hadn't understood. Now she did. The concubine Jhenna must have sacrificed herself to forge a weapon that could defeat and imprison the creatures she'd accidentally unleashed upon Shan. She had some hidden sorcery, clearly, and perhaps that was how the demon children had first fashioned a bridge to her from within their prison. For a thousand years her soul had dwelt within her family's sword, infusing it with power. Now her part in this long saga was finally over.

Cho Lin leaned back against the robed legs of the statue. Where did she go from here? The sword was broken. Without it, she had no way to banish the Betrayers. She was cold and hungry and alone in a ruined city on the edge of the world. The demons would be laboring to bring about the same devastation that had consumed ancient Shan. What could she do? Cho Lin covered her face with her hands. The hopelessness of it all was overwhelming.

But was she truly alone? She looked around the silent, empty chamber, her gaze lingering on the pools of shadow where the moonlight did not reach. Something had led her to this room and healed her wounds. Something had brought the fragment of her father's sword and left it here for her. Something clearly did not believe that she should abandon her family's ancient mission.

What was it?

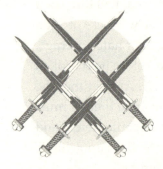

8: KEILAN

"WE HAVE TO go back."

Alyanna ignored him, her attention fixed on the landscape unfurling below. The red-tiled roofs of Theris and the towns clustered around the walls had vanished long ago, though Keilan hadn't noticed exactly when, as he'd been busy helping Nel keep Senacus from bleeding to death. By the time they managed to fully staunch the paladin's wounds, the strange disc carrying them had left the city far behind. Now they soared over a great crimson forest, though much of the canopy had been devoured by winter. There seemed to be little of any real interest beneath them, which was why Keilan thought the sorceress was simply ignoring him.

"We have to go back," he repeated, louder than before.

Keilan could have reached out and shaken her, as she was sitting cross-legged on the edge of the disc less than an arm's length from him, but he didn't dare. Truth be told, even though Alyanna had saved them from the genthyaki, Keilan was still afraid of her. Here was a sorceress as powerful as Cein d'Kara and as old and mysterious as his grandmother. From the brief snatches of Jan's memory that he'd experienced she was considered as ruthless and ambitious as anyone who had ever lived in the vanished empires. She had crafted the sorcery and led the cabal that had destroyed the old world. Yet she was smaller and slighter than Nel, and looked even younger.

Mustering his courage, he tried again. "Alyanna—"

She glanced at him sharply. "How do you know that name?"

Keilan swallowed, his mouth suddenly dry. "I . . . I saw you. Under the mountain."

Her eyes widened, and he could have sworn he saw a trace of fear in her face. "With the kith'ketan? How?"

"No, no," Keilan said, shaking his head. "With Jan. And there was a crystal . . ."

"Ah," Alyanna said, and she almost looked relieved. "The queen used your power to break through the barriers in the bard's mind."

"Yes."

"Clever of her." She studied him, her lips pursed. "I'm surprised you came with me, then. You must know it was I who challenged the queen and brought the shadowblades into Saltstone."

"You saved us in the lichyard," Keilan replied. "Also . . . we didn't have much choice. The Pure were coming." He turned his gaze back the way they had come. "But we have to go back. My friend is being held captive in the temple in Theris. I can't abandon him."

"Was your friend the old man whose form the genthyaki had stolen?"

Keilan nodded.

"Then he is already dead," Alyanna finished, turning away dismissively. "The genthyaki can only assume the shapes of those they kill. By drinking the souls of their victims, they absorb the knowledge necessary to mimic them perfectly."

Her words were like blows to his chest, and Keilan found himself struggling to breathe. Pelos was dead? His oldest friend . . .

no, more than a friend. He was like family. In the years since his mother's death he had, in many ways, been more of a father to Keilan than his own da.

"You're lying," Keilan said fiercely. "I know the kind of person you are. I saw what you did."

Alyanna snorted and shook her head. "I gain nothing by lying to you about this, boy. Even if your friend was still alive and scheduled to be executed at dawn tomorrow, I still would not return to Theris and save him. So at least you can take comfort that you did all you could."

"Why would you not go back for him? He's a good man."

Alyanna looked at him like he was a simpleton. "I don't care."

Keilan's anger rose, and he welcomed it, wanting it to consume the hollow ache inside him. "What *do* you care about?" he hissed, reaching out with his sorcery to try and wrest control of the disc from the sorceress.

She batted aside his attempt with contemptuous ease. "You won't catch me off guard again, Keilan. You have power, but it is still raw and unrefined. And would you know what to do if you seized the chavenix? We would go plummeting out of the sky. I can fly on my own, if I must. Can you?" She jerked her head in the direction of Senacus, sprawled insensate, and Nel, who was crouched beside him holding a sodden cloth to the deepest of his wounds. Blood stained her arms up to her elbows. "Can they?"

Keilan let his sorcery recede from the bright pulsing core of the disc. "No," he said softly, slumping in defeat.

Alyanna's face softened, and she sighed. "I am too harsh. Your friend is dead." She looked away. "I also lost someone recently."

The sorceress grew quiet, and Keilan retreated to his own thoughts as well, his gaze drifting over the edge of the disc. A river flashed far below in the early morning light, a thread of gold set in the dark brocade of the forest. When they'd first soared into the sky he'd been terrified – the disc was barely large enough for all four of them and their travel bags, and if it had tilted only slightly they would have rolled off and tumbled to their deaths. He'd dealt with his fear by focusing on assisting Nel in saving Senacus. It had helped, though, that the disc seemed as solid as the ground, and some sort of invisible bubble surrounded them that kept the cold winds at bay, reducing the sound of their passage through the sky to a muted howl.

"It's not dead," Alyanna said abruptly.

"It?"

"The genthyaki. It used sorcery to escape, though in a manner that should have been impossible. It's hurt, but those things are damnably hard to kill." Her frown twisted into a wry grin. "But you must realize that. You were the first one who cooked it with dreadfire."

"You know?"

She looped a strand of her black hair around her finger. "It was how I first learned about you."

Keilan remembered that terrible night: the wraiths swarming the caravan, men dying in the long grass, Xin convulsing as he felt his brothers' deaths through the bond they shared. "That thing was your ally?"

"Servant," Alyanna said bitterly. "Slave. It stumbled across you quite by accident – I had set it on another task. But once I was aware of your existence, I knew our paths would eventually converge." She looked into his eyes, and he could not turn away. "There are not so many like us left in the world."

"But now you and that thing are enemies?"

"It betrayed me. Or I betrayed it first, I suppose." She waved her hand dismissively, as if it mattered little which was true. "I arrived in Theris a few days ago and discovered that the Black Vizier of Menekar was already here, accompanying the inquisition as it pursued something of great import to the empire – and I knew that the fat Shan was the form the genthyaki was now wearing. I was also watching the temple, waiting for my chance to strike, and then there she was" – Alyanna nodded in Nel's direction – "leading the shapechanger away from the Pure and right to where you all waited. I suspected it had rather nefarious designs on you, and so I chose to reveal myself."

"Why did you save me? Where are we going?"

Alyanna waved his words away, and for the first time Keilan saw how exhausted she was. "Later, Keilan. But be comforted that I bear you no ill will. Great and terrible things are happening, and if we want to survive – if anyone is to survive – we need to be allies."

"You're talking about those children."

Again, Alyanna looked at him sharply. "You surprise me, Keilan. I see that we must share with each other what we both know."

She gestured over the edge of the disc at the rolling forests far below. "I need to rest. Help me find someplace suitable, and then we will talk more."

The midday sun was high overhead when Alyanna brought the disc down in the middle of an orchard. Through the rows of trees, a prosperous-looking homestead was visible. Like most of the farmhouses they'd seen in this part of the Kingdoms, it was constructed of stacked logs, with a fine thatched roof of white straw. No cries of alarm had gone up as they descended between the branches, so their arrival must not have been noticed.

"What is our story?" Nel asked Alyanna as the sorceress hopped from the hovering disc onto the grass.

"Story?" Alyanna bent down to scoop up one of the ridged green fruits littering the ground. After inspecting it for a moment and trying a tentative nibble she wrinkled her nose and tossed it over her shoulder.

"Yes, story. What do we tell these farmers when we show up at their door with a badly injured paladin? And how do we convince them to help us?"

Alyanna cocked her head, as if confused. "Convince them? I don't plan on wasting my time 'convincing' them of anything. We need food and rest. Why do you think I chose this place, so far from any other farms or towns?"

"So you're just going to take what you need?" Keilan asked.

"I'm not going to *kill* them," Alyanna said, sounding slightly exasperated. "Unless they refuse my demands. Or annoy me."

Nel stood up on the disc, her arms crossed, and looked down on the sorceress. "These are farmers. Peasants. I won't steal what little they have."

"What a kind soul you are," Alyanna murmured, her voice dripping with scorn. "But the end of the world is fast approaching. I suggest you set aside your morals for now and accept that difficult choices must be made if any of us are going to survive."

Nel held Alyanna's gaze for a long moment. The knife was glowering, her jaw clenched, and the sorceress matched her. Keilan edged away from the two women, sliding from the disc. The dry grass crackling under his boots was a welcome sensation after so long huddled on the smooth metal.

Senacus groaned in his sleep, his face twisting as pain shivered through him.

This broke the tension, and Nel looked away. "Fine," she spat out. "We get what we need, one way or another. But first we ask nicely."

Alyanna shrugged, as if this was a barely acceptable compromise. She grabbed her sack and slung it over her shoulder. "Remove the paladin and your bags from the chavenix. Keeping it in this shape is tiring."

Keilan and Nel wrestled the limp paladin from the disc, careful not to re-open his wounds, and then Alyanna stepped closer and began to mold the strange artifact back into a sphere. Keilan concentrated on the strands of sorcery as she lashed them together, trying to memorize the patterns she was making. There was a brilliant efficiency with how she manipulated the power flowing through her – even Cein d'Kara and his grandmother had not displayed such mastery. And her actions were effortless, like a skilled craftsman who had performed the same task so many times that the resulting perfection was the only possible outcome. A ripple went through the disc, and then it began to compress, folding in upon itself until it had returned to its original shape.

"What is that?" he asked breathlessly, awed by the beauty of her sorcery.

"A chavenix," she said, slipping the sphere into the bulging sack she carried. Keilan couldn't help but wonder what other wonders were inside. "A trifle, really. We used them to flit between the Star Towers during the years of the Imperium. Using them is quite draining, in truth, so they were never employed for longer journeys."

"Speaking of draining," Nel grunted, adjusting her grip on Senacus's legs, "let's get him inside."

Alyanna trailed a few steps behind them as they carried the paladin to the door of the farmhouse. Sheaves of dried herbs hung from the eaves, a traditional warding in the Kingdoms against evil spirits. There was also a sunburst carved into the wood above the door's iron knocker, and Keilan gave a little sigh of relief when he saw this.

Nel kicked the door hard. "Hello! Is anyone home?"

Frenzied barking erupted from somewhere inside.

"Please! A holy man of Ama is hurt! He needs help!"

Keilan thought he heard footsteps approaching, though he wasn't sure, as the dog was drowning out everything else. His shoulders and back were aching from holding Senacus, and Nel also looked like she was suffering. She slammed her boot against the door again in frustration.

"Let us in, please! One of the Pure is dying!"

"The Pure?" It was a woman's voice, soft and tremulous.

Nel leaned in closer to the door, her head nearly brushing the wood. "Yes, the Pure. We found him on the road to Theris. Must have been bandits."

Keilan heard the sound of a deadbolt sliding back, and then the door cracked open.

"Malkin has a bow," the woman said nervously through the gap. "He's a good shot. And Jeremia will let Dog loose if there's no paladin."

"We understand," Nel said, exhaustion weighing down her words. "Please."

The door swung open. A tall, pale woman with long blond braids stood in the entrance, worry lines creasing her face. Behind her, in the entranceway to another room, a boy about Keilan's age was holding a nocked bow, his eyes thinned with suspicion. Another much-younger boy with the same blond hair as the woman was straining to hold back the largest hound Keilan had ever seen.

"By the Radiant Father," the woman murmured when she saw Senacus, sketching a circle in the air. Then she waved frantically at the older boy to lower his bow. "Malkin, they're saying the truth. Oh, Ama save us."

"Ama save him, you mean," Nel said, moving into the house.

"This way, this way," the woman said, motioning for Nel and Keilan to follow her.

They did, though Keilan nearly dropped Senacus as the black hound lunged at him, jaws snapping. "Down, Dog!" cried the boy, struggling to hold onto the leash.

It looked like the hound might rip free and attack them, but suddenly it whimpered and lowered itself to the ground, its head between its paws. The boy nearly fell over as the weight he had been straining against vanished.

Keilan glanced back to find Alyanna stepping through the doorway. The dog whined as she approached, visibly trembling.

"Good dog," Alyanna said, smiling brightly at the boy holding the suddenly slack leash.

"Keilan," Nel prodded him, and he tore his eyes from the puddle spreading under the hound. Together they passed from the small entrance room and into a larger space. Three straw pallets were arrayed beside a hearth, along with a loom displaying a half-finished blanket or tapestry. Stools were scattered about, as well as crudely whittled wooden figures.

"Lay him there," the woman said, gesturing at one of the pallets, and then she went over to stoke the embers in the hearth.

With a relieved grunt, Keilan settled the paladin on the straw. Senacus squirmed in his sleep, his face twisting, but after a moment the pain seemed to pass and his expression grew calm again.

The woman was staring at the light trickling from his cracked eyes as if transfixed, her fingers clutching at her dress. She started when Nel laid a hand on her arm.

"Thank you. My name is Eria, and this is my brother Belgin." Nel nodded in Keilan's direction. "We are travelers from Vis."

"Vis . . ." the woman murmured, looking away from Senacus and seemingly seeing Nel for the first time. She looked her up and down with wide eyes.

"Yes," Nel continued as Alyanna entered the room. "And this is our servant, Gherta. She's a bit simple, so please excuse her if she says or does anything strange."

The woman did not even glance at the glowering Alyanna, instead staring at Nel's blood-drenched arms.

"Are you . . . are you hurt?" she whispered.

"His blood," Nel replied. "I did my best to stop the bleeding. But he needs better healing than I could give."

The woman eyes fluttered, and she shook herself, as if coming awake. "I've some bloodmoss we can pack the wounds with. We should get some hot water going, and there's Shalloch's root for the pain." She leaned over Senacus, her brow crinkling as she examined the cuts across his bare chest. "Don't look like they were made by metal. Animal's claws, I'd say. Maybe a bear . . ." Her face paled. "A big bear."

"What's your name?" Nel asked soothingly.

"Marialle. My husband is Faris Devensorn. He's away, bringing the goblin pears to market." She swallowed. "There was an attack like this last summer, not two leagues from here, on the old brook road. Ser Willes's son was murdered by some demon, and he was a knight. They say he was all cut to pieces, and that they were sending for the Pure to come hunt down what did it." Her frightened eyes returned to the savaged paladin. "Oh, may Ama protect us."

"He will," Nel assured her, guiding her gently away from Senacus. "But first we have to save his chosen."

This seemed to get through to the woman. "Yes," she said, smoothing the rumples her hands had made in her dress. She turned to where her sons were peering from around the edge of the doorway. "Malkin. Go down to the cellar and bring up an armload of the bloodmoss we dug out of the swamp this fall. I'll get a kettle of water going over the fire. I've some honey for the cuts – that should stop them from going black." She blinked, looking around. "Where's Dog?"

The smaller of the two boys had remained after his brother went to fetch what his mother requested, and he shuffled his feet like he'd done something wrong. "Back there," he said, pointing towards the door. "Dog's scared."

That seemed to shake her again, but she mastered herself in front of her boy. "Maybe he smelled something. I don't want you going outside, you hear?"

"I hear, Ma," the boy whispered. He was staring at Senacus without blinking, his eyes round as coins.

"Good," Marialle said, turning back to the paladin. "Ama's light, I wish Goodwife Roesia was here. She's got a healer's touch, but she's a half-day's ride through the woods, up on the Hangman's Knoll."

"Do what you can," Nel told her. "And we'll help."

"Right," the woman said, rolling up her sleeves. "Best get to work."

Marialle was more skilled than she claimed. Which made sense, Keilan realized. On an isolated farm, so far removed from a town or neighbors, someone would have to know how to treat wounds, set broken bones, and bring down fevers. First, she unwrapped the cloth strips – now stiff with crusted blood – Nel had used to staunch the bleeding. Then she cleaned the cuts, washing them with a pungent liquid she splashed from an earthenware jug. Keilan wasn't sure, but he thought it might be urine. Senacus muttered and shifted in his sleep as Marialle and Nel worked, sometimes even forming words. Keilan heard his own name, and the paladin spoke harshly to someone called Demian, admonishing him for the wrongs he'd done. Finally, the wounds were washed out again with water boiled in the now-blazing hearth, the dry clumps of moss the farmer's boys had brought up from the cellar were packed into the deepest cuts, and a salve was smeared over the ones that were shallower. Senacus drifted into a deep sleep after this, and though his face was pale and haggard it did seem like the pain had somewhat diminished.

Darkness had fallen by the time Marialle and Nel stepped away from the paladin. From their looks of grim satisfaction, they believed Senacus had made it through the worst and come out the other side. Alyanna had disappeared long ago, and Keilan thought she must have found a place to rest. She'd expended a tremendous amount of sorcery in her fight with the genthyaki, and then she'd kept them aloft for hours as they fled north. The power she wielded was daunting, but even she must have her limits.

Keilan and the two boys had watched the women labor to save Senacus, occasionally running to fetch a jar or bring more water. He'd tried to speak to Malkin, but the older boy had only offered up terse responses, refusing to meet Keilan's eyes as he wrung his hands together nervously. Keilan did catch the boy stealing scared glances at his jeweled sword, and that's when it had struck him: the boy thought he was a lord, and was too intimidated to even attempt a conversation. And yet in truth Keilan was the son of a poor fisherman, probably one of the few people to which the farmers of the Shattered Kingdoms felt themselves superior.

"Walk with me," Nel said to Keilan, holding up hands coated with blood and unguent.

He trailed her outside, and together they followed the trickle of running water to a small stream behind the farmhouse. The night was cloudy, the moon reduced to a smear of pale yellow, and Keilan stumbled several times in the dark.

"Can we trust the sorceress?" Nel asked as she washed her hands, keeping her voice barely above a whisper.

Keilan cast a nervous glance back at the farmhouse, though he suspected he would sense if Alyanna was weaving some sorcery that allowed her to listen in on their conversation.

"I think so."

"But she's the one who attacked the Scholia. And you said you saw her long ago, in the vision you had of the sorcerers who destroyed the old empires."

"Yes."

"She's a monster, then."

Keilan crouched beside Nel. Something splashed in the stream, and he nearly jumped back before he realized Nel had thrown a stone.

"She did terrible things. And I don't think she's changed. But I was inside Jan's mind, and I saw how he perceived her. Above all else, she is a survivor." The clouds parted, the moon materializing in the water. Another rock plunked down, rippling the hazy reflection. "She said she knew the world might end. Somehow, she knows of the demon children, and that they want to bring about the future the Oracle showed us. She desires to stop them, I'm sure of it."

"So we want the same thing. Do we tell her about the dagger?"

Keilan chewed on his lip, considering. "Let us keep it a secret for now. Until we're sure she can be trusted."

"I'm never going to trust her," Nel said, standing. "And I won't hesitate to put a knife in her if I have even the slightest suspicion that she's going to sacrifice us for her own gain." Keilan rose as well, joining her as she stared out at the blackness. "We don't even know where she's taking us."

"Tomorrow we'll get answers," Keilan assured her.

The plaintive cry of a bird drifted from the forest. Was there any sound more sorrowful than a solitary bird begging for company in the darkness? Keilan felt the sadness he'd been trying to ignore start to rise.

Suddenly Nel's fingers were lacing with his own. "How are you?" she asked softly, as if she could see into his thoughts.

Her touch made him shiver, and he had to force himself not to grab her hand more fiercely. "I loved Pelos," he admitted, trying to keep his voice from breaking. "He was family."

"I'm sorry. You have to hold tight to them in your heart, and wherever their spirits are, they'll know they are not forgotten."

There was something else as well, and it had been eating at his insides for days. He forced himself to speak of it, surprised by how difficult it was. "I killed a man, Nel. I stabbed him in the belly. It was . . . it was so easy. The look on his face when he realized he was dead. The terror. Like he was staring into a great abyss, and knew he couldn't escape." He swallowed, staring out into the darkness. "Is that what Pelos felt?"

"Don't suffer over that man," Nel said, the edge in her voice brooking no argument. "He was a soldier. His life was violence, and he knew very well it could end violently. We are trying to stop a cataclysm, and if others stand in our way, we will have to fight and kill."

"That's what Alyanna said."

"You were confronted by a soldier with a sword who wanted to take you captive and give you to the inquisitors of Ama so that they could torture you to death. Alyanna, on the other hand, was willing to kill the family that just saved Senacus because they had something she wanted. You are not like her. *We* are not like her."

She spat out these last words with a vehemence that surprised Keilan, then lapsed into silence. Keilan was quiet as well, concentrating on the feeling of her calloused hand in his.

"I'm scared," he told her suddenly, surprising himself, as he hadn't known he was going to admit that.

"I'm scared, too," Nel replied. "We'd be foolish not to be."

"I'm not scared for myself," Keilan continued, speaking quickly. "I'm scared for you. And Sella. And my da. Senacus is dying in there."

"He's not going to die," Nel said firmly. "At least not tonight."

"I'm scared what will happen if we don't stop those demon children. And I'm scared that stopping them might depend on us."

"I'm overwhelmed also, Keilan," she said, giving his hand a comforting squeeze. "If I think about the enormity of what's happening, I just lose hope. So I focus on only the next moment, the next task."

"And what is that?"

"Bringing Niara's dagger to the queen," Nel said confidently. "It was what we were going to do before Chale. She has the strength to oppose all these monsters." Keilan felt Nel twist around to stare back at the farmhouse. "And that includes her."

"What if that is not Alyanna's plan? What if she still considers the queen her enemy?"

Nel was quiet for a long moment. The bird in the forest trilled again, but this time there was an echo from somewhere else.

"Do you think you could use that flying circle?"

9: THE CRONE

THE RIDGE WAS already crowded by the time Willa finally arrived. Dozens of men and women milled about talking excitedly, though some reclined on chairs that poor servants must have lugged up the narrow switchback trail she'd just climbed. There was even a low table with a few pitchers of wine and bowls heaped with dry fruits, slices of salted meat, and an array of small pastries. The morning had all the makings of a lovely picnic. What a wonderful vantage from which to eat and drink and watch thousands of men hack each other to death below.

Scowling, Willa stumped towards one of the chairs. It was already occupied by a fat man with an oiled beard and beady black eyes, crumbs speckling the luxuriant fur lining of his robes. He looked at her with immense disinterest as she neared, then his gaze flicked away.

"The lady wishes to sit," Telion said from his customary place a few steps behind her.

"The magister also wishes to sit," the fat man drawled, not bothering to look at them.

Willa rapped his knee hard with the ebony sphere topping her cane and the man gave an aggrieved howl, his face purpling. He surged to his feet, his hands balled into fists.

"How dare you?" he hissed, looming over her.

She stared calmly up at him for a long moment, then brushed past him to slide into his vacated seat. The shock on his face almost made her crack a smile.

"Who do you think you are, crone?" he managed to say, despite nearly choking on his incredulous anger.

"It is *the* Crone," said a new voice, and they all turned to find that the magister with the streak of silver in his hair had sauntered over. Vhelan smiled broadly and bowed to Willa. "The infamous Lady Numil of Lyr."

"She wronged me!" spluttered the fat magister as Vhelan straightened.

"You should have given up your seat, Magister d'Kessen."

"Take care, boy," snarled the magister. "In Dymoria, those with gutter blood do not speak that way to their betters."

"Quite right. But your noble name means little in the Scholia, which I must assume you've forgotten. And since our beloved queen has named me as senior magister, I am, in fact, your social better right now. As such, it would be perfectly within my rights to insist on punishment for your rudeness. But I would prefer it not have to come to that. What do you think?"

The fat magister paled before Vhelan's dimpled smile. "Apologies, Magister Vhalus," he muttered, and then slunk away towards the edge of the ridge, where a knot of magisters were gesturing at something below.

"You can see, Lady Numil," Vhelan said smoothly, "as a commoner who once hailed from Lyr, I've encountered a bit of resentment about my new position from the Dymorian magisters with noble blood."

"Vhalus is quite a powerful name in Lyr. More than a few archons have come from that house."

Vhelan winked at her. "I think we both know, Lady, that I am as much a scion of the Vhalus clan as your good man here is a lost prince of the d'Karas."

"I always suspected my da was not my real da," Telion rumbled. "And I've heard it said the queen's father did do a bit o' adventuring in his day."

"Oh yes, I do know you, Vhelan," Willa said. "I remember several reports passing my desk about the young thief in the Warrens they called the Scholar. We try to cultivate good relationships with those individuals who might rise to prominence in the guilds. But before we could reach out, you vanished. We all thought you'd ended up stabbed in an alley, but finally word trickled back that you had been recruited to study at the Crimson Queen's Scholia. And now here you are," she spread her arms wide, "the youngest senior magister. We were right about your potential, it seems."

Vhelan bowed low again. "It is an honor to know I warranted even the slightest sliver of your attention. The children in the Warren were terrified of you, as I'm sure you are aware. The all-seeing, all-knowing Lady Numil. She would creep on spider-legs into our sleeping places, the whispers said, and drag us away to drink our blood if we were not careful."

Willa snorted. The inhabitants of the Warren would never have heard of the Lady Numil – Vhelan was being polite. She was the Crone to them, an apparition that haunted the Lyrish underworld. It was a legendary persona she had carefully cultivated over many decades.

The sound of a horn floated to her from over a great distance. Somehow she knew it was not wrought of silver and blown by a commander in the queen's army. No, there was a wildness to this echoing blast – she heard the mountains and the trees and the roar of tumbling rivers. This was a horn carved of bone, she'd wager, ripped from the body of a beast that roamed the northern wastes.

Vhelan heard it as well, as his face suddenly grew serious. He looked over his shoulder to where the magisters were gathered at the edge of the ridge. Then he held out his hand to her. "Come, Lady Numil, let us see what these barbarians look like."

"You did not join the queen when last she ventured into the Frostlands?" she asked, accepting Vhelan's help and letting him gently pull her to her feet.

The magister shook his head. "None of us did. Queen Cein wanted to defeat the Skein without sorcery – she feared that if we used our magic openly, then the emperor of Menekar could use it as a justification for war."

"This does not concern her now?" Willa asked as they moved to where they could see what was happening below.

"We are stronger than we were then. She has told me that she believes it is time we revealed ourselves to the world."

Now *that* was an interesting little morsel, but she would have to set it aside for now, to be chewed on later. There were other things demanding her attention.

The battlefield chosen by Lord d'Chorn certainly seemed to play to the strengths of the Dymorian army. It was a wide, snowy plain, pocked by small copses of pine trees. A thick forest bounded it to the west, and to the east the rumpled ground eventually rose up into true mountains. The Dymorian pikemen had arrayed themselves between a pair of low, barren hills, and had spent the past two days digging pits and setting sharpened stakes in front of their position. Companies of archers crouched among the broken scree covering the hills, ready to rain down death. Behind the massed pikemen were yet more archers, as well as the heavy cavalry, which would be prepared to charge when the Skein attack faltered, or perhaps they would be used to harry the barbarians if they tried to flank the Dymorian position. Such an attempted maneuver by the Skein king would be known well in advance by d'Chorn, as the famed Dymorian rangers were abroad on their swift horses, tracking the movement of the Skein horde.

And then, of course, there were the magisters of the Scholia, enjoying their morning repast here with Willa. Far away from the fighting so no arrow could reach them, but apparently close enough that their sorcery could still strike down the barbarians. The path wending up to this ridge was narrow enough that a handful of men could hold it for days, and a contingent of Scarlet Guardsmen and Willa's own Lyrish soldiers guarded the way.

It was an impressive force, far larger than the mercenary guilds Willa had seen fielded by the Gilded Cities in any of their conflicts. Only the padarasha of Kesh and the Empire of Swords and Flowers could muster such an army on this side of the Spine, and never had either of those great powers ventured this far north.

In the distance, across the snowy plain, the first of the Skein had appeared. They rode horses, stunted little things with shaggy manes, and they milled about with no apparent discipline. The men were little more than insects from this distance, but Willa imagined she saw great braided beards and long unbound hair. One rider galloped back and forth in front of the rest, and Willa saw him raise something to his lips. Soon after the sound of the horn came again, rolling across the plain.

"Less than I thought there would be," Vhelan murmured, his fingers playing with the golden amulet he wore. Willa made a quick estimate, made difficult by how the warriors were constantly shifting, and came to only a few hundred at most.

"This is just the vanguard," Telion said. "The first to arrive. That fellow there is letting the foot behind them know that they've seen us."

"Well, we should charge them, yes?" said Vhelan, a nervous edge to his voice. "Smash them with our cavalry before the rest arrive."

Telion cleared his throat noisily and spat, which Willa knew was his way of showing disagreement. "They'd turn tail once our horse came at 'em. Lead us back to their main host and try to put us in range of their bows."

Vhelan jumped as Telion slapped his shoulder with a huge hand. "Don't worry, Lyrishman," the big man said jovially. "There'll be fighting soon enough. But it'll be better if they come to us."

10: KEILAN

KEILAN AWOKE WITH an aching head, the memory of his unsettling dreams washed away by the morning light. He lay curled on a woolen blanket beside the hearth, and though the fire had died during the night, someone had thrown open the window's shutters to welcome the unseasonably warm day. In another room he heard the clatter of pots and the sound of something being chopped as a woman sang in a language he didn't know. If he closed his eyes he could almost imagine he was a child again, his mother preparing breakfast while his father snored away the day.

But the snoring he heard now wasn't his father's. Keilan shifted so he could look upon Senacus. The paladin seemed much the same as he had last night, though perhaps there was a bit more color in his pallid cheeks. A blanket covered him, and Keilan was tempted to pull it away and see how his wounds were faring, but he didn't want to disturb the Pure if he was sleeping well.

Keilan sat up, arching his spine to try and banish the stiffness that had settled in his lower back. Nel was right – he had gotten used to the soft beds of the Scholia. The accommodation at the pirate lord Chalissian's manse had been even more luxurious, and the guest quarters on his grandmother's island had been comfortable enough. He was no longer used to sleeping on the floor.

The other two pallets near the fire were empty – Marialle's boys had bedded down in them, but like every farm, there were chores to be done before the sun had risen. Senacus's unsheathed sword and Keilan's own jeweled blade were leaning against the wall, and piled nearby were the travel packs that the Lady Numil had given them so long ago.

Keilan blinked, coldness settling in his stomach. His pack was untied and open, clothes and various sundries strewn about.

The dagger.

Keilan scrambled to his feet and rushed over, dreading what he'd find. To his relief, he saw the carved rosewood box nestled at the bottom of his pack. Tamping down his apprehension he unlatched the lid and flipped it open.

There it was. A gleaming blade of dark crystal, similar to obsidian but more opaque, with blacker strands threading the strange material. Crimson Shan characters were carved down its curving length. Its hilt was unadorned silver, though its pommel was wrapped by lines of more spidery Shan symbols that seemed to squirm as he stared at them. Now that the box was open he could feel the sorcery coiling within the dagger like a serpent preparing to strike, and he hurriedly shut the lid again. The container somehow muted the dagger's sorcerous emanations, which would explain why Alyanna had not yet noticed what he carried.

Then who had rummaged through his pack? And why? Nothing seemed to be missing. Even his coin pouch with the little money he had left after giving most to his father was still there.

Shuffling steps made him look up. The younger of the two boys had entered the room carrying an armful of lotus roots. He put his head down and tried to walk quickly through to the kitchen where his mother was still singing and chopping, but Keilan stopped him with a word.

"You," Keilan said, and the boy froze. A lotus root squirmed from his arms and fell to the floor, and the boy's face colored like he had been caught doing something embarrassing.

"Did you look in my bag?" Keilan asked as the boy crouched to scoop up the wayward vegetable.

"No . . . my lord," the boy said haltingly as he stood again.

"You know who did?"

A moment's hesitation, then the boy nodded once. "Yessir."

"And?"

"Was your servant, sir. With the dark skin. She took something an' went outside." The boy paused, swallowing. "She's talkin' to herself in the orchard. I seen her."

Talking to herself?

"Please, my lord, I have to give these to my ma. She needs 'em."

Keilan waved the boy away, lost in his thoughts. Who was Alyanna talking to?

The orchard. He stumbled to the door and slipped out into the morning. There was a bit more bite to the air, but still it felt like an early spring was coming. He looked around, blinking, shielding his eyes from the bright sun.

There. Alyanna was at the edge of the orchard, on her knees, facing away from the farmhouse. She was hunched over something on the ground, and the boy had been right – Keilan heard her voice rising and falling, like she was carrying on a conversation. Confused, he peered among the trees, searching for who could be out there.

He crept closer, hoping to catch her unawares, but Alyanna jerked her head around before he'd gotten within a dozen paces. Her lips were pursed, her eyes narrowed.

"Keilan," she said, and there was a surprising edge to her voice.

"Alyanna," he replied, stepping closer and trying to see what was set on the withered grass in front of her.

Surprise shivered him. It was the doll Sella had found on Niara's island, a lump of cloth with straw for hair and a mouth of stitches. Black buttons stared sightlessly at Alyanna and the lattice of branches beyond her. What was it doing here? Sella must have slipped it into his pack before she'd returned home – she had mentioned something about how the doll had likely belonged to his mother, and that he should keep it as a reminder of her. Then another thought came to him with a tingling chill: Sella had said the doll had spoken to her. Could it have somehow moved itself into his pack on its own? But that was impossible.

"You've been busy," Alyanna said, holding his gaze meaningfully.

"What?"

Alyanna's head snapped back to the doll on the ground. "I know who that is!" she said in exasperation.

Keilan took an uncertain step backwards. What madness was this?

Alyanna scooped up the cloth doll and shook it at him. "The babbling. How can you stand it? Whatever passed for a mind in this thing must have shattered into a thousand pieces."

Keilan swallowed, his eyes flicking from the doll's crudely stitched face to Alyanna and back again. "I don't understand," he said slowly.

Alyanna blinked, her brow furrowing. "You can't hear it?"

His wide eyes must have been answer enough, as her expression became more thoughtful. "Interesting. I wonder if that is because you haven't developed your Talent fully yet. Or perhaps Niara put some enchantment on the soul so that it couldn't bother her, and you also are unable to hear it because you share her blood. I've been listening to its cries ever since we fled Theris, though it took me a while to realize where the noise was coming from." Alyanna raised the doll to her face, peering into its button eyes. "The Silver Sorceress," she mused, and he sensed she was speaking to herself now. "In hiding for a thousand years, and now dead by the hand of her own grandson." She looked at him again with a slight smile. "This is why I never had children."

"It was an accident," Keilan whispered, staring at the doll fearfully. Sella has been right all along – there *was* a spirit inhabiting this little piece of cloth and straw. If that was true, then the rest of the story Sella had told him must also be true.

"What else is it saying?" he asked.

Alyanna shrugged. "Nonsense, mostly. Sanity is hard to maintain for a soul after being ripped from its flesh. And I suspect with Niara's death whatever sorcery she used here has started to deteriorate, hastening the descent into madness."

"So this . . . spirit was once a woman?"

Alyanna gave him a queer look. "I thought you understood. The spirit said she explained it to your friend." She brushed the doll's hair back in mock tenderness. "This was once your aunt."

"My aunt?" Keilan cried, aghast.

"I suppose in the end it was Niara's desire for solitude that resulted in this. After we performed our great sorcery beneath the mountain – and it was difficult to convince her to join that, let me tell you – she vanished. I searched for her for a while, but eventually gave up. I assumed she'd run afoul of one of Ama's faithful, or delved too deeply into dangerous sorceries. Now I have learned she retreated to a private sanctuary so that she could perform experiments even more ambitious than my own." Keilan heard what he thought was grudging admiration in Alyanna's voice. "But such work required more sorcery than any single Talent could draw from the Void. And so Niara tried to make her own Talents." She shook her head, as if awed by the audacity. "Many children over many years, all in the hope that one of her blood would be born with the same depth of Talent as herself. And in the end, it was the daughter who got away that gave birth to the one she was looking for." Alyanna paused, and her next words were delivered like she was explaining something to a simpleton. "That would be you, Keilan."

His head was whirling as he struggled to make sense of what Alyanna was saying. "How did the spirit of my aunt end up in the doll?"

Alyanna's brow furrowed. "Its constant babbling is confusing. From what I can piece together, Niara did not want her daughters – and her children were always daughters – to grow old and die. The idea of caring for her babies until they were crones, and then having to watch them slip away into the dark – all while she remained forever young – must have horrified her." Alyanna stared at something he couldn't see, her voice growing distant. "The idea terrifies me as well, in truth." She shook herself, returning her attention to the doll. "So before they grew too old, she destroyed their mortal bodies and bound their souls to these dolls." Alyanna thrust the limp doll towards Keilan. "This one is the reason you exist. Somehow, she learned how to speak with the living. She claims she was the one who told your mother what would happen to her, how her own mother would sacrifice her flesh and blood and bind her forever to cloth and straw. It was why your mother fled Niara's island."

Keilan accepted the doll from Alyanna, turning it over. There was nothing to suggest a soul was trapped inside, struggling to be heard. Was there a room somewhere back on his grandmother's island filled with dolls like this, each with a soul inside like a weakly guttering flame? How could they stave off madness? Trapped and alone forever, slowly edging towards oblivion. The thought made him shiver.

"What should we do with it?" Keilan asked, tracing with his fingertip the jagged stitching of its mouth. "No, not it. Her."

Alyanna held out her hand to take back the doll. "I will wring what knowledge I can from this thing. Niara was a brilliant sorceress, in many ways my equal. If what the doll says is true, her ambitions may actually have outstripped my own."

"Will you make her suffer?"

"She's already suffering. Her mind is slipping away while she's trapped in the body of a doll. But perhaps she can still be of some use."

"Some use," Keilan said quietly. He reached down into himself, grasping his sorcery and twisting it into one of the few spells Niara had taught him.

"No!" Alyanna cried as blue flames erupted from his hand, enveloping the doll. "What are you doing?" she hissed angrily as the cloth and straw blackened and turned to ash.

"She was my aunt," Keilan said, steeling himself in case Alyanna tried to use her own sorcery to dampen the flames. But the sorceress just watched him with her jaw clenched. "And she deserves to be at peace."

"Fool," Alyanna said, but she sounded more tired than angry. She stared at the doll until it was utterly consumed, her mouth set in a thin line. "Sentimentality is a weakness, Keilan, one you must learn to transcend. There may be hard choices coming. Will you be able to sacrifice that girl inside the house if it is necessary to stop the Chosen?"

Keilan released his sorcery and the blue flames vanished. All that remained of the doll was a few twisted black scraps. "I would find a way without giving her up."

"There is not always that choice," Alyanna said fiercely. "You must be prepared to do anything. The creatures we are trying to stop . . . they are not encumbered by any morality. Their only desire is to end the rest of us. To make the world suffer for what was done to them."

"And what was that?"

Alyanna frowned. "I don't know, exactly. But I have my suspicions. I believe they were human children once, and sorcerers corrupted their bodies and spirits, twisting them into monsters. And now only one passion animates what remains: vengeance."

"How are we going to stop them? Where are you taking us?"

Alyanna looked to the north, tucking a stray strand of her hair behind her ear. She was disconcertingly beautiful, Keilan thought. How could someone who looked so young and innocent harbor such an ancient and vicious soul?

"We are going to the Crimson Queen. She is marching into the Frostlands with her army to confront the Chosen."

"The Chosen? You said that before. You mean the Shan child-demons? I have heard them called the Betrayers."

Alyanna snorted. "It seems they have a more generous understanding of their own nature."

"And wait," Keilan said, confused. "I thought the queen was your enemy?"

Alyanna shot him an annoyed glance. "She was. But there is a greater threat now. We have . . . settled our differences, or at least set them aside. I contacted her to warn her about the dangers posed by the Chosen, but she was already aware. She said the bard, Jan, was captured by them. If we can free him, the strength of four Talents should be enough to overcome the Chosen and their allies."

"We are going to the queen," Keilan said slowly. It seemed that they would not need to steal Alyanna's flying disc after all.

"Yes. But we cannot dally here for too long. We must leave the paladin – he will not recover in time. And every hour we delay makes it more likely we will arrive too late to help Cein d'Kara in the Frostlands when she will need it most."

The Frostlands. The very name sent a thrill through him. It had been a mythical, far-off place when he was a boy listening to tales at his mother's knee, a once-glorious realm of warriors and wizards and dragons, now forever locked in ice and sorcery. Preserved like bones in rock, dead but not decaying.

Keilan rubbed his palms together, trying to brush away the last black fragments of the doll. He jumped as Alyanna's hand flashed out and grabbed his wrist, turning his arm over.

"What is that?" she asked, her brow creasing.

Keilan's heart fell when he saw that the veins near his wrist had once more become black and inflamed. He had been feeling better since the episode in Chale, and he'd hoped he was finally recovering from this affliction.

"I have an infection," Keilan said. He tried to pull his hand away, but Alyanna held tight, her slim fingers tracing the distended black lines, lingering on the faint red mark where Niara had cut him with the dagger.

She shook her head.

"An infection? No. This is not natural. I feel traces of sorcery . . . and something familiar. Where did you get this cut?"

The look on her face was making Keilan worried.

"On the island. My grandmother's island."

Alyanna's concern turned to confusion. "This is Niara's sorcery? But that doesn't make sense. I've seen veins like this before, under the corpse-flesh of the Chosen. And their taint is here, though subtle. You must have been exposed to them." She tilted her head to the side, her face thoughtful. "Saltstone? You were there the night of the attack, as were the Chosen. You did not come into contact with them at that time?"

"I . . . I don't think so."

She sighed, her frustration plain. "The doll told me in its ramblings that you killed Niara. Was she allied with the Chosen? Were they on the island as well? Why did you seek her out?"

Keilan swallowed, flustered under the barrage of questions. Should he tell the sorceress everything? He knew from his time in Jan's mind that Alyanna was consumed with her own selfish ambitions, and was capable of great evil . . . but they were united now by a common purpose. He flicked his eyes towards the farmhouse. Nel had told him to keep the dagger secret, yet Alyanna might be the only one who knew how it could be used against the demons.

He made his decision. Taking a deep breath, he told the sorceress what had happened since the attack on Saltstone: their pursuit of Senacus south to Lyr, the summons by the Oracle, the vision of what might happen if the Chosen were not stopped. Alyanna's face was impassive, though a flicker of consternation passed across her face when he spoke about the vision he'd had: the black temple in the ruins of the Selthari Palace formed of twisted corpses, and the arrival of Niara to challenge the demon children.

"So after the end of the world, the Silver Sorceress finally emerges," she said with a trace of bitterness, shaking her head. "Of course. That would be very much like Niara."

"They had sent one of their number to kill her. She was carrying its head when she arrived, and threw it in the grass at their feet." With a shiver, Keilan remembered the mouth of the Chosen opening and closing like a fish taken from the water.

"They feared her," Alyanna mused. "But why?"

"She had a weapon. A dagger that could hurt them. Niara claimed it could even destroy the demons. This was what cut me, on her island."

Alyanna leaned closer, interested. "Why was this dagger special?"

"My grandmother said that centuries ago a warlock of Shan had sought her out. He wanted to banish the Betrayers forever, but there was no one in the Empire of Swords and Flowers who could perform the sorcery necessary to craft this dagger. They had blood and hair from one of these children, taken long ago."

"Yet in the end they did not use the dagger to destroy them."

"She said the warlock betrayed her, and so she kept it."

Alyanna tapped her lip with her finger, deep in thought. "But it must truly be capable of ending the Chosen. And that was why the Oracle sent you to find her." She focused on Keilan again, her eyes intense. "You have it, then? This dagger?"

He hesitated for the briefest of moments, then nodded. What was done was done – he hoped he had been right to tell her.

She clapped her hands together, smiling broadly. "Excellent. This must be the stream the Oracle was hoping would come about by sending you to Niara's island. You returned with this dagger and have brought it to me."

"We were bringing it to the queen," Keilan said quickly.

"The queen has power, I'll grant you," replied Alyanna, "but she is still a child. I have wielded artifacts the likes of which she has never imagined. I want to see this dagger, Keilan." She reached out again and touched his arm. "This is what concerns me now, though. Something of their essence has infected you. Have you felt different since you were cut?"

"I've been . . . quick to anger," Keilan admitted. "Sometimes I feel lightheaded, though I thought I was getting better. And my dreams have been troubled, but I don't remember them."

Alyanna chewed her lip. "You are almost certainly in danger. We don't have time now, but when we reach the queen I want to examine you more thoroughly and see if I can draw out this poison."

"You think we should leave soon?"

The sorceress nodded. "As I said, we have no time to waste."

"But what about—"

"Keilan!"

They turned to find Nel hurrying towards them.

"Keilan, it's Senacus! He's awake."

The paladin's eyes had opened, flooding the room with Ama's radiance. He turned his head weakly as Keilan came through the entrance, and from his expression he looked to still be in considerable pain.

"Thank the Father," he whispered, struggling to sit up.

"Please, my lord," cried Marialle, hurrying to his side. "Rest. You'll tear open your wounds again."

Grimacing, Senacus sank back onto the pallet. His silver hair was plastered to his head, as if he was suffering from a terrible fever, and his skin was sallow. He looked like a corpse.

"How did we live?" he asked softly.

"We were saved by—" Keilan glanced at Marialle, who was watching with wide eyes "—someone very strong."

Senacus's eyes flickered to the farmer's wife. He had caught that look. "Goodwoman," he said, addressing her. She stepped forward, gaze downcast, her hands kneading her dress like it was a piece of dough. "Thank you for your hospitality. But I must make a request. I need to speak with this boy and woman in private. Will you leave us for a moment?"

Marialle gave a jerky nod and then scurried away, back towards the kitchen. Senacus waited a heartbeat longer, then gestured for Keilan and Nel to come closer.

"What happened?" asked the paladin.

"A sorceress," Nel replied. "She rescued us from the shapechanger. We fled on a flying circle and found refuge on this farm."

Keilan noticed how Senacus was licking his lips and hurried to fill a cup from a pitcher Marialle had left behind.

"A sorceress," the paladin repeated as he accepted the cup and drank deeply.

"Not just any sorceress," Keilan said slowly. "She was the one who orchestrated the attack on Saltstone."

Senacus froze, then slowly lowered the cup. "I knew I had been a puppet when I saw my companion use sorcery that night."

"The shadowblade," Nel said, her voice twisted by hate.

Senacus nodded slightly. "Yes. And if what you say is true, then this sorceress is the puppeteer. She must be the one who influenced the High Mendicant to send me west to find you, Keilan. She wanted you."

"I did."

Alyanna stepped into the room, her head held high. Even dressed in a simple robe and shawl, Keilan realized, she radiated the same presence as the queen of Dymoria and the prince of Vis.

The Pure's face had gone utterly still. Keilan suspected that if his body was willing, Senacus would have lunged towards where his white-metal sword leaned against the wall. "You hide your sorcery from me."

"A simple enough trick," she said. Her tone was confident, but Keilan noticed that she did not approach the paladin.

"Show me," Senacus said through gritted teeth.

Alyanna cocked an eyebrow. Nothing seemed to change for Keilan, but Senacus suddenly sucked in his breath.

"By the Radiant Father," he breathed hoarsely, then blinked, as if a bright light that only he could see had suddenly been extinguished. "What are you?"

"Something more brilliant than your blessed light," she retorted. "Ama has no power over me, paladin."

Senacus fell silent for a moment. Invisible lightning seemed to crackle in the air between the Pure and the sorceress.

"She is helping us," Keilan ventured. "She knows the threat those children represent."

Senacus glanced at him. The paladin's face glistened with sweat, as if the conversation was straining him greatly. "She sent me to bring you back to her," he said.

"Keilan is a prize," Alyanna said. "The harbinger of a new age. Every Talent covets him, for with his power added to their own, great things become possible. It is true I wanted him by my side."

"To do what?" Senacus pressed.

"Great. Things." Alyanna delivered these words slowly and clearly.

"Don't trust her, Keilan," the paladin continued, his desperation clear. "She schemes. She—" His burning eyes widened. "The Weaver. Demian was speaking about *you*. You are the Weaver."

"Do not say his name!"

Keilan jumped at Alyanna's outburst. The skin on his arms prickled as he felt her swell with sorcery. Her sudden rage was jarring.

"Where is he?" Senacus continued, clearly unafraid of the sorceress and sensing weakness. "Does he live?"

Alyanna whirled to face Keilan. He could almost see the sorcery brimming in her dark eyes. "Say your goodbyes to the Pure," she spat. "We leave soon." Then she turned on her heel and strode from the room, the crackling power dissipating in her wake.

Keilan shivered, unnerved by this sudden glimpse of Alyanna's unbound strength. She could draw at least as much sorcery into herself as the queen or his grandmother.

"You are remarkably good at making friends," Nel said dryly.

"That is one I don't want to be friends with." Senacus stared at Keilan pointedly as he said this. "And neither do you."

Keilan grimaced. "We need to go with her."

"You don't," said the Pure.

"We do," rejoined Keilan. "We are somewhere in the middle of the Kingdoms with no horses. Do we have days to find our way to a town where we can buy mounts? Weeks to travel to the Frostlands?"

"The Frostlands?" Nel's face crinkled in confusion. "We need to go to Dymoria."

Keilan shook his head. "I spoke with Alyanna. She's also traveling to the queen, but she knows the queen will be in the Frostlands. Cein d'Kara has declared war on the Skein."

Nel blinked in bewilderment. "How does the sorceress know this?"

"She has communicated with the queen somehow. They are allied now against the demon children."

"Do not believe anything she says," Senacus hissed, wincing. He was panting, struggling to sit up.

"I won't," Keilan said, crouching beside the paladin. He found Senacus's hand and gripped it fiercely. "I promise. But she has a way for us to reach the queen. We need her. And she needs us to stop the Betrayers."

The Pure sank back onto his pallet, clearly exhausted. "I can't travel yet," he said, his voice hollow.

"I know," Keilan replied. "Rest here and get strong again."

The paladin nodded slightly, staring at the wall. He looked utterly defeated.

Keilan leaned in closer to the Pure. "I forgive you."

Senacus glanced at him sharply, his surprise evident.

"I've learned things about my grandmother," Keilan explained. "Terrible things. She . . . she was a monster. Whatever she planned on the island, whatever she wanted me to help her with . . . it's for the best that she failed." He paused, struggling to pull up the last words he had to say. "You were right. She had to be stopped." With some effort he quashed the last of his resentment towards the paladin. Niara had sacrificed millions to gain everlasting life, and murdered her own daughters if they were born without great sorcery. She had been evil. Keilan repeated this thought, trying to bludgeon himself into believing it totally. She had been evil.

Senacus squeezed his hand, and a prickling heat crept up Keilan's arm. "I will pray for you, Keilan," the paladin promised. "The Radiant Father knows you fight to save us all."

11: CHO LIN

THE NEXT MORNING, Cho Lin would have believed it had all been a strange and vivid dream, except that the broken shard of her father's sword was still there, gleaming in the light trickling through the gaps in the ceiling.

She climbed to her feet, amazed by how good she felt. The aching cold that had settled in her bones ever since she'd entered the Frostlands was gone. Cho Lin pulled aside her furs, examining the faded red lines where the demon had slashed her. She almost couldn't tell them apart from other wounds she'd received years ago. A great sorcery had been done to her, and while the thought did give her a little trickle of unease, she also knew that she would otherwise have died.

It must have been the tears of this statue. She'd drunk nearly half of the small basin's contents, and from the look of it many days would pass before the beads of moisture running down the stone cheeks refilled the container. Cho Lin circled the statue, looking for some hint as to its provenance. Her fingers brushed the stone folds of its robes and lingered on the outstretched arms that had held the remnant of the Sword of Cho. The detail was remarkable.

"Thank you," she whispered in Shan.

The statue did not answer, of course.

Could it be a representation of the Pale Lady, the spirit that had led her here? Cho Lin thought not. The statue's robes were concealing, but also plain, and her soft features suggested compassion. She looked like one of the itinerant nuns who wandered the Empire of Swords and Flowers spreading Sagewa Tain's vision of the Enlightenment, sworn to poverty and dedicated to aiding those in need. The ghost, on the other hand, had been dressed in rich vestments and wearing a diadem on its brow. Its sharp cheekbones and the way it glided with its back straight and head held high suggested it had once been a noble. Jan had told her once that Nes Vaneth had been ruled by sorceress queens, and that he had been the lover of the last who ruled here, before the ice swallowed the holdfasts. Could this be her unquiet spirit? And if so, why was she helping her?

Cho Lin's stomach growled, interrupting her musings. She was ravenous – her last meal had been days ago, a handful of rotten vegetables and bone scraps. Her body felt whole and strong, but that would fade quickly if she did not find something to eat.

She would have to leave the safety of the ruins. There was food in the Bhalavan – every morning, the remnants of the previous night's feast littered the tables. Most of the Skein would be sleeping, this early in the day, their heads still sodden with drink. Perhaps if she pulled up the cowl of her furs, she could sneak inside pretending to be a thrall. The thought of eating cold, greasy chunks of meat made her stomach gurgle again in hunger.

But then what? Return to the ruins and wait for the Betrayers to come searching for her? And the demons would seek her out when they returned, of this she was certain. They hated her – no, they hated her family. Cho Xin had bound them a thousand years ago by slaying their corporeal bodies with the Sword of Cho.

Her eyes drifted to the shard of metal at the statue's feet. The Betrayers had feared this weapon, but it was no more.

Or was it?

She knelt beside the rippling steel, pressing her fingers to the cold metal. Was the soul that had infused the sword with power truly gone? Could it be enticed back if the sword was whole once more?

Cho Lin's heart beat faster, her excitement rising. Something – the spirit? – had brought this piece of the sword to her. And there must be a reason why.

The warlocks of Shan had made this weapon long ago. If she returned to the bone-shard towers with all the pieces of the sword, perhaps they could reforge what had been broken. The despair that had been hovering at the edge of her mind ever since the shapechanger had snapped the sword lifted a little. She had a purpose again.

Cho Lin breathed out slowly, reaching for the Nothing. She grasped it immediately, and the emptiness flooded her limbs with strength. It was as if a wound in her soul had been filled, and she was whole once more. But where were the other pieces of the sword? The last place she had seen them was in her cell in the Bhalavan, the fragments spinning into the gloom as the blade shattered. Could they still be there?

Cho Lin's fingers brushed the ivory handles of her butterfly swords.

She was going to find out.

Fat snowflakes were slowly drifting down among the ruins. Evidently it had been snowing for a while, as a layer of unblemished white covered everything. A great stroke of luck, probably, as otherwise the Skein may have been able to track her to the sanctuary where the Pale Lady had led her. Nevertheless, Cho

Lin kept herself alert as she moved through the shattered remnants of Nes Vaneth.

She saw nothing living, nor any evidence that hunters had come looking for her. Did the Skein truly fear the ghosts of Nes Vaneth enough that they would refuse to pursue her? Or did they assume the city had swallowed her, and that she was already dead? Certainly her wounds must have looked fatal to those watching in the arena.

Rather than approach the Bhalavan from the great avenue, she circled around the mighty structure until she came to the great empty space where the Skein from the north had been encamped. There had been over a hundred great tents here, at least, when last she'd gazed upon the field; the tribesmen of the Crow and Stag and White Worm that could not fit inside the Bhalavan's great sleeping hall. Now, though, there were only a few dozen tents scattered about, though the snowy ground was pockmarked by the blackened remnants of countless campfires, still visible despite the recent snowfall. Cho Lin thought back to how empty the Bhalavan and the city had seemed as the priest of the Skin Thief had marched her to the arena where the creature had waited. Such a spectacle should have attracted enough Skein to fill the benches to bursting, but the watching crowd had been sparse. The king of the White Worm, Hroi, and the thanes of the Stag and Raven had been absent as well.

Where had the Skein gone?

Cho Lin followed the curve of the Bhalavan's wall until she came to the great bronze doors that were forever cracked open. Pulling up her cowl and tucking away a few stray strands of her black hair, she slipped inside the hall.

The cook pits were empty, the great braziers cold. A handful of Skein sprawled at the long tables, sleeping off the night's excesses. Thralls, the women brought back from raids as slaves, moved as silent as shadows among the benches, cleaning up the remnants of the previous night's feast. Some among them might have recognized her, but they did not say anything or even appear to glance in her direction as she approached one of the tables and began gathering food. Her belly grumbled, imploring her to fall upon the scraps there and then, but Cho Lin ignored it and instead wrapped a few untouched chicken legs in a piece of cloth and stuffed that into her furs.

A tremor of fear went through her as her gaze was drawn to the far recesses of the great hall and the entrances to the shadow-choked passageways. She hoped she could remember the way back to her cell, but it had been a tangle of narrow corridors, and she hadn't been very aware of her surroundings on either of the occasions she'd moved through them. Somewhere in that gloomy labyrinth was also the tunnel that led to the throne room of the old Min-Ceruthan queens. The memory of the sorcery clotting that chamber made her skin prickle. Dancing blue flames within a wall of ice, the high nobles of the old holdfast encased in stone, forever cowering before the sorcery their queen had used to preserve her child.

Jan's child. As she drifted towards the back of the great hall, careful not to disturb the sleeping Skein, Cho Lin's thoughts turned to her old companion. Did he live, or had he finally succumbed to his terrible injuries? Had he suffered an even worse fate? She shuddered, remembering the shaman of the White Worm placing Jan's desiccated eye in his mouth and chewing slowly. Cho Lin dispatched a quick prayer to the Four Winds that if he was dead, at least her worst imaginings had not come to pass.

She lingered for a moment when she came to the statues guarding the largest of the passages. They were clad in archaic armor, greaves and cuirasses incised with swirling patterns, the heads of both hidden by crested helmets. A falcon perched on the shoulder of one, a snake coiled around the arm of another. She hadn't noticed it before, but the head of a small animal – maybe a ferret – was poking out from under a gorget. Once more she was impressed with the startling detail of the stone warriors . . . but now she had her suspicions that these statues had been flesh and blood before the coming of the ice, just like the courtiers and nobles in the throne room below.

After a quick glance to make sure none of the Skein or thralls in the hall had taken an interest in her, Cho Lin slipped beneath the arched entrance. A fierce cold filled these passages, and the only illumination came from where wan daylight trickled through chinks in the walls. As she pressed deeper, the light disappeared entirely, until she was moving through near-total darkness. Her heart thundered as she imagined what ancient horrors might still inhabit this cursed ruin, and it was only through tremendous effort that she kept herself from turning and fleeing back to the great hall.

She closed her eyes and mastered her breathing, summoning up her etiolated memories of this place. The Skein had marched her down a main passage, then taken a narrow corridor that curved away to the right. Cho Lin placed her hand on the frozen, pitted stone beside her, retracing her stumbling steps from that terrible night. The corridor had forked and they had stayed right, then traversed a passage low enough that the Skein were forced to crouch, though she could walk upright. Cho Lin raised her arm, and a little thrill went through her as her fingers brushed the ceiling.

The seamless black ahead of her was suddenly marred by a sliver of light creeping out from beneath a door. Her mouth dry, Cho Lin pushed on the frost-rimed wood, sending out another fervent prayer that the Skein had not bothered locking it after removing the prisoners. She exhaled in relief as the door swung open, its ancient hinges squealing.

Cho Lin had expected a great wash of emotions when she again gazed upon where she had been imprisoned. Now, though, staring at the filthy rushes and black iron bars, she only felt a curious detachment, like it had been someone else who suffered for all those weeks. It was actually a relief to stand in this chamber, as the light spilling through the prison's narrow window had banished the imagined horrors of the dark corridors outside.

Cho Lin shook herself, trying to focus on the task at hand. She walked over to where she thought the shapechanger had broken the Sword of Cho and then knelt, sifting through the dirty straw and bone scraps. Nothing here. Chewing on her lip, she stood again, peering into the depths of the prison. The demon in the body of her father had sundered the blade with such force that the shards had gone spinning away, and then casually tossed the hilt to the side. She had heard it clatter against the wall even though she'd covered her face, overwhelmed by the horror of it all.

Cho Lin gasped when she saw a chunk of blackness she'd overlooked at first; it blended almost perfectly with the shadows. She crept closer, nervously expecting it to be some rusted manacles or discarded tool, and it wasn't until her fingers closed around the black dragonbone hilt that she allowed herself to believe she had found her father's sword.

Cho Lin searched the prison for what seemed like an age, and the pale light had begun to darken by the time she was certain she had gathered all the pieces of the blade. None of the shards were as long as that which had been placed upon the outstretched arms of the statue. Carefully, she laid the shattered sword out on the stone, cursing herself for leaving the final piece back in the ruins. She hadn't wanted to be encumbered, and she'd known she would return to her hidden sanctuary, but it would have been better if she could be certain she had collected all the sword's fragments.

Could it be reforged? Despite the veil of mystery and power the warlocks of Shan draped themselves with, it was common knowledge in the empire that the order was a shadow of what it had once been. And was the sword's magic gone forever, or would the soul she'd experienced return to the blade if it was made anew?

Sighing, Cho Lin swaddled the pieces of the sword in a length of cloth, then tucked that under her arm. If the warlocks could not help, perhaps she'd have to return to the kingdom of the Crimson Queen and beg her assistance. Jan had said she was a sorceress unlike any other that been born in the turning of an age.

She paused, considering this. Shan was a thousand leagues away, while Dymoria bordered the Frostlands. Despite his imprisonment, Jan had claimed Cein d'Kara's intentions were just. Would the queen hear her out if she came before her bearing the broken blade, or simply clap her in irons when she realized that Cho Lin was the one who had spirited away her prisoner?

Steeling herself, Cho Lin plunged once more into the blackness of the Bhalavan. It seemed to take longer to find her way back to the great hall, and she had a fleeting moment of panic when she thought she must have taken a wrong turn. Not long after that, though, she noticed a very welcome glow creeping around a bend in the passage ahead, and heard the faint sound of gruff laughter.

The Skein had roused themselves. Cho Lin pulled her cowl down low and emerged from the corridor hunched over and shuffling, as she'd seen the thralls doing when they wanted to avoid drawing attention to themselves. She didn't even glance over at the tables, afraid she might be recognized. The midday repast must recently have been served; the sounds of clinking metal and raucous conversation carried to her as she hurried across the hall, and the smell of cooked meat made her mouth water. She couldn't wait to get back to her sanctuary and tear apart the chicken secreted inside her furs; she'd allowed herself only a few nibbles while she searched for the sword.

Cho Lin half expected a cry of alarm to go up, but it did not come, and her racing heart finally started to slow as she reached the great bronze doors. She couldn't hold back a giddy little grin at how brazen she had been. She'd done it! She had stolen into the Bhalavan and come away with the sword of her ancestors. There was hope still that the Raveling could be averted—

With a surprised grunt, she collided with someone entering the hall and was knocked onto her backside, nearly letting go of the bundle, which would have resulted in the sword's fragments spilling across the threshold.

The Skein she'd walked into had staggered back but managed to stay upright, and now he loomed over her, framed in the brightness of the day. He had dropped something, a tattered piece of fabric, and with a muttered curse he bent to pick it up. Their gazes met. His face was ancient, riven by age lines and faded scars. She did not recognize him, but his eyes widened and his mouth gaped open in astonishment. Cho Lin glanced at what he clutched in his hand, and her heart fell when she saw a collection of cured leather swatches roughly stitched together – bits of many different faces of many different colors sewn into a mask.

The priest of the Skin Thief.

She kicked out, driving her boot into his stomach just as he started to shriek something. Whatever warning he would have cried was replaced by a whoosh of air as she knocked the breath from his lungs. He fell to his knees clutching his belly, staring at her in hatred as he gaspingly tried to form words. Cho Lin lunged to her feet and dashed past him, bursting through the doors and nearly barreling into the party of Skein warriors who had been trailing behind the priest.

She skidded to a halt as they stared at her in slack-jawed surprise. The Skein were armored in gray leather pebbled like a lizard's skin, and their faces were tattooed to resemble snarling beasts. Bones were threaded in their greasy hair, and one wore a necklace of shrunken, monstrous heads. These were the Flayed, the elite warriors of the White Worm, garbed in the hides of wraiths and sworn to the Skin Thief.

Cho Lin put her head down and ran for the white stone ruins closest to the Bhalavan. Behind her, she heard cries of alarm and the grating bellows of the priest she'd struck down. She ducked around a shattered wall, leaping over the tumbled remains of a pillar sunk in snow. Would they dare follow her into Nes Vaneth? She paused, glancing back, and a spear flashed past her and clattered off a great faceted chunk of black ice. She was certain that if she'd kept running it would have sunk into her side.

The Flayed were close behind her, clambering over the tumbled stone. The one that had thrown the spear barked a harsh curse and drew a red-bladed, sickle-shaped sword, then pointed the curving edge towards where she had stopped. The others responded with a ululation that chilled her blood, charging towards her.

For a brief moment, Cho Lin considered throwing down the bundle with the fragments of her father's blade and drawing her own butterfly swords. But behind the Flayed and the white stone ruins loomed the gray vastness of the Bhalavan. The priest would certainly rally the Skein inside, and even though they were terrified of what lurked within Nes Vaneth, the sound of clashing steel this close would carry to them, and even their superstitions would not be enough to keep them from braving the edge of the dead city.

With a snarl of frustration, Cho Lin turned and fled. She reached for the Nothing, that pure well of strength at the core of her Self, and the world around her seemed to grind to a halt. The fat snowflakes that had been drifting around her a moment ago now hung suspended, and when she glanced behind her she saw that the Flayed rushing towards her now appeared to be wading through an unseen morass.

She ran. In moments she outdistanced them, but she did not slacken her pace until she arrived at the listing doorway that led to the sanctum where she had convalesced, and the statue with its basin of healing tears. Cho Lin paused, panting, her breath steaming in the cold, and looked back the way she had come. She'd churned the snow with her passage, leaving a trail that was impossible to miss. Cho Lin couldn't see any sign of the Flayed, but they would have no trouble following her. Should she try and hide her tracks? No, the Skein were used to hunting over snow – Cho Lin doubted she could fool them.

Then a fight it was. Hopefully, only the Flayed would pursue her here. If all the warriors in the Bhalavan suddenly swarmed out of the ruins then it would likely be time for her to join her ancestors beyond the veil. Glancing to her left, Cho Lin saw that down a small alley the close-packed ruins opened into a larger space. That would do.

Leaving the entrance to her sanctuary behind her, Cho Lin hurried through the narrow passage and found herself in what must have once been a market or a place for gatherings. Several other roads emptied into this circular space, as if she stood in the hub of a wheel, and a pair of great clawed feet of white stone suggested that at one time the statue of a rearing dragon had lorded over this part of the ruins. The rest of the statue might be here as well, as snow-covered mounds were strewn about. Most of the buildings bounding this space were nothing but tumbled stone, but a few still loomed above her, their second stories somewhat intact.

The faint sounds of pursuit drifted to Cho Lin, guttural Skein cries that were out of place in the utter calm and silence of the fallen city. She glanced behind her, back through the alley, but they had not yet come into view. For a moment Cho Lin considered leading the Flayed deeper into the ruins, but she doubted she would find a better spot for an ambush anywhere else. Mastering her nerves, Cho Lin quickly dug a hollow in one of the drifts and then placed the bundle with the Sword of Cho within. After covering it with snow and smoothing it over she went to the statue's feet and leaped up onto one of its great clawed toes. Perched rather precariously, Cho Lin embraced the Nothing within her, flooding her limbs with the strength of the Enlightened. She spent a moment repeating the mantra of Red Fang to herself – *the self my nothing the self my nothing* – striving for that perfect concentration that allowed for the greatest of feats.

Then she leaped. Her muscles bunched, exploded, and she soared like a tiger, whiteness flashing beneath her. She landed on one of the snow-covered mounds, and it took all her balance to keep from sliding off. Then she jumped again, onto another of the hummocks scattered about the space, this one close to a building. Once it must have been a magnificent villa, but its roof had fallen, though somehow this had not caused the second story to collapse. With a final great effort, she threw herself up and among the shattered snow and masonry overlooking the ruins, her heart fluttering as her boots just cleared the edge. She went to one knee, her hands sunk in the snow, her legs thrumming from the tremendous effort. She'd made larger jumps while training upon the jagged karst cliffs of Red Fang, but not very many.

When Cho Lin raised her head, she found herself staring into the eyes of a child.

She nearly screamed, and had to stop herself by pressing her knuckles to her mouth. The girl was barely old enough to stand, blond curls tumbling around a face so still and white she looked like a porcelain doll. But her eyes were too perfect to be fashioned of glass: vivid blue and flecked with green, widened by terror. Her small hand was outstretched, splayed against the dark ice that imprisoned her. Cho Lin bowed her head, overcome by the horror of it all. An innocent child, the flame of her life snuffed out, and for what? How could anything justify what the old sorcerers had done?

A faint crunching came from below. Cho Lin turned from the dead child and crept to the edge of the ruin, careful to keep herself hidden. The four Flayed warriors were just now emerging warily into the open, and given how their eyes were darting about they must also have realized this space would make an excellent place for an ambush. Behind them came the bent-backed priest of the Skin Thief, his ragged black robes stirring in the breeze. He was holding a curved flensing knife like those used to cut away the fur of hunted animals and remove their organs. The sight of it made her stomach twist.

The Flayed warrior in the lead followed her tracks up to the statue's shattered base. He made a circuit of the plinth, searching for where she had gone. He barked something in Skein and his fellows fanned out, their heads down as they looked for her footprints. Cho Lin considered slipping out the back of the building she crouched upon and fleeing, but she suspected that eventually the hunters would pick up her trail again.

She wanted to finish this . . . and she had a score to settle with the priest.

One of the Flayed wandered close to the building in which she waited. He peered into the ruins of the first floor, tensed and ready to hurl the spear he brandished. Another Skein barked something from the other side of the plaza and he turned to shout a reply. Without hesitating, Cho Lin drew one of her blades and leaped. The Skein must have heard the scuff of her boots, as he whirled around just as the point of her butterfly sword pierced his chest. The force of her weight behind it sent the blade bursting out his back. She let go of the hilt, absorbing the fall on her shoulder and rolling to her feet in the snow in one smooth motion.

The Flayed was still alive, splayed out with his hands wrapped around the length of steel emerging from his furs. He looked at her wildly, blood pouring from his mouth as he gasped for breath that would not come. She gripped the ivory hilt and yanked her sword free. It came loose with a sucking sound, and she heard the warrior's death rattle as she unsheathed her other sword and turned towards the rest of the Flayed.

The first to reach her was a giant with a bristly blond beard, his tattooed face contorted with rage. He wielded a great double-bladed ax like it was a hatchet, swinging it in a flashing arc. Cho Lin stepped back nimbly and the ax sliced only air, then she lashed out with the sword in her left hand. The wraith-leather armor parted and her blade sank into the flesh beneath, but the huge Skein seemed not to notice. Somehow he arrested his swing despite the strength behind it and reversed the blow, chopping at her neck. Her grasp on the Nothing gave her an extra moment to react, and she threw herself forward as the ax whistled over her head. She lost her grip on the sword she'd stabbed the Flayed with, but she managed to hold on to the other, and as she rolled to her feet she thrust the blade into his belly. She scrambled away before he could catch her with another swing.

Cho Lin shouldn't have worried, though. The ax slipped from the warrior's hand a moment later when he toppled face-first into the snow. The last two Flayed were approaching her more warily, each brandishing a sickle-shaped sword with steel the color of dried blood. A spider had been inked on the face of one of the men, six eyes clustered on his forehead amid a tangle of legs, while the other made her think of a lizard, a forked tongue dangling down his beardless chin. The Flayed split up to come at her from different angles, and she turned to keep both of them in her field of vision. Most warriors would dread fighting two at once, no matter their skill, but the monks of Red Fang almost always practiced sparring against multiple opponents. She could tell that although these two Skein were both skilled swordsmen, they had not been trained to fight in unison. If they had, they would have rushed her at once and forced her to defend two attacks simultaneously. Instead, they were trying to close on her slowly as she shuffled backwards.

A mistake.

Cho Lin suddenly exploded towards the Flayed with the spider crouched on his face, her left-hand butterfly sword a blur. He warded away the strike and hopped backwards to give himself more space, but rather than pressing her advantage Cho

Lin smoothly pivoted to meet the onrushing sword of the other Flayed, as he had lunged at her when she'd gone for his clansman. Her right-hand sword caught the red-steel of his sickle blade and turned it aside, and then she brought her other blade around and plunged it into his neck. The Skein went down clutching the wound, blood spurting between his fingers, and she threw herself at the other Flayed. He tried to stop her whirling blades but she pushed past his attempts and sliced his sword-hand off at the wrist, then buried a length of steel in his side. She must have pierced his heart, as he was dead before he fell to the snow.

The fight had lasted only moments. Across the plaza the black-robed priest stared at her, unmoving, and though Cho Lin couldn't see his face she imagined it was be twisted in shock. She took a deep breath and let it out slowly, concentrating on the blood thrumming in her veins. Every aspect of the world sharpened as she hung suspended in the Nothing within the Self: the faint breeze rasped loudly as it swirled over the snow, the pale blue sky was dazzlingly bright, and the smell of blood and voided bowels were heavy in the bitingly cold air.

She took a step in the direction of the priest. As if a spell had been broken, he turned and ran, his arms and legs flailing in the awkward gait of an old man who had not had to move quickly in many years.

Before he had gone a dozen steps, he skidded to a stop, the blade of her butterfly sword resting on his shoulder. Slowly, he turned to face her, and this time she could see the whites of his eyes beneath his mask.

"Shan demon," he hissed, the hand that held the flensing knife shaking.

"You call me demon?" Cho Lin said incredulously. "What about the thing you tried to feed me to?"

"That is not demon," the priest grated in his stilted Menekarian. "That is servant of the Skin Thief."

"One man's god is another man's demon," murmured Cho Lin. The unnatural vividness of her surroundings had begun to fade as her hold on the Nothing faltered. The sword she held to the priest's neck suddenly seemed to grow heavier.

"Kill me," the priest spat out harshly. "I wish to meet *my* god."

"Not yet," Cho Lin said. "I have questions."

"No answers for you," the priest replied, though Cho Lin thought she heard a tremor in his voice. Perhaps he was afraid of how the Skin Thief would look upon a servant who was present when a girl defeated his chosen warriors.

"There was another prisoner in my cell. The skald. He arrived in Nes Vaneth before me, and for a time was favored by the king and his thanes."

The priest said nothing, so Cho Lin pressed the edge of her blade against his neck. A trickle of blood slid down the furred collar of his robes.

"South," the priest said grudgingly. "Hroi take him south when he go to fight the queen."

"Queen?"

"The red queen. She brings her army into the Frostlands." The pain in his words was now mixed with anger.

The Crimson Queen of Dymoria had entered the north? And she had come to fight the Skein, who had allied with the Betrayers? Cho Lin's thoughts wandered to the shattered pieces of her father's sword. The warlocks believed she was a great sorceress. If she truly opposed the Betrayers, then perhaps she *was* the one to whom Cho Lin should bring the sword.

The priest seemed to notice her distraction. "You have no hope, spider-eater. You are doomed."

"I had little trouble defeating your Flayed."

The priest chuckled, a horrible rasping sound. "You can kill all the Flayed. It does not matter. The Skin Thief walks the land again. His children and servants labor to bring about *Gravishna*."

"What is that?"

"The end," the priest gloated. "The end of the world, Shan. The Worm shall rise and swallow the sun, and in the time of decay there will be sweet feasting for those who held fast to the faith."

The priest's words had an unsettling resemblance to the catechism of the Raveling. It was no wonder the Betrayers had found fertile ground in the far north for their breed of madness.

Cho Lin opened her mouth to demand he explain himself, but paused when he suddenly went rigid, his attention fixed on something behind her.

"Away!" he cried, his voice raw.

Cho Lin glanced over her shoulder and couldn't hold back a startled gasp. The Pale Lady stood in the center of the plaza, watching them with cold blue eyes, her white dress and long golden hair untroubled by the breeze. She was no illusion, though – the silver diadem on her brow gleamed like it had been freshly polished, and as Cho Lin watched, the lady slowly raised her open palm. A vivid scar marred the otherwise unblemished whiteness of her hand, red and festering.

"Who—" Cho Lin began, but then a sound made her whirl around and she had a momentary glimpse of the priest of the Skin Thief lunging towards her, flensing knife aimed at her throat. Reacting purely on instinct, she slashed sideways with the sword that still rested on the Skein's shoulder. Her blade bit into his neck – not deep, but hard enough that his strike was unbalanced and his hooked knife only grazed her cheek. The priest recovered quickly; with one hand clapped to his neck, he came at her again, but this time she was ready, and she buried her sword in his belly. He stood there, swaying, the flensing knife tumbling from his hand as he stared down at where she'd stuck him. Cho Lin finished him with a swing from her other sword, the mask of stolen faces fluttering free as his head tumbled to the snow.

Cho Lin touched her cheek and her fingers came away stained red, though she knew the cut was not serious. Unless he poisoned his knife, but she suspected that the barbarian code of the Skein would consider that dishonorable. Nothing she could do about that now, though. She turned back to where she'd seen the Pale Lady, fully expecting her to have vanished.

She was still there, regarding Cho Lin with a solemn expression.

"Who are you?" Cho Lin asked, sheathing her bloodstained swords.

But the apparition offered only silence.

"What do you want?"

Cho Lin took a step towards the lady, and with exquisite slowness the spirit turned from her and began to walk in stately, measured steps in the direction of one of the small streets that emptied into the plaza.

Cho Lin quickened her stride, but to her surprise she found that no matter how fast she moved, the lady stayed the same distance ahead of her. When she reached the center of the plaza, where the lady had been standing and watching her, Cho Lin saw that the snow was undisturbed.

"Wait!" she called out to the spirit, and then quickly dashed to where she'd hidden the Sword of Cho. Frantically, she dug up the bundle from the drifted snow, and though she again feared she would turn and find the ghost gone, the hazy white figure had paused at the edge of the plaza, as if waiting for her.

She hurried to follow.

The Pale Lady led Cho Lin deeper and deeper into the dead city, the architecture changing as they moved farther from the Bhala-van: columns and graceful flourishes of white stone gave way to more solid, squat buildings carved from gray rock threaded with veins of black. The doorways that still stood among the devastation here were nothing more than slabs of stone; in contrast, the area of the ruins where she'd recuperated from her wounds had been littered with the remnants of arched entrances. Those had reminded Cho Lin of what she'd seen in Kalyuni ruins back in the Empire of Swords and Flowers – she suspected that she now moved through a much older part of the holdfast, perhaps from before the Min-Ceruthans had established contact with the south.

Cho Lin stopped trying to catch up with the spirit drifting ahead of her, as every effort to close the distance had failed. Nor did the Pale Lady respond to any of her shouted questions or entreaties.

There were other wonders here, sights that Cho Lin suspected no living eye had glimpsed for a thousand years. She passed down a narrow avenue flanked by trees wrought from twisting metal, copper and bronze branches twining overhead to form a gleaming bower. Later she had to step over a narrow channel, through which sluggishly flowed what looked to be quicksilver. And the most startling discovery, which drew her gaze from the Pale Lady and made her stare open-mouthed in awe, was the black-bone skull of a dragon lying among the ruins. The beast's mouth was large enough to swallow a horse whole, and the building behind it had been utterly flattened, as if the creature had come crashing out of the sky. Of the rest of the dragon's body there was no sign.

Beyond the fallen dragon was a broad, low structure, its walls great jagged boulders pushed together. All of these rocks were of differing heights and widths, so that the structure almost resembled a mountain range, though the curve of the building and the gap that had been left for an entrance made it clear that the stones had been placed here long ago. Cho Lin felt the age of this place; it was from a time before the skilled masons of Nes Vaneth had hewn the rest of the city from the flesh of the north. She wasn't even sure that these stones had been placed here by human hands. The lack of symmetry among the boulders – some tall and tapering, some short and rounded – yet all fitted together with an unnatural precision . . . it did not seem like a design that had emerged from the minds of men. And there was an otherness to the place that lay heavy on her soul.

Within the center of the stone ring gaped a hole. Wide stone steps led down into the darkness. Cho Lin just glimpsed the golden head of the apparition she had followed here before it vanished from sight. Tamping down a little tremor of unease, Cho Lin approached the hole; a film of blackness seemed to cover it, keeping the light from revealing what lay below. She glanced at the towering monoliths rearing up around her, and she couldn't help but imagine that they were waiting and watching to see what she would do.

She put a foot upon the first step – it was slick, and she nearly slipped – then another, and another, until her leg was swallowed by inky darkness. There was a warmth trickling up through the stones, which must be why the steps were clear of snow. Or perhaps some sorcery still lingered here. This had clearly been a sacred place for the Min-Ceruthans, built to shelter whatever had persisted under the earth. Cho Lin descended into the abyss, her hand on the ivory hilt of her sword.

The blackness was so complete that it seemed to pulse around her, shapes roiling in its depths. Her breathing thundered in her ears – whatever barrier kept out the light also stopped the sounds of Nes Vaneth from penetrating the hole. She'd thought the dead city was absolutely silent, but now, as every scrape of her boots traveled back to her, she realized what true silence was. This would be the perfect place to try and grasp the Nothing, if she could overcome her gnawing fear of what could be lurking down here.

A slight breeze swirled around her, and Cho Lin shivered. She rubbed at her arms as her flesh goosepimpled. Something felt wrong about the wind – if it was being pushed through a tunnel down here, it should feel like it was all coming from the same way, rushing up to meet her as she followed the steps down.

What she felt, though, was more like a thousand ghostly fingers lightly brushing her skin and stirring her hair. It grew stronger as she went deeper, her hair teased in contrary directions, the gentle caresses hardening into actual pressure. Cho Lin yelped as her wrist was pinched, her hand going to her sword as she fought to keep from panicking.

"Stop it!" she cried, but her words were instantly swallowed. There was no echo down here, even though she must be descending into an underground space. The urge to turn and dash back up the stairs was nearly overwhelming, but the Pale Lady had saved her life and returned a piece of her ancestors' sword, and she had wanted Cho Lin to follow her into this terrible place. Steeling herself, Cho Lin ignored the spectral fingers tangling in her hair and forced herself onwards.

A presence waited several steps below her. She wasn't sure how she could sense it given that the darkness swaddling her was so complete, but even though she tried to convince herself that it was only a phantasm conjured up by her terrified imagination, she *knew* it was there.

"Hello?" she ventured, hesitating before taking another step. No answer.

She drew one of her swords. "Speak," she commanded, but still the presence remained silent.

Swallowing back her fear, she shuffled forward, easing herself slowly onto the next step.

Is anything truly there? Perhaps this was all a trick of her mind.

A smell came to her, something she knew from memory, but so incongruous for this place that she nearly dropped her sword in shock. It was the fragrance of burned herbs and rare wood, the same incense with which servants carrying swinging censers had anointed the robes of the celestial courtiers before they entered the Jade Court. When she was a child, it had clung to her father's robes, back in the days when he had been at the right hand of the emperor.

"Father?" she whispered into the darkness.

No reply, but the smell grew stronger, as if the presence was drawing closer.

It *felt* like him. When she was a small girl, she had lain awake in the darkness of her sleeping chamber, her head hidden beneath silken pillows so that the ghosts could not find her. Sometimes during the night she would sense him standing on the threshold of her room, watching her, and her fear would vanish, even though he never said a word or came closer to her. That was how she felt now. Holding back a sob, Cho Lin stretched out a trembling arm, not sure what she expected to feel.

Her fingers brushed embroidered silk. A wrenching cry shuddered up from deep within her, and her legs went so weak that she nearly stumbled and fell forward.

Ice-cold fingers closed around her wrist. It took all her willpower not to lash out with the sword she held in her other hand. If the grip had been painful, she probably could not have held back, but the hand was gentle, steadying her.

"Father, I'm sorry," she spoke into the darkness. Tears coursed down her cheeks; she wanted to wipe her face, but the cold hand held her fast. "The sword is broken and I cannot stop the Betrayers. Not by myself."

The grip on her wrist twisted her arm gently, turning her palms up. Cho Lin let out a little gasp as something sharp pressed into the center of her hand – a fingernail, if she had to guess. Slowly the nail began to move, sketching something, and after a moment Cho Lin realized what it was: a Shan character, written in the classical style. She recognized the word even before it was fully written, and again she felt a great upwelling of emotion.

Proud.

The dam within her broke, and she drew in a series of gulping sobs. All she had ever wanted was to be worthy, for her father to know that she could take up the ancient burden of her family.

The hand touching her vanished.

"Father?" Cho Lin said, questing out again. But the presence was gone, as if it had never truly been there.

The character that had been traced into her palm still tingled, though, and she clenched her fist. She would be strong. She had to be strong.

The darkness was no longer absolute, as in the distance a blue flame coiled and flickered. Nor was it endless: the steps she was descending terminated not far below on a floor of smooth black stone. There were no walls or ceiling that she could see – she stood upon an endless dark plain, with only the distant fire to guide her way.

It seemed to take quite some time before she managed to reach the flame. No heat emanated from it, nor did it crackle or hiss like a true fire. It filled a wide silver basin embedded in the floor, and there was nothing feeding the flames that she could see. Something about this fire seemed familiar, and after a moment she realized where she had seen its like before: in the throne room of the Min-Ceruthan queen, deep beneath the Bhala-van, she had glimpsed the same blue flames recessed deep within the wall of ice.

Across from her, through the dancing tongues, she saw the woman she had followed here watching her.

"What is this place?" she asked the silent ghost, but as she expected the Pale Lady did not reply.

A shiver of movement came from within the flames. An image was forming within the swirling fire, and as Cho Lin concentrated, sweat beading on her face, it became clearer.

She saw snow and stone, a few stunted pine trees clustered on the side of a hill. A door was there, sunk into the earth, a vast slab of gray rock. The true immensity of the portal became apparent when she noticed a crescent of tiny figures standing in the snow just outside it. The door must have been a thousand span tall, at least, higher than any city gate she'd ever seen. Slowly, the vague black shapes resolved as the image sharpened, and Cho

Lin sucked in her breath. Children dressed in tattered rags, their long, snarled black hair a stark contrast to their corpse-pale flesh.

One of the Betrayers stepped forward and placed its open palm on the door. The stone seemed to shiver, snow sifting down from higher up the hillside, but the portal remained closed. After a long moment, the Betrayer turned to rejoin his brethren, but then his empty eye sockets jerked upwards, seeming to stare directly at Cho Lin through the flames. She let out a little cry as a blast of cold air struck her in the face, and she struggled to keep watching as the scene began to recede, as if she were a bird soaring upwards, the Betrayers dwindling into tiny black points speckling the snow. As she spiraled higher, she saw for the first time the shape of the hills where the door was set. It was like something she'd seen before, in the memories of the Shan courtesan Jhenna. It reminded her of the way Sleeping Dragon Valley had rippled as if there was something vast slumbering beneath its surface . . .

Cho Lin stumbled back just as the flames vanished, plunging her into darkness.

"No," she moaned, terror seizing her. How could she ever find her way out of this dark and terrible place? Something like a wave washed over her, knocking her down, and her head struck the stone hard. She squeezed her eyes shut, wincing from the pain. A moment later she was surprised to find that a gray glow had begun to creep around the edges of her closed eyes, and it felt like she was no longer lying on hard ground, but cold snow.

When she opened her eyes, she found herself sprawled in the center of the stone ring, a granite-colored sky above. Beside her was the hole she had descended into and the bundle with the shards of the Sword of Cho.

She drew in a shuddering breath, shielding her eyes from the day's wan light. A vision. She had been granted a vision down there. She had learned something very important.

Whatever creature the Betrayers had summoned long ago – the thing that had become known as the Raveling as it tore apart the ancient land of the Shan – a similar beast was here in the north.

And they were trying to wake it.

12: THE CRONE

THE GOOD CHEER of the gathered magisters had vanished with the arrival of the main Skein host. The few hundred mounted warriors had been joined by thousands more that came trudging over the hills on foot, and they had established a camp close to where the Dymorians crouched behind their entrenchments. It did not appear to Willa like the Skein had put any effort into fortifying their position – almost as if they were daring the Dymorians to attack them. Which, of course, would mean abandoning the rows of sharpened stakes and earthen bulwarks that they had spent days building.

The queen had so far shown restraint. And it was a wise course of action, Willa decided. She could see no supply wagons with the barbarians. They must be feeding themselves on whatever they had carried in their packs and the game they could find in these harsh lands. General d'Chorn had been right – the Skein could not wait out the Dymorian army. They would have to attack or retreat once their food was exhausted. Yet despite the knowledge that the Skein would have to throw themselves at the Dymorian fortifications, Willa was still nervous about the coming battle, and this sentiment seemed to be shared by the magisters watching from the ridge.

She was having trouble putting her finger on the source of this unease. The Skein did not greatly outnumber the Dymorians – the chaos of the barbarian encampment made it difficult to get an accurate count of the host, but she would have guessed that the two armies were of roughly equal size. She saw no siege weapons like those used in the Gilded Cities, no ballistae or catapults that might weaken the Dymorian position from afar, and she was certain that the bows of the Skein paled in strength to the famed ebonwood bows of the Crimson Queen's archers. By every tenet of modern warfare, the coming battle should be a massacre – and yet she could not shake her nagging sense that the barbarians were not at as great a disadvantage as they appeared.

"Can you see the different tribes?" Telion asked, shielding his gaze from the red dawn as he studied the Skein.

Willa squinted at the enemy camp. Damn her eyes; from this distance it looked like a kicked-over anthill, the barbarians scurrying about as they attended to their morning duties. "They all appear equally primitive to me."

Telion gestured at the left flank of the Skein horde. "Each of the tribes has their own standard. I was talking to a few soldiers last night, and they told me the Skein across from us are the Stag, Crow, and White Worm. See that one there?"

Willa looked to where he was pointing. Rising above the chaos was a tattered black banner, snapping in the wind. "Yes."

"And there," Telion continued, indicating a flap of what looked like red-brown hide topped with several great pairs of tines. "Each of the Skein clans takes an animal as their symbol. They would be the Stag, I assume. The first must be the Crow."

"Can you see what's on the last?" Willa asked, peering at the third and final standard. "Is that a skull?"

"Wyvern, I would say," Telion agreed. It perched on top of a long pole, long strips of fabric or leather dangling from its lower jaw. "In the north, 'worm' is an old name for dragons and wyverns." Telion cleared his throat and spat. "They must be the Skein of the White Worm. They're from much farther north. A harsher people, is what I heard. They worship crueler gods than their southern cousins."

"And the thane of this tribe is the new king."

"That's what I heard."

"Hm," Willa murmured, drumming her fingers on the ebony sphere atop her cane.

Telion glanced at her when he heard the clack of her rings striking the stone. "Something is bothering you." It was a statement, not a question – Telion knew her too well.

Willa frowned. "I'm worried, but as you know, I've always been a worrier. I probably wouldn't have lasted this long if I wasn't. I trust my instincts . . . and right now, they are telling me that we are not ready for this fight."

"The Dymorians know what they're doing," Telion assured her, though his confidence sounded slightly forced. "I've been down in the camp wandering about."

Drinking and dicing, Willa thought, but she kept this to herself.

"These soldiers are professionals. Not like the armies of the Cities, commanded by the fourth sons of archons and dukes. They know how to fight and how to win wars. The queen is clever, and then there's this lot," he waved his hand, indicating the magisters on the ridge, "who everyone seems to think they'll end up being the dragon on the tzalik board."

Just at that moment, a spindly magister with tonsured hair tripped over his own feet and went sprawling. Most of the cup of wine he had been carrying ended up on the robes of other magisters, eliciting angry cries.

Telion raised his eyebrows at this, shaking his head. "Let's pray to the Silver Lady they're a bit more impressive when it comes to throwing lightning bolts."

"Do you think the battle will be today?" Willa asked, returning her attention to the armies on the snowy plain.

"The battle will start very soon," Telion rumbled. "Too much activity on the Skein side. They're getting ready."

Willa's heart skipped a beat at this. "Should we tell the magisters to prepare themselves?"

"That Lyrish thief will get them in line when the time comes," Telion said, then spat again. "I hope."

Telion's assessment proved correct. The Skein spent the early part of the morning girding themselves for war; sunlight glittered on countless spears and axes as the barbarians took up their weapons and arrayed themselves across from the waiting Dymorians. They seemed to have little discipline to their ranks, with most of the warriors milling about in no formation, but at the very least the army had been separated into three prongs, each with one of the clan standards at its front.

Four mounted Skein trotted forward towards the Dymorian line. As they neared, Willa could see that one of them wore a helm that sprouted a huge set of antlers, while another wore a headdress of midnight-black feathers and carried a longbow of pale white wood. The thanes of the Stag and Crow, she assumed. The other two riders were much less impressive: one was a thin young man in ragged black robes, while the other was dark haired, clad in gray leather armor and a cloak of many different-colored patches. The new king, Willa thought, though he did not dress like one.

"Do they wish to parley?" Willa asked. Beside her, Telion shrugged.

The Skein king had wheeled his horse around so that he faced the massed ranks of his countrymen. He seemed to be exhorting them, punctuating whatever he was yelling by thrusting his fist into the air. Then he reached back to something tied to his horse's barding and raised it into the air: it looked to Willa like a man's head, but its face shone red and wet, as if the skin had been cut away. The king brandished the grisly trophy by its hair, shaking it in front of the other Skein, and they bellowed back their support and raised their weapons in unison. With a mighty heave, the king sent the head flying towards the Dymorian lines, but before it landed, the thane of the Crow nocked his bow and fired. The arrow pierced the head, sending a spray of gore across the snow.

"It appears he does not wish to parley," Telion said flatly. His hand had drifted to one of the silver hilts protruding over his shoulder, as if he wanted to draw his sword.

Willa expected that this performance by the Skein king and his thanes would end with the barbarians surging across the snowy plain, but instead an eerie calm settled over the battlefield, as if both sides were holding their breath in anticipation of something that had yet to arrive.

"What are those?" Telion asked, and a moment later she saw what had drawn his eye.

A half-dozen great sleds were slowly being hauled through the massed Skein, pulled by shaggy oxen with long curving horns. The sleds carried something box-shaped, but the true nature of the objects were hidden beneath black tarps. These had been nailed down so that nothing of what they covered could be seen.

Willa's uneasiness deepened. The magisters on the ridge with her and Telion muttered and shifted.

"Should we strike at those things?" someone asked, but Vhelan shook his head vigorously.

"The queen said to wait until the battle is joined. She doesn't want us to give away that we are here."

"What's under there?" Telion murmured. "Weapons?"

"Animals," Willa replied, and when she said this, she knew it to be true. It was not a box the black tarp covered, but a cage. For the same reason a falconer kept his bird hooded, the darkness would keep whatever was inside calm.

Until it was time to hunt.

"Animals?" Telion repeated dubiously. "What beast could trouble an entire Dymorian legion?"

The sleds had stopped well in front of the Skein lines, farther even than where the king and his thanes lingered, but still beyond the reach of the Dymorian archers. Handlers unhooked the oxen and led them plodding away, while other Skein swung axes at the taut ropes lashing the tarps to the sleds. The black cloth fell away, revealing huge cages with bars of iron as thick around as a man's waist. Inside each of these prisons was curled something strange, creatures unlike anything Willa had seen before. They resembled white-scaled snakes at first, with the way they were coiled, but then she noticed the many small, stunted legs running the length of their looped bodies. One of the serpents raised its wedge-shaped head, its slitted orange eyes blinking like it had just been awoken from a very long sleep, and opened its mouth wide to reveal rows of curving fangs. The screech it made was like a raptor's cry, but many times louder, and Willa winced as some primal fear shivered through her at the sound.

"Garazon's black balls," Telion breathed.

The ax-wielding Skein struck next at the chains fastened to the front of the sleds, and after a few strong blows, the links shattered. As the barbarians scrambled back to their waiting countrymen, the doors on the cages slowly swung wide.

Willa was expecting the coiled serpents to explode from their prisons, but the beasts remained within, seemingly paralyzed by the brightness of the day and the masses of men. A few more Skein crept forward brandishing lit torches, thrusting the flames through the bars at the back of the wagons. Now more shrieking hisses erupted from the beasts, and grudgingly they slipped from the sleds and onto the snow.

The size of the creatures surprised Willa – while coiled, it had been difficult to tell just how long the serpents were, but now she could see that each was the length of a dozen men laid head to foot. It didn't seem like they would make very effective war beasts, though, as they appeared frozen by the noise and the sight of the gleaming armies. One burrowed its head in the shallow snow and frantically tried to dig deeper with its stunted front legs, while another started to slither off towards the nearby forest.

"Well, let's hope that was the Skein's secret weapon," Telion said, the relief in his voice evident.

Willa was just about to reply when every one of the serpents suddenly stopped what they were doing and twisted their heads around to stare at the Skein king.

No; not the king.

The thin man in the black robes, barely a shadow beside the massive thanes, kicked his horse forward. As he rode out among the beasts every slitted orange eye tracked him closely.

"Do you feel that?" said one of the magisters near Willa, a ragged edge to his words.

"Aye," another replied. "It's like the queen."

"He's a sorcerer," murmured Vhelan, running a shaking hand through his silver-streaked hair.

The magisters on the ridge turned to stare at Vhelan, like a parody of what was happening down on the snowy plain. He blinked, as if surprised by their attentions.

"What do we do?" asked the same fat magister whose chair Willa had stolen the first day on the ridge.

Vhelan swallowed. "What can we do? You all feel that power, yes? Only Queen Cein could hope to—"

A cascade of shrieking cries came from below and Willa turned just as all of the serpents lurched into motion, scuttling with tremendous speed towards the lines of Dymorian pike men. Their legs churned the snow, sending up sprays of white.

For a moment the Dymorians seemed stunned by what was approaching, but then the archers behind the first rows of soldiers bent their bows and sent a volley of arrows arcing into the sky. Most of the shafts landed in the snow, but a fair number fell upon the onrushing serpents, speckling their white scales. If the arrows pained them, they did not show it, and to Willa's eye they didn't slow in the slightest as they crossed the snowy plain. This was unnatural – no simple beast would ignore such wounds and charge a waiting army. Her gaze found the thin man, the sorcerer of these people. Was he the only one? No matter how powerful he might be, there were dozens of magisters on the ridge with her, and somewhere down below waited the Crimson Queen.

The serpents struck the first layer of Dymorian fortifications, tearing great holes in that barrier of sharpened stakes like it was made of silk. The pits and earthen bulwarks beyond these defenses proved no more effective, as the beasts scuttled over them easily. The distance between the front ranks of the Dymorian pike-men and the monsters was vanishing quickly, but the line did not waver in the slightest, much to Willa's surprise. Hundreds of pikes were lowered to meet the charge, and Willa found that her hands were squeezed so tight that her nails were cutting into her palms.

The sound of the great serpents smashing into the Dymorians drifted all the way up to the ridge, metal rending and steel striking scales as hard as iron. Overlaying these clashes were the screams of men and the monsters' roaring. Huge jaws snapped, biting men in half, and stunted legs tipped with curving talons raked indiscriminately, slicing open bellies and scattering limbs. Many of the pikes skittered off the monsters, but more than a few found gaps between the scales, lodging there and causing black blood to spray forth. Within moments, each of the serpents was spined with pikes and arrows like a sea urchin, but still they thrashed deeper into the Dymorian ranks, driven on, Willa assumed, by the will of the Skein sorcerer.

They were faltering, though, their movements slowing as more and more swords and pikes pierced their hides. The first one to die was slain by a brave contingent of Dymorian cavalry that peeled away from the main host and rode directly at the serpent, lances lowered. Some of the horses shied away when they caught the monsters' scent, but one officer with a bright red plume streaming from his helmet managed to control his mount and urge it on, then plunged his lance directly into the serpent's eye, killing it instantly.

One by one the other serpents perished, hacked to pieces or finally succumbing to countless wounds, their white scales streaked with red and black blood. A ragged cheer went up from the Dymorians as the last of the great beasts shuddered and went still, its orange eyes glazing over in death. But the relief was short lived, for with a mighty roar the left and right prongs of the Skein host surged forward, charging across the snowy plain, the sound of thousands of guttural screams raised as one great war cry chilling Willa's blood.

Willa held her breath as the Dymorian officers rallied their soldiers and tried to reform the lines. Again, she was impressed with the discipline of the queen's army; despite having been shattered by the rampaging serpents only moments before, the wall of bristling steel was quickly made anew. The fortifications they had constructed over the last few days could not be repaired so easily, and the vanguard of the Skein horde poured through the huge gaps made by the serpents. More flights of arrows darkened the sky and fell upon the northerners, but the crush was so great that Willa could not see any appreciable thinning of their number.

The leading edge of the Skein wave collided with the Dymorian line. Wild-bearded warriors swinging great battle-axes leapt to meet soldiers who had braced the butts of their pikes in the snow. In some parts of the long line the barbarians were thrown back; elsewhere, the shock of the Skein charge broke through the first line and crashed into the swordsmen who waited behind their fellows. Even from this distance Willa could see that the Dymorians fought with practiced efficiency, well-drilled cuts and thrusts that played to the strengths of their formation, while the Skein laid about with wild, sweeping blows, so caught up in the battle frenzy that they ignored any wounds they took unless they were grievous.

"Magisters!" Vhelan cried, striding to the edge of the ridge. "It is time!"

The dozens of robed men and women joined the sorcerer, looking down on the seething battle below. Willa's skin prickled as they began chanting and fluttering their fingers, and the very air seemed to grow heavier, pregnant like before a thunderstorm.

"This'll be interesting," Telion muttered, and Willa nodded. Interesting, but also terrifying. Only Cein d'Kara could call upon the might of a sorcerous school – now that she had shown herself willing to deploy them in war, the balance of power in Araen had shifted forever. How many cities and kingdoms would be driven into the arms of Menekar because they feared the might that was about to be unveiled here?

A big, broad woman who looked like she would be more at home milking cows was the first to finish her incantation. Crackling light flashed from her outstretched fingers and flew down to strike among the Skein; snow and dirt exploded upwards, knocking several of the barbarians from their feet. Hundreds of pairs of eyes turned to the ridge just in time to witness havoc unleashed.

Fire and lightning and glittering shards rained down from the gathered magisters, falling among the Skein like the wrath of the gods. Willa clutched at Telion's arm, her breath stolen from her by the display.

How could mere men and women master such forces? And more importantly, how could anyone be trusted to wield such power? Even if the queen defeated the Skein and destroyed the demon children before they could bring about the cataclysm she had glimpsed, the world had now changed forever. It frightened her. She was so old and tired, but Lyr would need someone wise to navigate these dangerous waters or her city would be dashed against the rocks.

The magisters kept their sorcery away from where the Skein were already fighting the Dymorian soldiers, concentrating their assault on the barbarians still streaming across the plain towards the pitched battle. The snow was pocked by the barrage, scarred black by the scouring and littered with smoking corpses. Willa almost felt pity for the northerners trapped below, unable to escape from the devastation falling from above.

Something caught Willa's eye. One of the Skein was now sheathed in a smoky gray sphere, dark enough that he had been reduced to a hazy outline. Willa suspected it was the sorcerer who had compelled the serpents to attack the Dymorian lines. The magisters' sorceries raged around him, and a bolt of silver lightning struck the barrier, crawling along its edges before dissipating. The figure lifted from the snow, rising smoothly into the sky until he hovered at the same elevation as the magisters on the ridge.

Vhelan was pointing at the Skein sorcerer and screaming something, but his words were lost in the crash and rumble of the spells erupting from his fellows. A few magisters did turn their attention to this new threat, but their attempts at piercing the dark shell enclosing the sorcerer proved fruitless.

Willa saw the shadow slash the air with his arm violently, and a wave of glistening black energy billowed from the sphere.

"Down!" Telion cried, grabbing her and pulling her farther away from where the magisters were clustered at the edge of the ridge. Still, she saw what happened as the dark magic reached the sorcerers of the Scholia. Prismatic barriers flashed into existence around the magisters in the path of the sorcery, but most of these wardings immediately popped like soap bubbles as the blackness overwhelmed the defenses. When the sorcery hit the magisters, it made their skin bubble and smoke, and several dropped to the ground, clawing at their flesh as it sloughed from their bodies.

A few of the magisters had been successful in repelling this darkness, including Vhelan, though the blue shield hovering in front of him was now riddled with holes like it had been splashed with acid.

Screaming to be heard over the cries of the wounded magisters, Vhelan again gestured at the sorcerer encased within the dark jewel. "Everything! Give everything! Empty yourselves of every drop, but slay that Skein!"

Before the magisters could regroup, Willa saw the figure make another cutting motion with his arm. No visible energy flowed forth this time, but pillars of stone erupted from the ground around where the magisters stood, sending several flying into the air. Willa was lifted as well, but not because of the heaving earth; Telion was carrying her, his great arms wrapped around her like she was a child. From over his shoulder she saw a haze of falling earth and dust, magisters stumbling through the devastation. Then Telion ducked behind a boulder and set her down gently.

"We stay here," he told her, his wide eyes smears of white in his grimy face. She imagined she didn't look any better.

The magisters were shouting to each other. She heard Vhelan trying to rally them, while others were crying in pain or fear or anger.

One hysterical voice cut through the din. "She comes! She comes!"

The rock Telion had sheltered them behind was on the southern edge of the ridge, and Willa had a clear view of the fighting below. She scanned the churning masses of men, her heart in her throat. Where? Above the Skein horde, the sphere containing the sorcerer was still, a black pearl set in the white of the sky. No more sorcery flowed forth, as if the one inside had decided that the magisters of the Scholia were no threat, and now he waited for the true challenge.

And there she was. "The queen!" Willa cried, clutching at Telion's arm.

Behind the Dymorian ranks, Cein d'Kara was ascending into the sky. Her unbound red hair flowed behind her, rippling in the wind made by her passage. She wore the same fine white armor that Willa had seen in the queen's tent during the council, and though it was hard to tell from this distance she thought she also bore the glittering sword of the Min-Ceruthan sorcerer. From somewhere below, an arrow lofted towards her; Willa's breath caught in her throat, but the shaft vanished in a puff of flame and smoke when it struck some invisible barrier.

Cein d'Kara arrived at the same elevation as the Skein and then arrested her flight. Far below the two sorcerers, the battle continued to rage, but Willa thought its intensity had slackened, as many eyes had turned heavenward to witness what was about to happen. Willa shivered. It was as if the patron gods of two peoples had descended into the mortal realm to settle this war, like in the old sagas.

The black sphere sheathing the Skein melted away. Willa was shocked to see how young he truly was, barely older than that boy Keilan she had sent into the south. Despite his youth, his face was almost like a skull, skin stretched taut over his sharp-boned features. He did not smile, nor did the queen. They stared at each other with an intensity that unnerved Willa, as if some contest was taking place that she could not see. Nothing about their appearance was similar – he was thin and emaciated, dressed in ragged black robes, while the queen was flushed with radiant life and power, her immaculate white armor shining.

The air around both sorcerers shimmered, strange colors leaking into the sky beyond them. An unnaturally warm wind gusted, rippling the furred hem of Willa's robes. She glanced at Telion, and saw the fear she felt mirrored in his eyes.

And then the storm broke.

Golden energy shot forth in twisting braids from the Crimson Queen just as bile-green strands of shadow erupted from the outstretched hand of the Skein sorcerer. Shimmering wards flared into existence to obstruct these sorceries: the golden light fractured into countless cutting blades that tried to slice through the dark sphere before finally dissipating into glittering motes, while the grasping strands oozed along the outside of the pale red barrier that protected the queen, as if searching for an opening. Another blast of sorcery emanated from Cein d'Kara, slicing through the attenuated green strand at its thinnest point, and, once severed, the Skein's magic evaporated. Each of these spells sent concussions of sound rolling over the battlefield and those crouched on the ridge; Willa's head was ringing as if lightning had struck just beside her.

Tides of sorcery surged and retreated in the air between the two hovering figures, seeming to split reality open along its seams; in the ragged wounds fissuring the sky, Willa glimpsed swirling colors and glistening darkness, like she was peering through a pinhole into other, alien realms. At times the flashes and explosions were too bright to look upon, but each time her vision cleared the queen and the Skein were still there, hurling crackling sorceries in a fractured sky. These two sorcerers did not merely resemble gods, Willa thought, silently amending her previous observation. They *were* gods, at least compared to the rest of mankind.

It was enough to drive her into the arms of Ama – she understood, at last, why the Pure and the mendicants had attempted for so many centuries to keep sorcery from returning to the world.

Muffled shouting came from elsewhere on the ridge, and moments later a dozen different sorcerous attacks rippled towards the Skein sorcerer. Each of these blasts appeared pathetically small and thin compared to the massive energies being wielded by the two hovering sorcerers, but together they seemed to be having some effect. With the bulk of his power focused on repelling the queen's assaults and forming his own counterstrokes, it appeared that the Skein could not divert enough attention to what the magisters were doing. Shimmering silver cracks were appearing on the outside of the black jewel that protected him. A shard of glittering darkness even fell away, though it vanished before tumbling to where the armies fought below.

Screams came from the other side of the boulder they sheltered behind, where the surviving magisters were gathered. Not cries of triumph as the Skein sorcerer's wards flaked away. No; Willa heard terror. She shared a quick glance with Telion, and then crept to the edge of the rock and peered around it.

The fat magister whose seat she'd stolen was sprawled on the ground a dozen paces away. His face was turned towards her, his eyes wide and glassy, blood trickling from his open mouth. Crouched on his huge belly was one of the ragged, pale-skinned children Willa had glimpsed in the Oracle's vision; the demon's arm was plunged up to its elbow in the magister's stomach, and as she watched in horror, the creature pulled out a handful of glistening entrails. Most of the other sorcerers of the Scholia were still on the lip of the ledge, sending waves of sorcery towards the Skein, but a few had noticed the unnatural child and had redirected their attacks. Coiling blue snakes lashed at the demon, blistering the corpse it perched upon and igniting the dead magister's bloodstained robes, but the sorcery slid across the child like water, dripping down to sizzle upon the ground.

Cries of alarm went up as more and more of the magisters turned to confront this new threat. Suddenly there were more of the demon children, loping with an unnatural, ape-like gait, leaning forward and using their hands to propel themselves. The magisters' spells shattered the pillars of stone thrust up earlier by the Skein sorcerer and sent rock and dirt exploding upwards; a veil of dust and smoke settled over everything, and Willa couldn't see farther than a few span in front of her face.

More anguished cries, trailing into silence. Willa drew back from the edge of the boulder, trying to keep her breathing steady. She started as Telion leaned closer to her.

"We need to get out of here," he said. His voice was somehow calm, damn the fool.

Willa could only nod jerkily. Her hand scrabbled in the dirt for her cane. She would have to run down the side of a hill, fleeing demons, and find refuge somewhere in the battle swirling below. She had a sudden, almost overwhelming urge to start giggling at the absurdity of it all, but she swallowed it back. Telion would think she'd gone mad.

Through the churning dust she could still see the glowing wards of the queen and the sorcerer. Something had changed, though. Only moments ago, many lines of glittering sorcery had been bombarding the Skein, but now the red barrier protecting the queen was being lashed by thick ropes of twisting black power.

"No," Willa breathed as the wards protecting Cein d'Kara disappeared in a muted flash and the faintly glowing figure of the Crimson Queen tumbled from the sky like a falling star. Her sorcery guttered and vanished before she fell among the warriors fighting below, and so Willa could not see where she landed.

Numbness filled her, and she struggled to comprehend what had just happened.

The Crimson Queen of Dymoria was dead.

"We go now," Telion said, and again she was lifted, pressed against his chest.

They stumbled through the roiling dust, her eyes stinging, and several times her protector nearly fell. But somehow he kept his feet, and she realized that he had found the narrow path that descended from the ledge. The air was clearer here, and below her on the switchback trail she could see the scattered corpses of the guards she'd brought from Lyr – they had been torn asunder, as if by the talons of a great beast. Dozens of warriors reduced to bloody chunks. She felt her gorge rise.

Suddenly Telion slowed and stopped, then gently set her down.

"What are you doing?" Willa cried, unable to tear her eyes away from the carnage below.

"Get away," Telion said simply, and she heard the ring of his silver-hilted swords leaving their sheaths.

She turned. He stood upon the narrow path, facing the direction from which they had just fled. Something was moving in the swirling dust, a shadow coming closer. It was a child, dragging behind it the severed head of a woman by its long hair.

"Telion!" she cried desperately.

"Go!" he shouted over his shoulder, and then he charged into the haze, swinging his swords.

A moment of silence. Willa felt like her legs were going to give way beneath her as she waited. Then the screams began.

Sobbing, Willa turned and began to hobble down the rocky path. Telion's ragged, pained cries followed her, until they abruptly ceased. Her cane caught between two stones and twisted out of her grip, and her arms flailed as she lost her balance and went tumbling forward. Her face smashed something hard, and she knew no more.

13: KEILAN

THE DARKNESS SLIDES *across her skin like cool water. It swaddles her, envelops her, seeping inside her nose and mouth and filling her with the comforting numbness of the abyss in which she floats. She kicks her thin legs and feels the substance of this place roil and eddy. It summons a fragment of a memory: her, slipping like a fish through the glittering waters of a slow-moving river, Elder Brother watching her from the muddy bank.*

The moment sinks again as soon as it surfaces, leaving nothing behind except a vague unease. She pushes it aside—for the thing in the dark is suddenly stirring.

It shifts, displacing great washes of cold darkness from far deeper in the abyss. She steels herself, straining to keep herself from spinning away into the black. The thing spasms, and she can feel it rising through layers upon layers of its dreams, edging toward wakefulness.

That must not happen.

In the cold and black, she begins to sing. She does not know where she learned this lullaby, though there are sensations she associates with it: warmth, safety, the smell of dried herbs and flowers.

Moonlight ripples on the lake
See the heron's shadow in the weeds

Little frog, beware the flashing beak
The hungry fish
The crafty snake
Burrow into your muddy bed
And wait for mother sun to wake

The thing in the darkness stills. Elsewhere, in the great distance, other voices fall silent – her brothers and sisters, also finished soothing the creature that shares this abyss with them. She wants to swim to where they float, but she knows they will recede faster than she can approach.

She has tried many times before.

The darkness shivers, briefly lightening before the black rushes in again, more seamless than a moment ago. Somewhere, the door has opened. It only opens for one reason: a new brother or sister has entered this place. Another presence for her to strive towards but never touch. She sends out her awareness, curious.

She recoils, shocked. The darkness around the stranger seethes with hate and anger. And power. The brother – and she feels it is a brother – rages and thrashes. Fear washes through her, and she wills a message to her new sibling. **Calm, brother! Do not wake the thing in the dark!** She does not expect her plea to be heard. It never has been before. But the distant presence quiets. And then she hears an echoing reply, carried to her by the swirling black.

Why not?

Keilan opened his eyes.

Something was touching his forehead. He reached up groggily, still half asleep, and swatted at whatever it was. His hand found a finger lightly pressed to his brow, and he twisted his head around to see who was there.

Alyanna was sitting behind him, cross-legged, her full lips drawn down into a frown. She blinked when their eyes met, as if she too was surfacing from somewhere else. Pink dawnlight had just started to fill the windows, though once again the two farm-boys had already risen from their pallets by the hearth to attend to their chores. Senacus was snoring softly, turned away from Keilan to face the cold ashes of last night's fire; he did this so that the trickle of light spilling from his eyes would not keep the rest of them awake.

"What are you doing?" Keilan whispered, raising himself up on his elbows and turning to face the sorceress.

Alyanna's face was troubled. She chewed on her lip, studying him in the early morning gloom. "What did you dream about, Keilan?"

Dream? Had he been dreaming? Keilan reached back to see if he could grasp any recollections before they squirmed away. Despite his best efforts, he couldn't remember anything in particular. There was a hollow ache lingering in his chest, though, like he had brushed against some great sorrow.

"I don't know."

Her eyes narrowed. "Truly?"

Had he been swimming? Floating in a dark sea? He couldn't be sure, so he said nothing.

"You were dreaming," Alyanna said. "And not only were you dreaming, you were dreamsending, of a sort."

"Dreamsending?"

"A sorcery I have some experience with, though I am not a master. It is . . . bridge building. Reaching out to create connections between minds. Although, in this instance, the bridge is already there."

Keilan swallowed. "Where does the bridge go?"

Alyanna gripped his arm, then turned it over. Black lines were etched beneath his skin, as if his veins carried something other than blood. Keilan sucked in his breath, frightened.

"To something that is no longer human."

"The . . . the children?"

"One of them. A girl. It was hard to perceive what was happening. There was darkness, cold, and something vast and terrible swelling in a great abyss."

"I don't remember," Keilan said softly, though now that Alyanna described the dream he could sense the truth in her words. "You could see?"

Alyanna nodded. "It was easier than I thought it would be, to be truthful. I slipped a tiny part of my awareness onto the bridge, so small I don't think either of you noticed. And it is my memory now. I can share it with you."

Keilan pushed aside the lingering dread of the dream he could not recall. His fingers lightly brushed the swollen veins in his arm, which to his relief seemed to already be dwindling, their darkness fading. "Yes. I have to know."

Alyanna returned her fingers to Keilan's forehead. "Relax. You should try to be open to what I'm about to share. Let me pour my memories into you."

Keilan calmed the nervous flutter in his stomach. *Be open? What does that mean?* Then he felt it, a prickling sensation in his head like a spider scurrying along the inside of his skull. It was unnatural, invasive, but he tried to keep from pushing it aside in disgust. Sensations flashed in his mind's eye – drifting in a cold darkness, the presence lurking below – and then these solitary moments were replaced by a tumbling cascade that gave him the sense that he was experiencing something half-remembered for a second time.

"Is this . . . is this the child's dream?" he asked between gasping breaths. The sadness and fear and loneliness permeating these memories brought tears to his eyes.

"No," Alyanna replied, pulling her hand away. "I don't think so. I doubt very much that these creatures need to sleep at all. I think the bridge that was made is allowing your dreaming mind a glimpse into the deepest recesses of the once-child's consciousness."

"So that really happened? Floating in the dark trying to keep a monster from waking?" Keilan shuddered at the thought.

"I believe so," Alyanna said. "Though remember we are only experiencing the child's perception of what occurred. Maybe its mind had become untethered from its physical body and was drifting. I don't know what was truly happening. But I have my suspicions."

"What?"

Alyanna pursed her lips, and Keilan had the sense that she was deciding what he should know.

"Tell me, please," he begged. "If we're going to stop these things then we should share our secrets."

Alyanna gave a little crooked smile. "I suppose you're right, Keilan." She sighed, running her fingers through her long black hair. "Where to begin? Perhaps . . . perhaps with what has already happened to you."

"Me?"

"Yes. A half-year ago, the world trembled. It was like a bell deep under the ground had sounded, and all the great Talents felt the vibrations. It was what brought you to the Crimson Queen's attention."

Keilan remembered what Vhelan had told him long ago in the ruined city of Uthmala. The queen had noticed him when he'd done his dowsing aboard his father's fishing boat. He'd pushed too far into the deep and disturbed one of the Ancients, a great beast that slumbered at the bottom of the ocean. It had come close to waking, and from what Vhelan had said, that would have brought about a cataclysm to rival what had happened a thousand years ago.

"I can see in your face you know what I'm speaking about. You touched the Sleeper in the Deep with your sending. During the time of the Imperium, that creature lay at the bottom of a great lake, and the sorcerers of the Star Towers made sure that access to it was strictly controlled. No great Talents were allowed near the god-beast, except for a tiny order of sorcerous monks that lived on an island in the middle of the lake. Their duty was to make sure the Ancient stayed asleep."

"How did they do that?"

"The Ancients are sensitive to those with Talent, just as those with Talent are sensitive to them. If their sleep is troubled, great sorcerers can soothe them into a deeper slumber . . . but they can also drag them towards wakefulness, if they are mad or foolish enough to do such a thing. No Ancient has ever come fully awake, to my knowledge. The sorcerers of the Star Towers believed that if that was ever to happen, the resulting destruction would end the age of man."

Keilan thought back to the memories Alyanna had just shared. The child had existed in some strange abyss, with a terrifying presence lurking below which must be pacified whenever it verged on waking . . .

"You think these Chosen or Betrayers or whatever they are called were once tasked with keeping an Ancient asleep?"

Alyanna nodded, her expression thoughtful. "Yes. And let us follow the other breadcrumbs that are scattered about. The child-demons came from the Empire of Swords and Flowers. They were Shan once. The Shan arrived in these lands fleeing a great devastation that destroyed their ancient homeland utterly. The Raveling, they called it."

"A cataclysm," Keilan said softly.

"Indeed. And from that glimpse into the memories of one of the Chosen, they were forced to appease one of the Ancients against their will. They were prisoners."

"But they woke the Ancient."

"It destroyed their lands." Alyanna grimaced. "And now they are trying to wake another."

Surprise shivered through Keilan. "How do you know this?"

"Something has been prying at the edges of the seal that imprisons the White Worm of the north. Not enough to wake the beast, but it has disturbed its sleep. I can feel it, and I'm sure Cein d'Kara has as well."

"That's why the Betrayers are in the Frostlands," Keilan said slowly.

"Yes. And why we must go there quickly, so we can ally with the queen and her school of sorcerers."

Keilan shook his head, dazed by these revelations. "But why would the children do this?"

"Revenge," Alyanna replied. "Surely you felt the wrongness in that memory. Something terrible was done to them, and they want the world to share their pain."

Keilan thought back to the vision the Oracle had shown him. The shattered ruins of Menekar, all life extinguished. That was what they had to stop. Every city, every kingdom, ground to dust beneath the coils of the White Worm. He glanced again at Senacus, still snoring softly. The paladin had not trusted Niara, and in the end he'd been right. Yesterday he had begged Keilan not to join with Alyanna. But this was a greater threat than any lone sorcerer, no matter how wicked they were. This was the end of the world.

"When do we leave?" he asked quietly.

"Today," Alyanna said, suddenly rising. "There is no more time to waste."

Marialle helped Keilan replenish their supplies, bringing up from her cellar several wheels of aged cheese, slices of dried fruit and mutton, and enough hard bread to keep hunger away for a fortnight. While they separated out everything into portions for each of their travel bags, Keilan told the farmer's wife that Senacus's presence here should be kept a secret, that there were enemies out there looking for him. She listened solemnly with wide eyes, and set down her knife to make the sign of Ama's sun in the air in front of her. Then she swore on her children's souls that they would tell no one about the Pure, and assured Keilan that Senacus could stay until he was fully recovered.

It was late morning when it happened.

Keilan was preparing a cold compress for the still-sleeping paladin, washing a cloth in the stream outside the farmhouse, when the first reverberations hit him. The air seemed to tremble, and a wave of prickling numbness washed through Keilan that was so strong he actually dropped the cloth in the water. Shaking, he checked the faded cut on his arm before bending to retrieve the cloth, fearing that another of his spells was coming on. His veins were fine, though, no sign of the blackness that had swollen them earlier in the day.

Another great rush of sorcery, and his head spun. Keilan staggered away from the stream. What was this?

Alyanna appeared in the doorway of the farmhouse, her hand on the frame to steady herself. The expression on her face was bleak.

"What's going on?" Keilan asked, stumbling towards her. He realized he'd dropped the compress again, but the thought of trying to find it in the grass was nauseating. It was all he could do to remain standing.

Alyanna looked at him with hooded eyes, her mouth set in a thin line. "Something that has happened only once in the last century, and was vanishingly rare even before that. Two great Talents are fighting to the death. In the days of the Star Towers, we did not" —Alyanna grimaced, and shook her head as if to clear it— "we did not allow such conflict. Any sorcerers who unleashed this amount of power would be considered anathema and hunted down."

"When did it happen last?"

Alyanna mouth twisted into a rueful smile. "Only a few months ago. Atop the queen's tower at Saltstone."

"Ah." Keilan had been half-conscious elsewhere in the fortress, which must be why he'd never felt like this before.

"This is greater than the duel between Cein d'Kara and myself. We were forced to focus our sorcery and keep it contained, lest we shatter the tower we stood upon. Whatever is happening in the north" —she winced as another wave washed over them, staggering Keilan— "is completely unfettered. The devastation must be awesome."

"Is it the queen?"

"Who else could it be?"

Keilan swallowed, staring off towards the north. "Then we are too late."

"It would appear so."

"Do you think she'll win?"

Alyanna shrugged. "She has great power, even for a Talent."

"She bested you."

Alyanna made a face. "With help. I was ambushed by several of her magisters – weak, pathetic creatures, but in a contest like that, any distraction can prove the difference."

"So what do we do now?"

"We leave. Immediately. If the queen destroys the children, we can celebrate, but if she does not . . . then it still falls on us to stop the Ancient from awakening."

14: CHO LIN

CHO LIN SPENT the rest of the day recuperating from her ordeal. She'd escaped significant injury during her fight with the Flayed, and even the small cut on her cheek faded into nothingness a few hours after drinking a gulp of the silvery water at the shrouded statue's feet. Most of what had been in the basin when she'd first come here had by now been consumed, but there was enough left that she made a short foray back into the ruins to search the corpses of the men she'd killed for any kind of container to store what remained.

Cho Lin had half expected to find the plaza where she'd ambushed the Skein to be empty, their bodies swallowed by the dead city, but the Flayed and the priest were still there when she arrived, though now they were covered by a light dusting of snow. She searched for anything that could be of use, wrinkling her nose in disgust – the smell of spilled innards and voided bowels was bad enough, but the stench rising up from their greasy furs and matted hair was even more stomach-turning. She doubted any of these men had been washed since their mothers last dunked them squalling into a wash basin.

On the body of the blond-bearded giant she found a stoppered wine skin – at least she thought it was wine, until she unsealed the top and took a quick sniff. The spirit inside was strong enough that the smell made her eyes water and her nose itch, but still she emptied out the skin's contents into the snow and tucked the container inside her own furs. This was not a time to be squeamish. Scavenging from the other Flayed yielded a few pieces of dried and salted meat – horse, by the smell of it – and an assortment of coins and other treasures: a small gold figurine of a serpent that looked like it had once been part of a tzalik set, a knife with a silver hilt inset with moonstones, and, to her great surprise, a jade hairpin that looked to be of Shan make that one of the warriors had been using to secure his rucksack. Cho Lin would have preferred to not take from the men she'd slain – this was the way most vengeful spirits tracked their killers – but she suspected having some things to trade would improve her chances of surviving the Frostlands.

When she returned to the sanctuary to which the Pale Lady had led her, Cho Lin devoured the food she'd taken from the Bhalavan, saving the horse jerky for a later time. If she had been told as a young girl that one day she would be stripping meat from bones discarded by barbarians and savoring every bite, she never would have believed such a thing. Yet here she was, licking cold grease from her fingers and wishing she'd scrounged more scraps from the feast hall.

After her belly had finally quieted, she spent some time cleaning her butterfly swords. She used snow that had drifted in through the hole in the ceiling to rub the gore from the blades and where it had collected in the etchings of the intricately carved ivory handles. This made her think of Verrigan, standing at the balustrade above the pit, having just thrown down these swords. There was no doubt that he had saved her then, just as he had saved her when she'd been ambushed by the wraiths. Cho Lin wondered what had happened to him. Some terrible punishment, most likely, and she felt a pang of sadness. He must have known that helping her would be his death, and yet he had done it anyway. Her fingers traced the contours of a tiny wolf's head engraved into the hilt. In Shan, wolves and dogs were symbols of loyalty, and Verrigan had been a true and loyal friend. She would not let his sacrifice be in vain.

The fragments of sky visible through the broken roof darkened while she rested and recovered her strength. By the time the first glimmering stars had emerged, she felt better than she had in many days – the hollow ache in her belly had been assuaged, the wounds she'd received in the arena and fighting the Flayed were nothing more than a distant memory, and for the first time since she had woken to find Jan had slipped away from her she had a clear direction in which to travel. She must bring the remnants of her family's sword to the Crimson Queen and see if the blade could be reforged, and also inform the sorceress of the Betrayers' desire to wake the great beast in the north.

Cho Lin thought back to her own journey through the Frostlands. It had taken her ten days on horseback to reach Nes Vaneth after she'd passed through the Bones, and she would have to assume that the Dymorian army the priest had spoken of would not march too deeply into these inhospitable lands. She would need supplies and a horse if she wanted to entertain any realistic hope of surviving the Frostlands and reaching the queen.

Finally, when the night was at its darkest, she was ready to leave this place. The bundle with the shards of her father's sword was slung across her shoulder; the skin she'd scavenged was filled to the brim with the healing water; and her butterfly swords were again at her side. She even pulled back and bound her hair with the jade pin she'd found. She felt like she had been truly reborn in this place. Before she departed through the shattered wall, she stood before the statue and placed her hand on the shrouded girl's damp cheek.

"Thank you," she whispered, and it might have been her imagination, but she felt like there was a presence watching her in the chamber.

THE SHADOW KING

Cho Lin slipped from the crumbled building and into the tangled streets of Nes Vaneth. The moon was hidden behind a veil of clouds, draping the ruined city in shadows. Once, the darkness might have frightened her, but even though she knew this place was haunted, she did not think the spirits that persisted here wished her ill. They mourned what was lost, yet they did not covet what the living had, unlike the hungry ghosts of the Shan. Cho Lin searched for any glimpses of the Pale Lady as she passed through the ruins, but the spirit that had saved her and shown her the secrets of the city did not reveal itself.

She retraced her way back to the great avenue that led to the Bhalavan, and then cautiously approached the darkened feast hall. No light spilled from the cracked-open doors, but torches had been set in the snow near the entrance, and Cho Lin noticed several dark shapes slouching in the shadows. Someone had wisely posted guards since she had been here last. Cho Lin frowned, uncertain what she should do. There was nothing she needed in the Bhalavan, but the stables were beside the feast hall, and she doubted she could lead a horse down the avenue without being seen. Still, she needed a mount. Braving the Frostlands without a horse would be suicide.

Keeping far from the edges of the puddles of light cast by the torches, Cho Lin crept towards the long, ruined building the Skein used as a stable. Offering up a quick prayer to the Four Winds that she would not be noticed, she dashed inside, quiet as a hunting cat. No cries went up behind her, and she let out a sigh of relief – just before her foot kicked something soft curled among a pile of hay and rags. The shape grunted, and before whoever it was could come fully awake Cho Lin threw herself down on top of them, the jeweled dagger she'd taken from the Skein in her hand. She was just about to plunge the blade down when she realized from the high-pitched gasp and slender limbs that this was only a boy. Cursing her luck, she pinned the thrashing shape, covering the boy's mouth so he couldn't scream.

"Quiet," she hissed in Menekarian, laying the steel of her dagger against his neck, "or I'll cut your throat."

Cho Lin wasn't sure if the boy understood her words, but the prick of the metal must have conveyed what she wanted, as he went very still. She could feel the rise and fall of his chest beneath her as he drew in deep, panicked breaths.

What did she do now? She didn't want to kill a child. But without a horse there was no hope of her reaching the Dymorian army and the queen. Could she keep him quiet? Or should she take him with her, and then release him when she'd at least put a few leagues between her and the city? Whatever she decided, she needed to do it quickly.

The boy had mastered his breathing, and he didn't seem like he was about to scream a warning. Quite a brave lad, Cho Lin admitted.

He mumbled something into her palm. Cho Lin bit down on her lip, unsure what she should do. The boy tried to talk again, and Cho Lin increased the pressure of the blade on his neck.

"I'm going to remove my hand," she said, imparting as much menace as she could into her words. "Speak softly."

She lifted her hand, readying herself to slash his throat if he began to yell.

"I know you," the boy whispered. "You Shan."

"Yes, me Shan," replied Cho Lin.

"You see me."

That surprised Cho Lin, though certainly she'd seen hundreds of Skein in her days in the Bhalavan.

"Uncle give me your horse. I take horse here."

For a moment she was confused, and then she remembered the boy that had dashed up to Verrigan when they'd first arrived at the Bhalavan. He'd said the boy was his nephew, and the memory of him tousling the boy's hair affectionately made her breath catch in her throat.

"Yes," she said slowly. "I remember."

"I hear . . ." His voice trailed away, and she could hear his pain. "I hear Uncle give you swords. Throw down, then you kill demon."

Cho Lin nodded, though she wasn't sure if he could see this in the dark. "Your uncle was a friend."

The boy shifted under her slightly. "I no say you here. Promise."

Something in the way he said this convinced her, and she pushed herself from the boy, then reached down to help him stand.

"Your uncle . . . is he . . ."

The shadow shook its head, and her heart fell.

"The priest . . . he . . ." The boy could not finish, and Cho Lin had to restrain herself from leaning forward to comfort him.

"I must leave the city," she said instead. "Your uncle was a good man. He saved me then, but now I need your help."

The boy was quiet for a moment. "What you want?"

"A horse. And a way so that the men outside do not see me when I leave."

Cho Lin tensed as the boy's hand closed around her wrist, but it was only so he could lead her deeper into the stables. Even in the dark she could tell that most of the makeshift stalls were empty, though the smell of horse was overwhelming. The Skein were apparently not so concerned with keeping their stables well mucked.

The boy stopped beside an occupied stall, his hand falling from her arm. "You horse," he said, and as if it knew it was being discussed her old mount snorted and stamped its hooves.

"My horse," Cho Lin said quietly, slipping inside the stall. She laid her hand upon its flank, and the horse bumped its head into her shoulder, as if in greeting. Verrigan had told her that this wasn't a good horse, and that he had thrown his previous master in a fight. But he'd been nothing but sweetness to Cho Lin during their ride to Nes Vaneth, and she'd come to suspect that there was a very good reason why the horse had disliked his old rider. Cho Lin stroked the horse's shaggy mane, unable to keep from smiling as tears prickled her eyes.

"Thank you," Cho Lin told the boy, hurriedly wiping at her face. Why was she becoming so foolishly sentimental?

"Come," the boy said, and she heard his footsteps moving towards the back of the stable.

"Wait," she replied, casting about for the horse's saddle and tack. She found it in the corner of the stall and as quick as she could she secured it on the horse, fumbling with the leather straps and buckles in the dark. The horse remained patient as she worked, and Cho Lin gave him another friendly pat.

"Good boy," she murmured, and the horse snorted in reply.

"Quickly," the boy said, materializing from the dark. "Follow."

Gripping the bridle, she guided the horse from the stall, falling in behind the shadow of the boy. He led her deeper into the stable, the blackness thickening around them.

She was just about to call out and make sure the boy was still in front of her when she walked into his back.

"Here," the boy said, and she peered into the shadows, looking for what he had brought her to see.

After a moment she noticed the patch of grayness in the black – part of the wall had collapsed here, a large enough gap that her horse could slip through. She stepped closer, squinting into the gloom. The hole was opposite the side of the stables that faced the Bhalavan, and some of the clouds must have cleared, as she could see the white stone ruins of Nes Vaneth glowing faintly in the starlight.

"Go," the boy said simply.

Cho Lin turned back to him. "Thank you," she said, and she thought the shadow ducked its head, as if embarrassed. "Your uncle would be proud."

She reached out and touched his arm lightly, and then she led the horse through the collapsed section of the wall. The night had gotten brighter, but there were no guards here and they passed unmolested across the empty field. When she reached the edge of the tumbled buildings she turned back and raised her arm in farewell. She saw nothing in the darkness, but she knew the boy was watching her.

Snow began to fall as Cho Lin passed through the dead city, for which she gave thanks, as it would hide their passing. She tried to keep the great avenue that sliced through Nes Vaneth in sight, wending her way through a tangle of side streets, since she knew it eventually reached the ruined gates. That was the way she had entered the city, and it was the way she wished to leave. Since it was so well trafficked, there likely weren't any beasts prowling about in the forests.

Through the gaps between buildings she saw several points of light flickering in the distance. That must be the gate, and of course it was guarded. It was not the only way out, however – the walls girdling Nes Vaneth were as ruined as the rest of the city.

The first section she came to was surprisingly intact, but as she followed its meandering length she soon arrived at a segment that was just great blocks of tumbled stone. She threaded her way through the debris, checking the ground carefully as she went so that the horse she was leading would not wedge a hoof between rocks or stumble over anything in the dark.

Then she was beyond the city, facing a dark swell of pine trees. She looked to her right, down the long sweep of the walls; the clouds had dwindled to tattered strips, and the pale moon painted the snowy ground and white walls with a ghostly sheen. In the distance she could see the bulge of the gate house, but it was so far away that there was no chance any guards could glimpse her. She turned back to the slice of Nes Vaneth visible through the gap in the walls. The city gleamed in the moonlight, partially obscured by falling snow; a dead place, but still inhabited by the ghosts of a lost people. Was the Pale Lady out there, drifting among the ruins, starlight in her hair and unmelted snowflakes collecting on her cold skin?

She shook herself, finally tearing her gaze from the lost city. As if in imitation of Cho Lin, her horse tossed its head, shaking loose the snow that had gathered in its mane. Cho Lin stroked its flank, murmuring nonsense to try and comfort the animal. She squinted into the falling snow. If they entered the forest, she could build a simple shelter once they were far enough from the city that a fire could be risked. They needed food, though. The few strips of meat she'd scavenged from the dead Skein wouldn't last very long, and she doubted very much that she'd find anything for her horse to eat once they entered the wilds.

She remembered the settlement just outside the gates of Nes Vaneth. When she'd approached the city with Verrigan and his war band, the longhouses had been in the process of being looted by the victorious Skein. It had been where the women and children of the Bear lived while the menfolk drank and feasted in the Bhalavan with their thane. The usurpers had looted the houses of furs and treasure and well-made furniture, but perhaps they had left whatever stores the Bear kept for the winter months untouched.

Cho Lin licked her lips, tasting the cold purity of the melting snowflakes. The longhouses should be abandoned, what with the bulk of the Skein army having gone south. The temple of the Stormforger where she had given up her swords might still be inhabited, so she must still be careful. But likely the priests would be asleep, and she could move as quiet as a shadow when she wanted to.

That was her plan, then. Scavenge what she could from the Bear longhouses, then put as much distance as she could between her and Nes Vaneth. With any luck, the Skein would never even notice that she had returned for her horse and left the city.

Cho Lin led her horse into the forest, heading in the direction she thought would take her to the abandoned Skein settlement. Only a thin trickle of moonlight filtered down through the trees, and there was utter silence except for the crunch of hooves in the snow and the jangle of her horse's tack. She jumped and nearly drew her sword when snow sloughed off a branch and thumped to the ground. The forest, she decided, was even more frightening than the haunted city.

Her instincts were true, and eventually the trees thinned and she found herself staring at the darkened longhouses. She was closer to the ruined gate now, but still she thought it unlikely that any guard would be alert enough to catch her skulking in the darkness. After casting about for a moment, she found a sturdy low-hanging branch and tied her horse's reins around it. The horse grumbled and stamped its feet, and Cho Lin scratched it behind the ear to try and calm it.

"I'll be back soon. You want to eat tomorrow, yes? Be quiet. Be good."

Then she slipped from the cover of the trees, dashing across the field to the closest of the longhouses. When she reached it, she pressed herself against the wooden wall, trying to sink into the pooled darkness.

Nothing. No shouts, no alarm. *Best get to it, then.*

The door of this longhouse was a splintered ruin. Inside was pitch black, but her eyes had adjusted somewhat from moving through the forest, and the saw shapes swelling in the darkness. She moved forward cautiously, things crunching beneath her boots. She crouched, feeling chips of wood and shards of broken crockery. Her questing fingers brushed something soft and cold and smooth; there was a body here, and she suspected it was a young child. She sighed, remembering the dead women and children strewn about in the snow that she'd stumbled across far to the south – they had tried to escape, but in the end they had met the same fate as those who had stayed behind.

A fresh hatred of the Skein rose in her. They were little better than beasts, murdering the helpless families of their enemies. But there was still goodness, such as Verrigan and his nephew. Although, Cho Lin admitted grudgingly, Verrigan *had* led the warriors who had fallen upon the fleeing Bear. A complicated people.

In her fumbling explorations of the darkened longhouse she nearly tripped over another corpse. She also discovered barrels pushed against one wall, and after prying off the lid of the largest of them she found it half-full of some grain – barley, she suspected, to her great excitement. At least her horse would not starve. After rooting around some more she gathered a few sacks that seemed to be free of holes, and she scooped as much of the grain into one as it could hold. When she opened another of the barrels she was assailed by the smell of fish, and to her delight she found it packed with salted and dried trout. Her mouth watered, and she had to restrain herself from tearing into the fish right there and then. She stuffed another of the sacks full, sending a quick thanks to the spirits of those who had lived in this house. Further investigations yielded a length of twine, a fur blanket, an assortment of dried mushrooms and tubers, and a shard of what she hoped was flint. A tool to easily make fires would improve her chances of surviving the Frostlands as much as her horse or the provisions she'd found.

Satisfied, Cho Lin exited the longhouse through the shattered door. Glancing at the other darkened longhouses, she couldn't help but wonder what useful things she might find inside. She shook her head, though, adjusting her grip on the heavy sacks she'd slung over her shoulders. She didn't want to weigh her horse down too much, and she shouldn't linger much longer.

She was just about to run – or perhaps waddle, given how laden down she was – back to where she'd tied up her horse when she saw a glimmer of light from deeper in the settlement.

Against her better judgement, she quietly put down the sacks she'd been carrying and crept closer, keeping to the deeper shadows beneath the eaves of the longhouses. If there were already men searching for her, she should know this.

The light was not from a torch, though. A flame burned in a wide, curved brazier outside of a circular building. A Skein temple, she knew, as it resembled the place where the priests of the Stormforger had confiscated her weapons. This one looked smaller and more slipshod, as if it had been erected recently and quickly. The flap of hide covering the entrance was mottled and patchwork, and it reminded her of . . .

Cho Lin shivered. She knew what god was worshipped here.

The brazier had been placed before a thick wooden pole, and the dancing fire illuminated the dangling legs of a naked man. His arms were outstretched, his wrists tied to a crosspiece. His face . . . at first she thought the flames simply weren't high enough to reveal what he looked like, but then she realized that the skin of his face had been stripped away. She knew who it was from the long yellow braids hanging down.

Choking back a sob, Cho Lin turned away from Verrigan and made her way stumbling back to where she'd left what she'd scavenged. Shouldering the sacks, she hurried towards the trees and her waiting horse, tears burning her cold cheeks.

15: KEILAN

AS THE SKY began to darken, Alyanna brought the chavenix down at a rest stop along the Wending Way. It was a cleared area just off from the road and bounded by a trickling stream, the blackened remnants of many fires attesting to the spot's popularity among the caravans that plied the Way. When the disc settled on the grass Alyanna stood, grimacing as she stretched and her limbs unkinked. Keilan also couldn't wait to get up and walk around. They had been sitting all day as they flew over the forests of the Kingdoms and the middlelands, and he had lost most of the feeling in his legs long ago.

It wasn't just Alyanna's body that had apparently grown uncomfortable during the journey – the sorceress's eyes were shadowed, and faint lines had appeared on her brow, as if she suffered from a headache. Keilan assumed this was from the stress of keeping the chavenix aloft for so long; the sorceress had mentioned that the artifact had only been used for short flights in the past because of the strain it inflicted on its users.

"Get a fire going," Alyanna said as Keilan hopped off the disc and began to pace back and forth, trying to make the tingling numbness fade away.

"Why don't you just use your sorcery to keep us warm?" Nel asked, dragging one of the packs from the chavenix.

Alyanna looked at her like she was a simpleton. "Do you want to freeze? It's difficult to maintain such sorceries while sleeping, and if the strands slip away from me in the night, you might just wake up with blackened toes. Also, I need rest. I'd forgotten how draining keeping this thing in the air is."

"I'll find some kindling," Keilan said quickly when he saw Nel's mouth opening for what he assumed would be a tart response.

Alyanna nodded, then settled herself beside one of the firepits, leaning against a rock with her eyes closed. Nel clearly thought better about saying whatever it was she'd been poised to say and instead turned away from the sorceress with a snort and a shake of her head, reaching for another of the packs they'd brought.

"Not that one," Alyanna said without opening her eyes, and Nel froze, her hand hovering over the sack from which the sorceress had first pulled the chavenix.

With a flick of her wrist, Alyanna made the sack float over to where she was resting and settled it beside her. "Touch the wrong thing in here and you'll get something much worse than frostbitten toes."

Keilan remembered the flail of living darkness with which Alyanna had scourged the genthyaki. What else was in that bag?

"Let me gather the kindling," Nel said, brushing past him as he stared at the unassuming sack. "I need some space from this one."

Alyanna cracked her eye open, smirking as she watched Nel disappear into the stunted growth near the road. Then she reached inside the sack and pulled out a small, tattered book bound in black leather. A flicker of excitement sparked inside Keilan when he noticed that the faded title was written in High Kalyuni, like his mother's books and the ancient tomes he had found in the Barrow of Vis.

Alyanna noticed him studying the book she held. "Don't bother, Keilan. This was scribed by the ninth High Gendern of Kashkana in a language that has been dead for a thousand years."

"*The Shadow of a Waning Moon*. Is that right?"

"You can read High Kalyuni."

"My mother taught me."

Alyanna expression turned more thoughtful. "You are just full of surprises, Keilan. You truly do have potential."

The praise was unexpected, and he felt color rising in his face. He quickly tried to change the topic. "What is that book about?"

Alyanna brushed the cracked and ancient cover reverently. "It is concerned with the great mysteries of the world. I've always been fascinated by the unknown. There's a large section devoted to the Ancients – or the Ashenagi, as the sorcerer who wrote this called them. There are some secrets to be gleaned, but he writes in a frustratingly oblique manner. It's hard to tell sometimes if he truly has any insights, or is merely leading the reader down a path to nowhere. I've always wished I could ask the one who wrote the damn thing directly."

"The book demands to be heard, but it cannot listen. It desires to communicate, yet it refuses conversation."

The sorceress paled. "Where did you get that from?" she said, her voice barely a whisper. She looked like she'd glimpsed a ghost.

"I read it in a book."

Her eyes narrowed, and as quickly as her control had slipped, she mastered herself again. There was nothing in her face to suggest that she had just been shaken by what he had said, though she was now staring at him intently.

"There are depths to you, Keilan. You are truly Niara's grandson."

A clatter rose up nearby, and he glanced away from Alyanna to see that Nel had returned and dumped a pile of wood on the ground. She looked concerned, her gaze flicking from Keilan to

Alyanna and back again, clearly aware that had something had passed between them in the short time she'd been gone.

"What's going on?"

Two days later, they found the battlefield.

Keilan knew they were approaching something, as for the first time since they had passed into the Frostlands the unblemished blue sky ahead of them was now stained by a greasy haze. The source of the smoke became apparent when they came close enough to see the bloody aftermath of the great battle that had been fought here. Hundreds, perhaps thousands of corpses were scattered about in the snow, while even more had been heaped into mounds and set aflame. Those fires had long since gone out, though threads of black still trickled from the charred bodies. The sight of so much death sickened Keilan.

Alyanna said nothing as she guided the chavenix down to settle in the churned snow near where the bulk of the fighting had taken place. Ravens lifted from the dead warriors in a flurry of wings, shrieking indignantly at the disturbance. The sprawled bodies were all Skein, Keilan realized, most feathered with arrows or blackened by what he assumed was sorcery. There was a smell here, beyond simply the stench of so many corpses. It was like what lingered in the air after a thunderstorm, and his skin prickled. It smelled like sorcery.

Nel stepped from the Chavenix, gazing around at the devastation with her lips pursed. She looked nervous, Keilan thought. Something was bothering her. And he could guess what that was.

"I don't see any Dymorians," she said.

"They are the ones that were burned," Alyanna said, still sitting cross-legged on the disc. She at least seemed unfazed by the horror spread around them.

"Then they must have won, yes?" Nel continued, a note of hope in her voice.

"No," Alyanna said simply. "They were slaughtered."

"But surely the victors would burn their own," Keilan said. "And leave the enemy to rot in the snow."

Alyanna shook her head. "The Skein are a strange people. They believe that the souls of fallen warriors are carried in the beaks of the dark-winged flock into the halls of the gods. The barbarians burn their enemies to deny them this honor."

"So where is the queen?" Nel said, her voice rising to a near panic. "And the magisters? What happened to them?"

Alyanna shrugged. "Dead, I assume." She jerked her chin in the direction of the closest pile of blackened corpses.

"No!" Nel cried angrily, whirling back to face the sorceress with her hands balled into fists. "You're wrong! They must have escaped!" For a moment Keilan feared she was going to hurl one of her daggers at Alyanna.

"You could ask them," Alyanna said, gesturing at something behind Keilan. He turned to see a half-dozen Skein approaching; most brandished double-bladed axes, but a few also held bulging sacks. Scavengers, Keilan guessed. His hand drifted to the jeweled hilt of his sword, but he knew that he could not stand before these men. They were tall and broad, with wild red and yellow beards, and beneath their dark furs, metal glinted. Keilan had never seen a Skein before, but the barbarians lived up to every story he had heard while clustered around the Speaker's Rock in his village. They looked as much animal as man.

The Skein quickened their pace when they realized they had been seen. Keilan saw their anticipation of what was to come, vicious smiles splitting ruddy faces. Chance and Fate appeared in Nel's hands, and reluctantly Keilan drew his sword and tried to set his feet into the Forms without slipping in the snow. His heart beat wildly as the barbarians broke into a run, bellowing as they lifted their black-iron axes.

Shimmering crimson lances flashed past Keilan. The sorcery pierced each of the barbarians' chests unerringly, ripping through the Skein like they were made of cloth. Some toppled over immediately, while others stumbled to a halt, staring down in shock at the charred holes in their chests before then collapsing. The last warrior standing actually dropped his ax and put his hand inside his body, not comprehending what had just happened, before joining his fellows on the ground.

They had all died in the space of a few breaths.

"Garazon's balls," Nel murmured, giving voice to what Keilan was feeling. They turned back to the sorceress and found her still sitting calmly on the disc, as if nothing had happened.

"Your instinct should always be to use your sorcery, Keilan," she said, climbing to her feet and stepping lightly from the chavenix. "It's ridiculous that with your power you always reach for your blade." She raised her face, squinting into the brilliantly blue sky. "Though I've known others like you. Men have such a romantic attachment to their swords."

"What should we do?" Nel asked, her daggers vanishing.

Alyanna's gaze traveled over the battlefield. "Let us see what we can learn from this place. The sorcery that was used might give us some insight into the capabilities of our enemies."

"And then?"

"We follow the Skein host, I suppose. We know the Chosen are allied with them."

The disc laden with their packs and bags lifted from the ground and came to hover beside Alyanna. Then she set off towards where the fighting had been thickest, the chavenix trailing obediently behind her.

Keilan and Nel glanced at each other.

"Do you think Vhelan . . ." he began, before Nel cut him off.

"We don't even know if he was here."

Keilan nodded quickly. "Yes, of course," he said, and then hurriedly fell in behind Nel as she moved to follow Alyanna.

They picked their way through a maze of dead Skein, skirting around the heaps of burned Dymorian dead. The blackened corpses piled together reminded Keilan unsettlingly of the structure the Chosen had emerged from on top of the ruins of the Selthari Palace. Death and horror followed in the wake of those demons . . . yet the presence he had touched in his dreams had not felt so evil. What had turned the spirit of the girl into a creature that wanted to murder the world? He shivered – away from Alyanna's cossetting sorcery, the bite of the Frostlands was prickling his skin. If they were going to stay in the north, they needed to find some warmer clothes.

Alyanna's low whistle pulled him from his thoughts. He followed where she was looking, and then couldn't hold back a startled gasp. A huge white-scaled serpent lay in the snow, bristled with countless arrows and spears. Orange eyes stared sightlessly in death, and its jaws were cracked open, revealing row upon row of curved teeth.

"I haven't seen one of these in a long time," Alyanna said, approaching the beast and laying her hand upon its scaled side.

"What is it?" Nel asked nervously, seemingly unwilling to get too close to the monster.

"We called them snow snakes in the south, though the only other one I've encountered was a dead specimen that had been brought to one of the Star Towers for study. I'm sure the Min-Ceruthans had their own name for the things. They infest the northern glaciers, tunneling vast nests into the ice that resemble what insects do under the earth. I heard that long ago the more adventurous Min-Ceruthans would lead expeditions into the far north to hunt these things for sport." She walked towards the thing's head, running her fingers along its sinuous length. "I don't think even the old holdfasts ever considered using these beasts in war, though. How clever."

Keilan imagined this great armored serpent smashing into the Dymorian lines and couldn't hold back a shudder. It must have been horrific.

Alyanna paused at the monster's open jaws and reached inside. Her face showed a slight strain, then Keilan felt a surge of sorcery and there was a crack like ice fracturing. When the sorceress withdrew her hand a moment later she was holding a curving fang as long as her forearm.

She said nothing, simply tossing the tooth onto the chavenix hovering beside her. Suddenly, a look of consternation passed across her face, and she glanced up at one of the rocky hills overlooking the battlefield. Without another word, she lifted from the snow and rose into the air.

"Alyanna!" Keilan cried, but the sorceress did not reply, intent on whatever had drawn her attention above. She did not glance back at them as she soared over the lip of the escarpment and vanished from sight.

Keilan and Nel shared a worried glance. What had she felt? He could sense strange sorcerous currents here, and perhaps they were emanating from above. It felt like when he used to swim in the ocean and would suddenly slip into an inexplicably cold or warm patch of water.

Alyanna reappeared, descending from above. She had a strange expression on her face, almost like she was deep in concerned thought, her lips pursed and her brow drawn down.

"What is it?" Nel asked. "What did you see?"

The sorceress shook her head slightly and beckoned for the chavenix to come closer. "Not what I expected. I think you both should have a look."

His heart beating fiercely, Keilan climbed on top of the floating disc. Nel did the same, and he could sense the tension thrumming in her. She was terrified of what they'd find above, and he knew why.

When they were settled, Alyanna made the chavenix soar higher. The rock wall of the cliff rushed past, and then they crested the edge of the ridge.

For a moment, Keilan struggled to understand what he was seeing. The rocky summit had been devastated: pillars of stone were thrust up from the ground, which, along with the lower reaches of the pillars had been blackened and scarred by flame. The formations looked unnatural, like something had pushed up from below, and given the debris heaped around their bases, whatever had happened had occurred recently. The sorcerous reverberations up here slipped past the warm bubble Alyanna maintained around the chavenix and made him shiver.

The sorceress set the disc down and indicated a tight cluster of the pillars with her chin. "In there," she said flatly.

Nel and Keilan slid from the chavenix and cautiously approached the unsettling rock formation. The residue of sorcery was so strong it was making him dizzy.

Nel was the first to glimpse what was within, and she gave a horrified gasp. Keilan rushed forward, his fingers scrabbling for his sorcery in case there was some threat.

It was a pyramid of human heads. He staggered, putting his hand on one of the pillars to steady himself. Mouths open in silent screams, eyes wide and glassy. There was no blood that he could see, as if each of the heads had been drained and cleaned before being carefully stacked.

Nel approached the pyramid slowly, as if in a dream. Her hands were shaking, and her eyes were moving over the grotesque pile like she was searching for something.

It was then that Keilan realized these were not soldiers. He saw the heads of women, some with gray hair, others only a few years older than him. And men of all ages as well. There was a softness and a smoothness to many of their faces, something he had seen before among those who spent their days hunched over books or attending to tasks inside.

Magisters. These were the sorcerers of the Scholia.

"I know them," Nel whispered.

Keilan touched her arm, wanting to drag her away, but she shook him off.

"Nel..."

"Do you see him?" Her voice was hollow.

Keilan looked again. "No." One head did draw his attention, though, perched at the very apex of the pyramid. "At the top. Is that...?"

"The Crone's servant," Nel murmured. "It is."

"What was he doing here?"

Nel shook her head slightly. "I don't know."

"Do you think Lady Numil is here as well?"

"I don't see her... head." Nel ran a shaking hand through her hair. "But maybe she's under the rest." She stepped closer to the pyramid, but Keilan grabbed her and pulled her back. She struggled against him, but he did not let go.

"No," he said as she twisted to face him, shoving him hard in the chest.

"Keilan, stop!" she cried, her voice cracking.

"I won't let you," he said, as calmly as he could, and she struck him hard on the cheek. He rocked backwards, his face burning, but still he held onto her.

"I need to know!"

"If he's here, he wouldn't want you to see!" Keilan said. Nel gave a final cry as she tried to twist from his grip, and then she collapsed. Gently, he encircled her with his arms as she shuddered against him, her small body wracked by sobs.

Over her shoulder, Keilan watched the grotesque pyramid. It seemed like more than a few of the heads were staring at him.

"Lady Nel?"

Keilan whirled around, still clutching Nel tight.

"Who's there?" he cried, looking around wildly.

A young man with dark red hair and an explosion of freckles was peering around one of the pillars of stone.

Nel pulled away from Keilan, rubbing at her face. "That's me."

Tentatively, the man stepped out from behind the rock. He was wearing a forester's garb, leather armor dyed green and dark brown, and the cloak he was wearing was clasped by a golden dragon eating its own tail. A ranger of Dymoria.

He looked stricken, as if he couldn't decide whether to be relieved or terrified. "Are you . . . are you ghosts?" he asked, staring at Keilan and Nel like he expected them to shimmer and vanish.

"No. We just arrived here from the south." Her voice was firm, the fragility she had just shown Keilan buried again.

The ranger blinked, running a shaking hand over his begrimed face. It looked to Keilan that he might start crying soon.

"Bless the Ten. I thought you were a vision put here by the demons. No one else has had the courage to come up here 'cause they feared what they'd find."

"No one else?" Keilan asked, hope kindling in his chest.

"The survivors. There's not many of us, and most are wounded."

Nel clutched at Keilan's arm. "Vhelan? Is he alive?"

The ranger's face crinkled in confusion. I don't know a Vhelan. Is he a soldier?"

Her nails dug into his flesh. "No. A magister."

"Only two magisters made it off this rock, I'm sorry to say. Magister d'Kalla and Magister Vhalus."

Nel gave a strangled cry, pulling so hard on his arm he nearly lost his balance. "Vhalus," she repeated breathlessly. "Vhelan ri Vhalus."

The ranger's hand drifted to his shock of red hair. "Young, but bit o' silver on his head?"

"Yes," Nel gasped, and again tears were streaming down her cheeks. "Yes."

Despite the horrors of all those heads staring at them, Keilan couldn't stop smiling. He wanted to hug Nel tight again, but she pulled away from him.

"What happened here?" she asked.

The ranger opened his mouth to respond, but then he stumbled back a step, his eyes widening and his hand going to the sword at his side. Alyanna glided out from between two of the unnatural pillars, ignoring them as she approached the pile of heads.

"It's all right," Keilan assured him. "She's with us."

The ranger continued staring at the sorceress uncertainly as she picked up the head of a plump female magister by its long hair and held it in front of her. She gave it a gentle push, examining it intently as it spun.

"The Skein had dark sorcery," the ranger explained. "And monsters. They unleashed the beasts first, punching holes in our lines. Then they came at us. We still would have won, I think, but there were demons. The magisters were slaughtered. The queen . . ."

His voice trailed away.

"The queen?" Nel prompted him, when it became clear he did not want to finish.

"She fell," he finally said.

Alyanna threw the head back on the pile, starting a small avalanche that disturbed the silence that had followed the ranger's words.

"She's dead?" Keilan asked.

The ranger shrugged, his face despondent. "We haven't found her body. Maybe the Skein took it so it could be defiled. They are a monstrous people."

"Why did you come up here?" Alyanna asked, pacing around the pyramid as she inspected it closely.

The ranger drew aside his cloak, showing two silver-hilted swords that were thrust through his belt. They looked familiar to Keilan.

"Lady Numil asked me to retrieve these."

Nel and Keilan shared a startled look.

"Lady Numil is alive?"

The ranger nodded. "She's back at the caves, with the rest."

"Take us to them," Nel commanded.

The ranger led them down from the ridge by way of a switchback trail. Keilan understood why the magisters must have thought themselves safe from the fighting – in places, the path narrowed so that they were forced to walk single file, and it seemed to him that a handful of warriors should have been able to defend against a much larger force.

But it had not been other warriors that had ascended.

The remnants of the defenders were strewn everywhere, and the snow was stained with dried blood and viscera. Keilan did not see a single limb or head attached to a torso – it was like how a child might meticulously pluck away the legs and wings of insects. Pale faces twisted in terror stared out from the black iron jaws of demons, and Keilan shuddered at the sight. Separated from the bodies, the Lyrish guardsmen's helms really did make it look like the heads were being swallowed by monsters. Keilan's stomach churned at the horror of it all.

Alyanna floated beside them as they picked their way down the trail. She at least did not seem disturbed by the carnage.

The ranger's eyes widened when she first stepped from the path and drifted into the air. "You have a magister with you, Lady Nel?" he asked her.

Nel shook her head. "She's not part of the Scholia, though she is an ally."

Keilan thought she wanted to add *for now*, but she did not – perhaps because she didn't want to wipe away the hope and excitement that had appeared on the ranger's face.

"What's your name, ranger?" she asked as they skirted the remains of a soldier that had been macabrely arranged so that legs were growing from its shoulders and a clenched, bloody fist emerged from the stump of its neck.

"Chelin, my lady," the ranger replied, and Keilan noticed that he was intentionally not looking at the desecrated corpse as he stepped around it. "I was with you and the boy here after the attack on Saltstone. I was one of the rangers chasing the paladin south."

"The archons let you go?"

Chelin bobbed his head. "Aye. Lady Numil went to see the queen, and after that a message came and we were freed. We arrived back in the city a few days after the army marched, but we caught up with them before they reached the Serpent." He shuddered. "Though now I wish we'd been left to languish in those cells. The last few days have been like a nightmare from which I can't wake."

When they reached the bottom, they found the chavenix waiting for them like an obedient dog. With some coaxing, Nel convinced the skittish ranger to climb onto the disc, and then they floated up and away, following his stammered directions. As the strewn corpses flashed by beneath them, he clutched his knees to his chest, his face white and sweaty.

"You'd best swallow back down anything that comes up from your belly," Alyanna said, smiling sweetly at the ranger. "If you are sick on my chavenix I will toss you over the side." He nodded jerkily, seeming to grow even paler.

"That way," he managed after a long silence in which he was visibly fighting his gorge, pointing at a tumbled pile of rocks at the base of one of the Bones. The stunted little mountain was pressed against the plains where the battle had been fought; there were no dead here, that Keilan could see – likely the Dymorians hadn't wanted to be trapped with the mountain's flank at their back, even if the stones scattered about would have made it hard going for attackers.

"There," Chelin said, indicating a narrow crack just visible between a pair of great boulders.

"How did you find this place?" Nel asked as Alyanna brought the chavenix down near the cave entrance.

Chelin wobbled as he stepped from the disc, holding a hand over his stomach. "The rangers scouted the whole area before the battle. When the queen fell, our lines broke. Men were fleeing blindly, being hunted down by the barbarians." He swallowed, looking at Nel guiltily. "The Skein were . . . were . . ." He paused, composing himself. "They were slicing away the skin of the fallen. I saw them. Sometimes the men weren't even dead yet. Taking trophies, I suppose. But the horror of it . . . I ran. And the only place I could think might be safe was these caves. Some of the other rangers who had found this place had the same idea." He looked away, and Keilan saw his shame. "I'm sorry, my lady. I'm a coward."

Nel shook her head. "You fled when it was hopeless. There's no dishonor in that."

The ranger nodded, visibly relieved by her words. "We stayed hidden until the fighting was over and they'd made those pyres. Then we crept out looking for survivors. We found twenty or so men who had been wounded on the field and somehow escaped being burned. A few more stumbled out of the forest after the Skein host departed."

"So how many are in the caves?" Nel asked as Chelin started walking over the rocks towards the gash in the mountain's side.

"About fifty. Oh, and the magisters and Lady Numil."

Fifty men. Keilan's blood went cold thinking about how the great Dymorian army had been reduced to just fifty men. How many thousands had been slaughtered on that field? Everything the queen had striven for was in ruins. The new age of sorcery had been murdered in its infancy.

The ranger whistled as he approached the cave, and a gawky boy with a mop of unruly yellow curls leapt up from behind a rock, nocking an arrow to his ebonwood bow. He smiled when he saw Chelin, showing the gap where his two front teeth should have been.

"Found some more, did ya?" he said, lowering his bow and coming out from behind the rock. "Weren't followed, were ya?"

Chelin shook his head and clasped the boy's arm. "No, Fars. This here is Lady Nel, she's a servant of Magister Vhalus. And those two are sorcerers."

The archer scratched his face, pursing his lips as he studied Keilan and Alyanna. Then his eyes alighted on the hovering chavenix and his skepticism melted away.

"Right," he said, the apple in his throat bobbing. "Come with me, lord an' ladies."

They passed through the cleft in the rock and navigated a short, twisting passage that forced Keilan to crouch and turn sideways at one particularly narrow spot. He was just starting to feel his panic rise from the stone closing around him when the tunnel suddenly opened into a much larger space. Torches had been lit among the boulders and stalagmites, illuminating groups of men clustered together. The roof of the cave was lost in the blackness, though Keilan saw dark shapes he assumed were rocks reaching down from the gloom above.

The archer pointed to a ring of torches set atop a mound in the cavern's center. "Commander d'Venish and Magister Vhalus are up there. Best you go see them first." Then he clapped his fist to his chest and spun about, vanishing back into the passage.

Chelin motioned for them to follow him, but Nel was already striding past. Keilan hurried to keep up with her, and they were nearly running by the time they reached the rise in the floor where the archer had said Vhelan was. Nel scrambled up the rocky slope and Keilan followed, scraping his knee bloody in his haste.

He reached the top a few moments behind Nel. Two men were discussing something in heated whispers – one was Vhelan in his red magister robes, now filthy and tattered, and the other was a young man with the imperious face of a noble. He was dressed in armor of fine make, his cuirass engraved with the twisting dragon of Dymoria, and the helmet he carried under his arm had a crimson horsehair plume. They were so intent on their argument that they did not realize Keilan and Nel had arrived.

"Hey, boss," Nel said simply, and Vhelan wrenched himself around, his jaw falling open.

"Nel?" he whispered, as if unsure whether she was real or not.

"Who is this?" barked the young soldier, his eyes thinning in suspicion.

Vhelan stumbled towards her, nearly tripping on his robes. "How?"

"We heard you needed some help," she said, grinning.

"Oh, thank all the gods!" the magister said, wrapping Nel in his arms and crushing her tightly to him. "I thought you were lost."

"Magister Vhalus!" grated the noble. "What are these people doing here?"

Nel pulled herself away from Vhelan and the magister turned back to the soldier, though he kept his hand on her shoulder as if he feared she would disappear. "Lord d'Venish, this is my oldest friend, Nel. And this is Keilan, an apprentice in the Scholia of our queen." Vhelan reached out with his other hand to clasp Keilan's arm. "How are you, my boy?" He studied Keilan for a moment. "You look different. You've changed – you're no longer a child."

The Dymorian commander stepped forward, his hand on the hilt of his sword. "And they just wandered into our hiding place?"

"I brought them, m'lord." Chelin said, panting as he finally crested the mound. "I found 'em on the ledge where the magisters . . ." He glanced at Vhelan, his voice trailing away.

"You went up there?" d'Venish said angrily, shifting his attention to the ranger. "Without asking for my permission?"

"Lady Numil, m'lord . . . she asked me to."

"The lady has no authority here," the noble said through gritted teeth.

"But . . . you said to afford her every respect—"

"Respect does not mean obeying her commands, soldier. She is a guest and nothing more. Remember that."

"Yes, m'lord," Chelin said, ducking his head and knuckling his brow as he slunk away.

Lord d'Venish gave an exasperated sigh, then turned back to the rest of them. "Fool could have led the Skein right back to us. We need to be careful before we finally leave these caves." He studied Nel and Keilan. "So you were on the battlefield. You were following our army up from the south, then? Must have been a rather rude shock." The commander paused, as if waiting for confirmation, and Keilan gave a quick nod. "Tell me, what does it look like out there? Any Skein still lurking about?"

"We saw some scavengers," Keilan answered without thinking.

D'Venish's eyes bulged and he glanced in the direction of the passage that led to the outside. "Were you followed? Did they see you?"

"No, no," Keilan added hastily.

The commander's face hardened, as if he didn't fully believe this. "God's blood. I need to tell our lookouts to be vigilant." He pointed a finger at Vhelan. "We will continue this later, Magister, but you know my position." Then he swept past them in a swirl of his dark cloak, his boots crunching as he descended the gravelly slope down to the cavern floor.

Vhelan waited a moment until the sound faded. "He's not stupid or incompetent," he finally said. "But he is under great strain."

"He's the highest-ranking officer who survived?" Nel asked.

Vhelan nodded slightly. "He's the *only* officer who survived. Which makes him the commander of the entire Dymorian army." Vhelan spread his arms to indicate the clumps of men huddled in the patches of light that were spread across the huge cave. "Such as it is."

"What happened, boss?"

"Disaster," Vhelan replied simply. "We lost."

"How?"

Vhelan motioned for them to follow him as he started down the slope. "The Skein had a sorcerer who was the equal of the queen. But she might not have fallen if he hadn't been allied with these demonic children. They threw their strength against her as well." There was a hitch to his words as he said this. "These children, Nel . . . they are evil made manifest. They . . . they butchered the other magisters."

"We know them."

Vhelan ran a hand through his hair. It looked to Keilan like the streak of silver in the black had grown larger since last he'd seen the magister. "Yes. I was there when the Crone told the queen about what you all saw in the Oracle's temple. Before she sent you on your ridiculous quest."

"It wasn't ridiculous," Keilan said quietly. "We found something."

Vhelan glanced at him sharply, but the look in his eyes quickly faded. "Truly? What does it matter now, though? Cein d'Kara is dead. Who else can stand against the Skein sorcerer and his demons?"

"There is someone," Nel said slowly. Keilan looked about, wondering where the sorceress had disappeared to.

"Is there?" Vhelan asked, excitement creeping back into his voice. "Did you find that sorceress from the Oracle's vision?"

"We did," Nel said. "But she died. I'm speaking of Alyanna."

"Alyanna . . ." Vhelan muttered, tapping his finger on his chin. "That name . . . I've heard it before. Wait." His brow drew down as he dredged his memories. "The sorceress the queen saw in Jan's mind . . . the one who challenged her atop Saltstone. *That* Alyanna?"

"That's the one."

Vhelan blinked, his surprise evident. "Hm. I tried to strike her down from behind when she was fighting the queen. Hopefully, she won't remember that."

The magister led them towards one of the larger lighted sections of the cavern. There were dozens of men here lying on furs, most with very obvious injuries: some had strips of bloodstained cloth wound around their heads or torsos, others had their limbs in makeshift splints or slings. Healthier soldiers wandered among the wounded, changing dressings or helping the men drink and eat. And a little way apart from the rest, so small and shrunken in her bed of furs she looked like a swaddled babe, was the Crone of Lyr.

"Lady Numil!" Keilan cried, rushing to her side.

The old woman turned her head towards him. Keilan's heart fell when he saw how pale and haggard she was. Yet despite her obvious discomfort, she still managed a shaky smile.

"Keilan. How good to see you. So you're the one they sent."

He slowed, blinking uncertainly. "Sorry? What do you mean 'sent'?"

She sniffed. "Well, I must be dead. Though it's unfortunate that I'm still in pain. I'd hoped I'd leave that behind at least."

"Dead?"

The Crone rolled her eyes. "Yes, dead. As are you, apparently. Otherwise why would I be seeing your spirit now?"

Nel appeared beside him and ducked her head in greeting. "It's good to see you again, Lady."

"Oh, and the thief, too." She started to sigh, but that quickly deteriorated into a hacking cough. "I suppose my deeds were not good enough to get me into where the righteous people end up. Shame."

"We're not ghosts," Keilan said slowly.

Lady Numil turned her head and spat out something green and viscous. "Hm. That's good, I suppose."

"Are you . . . are you all right?" Keilan ventured, and the Crone responded with a wet, rasping chuckle.

"No, I am not. Well, if I'm not dead now, it's just a matter of time. I'm dying, Keilan. Broken bones and this damnable cold, which won't seem to leave my lungs."

"I'm so sorry."

She snorted, turning back to them. "My death has been just over the horizon for quite some time. I'd have preferred to die wrapped in a soft blanket in my own bed . . ." Her words trailed away as the ranger Chelin suddenly appeared beside Keilan. "Ah. You're back. Did you find them?"

"I did, my lady," the ranger said, withdrawing the pair of swords from under his cloak.

Lady Numil's jaw clenched, and she blinked quickly, as if she was fighting back a tide of emotion. "Good. Good. Thank you, Chelin."

The ranger laid the blades beside her, and the Crone's hand slipped from the furs to stroke the twining silver serpents of the nearest sword's hilt.

"As I was saying, I knew my death was coming, but I still had tasks to accomplish." She peered at Keilan, her gaze suddenly sharpening. "As did you. Did you find the sorceress?"

"We did."

"And?"

Keilan glanced at Nel. "She's dead. But we have a weapon now, something that can kill the demons."

"Then it was not all in vain," Lady Numil murmured, the intensity of her stare fading as she subsided again into her furs. Pain shivered her face, and she moaned.

Moments later a man pushed past Keilan to crouch beside her. He put a flask to her lips and tilted it back; she coughed again, a dark liquid dribbling down her chin, but then her eyes fluttered closed as her breathing deepened.

"She'll sleep for a few hours," the man said as he stood, stoppering the flask.

"What's wrong with her?" Keilan asked.

"She fell and broke several ribs, and either one of them pierced her lung or she had a sickness before that's worsened as her body weakened." He frowned, then shook the flask. "Little we can do now except make her last days as comfortable as possible. This numbs the pain, but also addles the mind."

"Keilan!"

They glanced up as Alyanna suddenly strode from the blackness beyond the torchlight. "There's something we must discuss."

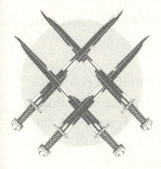

16: JAN

HE WAS JAN, the bard. Again.

For a long time he had been lost, wandering in a shattered labyrinth. His old reflections had stalked beside him, obscuring his sense of what was true and what was false. Jerrym d'Beln, exiled noble in the court of Vis. Jannil of the Narrows, mercenary captain of the Singing Men. Janus Balensorn, wandering minstrel turned crofter on the land of Ser Willes len Maliksorn. They were facets of himself, and each had lived and loved fiercely, until the barriers inside him had eventually flaked away and the compulsion to seek out Alyanna had driven him back to her. Then she would rebuild what had been broken, but with different material and technique, so he would have a new path to walk for a time.

The attack by the demons in the old throne room had broken him. The ghosts of his past selves had risen again, dragging him down into a realm of mist and mirrors. He hadn't been able to remember who he truly was; or, more precisely, the fragments that had been him in each of his incarnations had tried to convince him that they were what was real, and that the story of

Jan duth Verala was in truth merely another fiction spun by the Weaver of lies.

It was sorcery that had brought him back to himself. Like a bright light flaring in darkness, the surge of magic had torn away the clotting shadows and shown him the truth.

And that had nearly broken him again.

He huddled in an empty room illuminated by pale light trickling down from narrow windows. There was something wrong with his vision – he could only see out of one eye. A flap of leather covered the other, but he hesitated before pushing his fingers beneath it. He knew what he would find.

Instead, he concentrated on his surroundings. He felt like he was moving, the space swaying and shuddering slightly, though he did not hear the rumble of turning wheels. The room was empty, the wooden floor covered with mounded straw like he was some sort of animal. Cold iron encircled his ankle, connected by a chain to the wall.

There was something around his neck, too—Jan's finger drifted to his throat and found metal. A collar. He reached for his sorcery but it squirmed through his fingers like smoke.

So he had been captured. Was it the Kalyuni, still upset over Kashkana? Or had the fallowmancers finally discovered that he had been the one who stole their damn starlings?

He shook his head. No. Those thoughts were from a different Jan. Before the cataclysms. Before Alyanna.

His more recent memories slowly seeped back into his consciousness. He remembered his wife dying in his arms, her cheeks stained red by the Weeping. Then his journey across the white plains to the city of Menekar, chasing demons and finding a sorceress instead. The Mire. The Crimson Queen. The flood of his old self returning, then him awakening imprisoned within the ruins of Ravenroost. The Shan girl. Abandoning her and his promise so he could return to Nes Vaneth and what he knew awaited him beneath the Bhalavan.

It was then that his mind shied away from what had happened. Jan ground his teeth and pressed on, demanding to be shown how he had ended up here, a prisoner wrapped in filthy furs. In the throne room, he had found the child – his child? – gone, hacked from the ice. Then another sorcerer had appeared: the shaman of the new Skein king. His power had been overwhelming. Lask, that was his name. The shaman had removed the collar Cein d'Kara had put on him, then shown his sorcery was the greater by humbling Jan like he was a child that needed to be taught a lesson.

What had come after that was difficult to remember. There were brief glimpses of iron bars and cold stone, filtered through snatches of terrible pain and the numbing, dreamlike fog through which he had been drifting.

The room in which he huddled lurched sickeningly, and he bit down on his tongue. He was clearly still a prisoner of the Skein. Where was he, though? Not in Nes Vaneth. They were bringing him somewhere. But where? And why? His thoughts turned to Cho Lin, and he felt a pang of guilt and sorrow. He could only imagine what horrors the barbarians must have inflicted upon such a beautiful girl. If only she hadn't followed him into the Frostlands. If only he had honored his oath and gone with her to Menekar. Though in the end, they had found exactly what she had been seeking.

The demons. Whatever was beneath his eye-flap itched at the thought of those monstrous children. He remembered the intense shock he'd felt as one of those ragged children had moved out from behind a statue in the throne room. He could not escape those things. When he had hunted them, they had eluded him. It was only when he thought he'd abandoned the chase that he had found them. A lesson was there, somewhere.

Jan ran his tongue over his cracked lips. He was hungry and thirsty, but someone must have been feeding him and dribbling water down his throat while he slept. The Skein had been keeping him alive. To what end?

He came awake as his prison shuddered to a stop. Dusk had fallen outside, plunging the interior of the wagon into its own gloomy twilight. He heard faint voices, growing louder, and then a clanging sound from the other side of the far wall. Rusty hinges squealed as a door opened, and Jan blinked and shielded his face as brighter light flooded the room. Shadowy shapes milled at the entrance.

Someone spoke in the grating Skein tongue. "There's no more chains. We used them all on the—"

"They are not needed," came the soft reply. It was a familiar voice, and it sent a shiver through Jan.

"The king said—"

"Are you challenging my command?"

An awkward silence followed. "No, no." Jan could hear the speaker's fear as he stumbled over his words, though he tried to hide it. "It will be as you say, shaman."

Snow crunched as more figures approached the wagon. "Throw her in there!" barked the harsher voice, his nervous deference replaced with angry authority.

The wooden floor creaked as a pair of burly Skein climbed into the wagon. Jan slumped motionless, pretending to still be unconscious. Through his barely open eye he saw the barbarians toss a small limp body among the scattered rushes, and then they hurriedly exited the wagon without glancing back.

The soft voice came again. "Any strange noises from inside, or if the man becomes lucid, send for me immediately."

A grunt of agreement, and then the wagon's doors swung shut and Jan heard the sound of an iron bolt being replaced. Darkness rushed in to fill the interior once more.

He lay there for a few long moments as the wagon lurched into motion again, breathing quietly and studying this new prisoner. She was a shapeless mound in the blackness, unmoving.

"Hello," he finally ventured, but the shape did not stir.

Jan edged closer until the chain connecting him to the wall pulled taut. He could almost reach out and touch her, but in the fading light her features were lost in the shadows. She had long dark hair, slightly curled, and from what he could see her clothes seemed of expensive make. One of her outstretched arms lay in a sliver of light, and he saw to his surprise that she was wearing a bracer of fine white leather. What skin he could see was ghost-pale.

Jan chewed on his lip, uncertain what he should do. Let her keep sleeping, and hope she roused before whatever madness had gripped him returned? Or wake her now and learn what was happening outside?

He sighed, pushing himself backwards so that he could lean against the wall again. Best to let her rest. Who knew what terrible ordeals she had suffered? Surely he could wait a while, he told himself, drawing his knees up to his chest.

He lasted about a hundred heartbeats before his curiosity gnawed through his resolve.

Jan scooped up a handful of the dry straw covering the floor and packed it as tightly as he could, then lightly tossed it at the unconscious woman. He was aiming for her midsection, but instead he struck her squarely in the head, the ball of straw exploding.

"Apologies," he murmured. Had she stirred? He thought she might have shifted slightly.

He wadded together a larger clump of straw, and was just raising his arm to throw it when she spoke.

"Stop." Her voice was fractured by pain. It sounded familiar.

"Your Highness?" Jan whispered, incredulous.

With agonizing slowness, the woman pushed herself into a sitting position. She was in pain, Jan realized, with maybe even a few broken bones, given the way she flinched and shivered when she braced her arm against the floor.

"Jan," Cein d'Kara said. Her voice was flat, purged of emotion. The queen of Dymoria dragged herself closer to the wall and leaned her head against it exhaustedly.

"What are you doing here?" he hissed, forgetting his manners in his surprise.

She was quiet for a long moment. "I came for you," she finally replied.

"By yourself, Your Highness? Where is your Scarlet Guard? Your magisters?"

"Dead," she said with hollow finality.

Jan's mind reeled at the implications. "The Skein defeated your army?"

"Not the Skein," she said softly. "A sorcerer and his demon allies."

Whatever was under Jan's eyepatch began to itch again. "You mean the children . . ."

She nodded, moving her head against the wall. He thought her eyes were closed.

"My armies were about to slaughter the Skein. But they would have had no defense against sorcery after I fell, and my magisters . . ." Her voice trailed away. The pain he heard in her words might not be from an injury, Jan realized. She grieved for what had happened and who she had lost.

"They have collared me," she said angrily, her hand going to something around her neck.

Jan had less sympathy for her in this, given how she had been the one to put a collar on him first.

"My sorcery . . . I can feel it, hovering there, just out of reach."

He knew her frustration. For an accomplished sorcerer, the loss of power was like going blind or deaf. A fundamental way of interpreting the world had suddenly been lost to her. It was a terrifying sensation, and had reduced many great magi to tears. She was taking it fairly well, all things considered.

The silence stretched again. Jan's eyes had adjusted to the dimness, and he could see her more clearly. He was struck by how young she looked – in Saltstone, she had caked her face with whitening powder to make herself seem older, and carried herself with such confident imperiousness that even the oldest and most powerful nobles had afforded her respect. Now, though, that veneer had been scraped away, revealing the young woman beneath.

"You must hate me," she said softly.

That surprised him, enough that he did not know how to respond.

She took his silence another way. "I don't blame you," she continued bitterly. "Collared and imprisoned like an animal. As I am now."

"What happened on Ravenroost . . . I promise you it was an accident."

Her mouth twisted. "I knew that, even at the time. I was angry, though. Many of my oldest friends died when I blundered into that trap the Kalyuni sorceress had left in your mind. I wanted you punished. And I hoped she would come for you."

"Alyanna," Jan whispered. "I wonder where she is now."

Cein opened her mouth, but then hesitated for a moment before speaking. "On her way to the Frostlands," she said, and Jan sensed she wasn't sure she should be telling him this.

"She's coming *here*?"

"Perhaps. If her word can be trusted."

"So you've spoken with her?"

The queen nodded. "She sought me out in my dream. She claimed to want a truce between us; that there were dangerous creatures loose in the world, and that they would cause great harm if they were not opposed."

"The child demons," Jan said.

"Aye. And as chance would have it, I had just witnessed one of those things strike you down beneath Nes Vaneth."

"You saw that? How?"

"A simple scrying spell." She waved her hand weakly, as if it had been no great feat.

"You cannot trust her. Alyanna only acts in her own self-interest."

The queen laughed quietly, a rasping chuckle. It sounded like there might be fluid in her lungs, and that concerned Jan. How hurt was she?

"I will never trust her. But our interests were aligned on this. The Oracle of Lyr gave a prophecy that foretold that these demons could bring down the end of the world, and so they must be destroyed." She raised her slim hand and pressed it to the wood. For a moment her mask slipped, and Jan saw the pain in her face. "I have lost, though," she murmured. "I can only hope Alyanna or others have the strength to stop them."

"If Alyanna truly is their enemy now, they could not have a more ruthless or implacable foe," Jan said, trying to put as much confidence into his words as he could muster. "I've learned that she always wins, in the end."

17: KEILAN

"THAT'S MADNESS."

Alyanna ignored Nel's outburst, staring at Keilan with an intensity that made his skin crawl. The wizardlight she had summoned when they'd moved farther away from where the remnants of the Dymorian army were encamped painted her face with a spectral radiance, as if she were a ghost emerging from the utter blackness of the caves.

Keilan shifted uncomfortably under her gaze. "I don't understand."

For a brief moment, frustration flickered across her pale features. "You don't have to understand how it works, Keilan," she said with what he suspected was forced patience. "This is a sorcery that should take many years to master, but with my guidance, it is within your capabilities."

"And it's safe?" he enquired dubiously. Nel snorted and crossed her arms.

"There will be a brief moment of danger. I will be nearby, though, and if anything goes wrong, I promise to pull you back into yourself."

"And what will this accomplish?" the knife asked.

Now Alyanna did glance at Nel, and her cold disdain at being questioned was evident. "We are all masters of what happens in our own minds. Keilan would gain some measure of control over the child by drawing it into his dreamspace. We could learn much about these creatures, perhaps even how to sever the connection that binds this particular Chosen to Keilan." The sorceress shrugged. "I have my suspicions about the nature of these demons. Have you heard them speak, for instance?"

The question surprised him. Keilan thought back to the ruins of Menekar, the demons arrayed outside of the unholy temple they'd constructed. Their voices had been the hoarse whisperings of many children layered over each other. He nodded.

"At first I believed that the reason they speak as one is because they are truly one entity manifesting itself in several forms." She frowned, as if uncertain about her own speculations. "But after glimpsing the mind of the Chosen through the bond you share, another possibility has become more likely. Perhaps they speak with a single voice because one of the demons dominates the others. If we could draw another of the spirits away from the rest, I might be able to better understand how they are linked, and then apply this knowledge to cutting what binds you to them . . . or sundering their own souls from each other."

"The risks—"

"Must be taken," Alyanna interjected sharply, silencing Nel. She gestured towards the dark shapes farther out in the cave, clustered around the flickering oases of light. "These are desperate times. The queen is dead. Her armies are destroyed, and the broken men here cannot help us. Forget the Skein king and his horde for a moment." She raised three fingers. "We must contend with the Chosen, along with a sorcerous Talent strong enough to humble Jan duth Verala, and the genthyaki, which – even wounded – is a power that must be respected. We need to be bold, or we will fail."

Keilan floated in the black. The substance sliding across his skin was cool, but he did not feel cold. It was thicker than water, clogging his nose and mouth, and for a brief moment he couldn't contain his rising panic, as he feared he would surely suffocate if he did not surface. He thrashed about, his arms and legs churning the darkness, until suddenly he arrived at the realization that he did not need to breathe. Keilan mastered himself, calming his racing thoughts. Hovering there in the void, he was reminded of when he had used his sorcery – his dowsing trick, his father had called it – to find fish a lifetime ago.

There were other similarities. Under the water, Keilan had never been alone. The ocean had seethed with life, swarms of motes like fireflies in the dark, glimmering at the very edge of his vision. And although the sensation was different, he knew that this abyss was inhabited as well. This time, it was not lights in the distance, but pockets of even deeper blackness imbued with cold intelligence. And there was something else . . . a great presence pressing on the edges of his awareness, as if he was an insect hovering near something too vast to fully comprehend.

Keilan was frightened, drifting in this alien place. All that kept him from panicking was the feeling of the thread linking him with where he had come from. It stretched backwards, passing out of this strange realm; as Alyanna had explained it, she held the other end tightly. When he gave the signal, she would pull him back into his own sleeping mind and safety.

At least, that was the hope.

Tamping down his nervousness, Keilan began to orient himself in the black. Now that some time had passed, he could tell that the dreamscape of the Chosen was not seamless: in some areas darkness bloomed like spilled ink, while others pulsed with muted purple flickerings that suggested mysterious shapes lurked in the dark. It reminded him of violet lightning illuminating the bellies of storm clouds – as a child, he'd thought this was the Shael stalking the sky, watching the seas below for the Deep Ones. He wasn't sure even his most outlandish imaginings could guess what the colors truly were in this place.

He reached out with his consciousness as Alyanna had shown him, searching for that hint of familiarity. At first there was nothing, just the swirling coldness as he pushed through the black. The thread behind him grew more tenuous, stretching until he feared it might break. He was just about to turn and swim back to his own mind when he felt her.

She was nearby, and he willed himself to her.

Hello? It was a single soft whisper, the darkness trembling around him.

"Hello," he replied. As he spoke, a patch of deeper blackness shifted, as if something had turned towards him.

Are you a new brother?

"No," Keilan replied as the shadowy shape floated closer.

Who are you?

"My name is Keilan."

Kay-lan. That is a strange name.

"What can I call you?"

The black shape rippled. It was quiet for a long moment.

I don't know.

"But you had a name?"

I think so. I have been here a long time.

"How did you come to this place?"

A more violent spasm passed through the shape. *I don't remember.*

If he could feel his heartbeat, Keilan was sure it would be pounding. "Come with me," he said, reaching into the roiling blackness.

His fingers brushed something cold and clammy and soft. It trembled, as if afraid, but it did not pull away. His hand moved down the length of this thing, until he found where it tapered, and there he took hold of it. He felt hardness, sharp protrusions blunted by a smooth covering layer.

A wrist. He was holding a small, delicate wrist.

"Come with me," he repeated, feeling lightheaded. The thing he held did nothing, so he took this as agreement.

With his other hand he reached behind himself and found the thread that extended beyond this place. He gripped the warm, faintly vibrating strand and tugged, like a weighted pearl diver asking to be drawn back up.

The pull was sudden and violent. He would have screamed as he was yanked backwards if he hadn't been so surprised. The darkness swirled and eddied around him, and then it was gone, light rushing to fill the void. Streams of shimmering colors surged around him for the briefest of moments, and then a blinding white light obliterated his senses.

Dark swells rippled into the horizon.

He stood on a beach. Small waves broke upon the shore, then slid hissing across the sand. The cool water rushed around his ankles and retreated. In the gray sky, a crescent of honking birds flew towards a hazy copper sun.

He closed his eyes and breathed deep of the sea air, the familiar smell bringing back a rush of memories. What had he been doing before he came here? This was where he belonged. This was where—

His fingers were closed around a thin, bony wrist. He opened his eyes and turned, expecting to see Sella standing there, her mismatched eyes narrowed as she stared out across the waves.

Cold surprise churned his stomach when he saw it wasn't her.

He held the arm of a girl even younger than Sella, maybe eight or nine years old. Instead of a tangle of dirty-blond locks, this girl's hair was smooth and black and glistened like water at night. The strange child turned towards him, and with another jolt of shock he saw that she was Shan: her dark eyes were uptilted, and her nose was small and broad.

"This is the ocean?" she murmured, brushing away strands of her hair that the wind had pushed across her face.

"Yes," he replied softly.

"It is beautiful." She returned her gaze to the water. Keilan saw a tear slide down her pale cheek.

"Who are you?" he asked.

Her brow crinkled while she stared out across the sea, as if she was thinking hard. "My name is . . . Yan. Ko Yan."

Keilan swallowed. Awareness of who he was and where they were was slowly seeping back to him – along with the knowledge of what *she* was. He let go of her wrist, letting her arm fall, but she did not seem to notice.

"My brother is Ko Xien. He teases me sometimes. We live by the river with Mother." The lines of confusion on her face deepened. "No. The men took me to the red towers. My master now is Lo Jin." She glanced around, as if looking for this person. "Where is he? He will be angry if I am not there to fetch his tea."

A creeping sense of unreality was stealing over Keilan. He remembered now what this girl truly was, yet he was having trouble reconciling what he saw standing beside him with the images seared into his memory of the gaunt, ragged children emerging from their temple of twisted corpses to confront Niara. He watched Ko Yan with uncertainty. Had this child been buried deep within the Chosen for all this time?

"Your master is gone," Keilan said lamely, unsure how he should respond to her. "You do not need to bring him tea."

She was quiet for another long moment. Then she nodded slowly. "I see."

"I brought you here," Keilan said quickly, gesturing at the shimmering waves. "Do you like it?"

She pursed her lips, as if considering his question carefully. Her nature seemed to be the complete opposite of his oldest friend – where Sella was wild and impetuous, this girl was measured and thoughtful.

"Yes," she said finally. The surf rushed closer again, and she watched the foaming water with a look of concentration as it enveloped her bare feet. "I like it here." She crouched to examine a small shell that had been left behind as the water receded. "Do you—"

A sudden explosion of movement beside him sent Keilan stumbling backwards; he cried out in surprise as he lost his balance and fell heavily, his hands sinking into the wet sand.

Alyanna had appeared as if she had stepped from a crease in the very air, long black hair and purple robes billowing in the wind. Without hesitating, she grabbed the little Shan girl by the scruff of her neck and began dragging her down to the sea.

"What are you doing?" Keilan cried, lurching back to his feet.

The sorceress ignored him, just as she was ignoring the girl's frantic struggles. The child's legs kicked the air and her arms flailed helplessly as Alyanna carried her closer to the water.

"Kay-lan!" the Shan girl screamed.

"Alyanna, stop!" Keilan commanded, running after her.

The sorceress waded out until the waves surged around her knees. Then she thrust the girl's head under the water and held it there. Ko Yan's small hands grabbed desperately at the hem of Alyanna's sodden robes.

Sloshing through the swells, Keilan took hold of Alyanna's arm. "Wait! Don't do this!" he cried, pulling hard.

It was like trying to move a mountain. Alyanna did not even take notice of his efforts as she pushed the girl's head deeper beneath the water. The small fingers clutching at the sorceress's robes slackened.

"Alyanna!" he shouted, just before cold hands began to squeeze his lungs. Keilan collapsed in the water, spluttering as he tried to keep his head above the waves. Something was pressing upon his chest, robbing him of his breath.

"Abominations!" he heard Alyanna shriek, but it came from a great distance, overwhelmed by the roaring in his ears. Darkness bled across his vision and he felt himself sinking . . .

Keilan came awake gasping for air, his fingers clawing at his throat.

He tried to sit up, but only managed to smash against someone who had been leaning over him. In the darkness he couldn't see who it was, but the contact seemed to dislodge something inside him and he managed a ragged, wheezing breath.

"You!"

Wizardlight flooded the cavern, the radiance scouring away the darkness. Keilan blinked, momentarily blinded.

"You dare?"

The spots faded from his vision. Alyanna loomed above him, crackling with power. Dark lightning crawled along her arms and her hair writhed like it was alive. Her eyes were wide with surprise and anger, and Keilan saw murder in her face.

Across from her was Nel, and it must have been the knife who he'd collided with when he'd awoken. Her mouth was set and she was brandishing one of her daggers in the direction of the raging sorceress.

Alyanna gestured towards Nel, and Keilan felt a surge of sorcery. Fear stabbed him.

"No!" he rasped, certain the knife was about to be torn asunder by the sorceress.

The sorcery melted away before it could envelop Nel.

Alyanna's jaw dropped as Keilan gave a choking cry of relief. The sorceress's eyes narrowed and a filament of darkness whipped out to wrap itself around Nel, but as the glistening thread touched the knife, it too vanished.

Nel flinched like she was about to hurl her knife, but then she thought better of it. Instead, she held up the thing in her other hand; whatever it was gleamed white in the harsh wizardlight.

Bone. She held a knob of bone threaded by a silver chain. Nel was carrying the amulet Senacus had used to hide his power. She must have taken it from the paladin; Keilan remembered dimly that he had seen her scoop something from the ground when she had gone to retrieve the Pure's white-metal sword from where it had fallen in the lichyard.

"I was about to destroy one of them," the sorceress said to Nel with cold fury, stalking closer. Even though she had proven her immunity to sorcery, the knife still took a quick step back.

"Look at him!" Nel said, gesturing at Keilan with the point of her dagger.

Alyanna hesitated, her eyes narrowing, as if she expected some trick.

"Look!" Nel cried, louder than before.

What is she talking about? Keilan glanced down at himself. Black lines were etched into his skin, crawling up his arms. His hand went to his neck and he felt hard and swollen veins pulsing in his throat. And now that he could breathe again, he noticed the fire coursing through his body. He moaned, his head spinning.

"He was dying!" Nel cried, and through his haze Keilan felt her beside him, keeping him from toppling over.

"Touch me again with that *thing*," Alyanna hissed, "and I'll bring this mountain down on top of you!"

With a snarl of frustration she whirled on her heel and strode away, her wizardlight following her. The shadows rushed in as she departed, swallowing Nel as she knelt beside Keilan.

"Are you all right?"

Keilan took a deep, shuddering breath. The pain in his body was slowly abating. "Yes," he said shakily, reaching out to grip her arm in thanks.

"I had to wake you," Nel explained. "I could see that evil swelling in you. I thought you were going to die! I didn't know what to do, so I touched you both with the bone of the Pure . . ."

He felt her lift her hand, as if to show him what it held. In the blackness he could not see the amulet, but the dangling chain brushed his leg.

"What happened?" she asked.

Keilan tried to swallow away the dryness in his throat, unable to answer.

18: JAN

OVER THE NEXT few days, Jan drifted in and out of consciousness. The phantasms that had plagued him since his injury had vanished, but he was still weak and exhausted, and had trouble staying awake for more than a short while. Every time he came to himself, however, he felt like a small sliver of his strength had returned.

During this time he was unable to speak more with the queen, as she was always asleep when he woke. Once or twice he thought she was speaking to him, but these mutterings were actually conversations carried out in her dreams. She was afflicted by terrible nightmares: he was startled several times when she whimpered or moaned while tossing back and forth.

It was one of these cries that had woken him, he thought, though she had subsided into uneasy murmuring by the time he became fully aware of his surroundings. He lay there, his heart pounding. The night was dark, the interior of their prison black as pitch. He couldn't see her, but the small sounds Cein was making did give him some measure of comfort. No noises came from outside, and the wagon was still.

Slowly, the darkness became less complete. He could make out the blacker lump that was the queen, and he could see a few faint points of light through the narrow windows. He found his thoughts wandering. Why had the Skein kept him alive? The queen he could understand, perhaps, as she was a valuable hostage. Him, however? And where were they going? They had been traveling for days, and he assumed the direction was north, deeper into the Frostlands, as the air had grown steadily colder. But why—

His breath caught in his throat as fear swept through him. A tall, crooked shape lurked in the corner of their prison. Jan swallowed. It must be his imagination playing tricks on him. However, it did not dissolve into nothing the longer he stared at it; if anything, it seemed to grow more distinct. He couldn't help but remember the stories he'd heard in the Bhalavan of the Nightfather, the hoary old god who watched from the shadows, waiting, and could only be seen after death had come swirling down. Jan almost pinched himself to make sure he hadn't died in his sleep, but then sighed at his own foolishness. The gods of these barbarians were certainly not real.

The shape moved. It shuffled closer, detaching from the wall and coming to loom over the queen. Jan's mouth was dry, and though he wanted to yell out a warning, he managed only a hoarse rattling.

Pale light flooded the wagon as a sphere of wizardlight materialized above the shoulder of the White Worm shaman. Lask turned from staring down at the queen to regard Jan with his unnaturally blue eyes. His thin lips twitched when he saw Jan was awake.

"Sorcerer," he said softly. "You've returned to the land of the living."

Fragments of memories came to Jan. He remembered his face pressed against cold iron, the shaman on the other side of his prison. Lask had taunted him, showing him something. Then the shaman had put whatever it was in his mouth . . .

"Your strength impresses me. A lesser man's spirit would have perished long ago."

Jan propped himself up on his elbows. In the presence of the White Worm shaman the emptiness where his eye had been had begun to itch terribly, but with an act of will he kept his hands at his sides.

Despite his fear and hatred of this sorcerer, he couldn't restrain his curiosity. "Why are we here? What do you want from us?"

Lask studied him for a long moment without answering. His sunken cheeks were pools of shadows in the wizardlight's wan radiance. "I want to know how alike we are," he finally said.

Jan nearly choked in surprise. "Alike? We are nothing alike."

Lask tilted his head to one side, his brow creasing. "Surely you know that is not true. We are special, you and I." He gestured with a long fingernail at the motionless queen. "And she is, as well."

"We are all Talents," Jan hissed. "That is all we share in common."

"Hm," Lask grunted. "Let us find out if that is true."

He snapped his fingers and the queen shuddered awake, gasping.

"Your Highness," he murmured, stepping back as she moved her arms and legs weakly.

She managed to push herself to her hands and knees, staring up balefully at the shaman.

"Do you require anything? Satin pillows? Sweetmeats? Spiced wine?"

Cein d'Kara said nothing, her face twisted in hatred.

Lask turned back to Jan, and it almost looked like there was a trace of amusement in his eyes. He sniffed, his nose wrinkling. "At the very least we must clean these rushes. It smells like they have been soiled, and that is not fitting for a queen's chamber. Surely you have never suffered such squalid conditions." He raised a thin eyebrow. "That, at least, is one way we differ."

The shaman crouched beside the queen and stroked her cheek with his long fingernail. For a moment Jan was surprised that she did not flinch or try to strike his hand away, but then he saw how her jaw was tensed and her brow gleamed with sweat in the sallow wizardlight. He was holding her immobile with his sorcery, taunting her with how powerless she was while collared.

"Leave her be," Jan croaked, struggling to stand.

Lask watched him dispassionately. Jan felt no swelling of sorcery, but suddenly his limbs froze, hardening into stone. He toppled forward, his face striking the floor of the wagon. Then he was lifted by an unseen force and pushed roughly against the wall.

Lask's mouth quirked. "So many years have flowed over you, yet they did not lead you to wisdom. You know things, though, sorcerer. Secrets of the past." His finger drifted down to brush the metal collar around the queen's neck. "This artifact and others like it have been worn by the women of my adopted tribe for centuries. They thought them trifling baubles. It was not until the servants of the Skin Thief came to us that I learned the true power of these little circlets." The shaman settled himself cross-legged on the floor. "You think me a barbarian, but you are wrong. A barbarian does not know he is ignorant. He believes the old ways and the traditions his father taught him are in fact superior. A purer, more holy way of life." Lask shook his head slowly. "I suffer from no such foolish sentimentality. I have seen the wonders the Min-Ceruthans crafted." His gaze flicked to Jan. "Your people."

"And you think I can bring them back? Whatever you've seen is just a fading echo of what once was. That age is dead."

"The dead nourish the living," Lask replied. "It is the way."

Again, a hazy memory swam up from the depths. The shaman had said this before as he crouched outside Jan's cell, when he had – and now Jan forced himself to face what had happened that day, and the horror of it made his skin tingle – when he had *eaten* what remained of his eye. Jan's gorge rose. What kind of man was this?

"Are you like me?" Lask mused, tapping his chin with a bony finger. "Has there ever been another with my gifts? Or am I uniquely blessed? Those are questions I want answered." He stood suddenly, the wagon's door swinging open behind him. "Come," he said simply, then in a swirl of dark robes he vanished into the night.

Jan glanced at the queen. She was still on her hands and knees, staring after the shaman with a look of absolute loathing. The power holding him fast had slackened its grip, but he did not think he had the strength to follow the sorcerer, even if he wanted to. The wizardlight that had remained in the wagon flickered and went out, darkness rushing back to envelop them once more.

"What should we do?" Jan asked the queen, but before she could answer he felt invisible hands plucking at his clothes, and he was lifted to his feet. The manacle around his leg snapped open and something shoved him from behind, making him stumble forward a few steps. He would have fallen on his face again, but strands of sorcery held him up like a puppet on strings. Jan ground his teeth at the ignominy of it all. Such manipulations were simple enough for a Talent, but using them on another sorcerer, especially one who had been collared, was once considered an unforgiveable humiliation.

Lask certainly did not know this, and Jan doubted very much he would have cared even if he did.

Carried along by the sorcery, he stumbled out of the wagon. A bracing wind swept from the darkness, stinging his face, and his boots sank into snow. In the distance Jan could see the glimmer of many fires, and very faintly the sound of barking laughter carried across the empty plain. The moon was hidden this night, but the sky was ablaze with innumerable stars, sharp and glittering.

A pained grunt came from beside him as Cein d'Kara was compelled from the wagon. She swayed like she would topple over, but the sorcery kept her upright. Her face was a mask of frozen rage, her eyes fixed on the shaman as he strode in the opposite direction to the Skein camp.

Sorcery pulled at Jan, but more gently than before, as if he was being given the chance to follow under his own power. To his surprise, Jan found that he was able to slog through the snow without falling, though his legs and back ached horribly from the weeks he'd spent huddled on stone and wood. He heard the queen's crunching steps behind him, and he wondered if she also walked under her own volition.

The wizardlight hovered over Lask's head as he led them across the snowy field. At the edge of the radiance Jan glimpsed a tangle of dark trees and boulders; the shadows pooled in the crevices made it seem like there were faces leering at them from the stones. Jan shivered, shoving his hands into his armpits. The cold was like a living thing, creeping along his exposed skin, making his ears and nose burn. If he stayed too long out here he risked losing toes or fingers to frostbite, despite the layers of furs he wore.

The shaman must have wrapped himself in sorcery, since his thin black robes would have provided little real warmth. His head was uncovered; he hadn't even bothered to draw up his hood. Jan peered past him, into the night. Where was he leading them?

As if in answer to his unspoken question, a black shape suddenly swelled from the darkness. It was like the wagon they had just left, a box of wood on curved runners. Empty harnesses lay in the snow; no doubt the horses that had pulled the wagon during the day had been brought closer to the campfires after the Skein had stopped for the night.

Lask halted outside the darkened wagon and turned back to Jan and the queen. In the harsh light of his sorcery, his emaciated face with its sunken features made it seem like a skull was perched atop his robes.

"A huntsman found me in a place like this," he said, gesturing towards the shadowy brambles encroaching on his wizardlight. "A babe in the snow." He stared into the blackness, as if imagining that long-ago day. "Though that was pure chance, as I was not crying as I lay there among the roots of a dead tree. He feared I was unnatural, but still he returned with me to his home and offered me to his wife to replace the son she had lost that winter." Lask smiled bitterly. "How different my life might have been if that woman had loved me and raised me as her own. But such a life was not to be my fate." The shaman's face twisted. "She told her husband that I must be a demon cloaked in the skin of a man, a spawn of one of the Skin Thief's servants, and demanded that he return me to where I had been found. So he brought me again into the woods."

Lask fell silent for a moment, and Jan heard in the stillness the queen's chattering teeth. His own body was slowly going numb, but she looked to be suffering far more, whatever little strength she'd recovered being drawn out by the freezing cold.

"She needs to get warm, or she'll die right here in the snow," he told the shaman.

Lask glanced at them with disinterest, but a moment later a blanket of pulsing heat wrapped Jan. He nearly cried out in relief.

"Can you imagine?" the shaman continued, as if he had not been interrupted. "A newborn babe, abandoned in the depths of the Frostlands? What mother would do such a thing?"

"P-p-perhaps one who knew what you are," answered the queen, and Jan's heart fell. Surely the shaman would withdraw the cloak of warmth he'd cast over them.

Instead, Lask's mouth twitched in a slight smile. "What I am," he repeated, as if amused. "The huntsman did know what I was, it seemed. He did not throw me in the snow, as my own mother must have done. He brought me deep into the wilds, to the hut of a woman who was known to be a witch. He offered me to her, and later she would tell me that she accepted me because I did not cry, despite the coldness of the day and the trauma I had suffered." Lask tilted his head, as if reconsidering what he had said. "Or perhaps even then she could sense the power coiling within me."

"Your sorcery would not have manifested itself so early," Jan said.

Lask fixed piercing blue eyes on him. Even coddled by the magical heat, Jan felt a chill.

"I am not a sorcerer like you," Lask said, with such apparent seriousness that Jan could not hide his surprise.

"Of course you are."

The shaman shook his head, and Jan glanced at Cein d'Kara in confusion. The queen looked wary, as if unsure what the Skein meant by this. Clearly he was a sorcerer.

"I am not," he said simply, and turned back to the wagon. He climbed the wooden steps, and with a sweep of his hand a metal bolt slid away and the door swung open. "Come," he commanded, and then moved into the darkness within.

Jan hesitated, unsure of what he would find inside. Cein took a step forward and he reached out to grasp her robes, unable to tamp down his fear. The shaman was mad, that was clear.

Lask's voice floated from within. "The witch raised me. Sometimes she showed me such affection I thought I must truly be her child; at other times she lashed me with a whip of thorns and forced me to sleep outside. She was like the weather in winter: one moment the sun shines, the next a flensing wind cuts to the bone. I loved and hated her, it is true, but above all else I envied her."

The wizardlight drifted within the wagon, and Jan saw that the shaman was standing just inside the entrance. Beyond him, the far wall was still shrouded in darkness, but Jan sensed that something was there.

"I envied her power. The way the birds dipped their heads to her on the branches as she moved among the trees, the way she summoned fire from nothing, the way all the beasts and the men feared her. But I had none of her gifts. I was different; I could not weave the invisible forces of the world as she could. Yet living in the wilds had taught me a very important lesson: life is a circle. Strength is passed from one creature to another in an endless cycle."

Beside Jan, the queen sucked in her breath, as if she knew what he would say next.

"And so I killed her. I shattered her skull with a rock as she slept, then I ate her heart, as the bear eats the salmon or the falcon the mouse. And I felt her power bloom within me, and I knew that what I had done was a good thing. A true thing."

"You were always a Talent," Jan insisted, overcoming his shock at what the shaman had shared. "Sorcery does not pass like that from one to another."

"Perhaps," Lask mused. "But the witch was not the last sorcerer I consumed, and each time I felt my power grow. She was the strongest, though . . . until I tasted you, Min-Ceruthan."

Jan felt dizzy, his fingers going to his eye patch. The memories he had suppressed sharpened, and his gorge rose. They were at the mercy of a madman.

"And sorcery is not the only thing I can gain. How old do you think I am?"

Jan blinked, surprised by this sudden question. Lask looked to only have seen twenty or so years, his skin smooth and unblemished. Rather than say anything else, though, Jan merely shrugged.

"Nearly fifty winters," the shaman gloated, holding up his hand as if flaunting his youth. "I have barely aged since I consumed my mother."

He was lying. He must be. Such a thing was impossible.

"Come," Lask repeated, beckoning them inside the wagon. "Let us see how similar we truly are."

The force pulling at Jan became more insistent, and reluctantly he went up the steps and entered the wagon. As he stepped inside, the wizardlight flared brighter, revealing the far side of the space.

Jan staggered backwards, and if not for the shaman's sorcery he might have fallen. No. This was impossible. Ever since he'd realized that he was not truly a crofter in the Shattered Kingdoms, his life had been a litany of surprises and revelations . . . but nothing – nothing – had prepared him for what huddled against the far wall.

The cold wizardlight slid over the spines and claws and black chitinous flesh of a genthyaki. The creature was draped with chains, a half-dozen thick manacles of black iron encircling its limbs and torso and neck. Streaks of dark ichor encrusted its body, and its face had been scarred by fire. One of its clawed hands was missing, lopped off at the wrist; the injury was ghastly, as the stump had been cauterized crudely. For a moment Jan thought the monster was dead, but then he saw its nictating lids slide over its yellow eyes and he realized it was watching them.

A genthyaki. They were supposed to be extinct, destroyed by the combined power of the Star Towers and the holdfasts over a thousand years ago.

What was such a creature doing *here*?

"What is that thing?" Cein d'Kara asked. Her voice was remarkably steady given what a shock it was to see one of the shape changers in their true form for the first time.

Lask stepped closer to the genthyaki, and to Jan's great surprise, the monster flinched away from him.

The shaman turned to face them again, as if unconcerned by the span-long claws and barbed tail of the monster. Even hindered by the heavy chains, Jan thought it could reach out and impale Lask. Yet it did not.

"That is the question, Your Highness. I thought it was the Skin Thief himself, at first, the way it wore the form of other men."

He crouched beside the monster and pressed a hand to its glistening flesh; his fingers came away streaked with black ichor, and he showed them to Jan and the queen. "But do gods bleed? If they do, I claim that they do not deserve our worship." Lask wiped the creature's blood off on one of its curving spines. "It came to me when it was near death. Weak."

Jan wondered why the genthyaki was not using its sorcery – every one of the creatures had been powerfully strong, a few even as gifted as the greatest of human Talents. Then he caught sight of the tarnished dark-metal collar. The genthyaki's neck was far too thick for it, but someone had placed the magic-inhibiting artifact around its wrist as a bracelet. Even wrapped in chains and robbed of its sorcery, Jan knew how deadly these creatures were. He wondered if the Skein shaman understood what he had imprisoned.

"God or not, it has power." Lask bent down and picked up a dark-stained wooden bowl. A dagger had appeared in his other hand.

The genthyaki whimpered, baring its rows of fangs. Its tail lashed, thumping the floor, but it did not try to strike the shaman.

Lask approached the monster, then casually slashed its sunken chest with his dagger; black blood gushed forth, flowing down around the spiny thorns covering its flesh. The shaman held out the bowl so that some of the ichor spilled inside. The genthyaki panted, trembling in terror, a line of drool suspended from its open jaws. Jan had never realized that these things could even feel fear, and to see such a predator reduced to this unnerved him like nothing else he'd ever encountered.

Lask sheathed his knife and stepped away from the cowering monster, holding the bowl with both hands. "I thought the children served this beast, but in truth it served them. And it failed in its tasks." He raised the bowl to Jan and the queen, then closed his eyes and drank from it. A dribble of black blood escaped from the corner of his mouth and ran down his chin.

Behind him, the genthyaki whined and writhed. "I asked, and they gave it to me, so that I might grow stronger for the challenges ahead."

Color bloomed in the shaman's cheeks. As he lowered the bowl, Jan saw his lips were painted black. Jan felt lightheaded, the strangeness of this moment pressing down on him. The walls . . . the walls of the wagon seemed to constrict and expand in time with the shaman's slow breathing. It was almost like reality was threatening to be torn away, revealing . . . something else. The shaman's eyes flicked open, and to Jan it seemed like their unnatural blueness had deepened even further.

"Drink," Lask said, holding out the bowl.

The horror and disgust in the queen's face mirrored what Jan was feeling at the invitation.

"Drink," the shaman repeated, coming closer. "I told you I want to see how similar we are. I have never met others with power like mine. But are we the same?" He offered up the bowl to Jan.

"No," he murmured, shaking his head. "I won't."

Lask's expression did not change as he drifted closer to the queen. Steel rasped as he drew his dagger and pressed it to the queen's neck, just above the metal torc that suppressed her sorcery. "Drink, or I will empty her next." He brought his face closer so that his mouth nearly brushed her ear. "She will be sweet."

The queen's face was carefully blank, but Jan saw the hate and hopelessness in her eyes. She would not beg, he knew.

Jan raised his trembling hands, and the shaman gave over the bowl. He stared at the thick, inky liquid, his stomach churning.

A line of blood ran down the queen's throat and slid along the metal collar. He saw her flinch in pain, blinking away tears.

He raised the bowl to his lips and drank. It was warm and bitter, and he nearly gagged before he managed to swallow. Shuddering, he held out the bowl for the shaman. He wasn't sure what he had been expecting – a rush of power, clenching pain – but he felt nothing except a faint nausea. The walls did not breathe, the world did not ripple.

Interest was evident in Lask's face. "So we are not the same," he mused as he turned to the queen. "Now you," he said, holding out the bowl. "Perhaps the young are different than the old."

19: KEILAN

"UNACCEPTABLE."

Lord d'Venish delivered this pronouncement with cold finality, and Keilan's heart fell. Vhelan, though, appeared undeterred as he stepped closer to the glowering commander, spreading his arms wide.

"Please reconsider, my lord. Our situation calls for bold action."

D'Venish's eyes bulged, as if he couldn't believe what he was hearing. "Bold action, Magister?" He threw out his arm, indicating the lights scattered about the great cave and the men huddled around them. "The time for action, bold or otherwise, is long since passed. I have fifty men, barely half of them fit enough to march. Out there are barbarians and monsters in a vast frozen wasteland." He crossed his vambraced arms over his cuirass, his mouth set in a thin line. "No; the very idea is unthinkable. We would have to leave the injured behind."

Vhelan sighed, placing his hand on the officer's shoulder. D'Venish regarded this affront in mild astonishment. "You are correct, my lord. Our situation is dire. But eventually we will have to leave these caves; our rations are nearly used up, yes?"

"We can scavenge more from the battlefield," d'Venish said, shrugging away Vhelan's offending hand.

"To what end? How long can we persist in this place?"

"When I do decide to abandon this bolt hole, we will make a dash for the Serpent," d'Venish replied angrily. "In the opposite direction to where those bastard Skein have gone!"

"There is a great threat in the north—"

The Dymorian officer cut Vhelan off with a sharp slice of his hand. "Absolute raving madness. Demons waking gods to bring about the end of the world? What foolish nonsense. No, I won't listen to this anymore." He turned away as Vhelan opened his mouth again, showing his back to the magister. "Make yourself useful, sorcerer, and think of a way your magic can help us get out of this mess. I'm finished speaking on these matters." He beckoned for one of the soldiers waiting nearby to approach.

Vhelan looked like he was going to make another attempt at convincing the commander, but before he could, Keilan tugged on the sleeve of his robe and motioned with his head that they should leave.

The sorcerer considered this for a moment, then gave a little shrug and moved to follow Keilan as he clambered down the rocky mound that served as d'Venish's command post in the cavern.

"Unfortunate but understandable," Vhelan said when they reached the bottom and set off towards the fire where they'd left Nel.

Keilan glanced behind them at the shadowy silhouettes of the officer and his soldiers, their heads bent together in conference. The thought that d'Venish would ever even entertain the notion of accompanying them as they went off in pursuit of the Chosen and the Skein had always seemed to him exceedingly unrealistic. But Vhelan and Nel believed that having an armed escort would greatly increase their chances of making it through the Frostlands – especially if Alyanna's anger did not abate and she decided to truly leave them behind.

Nel was sitting cross-legged near a smoldering pile of kindling, dragging a whetstone along one of her daggers. A selection of small lizards and rodents were thrust close to the flames, impaled on wooden skewers. The sight made Keilan's stomach turn.

Nel looked up as they approached, then snorted when she saw their expressions. "I told you."

Vhelan settled beside her and reached for one of the skewers. He examined the leathery, crisped creature dubiously, then set it back down. "This was but the opening gambit," he said, with far more cheer than seemed possible. "Allowing us to take all the men always seemed a bit far-fetched. I fully expect that given enough time and patience I can wheedle at least a few of the rangers out of him."

"We'll need them," Nel grumbled, examining the edge of the dagger Keilan thought was Chance. "It might take weeks to get where the demons are going, and I have about as much chance of catching game as you do of finding winter grapes and squeezing them into wine."

At the mention of wine, Vhelan's expression turned wistful. "Ah. I was actually hoping we could look about for the supply wagons and see if any bottles survived the battle. I think a bit of drink might lift everyone's spirits."

Nel stared at him flatly as she sheathed her dagger. Vhelan offered a weak smile, shrugging. "Just a thought."

Keilan doubted very much if wine would be enough to improve the mood of the men. Most seemed broken, spending their days huddled around the flames, staring blankly out at the darkness. Keilan couldn't imagine what horrors they had experienced on the battlefield, but it must have been terrible indeed. Or perhaps they were wallowing in their hopelessness, having lost their queen and companions and certain that they would also die far from their homes.

Keilan certainly could sympathize. Vhelan and Nel were making plans like they thought there was still a chance of destroying the Chosen with Niara's dagger, but without the Crimson Queen or Alyanna helping them, Keilan had no illusions. The Skein sorcerer alone could destroy them all without lifting a finger.

If only Alyanna would return. The sorceress had stormed off in a rage after Nel interrupted her attack on the Chosen, taking her flying disc and sack of deadly artifacts and leaving the cave. That had been two days ago, he guessed; Keilan had found it very hard to keep track of time while inside the mountain. He was surprised she hadn't also taken the black-metal dagger, but maybe she had even more fearsome weapons. Or she believed that the dagger wouldn't be as useful as they'd hoped.

"The Crone was asking for you," Nel said, drawing him out of his increasingly bleak thoughts.

"Oh?"

Keilan had gone to visit her several times since that first day in the caves, but she had always been asleep or lost in deliriums brought on by whatever they were giving her for her pain. The soldier caring for her had confided in Keilan that he thought she only had a few days to live. That saddened him greatly; yes, Lady Numil was very old, older even than Mam Ru, but her mind had still been stiletto-sharp.

A stir from the soldiers around the nearest fire distracted him. When he saw what it was, he grabbed Vhelan's shoulder excitedly.

"It's her!"

Alyanna was striding towards them, bathed in the pale radiance of her wizardlight, the chavenix trailing behind her. Nel and Vhelan scrambled to their feet, both eyeing the approaching sorceress with wary apprehension. Keilan noticed that the knife's fingers hadn't left the hilt of the dagger she'd been sharpening.

Alyanna halted a few paces away and crossed her arms, her face serious. "I have news."

"Where did you go?" Keilan blurted, relieved that the sorceress had returned to them.

"I went out to learn what I could about our enemies. I thought it best to keep away from that one" —she jerked her head in Nel's direction— "while my anger was still hot. I went to the battlefield and the . . . sculpture, hoping to find some clues about the Chosen, perhaps an insight into their natures."

"What did you discover?" Nel asked.

Alyanna scowled at her. "Only that a tremendous amount of sorcery was unleashed here, and that you were exceedingly foolish to stop me from destroying that creature."

"Keilan might have died," Nel said quietly through gritted teeth.

"It was a risk I was willing to take," Alyanna replied tartly. "For all we know, the death of one of these things would destroy them all. Even the boy agrees with me." She glanced at Keilan expectantly.

"I . . . I don't think that girl was evil. It felt to me like she's lost and lonely."

Alyanna threw up her arms in frustration. "Well, I hope you didn't get too attached to her! We are still going to destroy them, yes?"

Vhelan cleared his throat. "Ahem. So what is your news?"

A triumphant smile spread across the sorceress's face. "Rejoice, magister. Your Crimson Queen is alive."

D'Venish was still deep in conversation with a pair of soldiers when Vhelan and Keilan returned, trailed by Nel and Alyanna. He saw them making their way up the mound and raised his eyes to the darkness above in obvious exasperation.

"I haven't changed my mind in the half watch since you left, Magister."

"We come bearing news of tremendous import, Commander," said Vhelan.

The Dymorian officer seemed taken aback by the giddiness in the sorcerer's voice. With a frown, he dismissed the grizzled soldiers he'd been speaking with.

"What is it?" he asked after the soldiers had drawn far enough away to give them some privacy.

"The queen isn't dead."

D'Venish reeled back like he had been struck. The annoyed impatience in his face changed to shock.

"Impossible," he hissed when he'd gathered himself, his eyes narrowing suspiciously. "Don't you dare jest about such a thing, Magister."

Vhelan shook his head, grinning. "I would never, Commander." He turned and swept a hand out towards Alyanna. "The sorceress who arrived with Keilan and my servant has sensed her. She must have been captured by the Skein."

Several conflicting emotions warred across the officer's face. "Who is she? And why can she sense Queen Cein, but you cannot?"

"My power is far greater than his," Alyanna stated, stepping forward. Keilan noticed she ignored his first question; if d'Venish realized she was the sorceress who had challenged Cein d'Kara atop Ravenroost then convincing him that they should be allies now would be that much more difficult.

"I have communicated with your queen before through her dreams. It is an art lost to the sorcerers of Dymoria. Last night on a whim I tried to reach out to her, expecting to find nothing but emptiness. Yet there was something. A distant flickering – I tried to draw her into my own dreams, but she would not come. Sometimes, if another mind is drifting between sleep and wakefulness, it cannot manifest itself completely in the dream worlds our consciousnesses create. But she is most definitely alive."

D'Venish's brow furrowed as if he was having trouble following what Alyanna was saying. "Her dreams, you say?" He turned back to Vhelan, his frustration evident. "Is this a ploy to get me to agree to your mad quest, Magister?"

Vhelan held up his hands, as if to quickly forestall this line of thinking. "Commander, no. This sorceress's power dwarfs my own – dwarfs any in the Scholia save the queen herself. She has the ability. And you must know I would never lie about such a thing. I do believe she is telling the truth."

The commander slowly pulled off his leather glove and wiped a hand across his forehead, then pinched the bridge of his nose. For a moment his hard countenance fell away, and Keilan saw how young d'Venish truly was – a junior officer thrust into a position of authority far beyond his years and experience. He had certainly suffered the same trauma as the soldiers he was trying to keep alive, but because he was the highest-ranking surviving officer, he had been forced to shoulder all the burdens. Keilan felt a pang of sympathy for the commander.

When d'Venish dropped his hand and looked up again, it seemed as if he'd come to a decision. There was still wariness in his face, but Keilan saw hope as well. The commander took a deep breath and let it out slowly.

"If there's any hope the queen is alive, we must try and rescue her. Our lives are nothing when weighed against hers."

Vhelan clapped his hands together. "Excellent!"

D'Venish's hand slipped to the pommel of his sword as he gazed out at the scattered flames flickering in the cave's darkness. "A score of the men are too injured to travel. I'll have to leave a few others behind to care for them, and at least two of the rangers should head south. Vis is much closer than Herath – perhaps they can convince the prince to rescue those we leave here." He turned back to Vhelan. "And that leaves thirty men. Not enough to overcome a Skein warband, but perhaps large enough to rescue the queen." His voice was strengthening as he spoke, as if he was growing more excited about the idea.

"Commander!"

They all turned as another soldier appeared atop the rocks. He was gasping for breath, as if he had run here.

"Ben?"

"Commander, the Lady Numil has awoken. But Xan says she doesn't have much longer. She's requesting to see the newcomers."

The Crone of Lyr looked to have aged a decade since Keilan had last stood in her presence. The lines on her face had deepened, her tiny black eyes receding into the waxy folds of her skin. Her skeletal fingers were curled into claws and clutched at the hem of the blanket drawn up to her chin. He might have thought she'd already sunk down into the Deep, except that her hands were shivering.

Her head shifted slightly as they approached. The torchlight made her eyes glitter like flecks of obsidian.

"Took your damn time," she muttered. Her voice rasped as she struggled to draw forth words.

"I'm sorry," Keilan replied. "I thought you were sleeping."

"I'm done with sleeping," snapped the Lady Numil. "The ones here want me to just float away into oblivion." She shook her head. "Bah. I'll stride into the dark with my wits about me, thank you very much."

"A little more rest, good lady, and you'll be back on your—"

The Crone interrupted Vhelan with a snort. "Ha. I'm never leaving this horrid cave, I know that. I'm no fool." She squinted at the magister. "Wait. Vhelan, eh? Surprised to see you alive. How did you manage to survive those demons?"

Vhelan blinked, apparently surprised by the Lady Numil's questioning. "Sorcery enveloped the ridge. I remember a bright flash, then darkness, and when I awoke I found that I'd tumbled onto a ledge below where we'd gathered. I could hear sounds coming from above . . . the demons desecrating the bodies, I believe."

The Crone's mouth twisted as a spasm of pain went through her. "Eh. You always had the Silver Lady's own . . . *ng* . . . luck."

"The queen is alive," Keilan interrupted, and her eyes snapped to him.

"Truly?"

He glanced at Alyanna, who had stayed back, half-hidden in the darkness. "Yes. We are going to try and rescue her."

A thin smile crept across the Crone's face. "Good. Perhaps there's hope yet."

Keilan crouched beside her and covered her hand with his. "There is, Lady Numil. We will find the queen and destroy the demons with the weapon we found. I promise you."

"You promise me," she murmured, her gaze unfocusing. "Sweet boy."

"Lady Numil!" Keilan cried, his fingers tightening around her hand.

For a moment, her attention sharpened again. "Eh. The darkness is creeping closer, Keilan. But you've lifted my heart. Take comfort in that. Oh." She pulled her hand free and pointed with a shaking finger at where packs and blankets were heaped near the torches. "The swords."

For a moment Keilan was confused, and then he saw the twisting silver serpents of the sword hilts emerging from the piled supplies.

"Telion . . . he was a good man. He . . . had a son." The Lady Numil grimaced, struggling with every word. "Just a boy. But those swords should go to him."

Keilan nodded, and the Crone let her hand fall. The strength seemed to be slipping from her as he watched.

"Good lad," she said. "Now . . . go save my city."

Her eyes fluttered closed.

20: CHO LIN

RECESSED AMONG A thick copse of pine trees, Cho Lin watched the men approach. She'd heard them from far away, their harsh laughter and voices raised in raucous song, but she hadn't been sure of their number until they crested the snowy hillock and emerged onto the field bounded by the woods in which she waited. Given the clamor, Cho Lin had been expecting a great host; she was slightly surprised when she saw it was only a couple dozen Skein. More than a few of their faces were flushed by drink, and they swayed unsteadily upon their shaggy horses. Some were taking lusty swigs from bottles of green and blue glass, and this also surprised her, as she'd not seen any such containers during her time in Nes Vaneth. The Skein drank ale and mead from tankards and horns, not wine from glass bottles.

Cho Lin receded among the branches as they neared where she hid, though she suspected they were too deep in their cups to notice her unless she walked out into their path and waved her arms. Now that they were closer, she saw the deer tines affixed to some of their helms – these were Stag warriors, like

Verrigan had been, sworn to the thane Kjarl. Her stomach sank as the implications of this came to her. The Stag were allies of the White Worm, and must have gone south with Hroi's army to confront the Dymorians. If they were returning to Nes Vaneth in such high spirits, drinking southern wine, that could only mean they had defeated the invaders. Utterly defeated, for if the Dymorians had merely been beaten back she suspected the Skein would have chased them across the Serpent. The threat must have been extinguished—which meant the Crimson Queen was dead if she had accompanied her army into the Frostlands.

If that was true, Cho Lin needed a new plan.

The thought that she could convince Cein d'Kara to reforge the Sword of Cho had always been unlikely. By the Four Winds, she didn't even know if that would restore the blade's potency. But that vanishingly slim chance had been what she was clinging to, and seeing the Skein returning triumphant made her feel like she'd swallowed an iron ingot.

She wished she could confront them about what had happened to the south, but if they remembered her at all, it would be as a prisoner.

Grinding her teeth in frustration, Cho Lin slunk away, retreating deeper into the woods. Her boots crunched in the snow and a flurry of bright red birds burst from the branches above her, rising shrieking into the sky. She did not worry about drawing the attention of the Skein, as the savages were clearly not worried about encountering enemies on their way back to Nes Vaneth.

Her horse snorted and tossed his head when he saw her approaching, his breath steaming in the cold morning air. She unlooped his reins from around the dead tree where she'd left him tied up and patted his cheek affectionately. His wet nose nuzzled her hand and she offered him a handful of oats before swinging herself up into the saddle.

Cho Lin gave the horse a moment to finish his breakfast, and then she kicked him lightly in the flanks. Grumbling, he resumed the plodding pace she'd gotten used to in the days since leaving Nes Vaneth. She suspected they could make better time if she left the forest, but there was far less likelihood of encountering others here among the trees. And now she knew the warriors who had gone to fight the Dymorians would be returning north. Hopefully, those thousands of Skein in their small warbands would avoid the woods; though there might be foragers, she reminded herself, so she should still be careful.

Cho Lin wished she knew what other dangers might be lurking. During the day the woods seemed empty, but she had seen tracks in the snow that had unnerved her – paw prints as large as dinner plates, and once she'd come across the eviscerated corpse of a large buck, its stomach flensed open and the remnants of its organs strewn about. A bear's work, she'd hoped, but truly she did not know what large animals dwelt in the Frostlands. At least the pine trees of these woods were spaced far enough apart that she wouldn't be taken by surprise while the sun was high.

The nights were more frightening. She kept her fires small and tried to build her shelters in the lees of boulders or dead trees, but still she felt a creeping dread when she stared out into the darkness, and every creaking branch or clump of snow sloughing from somewhere higher brought her hands to the hilts of her butterfly swords. For that reason, she hadn't been sleeping very much, and despite her best efforts to remain wary of her surroundings she kept finding herself nodding off in her saddle.

The waking and the dream world seemed to be blurring for her. If it wasn't for the incessant prickling cold, she wouldn't have been surprised to suddenly awaken in her cell back on Red Fang, the air clotted with the smell of incense. Her entire ordeal in Nes Vaneth – particularly after Jan had led her down into the bowels of the Bhalavan – had taken on the hazy edges of a half-remembered dream. Had she really followed a spirit below the ruins and been confronted by the ghost of her father? Could she trust the vision she'd seen in those blue flames?

Assuming that everything she had experienced was real, what should she do now? Cho Lin pondered this as she guided her horse around a fallen tree blackened by rot. Perhaps the queen still lived, despite the celebrations of the returning Skein. She could have been captured, or escaped with the remnants of her army. Cho Lin clung to these thoughts as she rode – she had no idea what other course of action she could take if the sword was unable to be repaired. She could try and find the door set in the mountain she had seen in the vision, the one the Betrayers were trying to open, but attempting to find that particular location in the vastness of the Frostlands would be like searching for a particular blossom in the imperial gardens of Tsai Yin. The truth was that even if she managed to track down the Betrayers, she had no way to fight them. All the old stories she'd been raised on had been very clear that no normal steel or iron forged by men could harm them.

Something pulled her from these bleak thoughts. She blinked, returning to herself as she gazed around the empty clearing. What was it? Nothing moved among the trees. Even the birdsong had stopped. That was a bit odd, she realized, as she'd grown accustomed to—

The ground exploded. Her horse whinnied in terror and reared back as a shape erupted from where it had been hidden under the snow; Cho Lin glimpsed white fur and yellow eyes and then she was thrown from her saddle. She landed hard, her breath driven from her, and a moment later a hoof came down a half-span from her head, spraying her with snow. Fighting through the shock, Cho Lin rolled farther away from her panicking horse and leapt to her feet, trying to make sense of what was happening.

A great beast clung to her horse, trying to bring it down. Its claws were sunk deep in her mount's flank, a long tail lashing the air. Her horse stumbled and screamed, tossing its head in desperation as jaws snapped for its throat. The beast looked like a huge white-furred tiger, though its snout was long and lupine, and there were too many legs scrabbling to find purchase in her poor mount's flesh. Six, she counted in a quick glance.

"No!" Cho Lin cried as the beast's teeth found her horse's throat and a spray of blood arced into the air.

She reached for the Nothing, drawing her butterfly swords as the cat-wolf ripped away a chunk of flesh, its white fur spattered crimson. It was so intent on savaging her dying horse that Cho Lin suspected she could have fled. But she was angry now. She watched the light fade from her horse's eyes, its back legs kicking feebly in the snow.

Cho Lin stalked forward. The creature raised its dripping jaws, a flap of skin hanging from its mouth. Its yellow eyes found her and the beast growled a warning, shifting its weight, its legs shivering as if it was preparing to leap.

"Come on!" she cried, clashing her blades together.

In response, the beast roared, baring fangs as long as her forearm.

Cho Lin charged.

This was not what the creature was expecting. She thought she saw a flicker of surprise in its eyes before it bounded from the horse's corpse. Despite its great size it landed lightly in the snow and whirled around to face her, the fur on its back bristling.

Cho Lin followed it, leading with her butterfly swords. The creature swiped at her, its claws flashing, but with her grasp on the Nothing it seemed to be moving in water; she dodged the blow and her blade lashed the blood-stained paw. The cat-wolf yowled and jumped backwards. Its gaze flickered between the steaming, sliced-open corpse of her horse and Cho Lin, as if deciding whether its kill was worth fighting this strange clawed little animal.

In this moment of hesitation Cho Lin closed the gap and leapt. Every detail of the roaring monster was etched in excruciating detail: she saw its pupils tracking her as she hurtled closer; the droplets of blood dripping from its wound as it cradled its paw; the notch in one of its ears.

She drove her swords point-first into the monster's throat. The blades slid in, half of their tapering lengths vanishing into the white fur. She let go of the hilts as her momentum carried her past the beast, tucking herself so that she struck the snow with her shoulder, and then rolled to her feet in one smooth motion.

The beast writhed, blood spurting from its ravaged neck. Cho Lin stood there, panting, and watched as its frantic movements and heaving chest slowed. Its tail was the last thing to show any life, and when it finally finished twitching, she strode up to the beast and ripped her swords from where they'd been embedded. A final gushing of blood accompanied this, soaking the white fur of its chest.

She glanced at the dead beast, then at the ruin of her horse. The supplies she'd dragged from Nes Vaneth, which she'd hoped would be enough to last for weeks, were strewn about in the snow. It was far too much for her to carry.

"Black hells," she muttered, staring into the glazed eyes of her unfortunate mount. What was she going to do now?

21: ALYANNA

WHAT A MOTLEY band they were.

Alyanna drew her knees up to her chest and held out her hands to the crackling flames, studying her companions seated around the campfire.

Useless, most of them, destined to be little more than fodder for the demons and their Skein allies. Perhaps if she was lucky they would prove distracting enough in a battle that she could land a mortal blow on one of her enemies. The Dymorian rangers, at least, had demonstrated their worth. Leaning forward, she turned the stick in front of her so that the other side of the scrawny bird skewered on its tip could crisp. She'd already torn apart one of the birds they'd brought back to camp, its greasy bones now scattered on the snow.

The Lyrish girl was watching her from across the flames, her chin glistening with the grease of her own dinner. The sounds she'd made as she consumed the pigeon had driven little spikes of annoyance through Alyanna; she'd gritted her teeth with every smack of the fool's lips, and she'd started to think that Nel was cracking the bones and sucking the marrow so loudly on purpose. Alyanna considered trying to find a way to dispose of the girl; along with being disrespectful, she was also dangerous while she carried the fingerbone of Tethys. But if Keilan discovered what she had done then she'd lose one of her greatest advantages in the coming battle. Also, the relic of Ama should be just as effective in inhibiting the power of the Chosen and the Skein sorcerer.

Beside the Lyrish thief sat the younger of the two magisters that had survived the calamitous battle. Seril was pale and fine-boned, with large dark eyes and a nervous habit of brushing aside her honey-colored fringe. Alyanna found that endearing. Seril was very shy and soft-spoken, and hadn't even managed to meet Alyanna's eyes when Vhelan, had introduced them. She reminded Alyanna of a lover she'd had in Mahlbion before the cataclysm, a junior artificer in the Palladia. The resemblance truly was uncanny, in both appearance and demeanor. Sometimes Alyanna wondered if existence was a wheel, and if men and women were all fated to be reborn again and again down throughout the ages. Many times she could have sworn she'd encountered the same person centuries ago – though, if that were true, she supposed she had broken her own wheel.

Or at least caught it in a rut for a good long while. Alyanna's fingers drifted to the corner of her eye. A few years ago, nothing had been there; now, she could feel very slight wrinkles. The souls that had preserved her youth for a thousand years had apparently been exhausted. Disturbing, but that was a problem for after she had dispatched her old servants back to the abyss.

Alyanna nodded at Seril, and the pretty magister offered back a slight smile, then ducked her head, as if embarrassed. How charming. Alyanna would have been tempted to try and relive those pleasant memories she'd once shared with the Palladian artificer, if she wasn't certain that this sorceress's chances of surviving what was coming were anything but vanishingly small.

Alyanna's gaze continued to drift around the fire. The senior magister, Vhelan, sat between Seril and Keilan. His gift was potent, stronger than his attractive colleague's, but still his power was only a tiny fraction of a true Talent. He could prove useful, though she would have to watch him carefully. Vhelan cultivated the persona of an incompetent fop, but Alyanna could see the calculations that were going on beneath this guise. Cein d'Kara must have recognized this as well, to elevate him to the position of senior magister at his age. Vhelan flashed an easy smile when he noticed her gaze lingering on him. *I see you*, she thought, wondering if he was thinking the same.

Keilan was staring blankly into the dancing flames, his face drawn. Whatever darkness the black dagger had poisoned him with weighed on him constantly. She had seen how he winced in bright sunlight and massaged his temple like he was suffering from a headache. Alyanna wondered if destroying the Chosen would cleanse their taint from him, or kill him as well. She hoped he could be saved – so much was possible when the power of Talents was combined, and he was young and malleable. Dangerous as well, though. He had slain Niara Lightspinner, perhaps the greatest sorceress Alyanna had ever encountered, and he had also badly wounded her own genthyaki servant. She would be wise not to underestimate him.

Alyanna pulled her bird skewer from the flames and stood, then began to make her way towards the boy. A burst of laughter came from one of the other fires, and she glanced at the silhouettes of the soldiers as they celebrated being under the open sky again. Alyanna had thought the survivors traumatized by their crushing defeat on the battlefield, but it seemed it had at least partially been the weight of all that stone pressing down on them while they hunkered under the mountain. She was always surprised at the resiliency of the human spirit.

Beyond the light cast by the fires lurked the dark wilds of the Frostlands. The soldiers were in good cheer tonight, but that would likely change after a few days of travel through the frozen wastes . . . and certainly if they survived to reach their destination. She knew better than anyone what dangers waited to the north.

Keilan glanced up at her as she came to stand over him. His face looked so open and innocent she had to keep herself from rolling her eyes.

"Come with me," she said.

"Where?"

She gestured vaguely into the dark. "Not far. You need to learn some simple spells if you're going to survive what's coming."

That intrigued him, she saw. Good. But still he glanced at Vhelan, as if asking if he could go with her. A true Talent, looking to a mere sorcerer for permission? Galling.

The magister glanced up at her as he stripped meat from a wing. He shrugged, and though he did it carelessly, like it mattered not what Keilan did, she saw the tension in his face and the quick look he threw towards the girl who carried the relic of Ama. Alyanna bit the inside of her cheek so her smirk wouldn't show. They did not trust her, but what could they do? She was their only hope to defeat the Chosen.

Keilan rose and followed her into the night. They had camped in a wide, snowy field, and away from the warmth of their fires the wind rushing across the emptiness was bracing. With a flicker of sorcery, Alyanna wrapped them in a blanket of soothing warmth. She did it slowly, twisting each strand with careful precision, hoping he was watching.

After they had gone a few hundred paces, she stopped and turned back to Keilan, summoning a small sphere of wizardlight. The boy watched her with that look of quiet concentration she'd grown accustomed to seeing. So much like his grandmother, and yet he'd known Niara for only a few short days. The blood ran true.

"Sit," Alyanna commanded, gesturing at the snowy ground.

He settled himself cross-legged, and she sank down beside him. "You know some sorceries."

He hesitated, and then nodded. "Just a few. Niara taught me on the island."

"Show me."

He licked his lips, furrowing his brow, and then a second wizardlight sprang into existence beside hers. His weaving of the strands was slightly fumbling, but no more than she would expect from a new apprentice.

"And?"

The light vanished. "I can summon blue fire."

Alyanna sighed, remembering how he had immolated the cloth doll. "Yes, unfortunately I know that."

"I can also do another thing with fire, but I need a flame already. I can twist it into the shape of a man and make it walk about. I saw a Kindred sorcerer do it."

A simple cantrip and largely useless. But there was something intriguing about what he'd said. "You watched him and then recreated what he did?"

"Yes."

"He did it several times?"

"No, just once."

Interesting. With a thought, Alyanna withdrew her cloak of warmth from Keilan. He blinked in surprise as the freezing cold rushed in to seize him, then looked at her questioningly.

"Recreate my sorcery. I saw you were paying attention to what I did."

Keilan swallowed, rubbing his hands together. He shivered as the wind gusted, though to her it felt like a warm breeze. *These elements should be an adequate spur.*

His brow furrowed, and Alyanna saw him reach for the squirming strands that welled up from within. Of course he would fail this first time, but after a few more demonstrations she hoped—

The spell blossomed, hotter than her own weaving; his control was not so fine, and she felt a buffeting surge of warmer air from the sorcerous cloak as he settled it around himself.

She fought to keep the surprise from her face.

"Very good," she said calmly. "Though the binding is rough, and that's why the edges of the sorcery are leaking."

He bit his lip, and she saw him smooth out the imperfections in his weaving, tightening the strands. The warmth from his sorcery receded from her.

Her heart was beating fast. All Talents could learn sorcery simply from observing, but at his stage of development, to recreate a spell so well after seeing it woven only once was impressive. Extremely. The only other Talent she could remember doing the same was her opponent in the finals of the Gendern's tournament a thousand years ago, back when she was still an apprentice. It had been a young savage girl from the grasslands with silver hair, the pride of Kalyuni's Star Tower. That had been the first time she'd encountered Niara.

Yes, the blood ran true.

"And you can summon dreadfire," she said lightly, as if that too was no impressive feat. "You burned my genthyaki."

Keilan shook his head, still distracted as he continued tweaking the strands of his sorcery. "I did. But I don't know how; the monster was going to kill Nel, and I brought it forth by instinct."

"Perhaps for the best," Alyanna said. "Dreadfire is a dangerous substance. It is also incredibly draining, and if you fail to slay your enemy with the first strike then you likely won't have the strength to protect yourself from the counter."

"You speak of protection . . ."

"Wards, mostly. Have you tried to summon one?"

Keilan finally finished fiddling with his sorcery and let it be. Inwardly, Alyanna marveled at how elegant his weaving now appeared.

"No."

"Then that is the other sorcery you will learn tonight." Alyanna brought her wards into existence with a thought. This time she manifested them as a translucent blue shield.

"Your ward is the most important spell you will ever learn. You must be able to summon it in an instant, and infuse it with so much of your power that it can stop most any attack."

Keilan reached out, hesitating before his fingers brushed her shield of blue glass. He glanced at her questioningly.

"You may touch it," she said, and his fingers splayed against the barrier.

"It feels like metal."

"A ward will stop nearly any physical attack. Swords and arrows and the like. The more force behind the strike, though, the more likely it will crack. A common sorcerer like those magisters back by the fire might not be able to resist a strong warrior's blow. But Talents like us can survive an avalanche."

"An avalanche," he whispered, and she could feel his senses exploring the intricacies of her weave.

"Wards are also capable of stopping sorcery. The weakest magical flame would be deadly to the unprotected, so if you suspect that another sorcerer wishes you harm, you must raise a warding."

Keilan's face grew distant, as if he was remembering something.

"The more sorcery you pour into your ward, the stronger it will be. But if you devote too much of your strength to it you'll have little left over for anything else." Alyanna cocked her head to one side, considering again what she had just said. "Hm. Perhaps you *should* focus on making your wards as strong as possible. You have little in the way of offensive spells, and they take longer to learn how to use effectively. If we find ourselves in a magical duel, I want you to hunker down and keep yourself safe. Do you understand?"

Keilan nodded, still distracted by whatever memory she had inadvertently summoned.

"Focus, Keilan," she snapped. "Now, I want you to try and summon a ward. Are you ready?"

Another nod. Keilan braided his sorcery into a weave that approximated her own, and a pale blue cocoon materialized around him. He seemed surprised to see it swell into existence, and this momentary lapse in concentration made the barrier shimmer and vanish.

"Concentration is the key to sorcery," she said, sighing. "A mistake like that would doom you in a fight with another Talent."

"I'm sorry."

"Don't apologize, only do better next time. In fact, we'll be traveling for a fortnight before we reach the Burrow of the Worm, and I expect you to spend every free moment refining your control over your ward. I want it seamless and strong for when you truly need to summon it. Do you understand?"

"Yes."

"Good. Now that's enough for tonight. Tomorrow we'll have another lesson, and if you can perform those two spells flawlessly, I'll teach you two more. We will persist until we find the limits of what you can learn in such a short time."

For most students, even Talents, such a pace would have been unthinkable. But the boy had potential. Alyanna felt a little thrill as she watched him unravel and make again a section of his warding, searching for a more perfect weave.

They could do great things together someday.

Fine golden sand squirmed between her toes as the crash and hiss of waves swelled behind her. A searing blue sky burned above.

It seemed that dreaming of beaches was common, though this place was completely unlike where Keilan had brought the Chosen girl. That beach had been gray and stark and cold, drawn from his memories of growing up on the bleak coast of the Broken Sea.

This was very different. Hills covered in lush jungle rose up from the shore, a sweeping green canopy interrupted only by a barren promontory where a tumbled ruin of red stone perched, facing the ocean. The sand was warm, and almost silken in its texture. Alyanna turned, and was surprised by the color of the shimmering jade water.

This was not the Dymorian coastline, either.

Alyanna began to walk along the beach. Not far from her was a collection of primitive structures, set back near the tree line. She moved in that direction.

This was the dream of Cein d'Kara. Her attempts to draw the queen into her own dreams had been rebuffed, so instead Alyanna had gone to hers. She'd thought the queen's mind had been sealed from her – that she'd somehow learned how to insulate herself from dreamsending after Alyanna had so rudely summoned her sleeping self – but the path into Cein's dreams had been easy enough to follow.

Now it was just a matter of finding her here, and the huts seemed like the best place to start.

Alyanna had been in a place like this before, when she'd joined a research expedition to the jungle continent of Xi. The waters there had been the same blue-green color, the air like here swollen with humidity. They'd only dared explore the very fringes of the great dark forests, wary of the poisonous flowers and stalking plants, but that place did resemble the verdant greenery that seemed to be swallowing these hills.

Cein d'Kara had never been to Xi, surely – those lands were as far from Dymoria as anything in the known world, on the other side of the Thread and a weeks' sail past the Eversummer Isles. The only ships that dared ply that route left from Palimport, in Menekar, and Alyanna was certain she'd have known if the Crimson Queen had ever visited the empire.

So where was this?

Perhaps it was a purely fictional construct, her retreat from the harsh reality of the Frostlands.

But Alyanna didn't think so.

She approached the small village. Most of the huts were bamboo lashed together with vines, the roofs thatched with grass. She did not see anyone moving among the buildings, but she had the feeling of being watched.

"I knew you'd come back."

The words were spoken just behind her, and Alyanna jumped. She whirled around and found a woman standing a few paces away, watching her. She wore a dress of woven grass and a necklace of bright purple flowers around her neck. Her skin was darkened by the sun, and her eyes were a vivid shade of green. She looked familiar.

The woman tugged on a lock of her bronze-colored hair. "You said you'd return for her." She turned towards the ocean and squinted at the rippling green water, shielding her eyes from the bright sun.

Alyanna followed where she was looking. A massive caravel was moored not far from shore – Alyanna was certain it had not been there a moment ago. Its sails were unfurled but hung slack in the dead air; she could make out a twisting red shape on a field of white, and she knew it was the dragon of House d'Kara. The ship appeared unmanned, its deck and raised forecastle empty.

What was this? Alyanna stared at the woman, trying to decide where she knew her from. The cast of her face, the shape of her nose . . . she had more than a passing resemblance to Cein d'Kara. And as much as there were physical similarities, it was also in the way she held herself, the calm command in her green eyes.

Alyanna remembered vaguely some rumor that Cein d'Kara had not been born in Dymoria. She was the bastard of the old king, the whispers had said, sired when he had led an expedition into the Sunset Lands, the mysterious realm far across the western ocean. She had appeared at court as a full-grown child, that much Alyanna was certain, and upon her ascension to the throne several of the great Dymorian houses had repudiated her.

"Where is she?" Alyanna asked, and the woman pointed into the village, at the only building built of something other than bamboo and grass. It was a low, windowless hut of ancient stone blocks scavenged from some other older structure. The door was roughly hewn of red wood and incised with a great flower. Several limp bodies were impaled upon the jagged sword-like petals of the carving. Charming.

"Why is she——" Alyanna began, but the woman had vanished. She looked up and down the empty crescent of golden sand. She was alone again.

Alyanna was surprised at the mild dread she felt as she approached the red door – she must be influenced by Cein's own feelings for this place. Her childhood had not been a happy one, Alyanna guessed. She'd found that to be a widely shared experience among those who had achieved greatness – a life of ease and coddling did not often forge men and women capable of bending the world to their will.

Her apprehension swelled as she neared the door. Alyanna pushed it to the side, reminding herself that this was not her own feeling. Whatever childhood trauma Cein associated with this place was irrelevant to Alyanna.

She put her palm on the carved wood of the door, expecting it to be locked, but instead it swung open easily. Light flooded the darkened interior. A figure huddled on the sandy floor gave a pained cry and raised knobby arms to try and block the sun. It was a girl, perhaps eight or nine winters old, her pale skin smudged with filth and fading bruises. Her long, tangled red hair covered much of her nakedness. She whimpered and shied away as Alyanna stepped into the room.

"Cein?" she asked, but there was no response.

Alyanna crouched beside the trembling child and brushed aside the hair obscuring her face. The girl flinched, her eyes squeezed shut.

Every other time Alyanna had entered the dreams of another, her very presence had resulted in the dreamer gaining some measure of awareness. Cein seemed to be lost in the grip of a nightmare, though. Alyanna sighed in frustration; she needed to learn what had happened during the battle, the capabilities of the Chosen, and this mysterious Skein sorcerer Vhelan had described.

"Cein," she said more harshly, "listen to me. You are Cein d'Kara, the Crimson Queen of Dymoria. This is a dream. This is not real and we—"

The door slammed shut, plunging the room into darkness. Alyanna whirled around, summoning her wizardlight. The ball of radiance flared into existence, then flickered and vanished. In that brief moment she thought she saw something move.

Alyanna controlled her breathing, mastering her rising panic. This was just a dream. She was safe asleep in her furs beside the fire. She reached for her sorcery again, but nothing happened. Something had been severed inside her, like when that mendicant had cut her connection to the Void while the genthyaki smiled and watched in the guise of the Black Vizier.

This was not happening. Something had fooled her mind into thinking she was still Cleansed, but what was broken inside her had been healed. She fought to stay calm. The room around her was utterly black and silent – that surprised her, as she couldn't even hear the breathing or scared mutterings of the child Cein anymore. She reached out to where the girl had been, but her hands found nothing except cold sand.

Something was very wrong.

She heard the quick patter of small feet churning sand.

"Cein?" she cried, turning in the direction the sound had come from. "Don't be frightened. I am not here to hurt you."

we are not frightened.

Alyanna gasped as searingly cold fingers closed around her leg. She tried to pull herself free but the grip was like steel; then she was yanked hard and tumbled to the ground.

A trap. They had set a trap for her.

Desperately, Alyanna strained for her sorcery, but it remained stubbornly out of her reach. Her fingers scrabbled in the sand as she tried to get away from the Chosen holding on to her leg.

The burning fingers suddenly vanished. Gasping in relief, she crawled until her hands touched the wall. She put her back to the stone and tried to stand, but all strength had fled from where she'd been touched and she slid down again.

She heard them in the darkness, their footsteps whispering in the sand as they slowly approached.

mistress they croaked in their ragged whispers. *you hurt us*

This was a dream. If she woke up, she would be safe. She tried to will herself awake, but the pathways that had led her to Cein's mind had vanished.

She had to distract them while she figured out how to escape. "Which one of you is Ko Yan? You are a prisoner – I can help free you from this nightmare!"

Shapes swelled around her, shards of deeper blackness.

she is part of us.

"Us? Or you? She is your slave, like the rest of them. Let them go. You took your revenge on the Shan; the people of this land did nothing to you."

the shan are here.

"Then destroy them! Leave the rest of us be!"

A rasping chuckle. *you are just like all of them. selfish. willing to trade the lives of others to save your own. you are lo jin come again.*

"Who are you?" Alyanna cried as the shadows loomed around her.

we are wan ying. we are the first and the last

They fell on her. Alyanna screamed as something rent her clothes and pierced her skin; she raised her hands, trying to ward away the demons, but they batted her arms aside with ease. Sharp teeth tore chunks from her flesh as they dragged her down to the sand.

"No," Alyanna moaned. They were so heavy, so heavy and so cold. She couldn't breathe; the weight on her chest was like a great crushing stone. She could feel the warmth of her life streaming from her as the Chosen ripped her body to tatters. Cold fingers caressed her face, tangled in her hair. Something sharp was being pushed into her belly, and it wriggled like a worm inside her and she felt a scream building but when she opened her mouth nothing spilled forth. Jagged nails slid along her lips—

Light.

The demons savaging her hissed as the door swung open. They rose from her and she drew in a shuddering breath, coughing up blood.

Through a red haze she saw a shape rushing towards her, then arms were underneath her and she was being lifted.

"Alyanna!" someone shouted, and she tried to focus on who or what was carrying her.

It had sounded like . . . Keilan?

A burst of blinding radiance, then the sky was above her. The world seemed to melt, running like wax, the green of the trees and the golden sand and the overwhelming blue above blurring together and she was falling—

Alyanna came awake gasping.

She sat up, drawing in shuddering breaths as she tried to orient herself. She frantically patted at her body, expecting to find it slicked by blood and covered in gaping wounds.

Nothing. Her panic slowly subsided as she mastered herself.

Around her the other sleepers continued dreaming, undisturbed. She watched the gentle rise and fall of their chests, their small movements as they shifted to find more comfortable spots on the hard and frozen ground. The fire had diminished, but someone had added more kindling so that it would burn until morning.

"Alyanna."

She jerked her head around, seizing the strands of her sorcery. Keilan crouched behind her, the concern in his face genuine.

"Keilan," she managed, letting the power slide between her fingers. "Was that you?"

He nodded, his face pale.

"How?"

"I couldn't sleep." He held up his arm, and even in the semi-darkness she could see the black lines etched stark beneath his skin. "They were itching. Burning. I got up and then I saw you writhing. You weren't making any noise but something was very wrong. I tried to wake you but I couldn't."

"I tried to contact the queen by going into her sleeping mind."

Keilan swallowed. "That was her dream? The beach?"

"I believe so. Something from her childhood, I think. But it was a trap. They were expecting me."

"I couldn't see what was attacking you in the hut. It was the Chosen?"

Alyanna ran a shaking hand through her sweat-damp hair. "Yes." She shook herself, then glanced at Keilan questioningly. "How did you follow me?"

He shrugged. "When I touched you, I could sense a thread running from your body into . . . elsewhere." He glanced at the fading lines on his forearm. "You were like a beacon, burning bright in the darkness. I remembered how you'd slipped into my dreams, and I'd glimpsed the basic weave of the sorcery. I did my best to recreate what I'd seen you do and tried not to get lost along the way. Then I was on the beach and I could hear you screaming from the village. There were people standing outside, a lot of them, just watching silently. They didn't try to stop me when I pushed through the door – you were there, and there were shapes on you; I thought they were animals, but they fled into the shadows when I picked you up. I don't think they were expecting me."

"I imagine not," Alyanna said softly, pinching the bridge of her nose. She could feel a terrible headache coming on. "Thank you," she said, touching his arm lightly. "I was careless and they nearly caught me."

She couldn't be sure because of the semi-darkness, but she thought he was blushing. "We need you," he said. "I saw what these things will do. The world needs you."

22: JAN

THE WALLS HAD breathed.

He'd seen the wood inhale and exhale like the lungs of a great beast. As if the wagon itself had for a moment lived, or been infused by the spirit of something else.

Madness. He was going mad. The strain on his mind – the centuries of the Weaver's tinkering, the trauma he had recently been subjected to – must have broken something inside him. Though in truth there was an even more terrifying possibility.

What he'd seen in the genthyaki's prison . . . what if it had been real?

Jan had never been a scholar. He'd paid only cursory attention to his studies, preferring to while away the days of his youth in swordplay or mastering the sorceries that came to him so instinctually. While other sorcerers had immersed themselves in the lore of the ancients, seeking out clues to unravel the great mysteries, he had instead fought and wooed and sung his songs.

Now, though, he wished he'd paid more attention.

What he'd witnessed . . . it was like another reality had infringed upon this world. When Lask had consumed the blood of the genthyaki, something had shifted, or been torn. Jan had glimpsed another place, though he did not know what.

He wished he could discuss it with Cein d'Kara. But the queen had not been returned to their wagon since that night. Jan could only hope that the shaman had not decided to see what power he could draw from her flesh. The thought was sickening. The eating of others . . . it was anathema in every society. Rituals that involved cannibalism had been what instigated the revolt against Menekar's Warlock King. The first Pure, Tethys, had found fertile ground for rebellion because of the atrocities committed by the emperor and his court as they pursued immortality. Jan remembered that much from his lessons, at least.

As the days passed, his thoughts turned to other things. He wondered what had happened to Cho Lin. Her quest to destroy the demons she'd called the Betrayers had been a righteous one, and he'd been selfish in abandoning her when he'd promised to bring her to where their prison was being kept. Of course, the irony was that in the end he'd led her right to where the monstrous children actually were. Perhaps she still lived – she was a disciple of Red Fang, and Jan had never known more skilled or dangerous warriors.

He considered what had led him to betray Cho Lin's trust and travel to Nes Vaneth. His memories had come back in a raging torrent after the ceremony atop Ravenroost, the accumulated remembrances of more than a dozen lives. It had been overwhelming. A few moments had been etched crystal-sharp, and the first time he'd traveled back to the old throne room of the sorceress-queens, centuries ago, was the most vivid of all. He hadn't understood at the time, but the barriers Alyanna had erected in his mind to hold back the memories of who he had been before the cataclysm had been greatly weakened. He'd felt a compulsion to travel north, into the Frostlands, and had eventually allowed himself to be drawn beneath the Bhalavan. There, he'd found the babe hanging in the blue wall of ice – he'd wanted to try and cut it out at that moment, though he knew it would almost certainly be dead. But on the slim chance that the sorcery swirling in the chamber had somehow preserved the child, he had not interfered, fearing that by doing so he would break the spell and kill her. So he'd sought out his vague recollections of a great sorceress – Alyanna – and begged her to help him. She'd responded by obscuring that version of himself, and giving Jan a new life to live, as she'd done so many times before.

The cruel witch.

Or had she done it for his sake, as she had claimed? Would the guilt of what he had done to his lover and people have consumed him if she'd helped him? If the child had slipped from the ice dead despite her assistance, would he have ended himself as he'd wanted to do before Alyanna had fashioned for him a new life?

He wasn't sure, and that shamed him.

The girl in the ice. His daughter, it must have been, for only Liralyn would have crafted that sorcery for their baby. What had happened to the child? The Skein king had claimed that she lived, taken by a priest of one of their barbaric gods into the wilds of the Frostlands after he had crudely hacked her from her prison.

Was she out there, even now?

The wagon lurched to a halt.

Jan blinked awake, lifting his head groggily from the pillow he'd made from the stale rushes. Amber light trickled through the high slats; it was late afternoon, if he had to guess. He felt strange, like he was still dreaming. A prickling numbness was crawling down the back of his neck and making the rest of his body tingle.

Something was happening. The Skein never stopped for the day until the sun had sunk completely behind the mountains. They must have arrived at whatever location they'd been slowly creeping towards over these long days. It was as mysterious to him now as it had been during their journey – he knew of very few places of interest that had survived the black ice the sorcerers of the Mosaic Cities had called down. Most of the other holdfasts had been utterly obliterated in the cataclysm.

Loud voices swelled from outside the wagon, coming closer. Icy fear spiked in him as he heard the shaman's barked commands, but when the door swung open it was the same pair of Skein that brought him food and water each night.

"The king wants to see you," the one with the bristly red beard growled, climbing inside the wagon.

King Hroi, the thane of the White Worm. Not Lask. Jan was disappointed at himself for his surge of relief.

"Where are we?" he asked as they unclasped the manacle from around his ankle.

"The end of the world," the other Skein said, a sour-faced warrior with a missing ear and a scar curving down the side of his cheek. The red-bearded barbarian seemed to think this clever, as he snorted a chuckle.

They grabbed him roughly beneath his shoulders and hauled him to his feet. Jan could walk, but he let them carry the bulk of his weight – hiding his strength seemed like the best course of action.

They emerged from the wagon and Jan had to shield his eyes. This was the first time he'd seen the sun in many weeks, perhaps more than a month. This long, dark nightmare had begun beneath the Bhalavan, and he was about to discover how it ended. He turned slowly, his gaze traveling over the gnarled mountains. They did not look familiar, which was strange. As a boy he had traveled all over the Frostlands, hunting stag and wyverns and wraiths, and he had learned how to orient himself simply by looking at the closest of the Bones – each segment of the range had its unique characteristics, such as the shape of the peak or a face hidden in the stones of a prominent cliff. Here, though . . .

He sought any familiar landmark, but found nothing. His confusion deepened. The far north, perhaps. It had been a wild, dangerous land, and he'd heard it was where the clan of the White Worm made their home.

Wait. No.

The scrabbling in his head sharpened.

Why would they have gone there?

The Skein led him through a thicket of stunted trees, and with mounting dread Jan became more and more certain what they would find on the other side.

His heart fell when his suspicions were confirmed.

They stood on the edge of an escarpment that swept down into a broad, flat field. Most of the Skein host had already gathered there – it was smaller than Jan had suspected, only a hundred or so men. They were all members of the king's Flayed, the elite warriors of the White Worm, their faces inked to resemble different beasts and monsters. The army that had destroyed the Dymorians must have already disbanded or made its way back to Nes Vaneth. Most of the Skein would have refused to come here, Jan suspected. It had been a cursed, forbidden place for ages, long before he'd been born in Min-Ceruth.

The Skein were clustered at the base of a great hill that soared nearly as tall as some of the smaller Bones. It did not look like a mountain, though – there was no rock emerging from the unbroken snow, and the swell of it was too rounded when compared to the jagged peaks of the Frostlands. In truth, it resembled one of the burial mounds where his ancestors had entombed their dead, but on an enormous scale.

Fitting, given what was inside.

Set into the side of this hill was a door that defied comprehension. It was a thousand span high, at least, a slab of featureless gray stone recessed slightly so that no snow covered its sloping vastness. There were no designs etched into the door, or if there had been ages ago they had long since been effaced. Nor was there any suggestion as to how the portal might open.

This was the Burrow of the Worm. Jan could feel something squirming in his mind, a wriggling, alien intruder. And he knew it would be worse for the Skein setting up their camp outside the door – the psychic reverberations emanating from the Ancient dreaming under the hill had driven men mad before, but those with Talent seemed to be able to cope better than those without the gift, or even lesser sorcerers. The speculation Jan remembered was that the Ancient existed both here and in the Void, and those with Talent also had a strong connection to that realm. These Skein, however, would have no such familiarity, so it must have felt like they were descending into madness.

He didn't feel any sympathy for them.

One of the Skein muttered a warding against evil as they started to descend to where the others had gathered. Jan wondered if this prayer was directed at what was sleeping within the Burrow, or the demons arrayed outside the door.

Five ragged children stood there, tiny compared to the great gray slab of stone rising above them. A group of Skein stood a ways away, the black-robed priests of the Skin Thief with their masks of cured flesh. They looked like a flock of carrion birds inspecting the Burrow, as if it were a particularly large and rich corpse to feast upon. Jan grimaced as he noticed Hroi and Lask among them. The Skein king's face could have been carved from granite, and he was staring at the Burrow with such a look of intense concentration it seemed he was trying to crack open the door through an act of will alone. His mottled cloak stirred in the cold wind, and both his hands rested on a pair of sword hilts, the blades thrust into the snow. The strange metal of one of the swords almost resembled amber, and Jan knew that this must be the legendary Night's Kiss. But it was the sight of the other sword that sent a pang of surprise through Jan. Set in the carved silver hilt, a fire opal burned like a fallen star – there was no other blade like it in the world. Somehow, the Skein king had acquired Bright, the sword spell-forged for Jan by the weapon-smiths of Nes Vaneth.

His shock melted away before the heat of his anger. How was this possible? Bright had been taken from him when he'd been imprisoned by Cein d'Kara, and he'd assumed the sword had been added to the collection of ancient artifacts she'd shown him in Saltstone.

"You look angry, sorcerer."

Jan tore his gaze from Bright's rune-inscribed steel to find the shaman smirking at him.

"That's my sword."

Lask arched a pale eyebrow. "Did you hear that, my king? The Min-Ceruthan says your blade is his."

Hroi's cold gaze settled on Jan. The thane of the White Worm stared at him for a long moment, then dismissed him by looking away.

"He does not recognize your claim, sorcerer. The sword was taken from the queen of Dymoria after her defeat – if you have a grievance, perhaps it should be with her."

Lask withdrew his hands from the long dagged sleeves of his robes and indicated something behind Jan.

He turned to find Cein d'Kara stumbling across the snow towards them, three of the Skin Thief priests shepherding her on. They were keeping a good distance from her, as if wary of what she might do, though to Jan it looked like she was barely keeping herself from falling. Her face was pale and drawn, the red hair spilling from under her fur hood dirty and tangled. But still she held her head high, and her eyes flashed defiantly as she caught sight of Lask and the Skein king.

Cein stopped, drawing herself up, but then the priest behind her lunged forward and shoved her hard from behind so that she went sprawling face-first in the snow. Grating laughter issued from the other priests as the queen pushed herself to her hands and knees. She was trying to stand, but her arms were already trembling with the effort necessary to stop herself from collapsing again.

Jan went to her and gently helped her to her feet. Cein clutched at him, but her face was hard as iron. "You consort with demons, Skein," she spat, finding her balance.

"Careful, witch!" barked one of the Skin Thief's priests. "You speak of a god's servants!"

Cein jerked her chin towards where the ragged children stood in the snow facing the soaring door. "They are not divine. Your god is a lie."

Scattered gasps and angry muttering rose up from the priests. Jan heard a few shouted cries to kill the queen here and now.

The Skein king chuckled, swinging his amber-bladed sword up onto his shoulder. "You may claim our god is not true, Dymorian." He pointed with Bright towards the Burrow. "But here its dreams soak this land. It is waiting to be awoken."

"That thing is not a god," said Jan.

Hroi snorted. "No? What could be more god-like than the creature beneath this hill? We are gnats to it. When it finally slithers forth after so many ages it will devour this world and bring about a great reckoning."

"Why would you wish that?" asked Cein, her voice fractured by pain. She was trying to be strong, but Jan could tell she was suffering from some injury.

"We worship the Skin Thief," Hroi replied, "but we are the clan of the White Worm. We have always dwelt in the shadow of the Burrow. All our lives it has squirmed deep in our thoughts – we've felt its blind hunger, the vastness and beauty of its presence. Long have we wished to usher the Worm into the light."

"And let it destroy the world?" Cein asked, incredulous.

Lask stepped forward, and the priests of the Skin Thief stopped their muttering. He seemed to command even more respect that the Skein king. "When a thing is consumed, it is not destroyed, Dymorian. I showed you that. It changes, and its strength is passed to what devoured it." He lifted his emaciated face to the hazy sun, his eyes narrowing. "This world will end, but something will come after. And we who are prepared to seize that moment will feast richly and grow stronger."

"The Skein have long dwelled in the ruins of a lost world," interrupted Hroi. "Scavenging among the bones of the past. When the Worm wakes, it will feed upon the south, crushing kingdoms and empires. My people will follow in its wake and make ourselves masters of what remains."

"You wish to rule over an empire of dust," Cein said sneeringly.

Hroi seemed undisturbed by her mocking tone. "I do, Dymorian. Would you rather be a queen of a shattered land and a broken people or a peasant toiling for rich men in a realm of wealth and plenty?" He turned away. "I know what your answer would be, even if you would not admit it to yourself."

"You do not—" Cein began, but then she gave a pained cry. One of the demon children had appeared behind her – Jan hadn't seen it move – and laid its twisted hands upon her. She fell to her knees, torn from Jan's grip.

A moment later agony flared in his spine, and he too was forced to kneel in the snow. He tried to lift his arms, but all strength had fled from his limbs. Points of piercing cold drifted across his back as one of the children ran its fingers across his body. It had reached up beneath his furs and laid its hand upon his skin. Jan's head spun and he nearly retched from the pain.

Through the haze, he sensed Lask approaching. "Hold them," the shaman said, and to Jan it felt like a great fist was squeezing him, tearing the breath from his chest.

Fingers were at his throat, and then to his immense surprise he felt the collar around his neck snap open. He gasped as his sorcery returned in a raging flood, and he reached for the strands that were once again within his reach . . . but the pressure holding him from moving was somehow also keeping him from seizing his power. Cein grunted in frustration beside him, and he knew she could not claim her sorcery either, even though her collar had been removed. The paralysis stemmed from the touch of the demon children, a coldness spreading from where that small palm was pressed against his back.

Another hand, much larger, settled upon the top of his head. Fingers tangled in his hair, gripping him roughly, though the pain was a distant echo compared to the agony radiating from where the demon touched his spine.

From the corner of his eye he saw that Lask now stood beside him; the shaman had one hand on his head, and the other clutched Cein d'Kara's scalp, so tightly that blood was seeping from where his nails pressed against her brow.

What was happening?

It almost felt like . . . yes, the shaman was opening himself to them, ready to receive their power. But of course they would not send their strength into this man– whatever great act of sorcery he wanted to perform was somehow related to the slumbering Ancient. Jan would die before giving the Skein what they wanted.

Deep within him, something shifted. The paralysis that was keeping him from grasping his sorcery suddenly loosened. He clutched for the twisting threads flowing up from his connection to the Void, but once they were firmly in his grasp he found himself unable to weave them into a spell. He struggled, sweat beading on his face. The queen moaned beside him as she also strained to use her returning power.

Small cold fingers pried at the clenched fist within him that held his sorcery. This jarred him, and he nearly let go; the feeling of something else trying to release his power was shocking. He fought against this force, but it was immeasurably strong, and gradually he was forced to relinquish what he held. It was the demon children, he was sure of it, but it was nothing like he'd experienced before. *It shouldn't be possible!*

Cein screamed, a wordless howl of rage and frustration. He might have done the same, as the implacable fingers of the demons forced open his hand so that the strands he'd gathered lay there in his palm, exposed. And then there was the shaman reaching down inside him to take up his sorcery, gathering Jan's power into himself. He'd never experienced a violation like this before, his sorcery seized by another with cold indifference.

"Yes," Lask murmured, his voice thick with stolen power. "I have it."

twist it into the shape we showed you.

Many ragged whispers spoken as one, booming inside Jan. The demons were within him, their black roots sunk into his body, their spirits floating alongside his own consciousness.

He sensed the sorcery swelling in Lask as the shaman drained them. Then he was manipulating it, crafting the torrent of energy into something that seemed familiar, the edges sharpening as Jan watched in horrified fascination—

A key.

With a snarl, the shaman lashed out with the sorcery he had braided. Jan could see no physical representation of the spell, but with the eyes of a Talent he watched it sink into the huge door like lightning striking the sea. Power coruscated across the stone surface, glimmering shards that flared and then faded into nothing.

Jan gasped. He felt hollowed out, like Lask had reached down and scooped out his insides. Darkness pressed on the corners of his vision.

The door . . .

Jan waited for the sound of grinding, or for the stone to explode outwards in a shower of stinging fragments.

But the door did not open.

Lask staggered, leaning heavily on Jan where he still clutched at his skull.

"It did not work," he said softly, sounding exhausted.

it shifted. we felt it. you must try again.

The shaman shook his head. "I used everything they had, along with my own power. We must wait for them to recover their strength."

Through his numbing weakness Jan felt the cold metal closing around his neck again. Lask crouched in front of him, his face sallow and drawn, and then the shaman patted him on the cheek.

"We try again on the morrow, Min-Ceruthan."

23: CHO LIN

SHE WAS BEING stalked.

At first, it had been a nagging sense of being watched. Cho Lin had paused as she slogged through the snow drifts, peering into the trees, hoping for a glimpse of whatever was making the back of her neck prickle. But there had been nothing except the snow softly falling between the bone-white trunks of the birch trees and the dark, bristled branches of the pines. She'd dismissed it as her imagination, chiding herself for allowing these wilds to fray her nerves. With the supplies she'd scavenged from Nes Vaneth running low, she had much more important concerns.

Then she'd heard it: the snap of wood breaking. It might have been a branch giving way under the weight of winter, or a stag rubbing its antlers against a tree. Two mornings ago, Cho Lin had emerged from the little shelter she'd constructed to find a magnificent buck watching her from deeper among the trees. If only she'd been wise enough to keep searching the Skein longhouses until she found a bow – the thought of fresh venison had taunted her as the great deer had turned and picked its way among the trees. Even with the strength of the Nothing she had little chance of running down a stag; later, though, as she chewed on her dwindling rations of salt fish, she'd wished she had at least tried.

Perhaps the sound was a family of deer. But then it came again, a faint crackling. Deer would not keep pace with her. Something that was hunting her would, though. Cho Lin's pulse began to quicken and she watched the forest with a sharpened intensity.

There were dangers out here. Ghost apes, or wraiths as Verrigan had called them. She remembered the severed head of the wyvern the Skein king had brought back from his hunt, its jaws large enough to swallow her arm whole. Then there was the beast that had ambushed her and slain her poor horse. And of course the Frostlands must teem with other threats she could not even imagine.

Very faintly, she heard the crunch of snow. Whatever was stalking her was not the most careful of hunters. Which only made her heart beat faster – if a predator did not care if its prey was aware of it, that was because it had confidence in its speed and strength to catch the animals that tried to run away. Cho Lin let out a long, slow breath. She wasn't about to be dragged down from behind. No, if this thing wanted her, it would have to face her with her claws out.

Cho Lin ducked behind the stump of a large dead tree. Quickly, she flung her pack on the ground and slid her butterfly swords from their sheaths, the coldness of the ivory burning her fingers. She waited, her back to the scarred bark, listening for the approach of the hunter.

24: KEILAN

EVERY DAY WAS the same in the north: trudging across snowy plains and through silent forests until he could hardly tell one morning from those that had come before. The wonders he had hoped to glimpse in the Frostlands remained stubbornly hidden. He saw no dragons wheeling among the distant peaks of the Bones, or wraiths slipping between the trees. He flopped onto his bedroll each night with his legs burning and his ears numb, and woke the next morning still sore and tired.

Some evenings he lay swaddled in the furs he'd scavenged from the battlefield, and watched the sky pulse with strange lights, rippling veils of green and purple. Vhelan had surmised that farther north was where the bounds between realities frayed, the energies of the Void leaking into this world. Alyanna had snorted when she'd heard this and tartly informed him that there was nothing magical about the light; that it was a purely natural phenomenon investigated by a Kalyuni scholar a thousand years ago. Keilan knew she spoke from a well of knowledge deeper than any who lived in this day, but still he felt a surge of wonder as he watched the colors dance across the heavens.

His headaches were growing worse. Well, perhaps not worse, but certainly different. Ever since being cut by the black dagger he'd suffered from flashes of pain like sudden lightning storms, vicious enough for him to momentarily lose his vision or fall unconscious. Now the discomfort was constant, though not as intense. It felt like sharp nails were being scraped inside his head, and while he could still keep pace with the marching soldiers, he found that he had to keep his eyes on the ground so that the sunlight wouldn't sharpen the pain.

One morning, not long after they'd left camp, Nel noticed the tightness in his face and nudged his shoulder gently. "Keilan, do you feel sick again? Should we stop for a while?"

He shook his head curtly. "I'm fine."

"Let me see your arm," she asked, already rolling back the sleeve of the too-large fur jerkin he'd taken from a dead Skein. "Hm." Her brow furrowed as she inspected his forearm. "There's a little blackness, but nothing like before."

"Really, I'm all right," he said, sliding the sleeve back down. She frowned when she heard the slight annoyance in his voice.

"Go talk with the sorceress," she told him firmly. "Let her know what you're feeling. The demons know there's a connection between you now, and only the Silver Lady knows how they might strike at us next."

Keilan sighed and rolled his eyes, but still he sought out Alyanna at her usual place in the column, a dozen paces behind the last soldier and reclining on the chavenix. She looked like a satrap's wife being carried on a palanquin through some decadent eastern city. Alyanna lifted an eyebrow and sat up when she noticed Keilan standing there.

"You finally wish to join me?" she asked, patting the shimmering metal beside her.

"No."

Alyanna had offered him a spot on the chavenix before, but Keilan had always declined. He would have felt too guilty watching the others trudge along in the cold and snow while he remained warm and rested on the disc. After all, many of the soldiers bore wounds from the battle, though the worst of the injured had remained behind in the caves. Alyanna, of course, had no such qualms.

"I have a question for you, though," he said as he fell in alongside the chavenix, matching its leisurely pace.

She cocked her head to one side, waiting for him to continue.

"I feel . . . different. My head hurts, but it's not like the spikes of pain from before. It's more of an . . ." He paused, struggling for how to describe the sensation.

"Irritation."

"Yes," he replied, surprised.

"I feel it too, Keilan. It has nothing to do with the bond you share with the Chosen." She stared off towards the north, squinting at the Bones looming on the horizon. "It's the White Worm. I honestly don't know how the Min-Ceruthans remained sane with its presence always intruding on their minds. We Talents are particularly sensitive, but the others will take notice of it soon enough, particularly in their dreams. And it will get worse for them the closer we get to its lair." Alyanna rummaged in her bag for a moment and pulled out a thin book bound in red leather. "This was written by a fallowmancer of Vis who lived for a year just outside the great Burrow where the Worm is entombed. He recorded all the visions and dreams he experienced that he thought could be ascribed to the Ancient. Mostly they were so alien in nature he struggled to put them into words – there are pages of descriptions about feeling his coils pushing through substances that have no parallels in this reality, esoteric relationships with things that our human minds cannot comprehend. Very literally the dreams of the Worm seeping into his own."

"Did he ever come to understand it better?"

Alyanna shrugged. "Perhaps. When he returned he murdered several members of his order in a gruesome fashion, and then killed himself by leaping into a pit of hungry pigs."

The sorceress chuckled when she noticed his expression. "Do not worry overmuch, Keilan. I do not expect we will be here long enough that our sanity becomes endangered."

He lapsed into silence for a while, concentrating on the faint scrabbling inside his skull. Could he order these strange feelings into some kind of coherence? Or was whatever was trickling from the god-creature far too different to be parsed by a mortal mind?

"You should know," Alyanna said suddenly, pulling him back from his thoughts. "We are getting closer to the Burrow. Less than a week more of traveling, if my memory is correct. Which it is."

Alyanna reached across the chavenix and found Keilan's bag among where they'd piled their supplies. She pulled it closer, but she did not undo its drawstring, instead watching him carefully. "You know what I'm going to ask," she said.

He did. "You want the dagger."

She nodded slightly. "The Chosen will be there. I have felt their power – it is raw and vicious and unconstrained. None of you could stand before them for more than a few moments. If this weapon does what Niara hoped, and can sever whatever connection links their consciousness with the remnants of their physical forms, I should be the one to wield it. Only I can get close enough to strike."

Keilan had been expecting this argument for days, but still it unsettled him. Alyanna seemed to desire the end of the demons as much as anyone, that was true. Could she be trusted, though? He swallowed, searching her face for answers. She looked totally without guile, her eyes wide and innocent. He wanted to sigh at the sight. Whatever else she was, Alyanna was no innocent.

But what choice did they have? She was right. They were all helpless as babes when compared to the sorceress.

At least she'd asked.

"You should be the one to use Niara's dagger," he told Alyanna, and a smile spread across her face, as if his agreement was wholly unexpected and appreciated.

"Excellent, Keilan. That is the wise choice. Now I don't have to take it without your permission, and we can remain on good terms."

"So it wouldn't have mattered what I said?"

"Of course not," Alyanna said, opening his bag and drawing out the carved rosewood box. "Don't be naïve." She slid back the cover and gently lifted the dagger from where it had been nestled upon velvet. Bright sunlight passed through the blade, illuminating the strands of black threading the dark material. Removed from its case, Keilan felt the weapon's strange emanations, and for a moment he forgot the scratching in his mind that Alyanna had attributed to the sleeping Ancient.

"Your grandmother was always a great artificer," Alyanna murmured, turning the blade over to examine the lines of tiny Shan characters spiraling around its hilt.

"Do you know how to make it work?"

Alyanna brandished the dagger; it looked almost like a short sword in her small hand. "I imagine stabbing them is the first step."

"I could do that."

She lifted a questioning eyebrow. "Could you? You'd need to get close enough first."

A commotion near the middle of their small column made them both turn their heads. Some of the soldiers had stopped their march and were clustered near the edge of the forest they had been skirting. The rest of their band had noticed something was happening and were drifting closer to see what it was. With a last glance at Alyanna, Keilan left the side of the chavenix and went to join them, pushing between the broad shoulders of the Dymorian legionaries to see what had caught their attention.

Three figures stood knee deep in the snow, having just emerged from the trees. The two in front were familiar to Keilan – one was Chelin, the young ranger who had first led them to the cave with the remnants of the Dymorian army, and the other was one of his fellows, also garbed in forester green and brown. Both seemed to be in a state of shock, their faces pale. Chelin looked like he had been struck, or run into a tree, as a large purple bruise had flowered on one side of his face.

The last figure was a young woman, and she was standing slightly behind them, as if she wanted a buffer between herself and the milling soldiers. Keilan couldn't blame her – angry mutterings were rising as more and more of the Dymorians saw Chelin's vivid bruise. She didn't look very threatening to Keilan, and she appeared calm as she surveyed the crowd of soldiers. She was Shan, he suddenly realized with a jolt of surprise, although she was draped in layers of furs like he'd seen the dead Skein wearing back on the battlefield.

Chelin seemed dazed by the attention of all his comrades. After a moment of watching the soldiers with wide eyes he blinked uneasily and stepped forward.

"We found . . . this here is—"

"What's a spider-eater doing out here?" demanded one of the closest soldiers, his voice hard. "She struck you, Chelin?"

"Well, I—"

"A Shan in the Frostlands?" cried another. "Must be allies with the northmen. She's a spy come looking for us!"

"Can't trust a spider-eater," snarled another. "My greatda always said they was unnatural."

"This is—" Chelin tried to interject, but he was drowned out by the soldiers' rising voices.

"Warlocks . . ."

"Strange . . ."

"Thieves . . ."

Keilan thought the Shan woman looked remarkably composed given that the soldiers were edging closer to her. Did she even speak Menekarian?

"*Nel soon*, Lady Cho!"

Everyone fell silent and turned to look at Vhelan, who had pushed his way to the front of the mob. He inclined his head towards the Shan girl and knuckled his brow respectfully. "You are well met in these cursed lands."

"Magister," the woman said, and the soldiers drew back a pace, as if they had suddenly been confronted by a talking animal.

"You know her?" asked d'Venish, who had also just found his way through the soldiers. Keilan could see the suspicion in the Dymorian commander's face.

"I do," Vhelan said. "This is the daughter of a Shan lord. Very recently she was a visitor in Herath, and even arrived in Saltstone." To Keilan's surprise, Vhelan actually winked at her, as if this were a joke they were sharing.

"What is she doing out here in the middle of the Frostlands?" The noble turned his gaze to Chelin, who seemed to wilt under his commander's attention. "Ranger, what happened?"

Chelin's throat bobbed as he swallowed hard. "We . . . uh . . . we were scouting these woods and we found her. Thought she was a Skein, a scout or maybe a camp woman out foraging. You said we should be on the lookout for any of the northerners, commander, so we was going to bring her to you . . ." The ranger pulled off his fur cap and crumpled it in his hands, looking sheepish. "She came at us. Gave me this" —he touched the purple smear covering his cheek— "an' after she knocked us down she started asking questions. Said she wanted to come meet the rest o' us. Said she was looking for Dymorians."

Commander d'Venish stared at Chelin incredulously. "She wanted to find us so you simply brought her here? After she 'knocked you down?' Garazon's black balls, ranger, are you implying that this *girl* defeated you?"

Keilan didn't miss the fear that flickered across Chelin's face. "Pardon, Commander, but she ain't normal."

Growling in frustration, d'Vanish turned to the silent Shan woman, who had watched this exchange with a hint of amusement in her face. "You! You dared assault a Dymorian soldier?"

Vhelan stepped forward, poised to say something, but the furious noble waved him quiet.

The girl the magister had called Lady Cho showed no sign of being intimidated by the red-faced commander. "He and his brother tried to" —her delicate face scrunched up, as if she was struggling to remember the proper word— "ambush me. They were clumsy. And lucky that I realized they were not Skein, or they would be dead."

"So you hate the northerners as well?" d'Venish said scornfully, as if he didn't believe that could be true.

Cho Lin nodded slightly. "You are all northerners to me. But the ones here in the cold lands are my enemies, or at least some of them are." Her dark eyes traveled over the crowd of soldiers; they had fallen silent during this exchange. "Take me to your queen," she said loudly, addressing everyone.

She delivered these words with the casual command of someone who was used to being obeyed. D'Venish's jaw hardened, but he bit back whatever harsh reply he wanted to make.

"We are going to the queen at this very moment," Vhelan said quickly before the Dymorian commander found his voice. "She's in the hands of the Skein."

The Shan pursed her lips in disappointment. "Very well. Then bring me to the rest of your army."

The magister spread his arms wide. "*This* is what's left, I'm afraid."

For the first time, something broke through the Shan's look of cool detachment. Surprise and disappointment were clear in her face before she quickly brought her emotions under control. She turned to Vhelan, dismissing d'Venish as if he were a common soldier.

"Let us find somewhere and talk, Magister. There is much to discuss."

Lord d'Venish decreed that they would stop for the rest of the day, despite the sun barely having started its descent, and this mollified the soldiers somewhat. They were still grumbling, though, as they worked to set up camp, casting uncertain glances at the Shan as she followed Vhelan over to where a pair of Dymorians were heaping kindling. The pine branches they'd gathered proved stubbornly resistant to catching the sparks created by the soldiers' flint and steel, and it took a sorcerous nudge from the magister Seril for a flame to finally be coaxed to life. The Shan – who had introduced herself as Cho Lin – appeared unmoved by this display of sorcery as she settled beside the fire. Vhelan stretched out next to his fellow magister, across the flames from the Shan. Keilan found his own spot, squeezed in between Nel and Alyanna, who had finally come down from the chavenix. Lord d'Venish and two other senior Dymorians also joined them, one a ranger and the other a scarred older soldier. They all watched the Shan warily, as if expecting her to transform into a monster before their eyes.

Cho Lin seemed untroubled by their gazes. She sat in the same manner as the Shan who had accompanied their caravan along the Way, with her legs crossed and her back sword-straight. She watched silently as the soldiers tasked with preparing their camp heated a metal flask over the flames, then poured its contents into a cup and handed it to her. Keilan was struck by how she held the water, just like Cho Yuan had held his tea, with both hands cupping the clay cup like it was a priceless chalice. She took small, careful sips as she studied the others around the fire. She'd taken off her fur hat and unpinned her hair, and it fell like a glistening black waterfall around her shoulders. Her face was delicate and heart-shaped, with smooth pale skin and large dark eyes. Cho Lin looked only a few years his senior, Keilan thought, but she seemed much older. She was slender, but there was an obvious strength to her, and a pair of carved white sword hilts emerged from beneath her layers of clothing. Still, how had she survived by herself out here in the Frostlands? Or overpowered two Dymorian rangers without the slightest scratch to herself?

"The last time I met you," Vhelan began when they were all seated around the fire, "you said you had been sent by the great and powerful of Shan on a mission of some importance."

"You've seen her before?" Nel interrupted before Cho Lin could reply, her eyes flicking from the magister to the Shan girl.

"Twice, actually," Vhelan replied, and Cho Lin arched an eyebrow at this.

"I only remember the one time, Magister," the Shan said quietly, blowing on her hot water.

"Ah. I hope you take no offense, but the queen used her sorcery to watch you and Jan after our encounter on the road."

Cho Lin's face was unreadable, but she did set down her cup. "Then you saw what happened?"

"We did," Vhelan said, looking pained. "Up until the demons attacked Jan beneath the Min-Ceruthan fortress. That severed the connection Queen Cein had made. To be honest, I feared you were both dead."

Cho Lin spent a long moment studying the steam curling from her cup. When she spoke again, her voice held a rawness that Keilan hadn't heard from her before. "I nearly died. Many days I was their prisoner, and then I escaped into the dead city. I killed a demon the Betrayers had brought to this world, and also a good number of Skein before coming south."

"And the sorcerer, Jan?" This was spoken by Alyanna, who had been quiet as she watched the Shan. "What happened to him?"

Cho Lin frowned. "I was told the Skein took him south when they went to meet your army. That is all I know."

"Where were you going? Back to Shan?"

The Shan shook her head at Nel's question. "I knew the queen of Dymoria had come into the Frostlands. I have heard from many lips that she is a powerful sorceress." Cho Lin reached into the pack beside her and pulled out a length of dirty cloth tied up into a bundle. She undid the knot, revealing what was inside. It looked to Keilan like the shattered remnants of a sword. The blade had been broken into many shards of varying length, and there was a hilt carved from black bone. He felt a trickle of familiarity staring down at the broken weapon – had he seen it before?

Cho Lin's face was creased with sadness. "This was the Sword of Cho. It is a legendary weapon. The demons you saw beneath the Bhalavan – the Betrayers, we call them – were banished a thousand years ago by this blade." Reverently, she picked up the black-bone hilt, which gleamed like obsidian in the fading light of day. "Another demon broke the sword. I was taking these fragments to the queen so that she could try to reforge them. Without this weapon, I fear there is no hope of stopping the Betrayers."

"Give me a piece of the blade," said Alyanna, holding out her hand.

Cho Lin glanced at Vhelan questioningly.

"She is a sorceress, like our queen," the magister said.

"Greater than your queen," Alyanna added with a sniff, beckoning for the Shan to pass her the sword. "Cein d'Kara is a child."

Cho Lin hesitated for the briefest of moments, then she gently lifted one of the metal shards and passed it to Alyanna. As her fingers brushed the rippling steel, something flickered across the sorceress's face, and then her brow drew down. Keilan felt a trickle of sorcery flow from her and into the piece of the sword.

"This was a great artifact," she said slowly, running her palm down the length of the shard. "There was a soul here, bound within the blade. One with Talent. But it's gone now." She handed back the fragment to Cho Lin. "What remains is a fading echo. The barest trace of the sorcery that once infused the blade. It can never be remade."

The Shan closed her eyes and bowed her head slightly. It looked to Keilan like she had just received terrible news that she'd been dreading, but also expecting.

"Then we are lost."

"No," Keilan interjected, and he felt everyone's gazes turn to him. His face prickled under their attention, but he swallowed and continued on. "We have our own weapon."

Cho Lin raised her head again, and Keilan saw a flicker of interest in her dark eyes.

"A dagger. Made by a great sorceress under the directions of a warlock of Shan, with blood and hair from the demons mixed into the metal."

Cho Lin shifted, leaning closer. There was interest in her face now. "Do you have it? Show it to me."

Keilan glanced at Alyanna. The sorceress gave him a look that he thought meant she was displeased, but then she reached into the folds of her robes and drew out the black-metal dagger.

"If that is true, you should give it to me," Cho Lin said, and Alyanna chuckled before slipping the blade away again.

"I come from a family of demon hunters," the Shan explained. "I have trained my whole life to destroy the Betrayers."

"You were at Red Fang," Vhelan remarked slowly, as if just remembering something he had been told.

Cho Lin nodded. "I can touch the Nothing, and it makes me the equal of any warrior alive."

"The Chosen are not alive," Alyanna said tartly. "They do not care how strong you are or how fast you move. Can the Nothing protect you from their sorcery?"

The Shan woman met Alyanna's defiant stare calmly. "It is in my blood. My ancestor was the one who first bound them."

The corner of Alyanna's mouth rose. "And yet here we find you, wandering around in the woods with the magic sword of your family in many small pieces."

Vhelan cleared his throat loudly, looking slightly embarrassed at the turn the conversation had suddenly taken. "Well, what she means to say is that we are lucky to have met. We all have the same goals here – to destroy the demons and rescue the queen."

Cho Lin bowed her head slightly towards the magister. "You are right. The Four Winds pushed us together, and now we must stop the Betrayers from bringing down another Raveling."

"What *was* the Raveling?" Vhelan asked, leaning forward with interest.

"The force that destroyed the old lands of Shan. Some kind of . . . beast, I've come to believe. And the Betrayers are here in the north, trying to wake another like it."

"And how do you know this?"

Cho Lin turned towards Alyanna. "I was given a vision of a great door set in the side of a mountain, somewhere here in the Frostlands. The Betrayers stood in the snow, and I knew they were trying to wake the creature that sleeps within."

Alyanna's eyes narrowed. "Who showed you this vision?"

A look of consternation passed across Cho Lin's face. "A . . . spirit I met in the ruins of Nes Vaneth."

The suspicion in the sorceress's face deepened. "I want to see what you saw," she said, then rose and approached the Shan.

Cho Lin blinked in alarm as Alyanna crouched beside her.

"What are you doing, warlock?" she murmured as Alyanna raised two fingers. Sorcery glittered in Keilan's mind's eye as an incredibly complex weave was crafted. Cho Lin's hand flashed out to grip the sorceress's wrist before Alyanna could touch her forehead.

"This will not hurt," the sorceress said in mild irritation. "I promise."

Cho Lin hesitated a moment, and then she let go of Alyanna. The sorceress pressed her fingertips against Cho Lin's brow, closing her eyes, and the weave she'd fashioned flared as it entered the Shan girl's head.

Alyanna was quiet for a long moment, her eyelids fluttering. Cho Lin seemed unhurt by whatever was happening, though she was watching Alyanna's twitching face warily.

"Liralyn!" Alyanna suddenly hissed, her face twisting. She jerked her hand back as if she had been burned, and her eyes snapped open.

"What did you see?" Cho Lin asked, her curiosity overcoming whatever reservations she had about the sorcery. "Is that the Pale Lady?"

"It is a memory that should stay dead," Alyanna said sharply, grimacing as she turned away to stare out into the dark.

25: CHO LIN

"WHERE ARE YOU from?"

The question startled Cho Lin, not only because it was voiced by the pretty, pale-skinned magister who had kept to herself for the last two days, but also because it was put forth in somewhat passable Shan.

She had been distracted, watching ominously dark clouds approach from over the mountains, and for a moment Cho Lin found herself so surprised that she could only turn and stare blankly at the magister.

"Where are you from?" the young woman tried again, carefully enunciating the tones this time. Incorrectly, as it were, but Cho Lin still understood what she was attempting to say. Very few foreigners ever mastered the eight tones of the Shan language.

"Tsai Yin," Cho Lin finally managed, and a smile like the rising sun broke across the magister's face.

"Tsai Yin," she repeated, infusing the city's name with such breathless wonder that to Cho Lin she could have been naming some far-off, mythical locale. Which for her it probably was, Cho Lin realized.

"You know my tongue."

"Yes. A little," the magister said, changing back to Menekarian. "I studied it in the Scholia. The senior magisters – well, I suppose the queen, truly – believed that Shan would make a great ally of Dymoria. That we might have to stand together one day against the emperor of Menekar and his Pure."

Cho Lin gazed past the magister at the column of Dymorian soldiers laboring up the snowy slope. They'd left the flatlands two days ago, entering a rugged landscape of taiga covered in scraggly pine trees. Beyond these hills the Bones rose up to scrape the sky, their peaks shrouded in clouds.

"It seems she was right," Cho Lin said, offering up her own smile. "Dymoria and Shan have become allies. Although the threat is different."

"My name is Seril d'Kalla," the magister said, knuckling her brow as she switched back to her heavily accented Shan. "Of the Blackmoor d'Kallas."

"And I am Cho Lin, daughter of Cho Yuan. May the East Wind always blow at your back, Seril d'Kalla."

"And yours, Mistress Cho. I must apologize for how horribly I speak Shan. There was precious little chance to practice in Herath."

Cho Lin waved her words away. "You are doing well. Most Shan believe our language is too difficult for any barbarian to learn."

"So we are all barbarians to you?" Seril said, and Cho Lin felt a momentary alarm that she had insulted the magister. Then she saw that her grin had widened.

"No," Cho Lin assured her. "I've come to respect you northerners while traveling in the lands beyond the Sea of Solace. Though the people of *this* land," she said, adjusting her fur collar as a frozen wind gusted, "very much deserve to be called barbarians."

She meant it as a jest, but Seril's face fell at her words. "Yes," the magister said softly. "After the battle, they did such terrible things to the dead. They desecrated the bodies, cutting away their . . . their" —her expression clouded and her eyes grew distant, as if she was seeing again what had happened— "their faces. And then they burned the bodies like they were pigs that had come down with the yellow ear disease. Some of them weren't even dead. I heard the screams . . ." She shuddered, unable to continue.

"It sounds terrible," Cho Lin said softly.

The magister must have seen the unasked question in Cho Lin's face. "I lived because I wasn't up on the ridge with the other magisters. I was beside the queen, at her command post behind the army. After . . . after Her Highness fell and the lines broke, the Skein flooded through . . . they were butchering everyone, even the servants and the scribes. I could have fought. I could have summoned fire and burned some of them, at least, but I was so scared." She swallowed hard, her eyes glistening. "I'm not a warrior. I never wanted to hurt anyone. That's why the queen didn't put me up there with Vhelan." Seril glanced guiltily at Cho Lin, as if she was admitting something terrible. "I hid. I pretended to be dead. And I saw what the Skein did, may the Silver Lady spare me." She wiped at her eyes, her face miserable.

"It's all right," Cho Lin said, putting a comforting hand on the magister's shoulder and giving a gentle squeeze. "Not everyone has the temperament to be a soldier. Some people are too kind to imagine causing pain to others. It's not a weakness, truly. It is a laudable thing." She let her arm drop. "I was forced to become a warrior; I had no choice in the matter. I found, though, that it was what I was meant to be. I can kill without any concerns now. Without hesitation. Sometimes I wish I had the strength to care about my enemies."

Seril offered a trembling smile. "I'm just a coward."

"I don't think so," Cho Lin replied, shaking her head slightly.

Their conversation meandered as they trudged through snowy valleys and forests of white-barked trees. The sky continued to darken, and Cho Lin heard the soldiers behind her start to mutter about the impending weather. The commander who had first challenged her yelled a set of commands that sent a few of the Dymorians dressed in green and brown leather loping ahead, presumably to scout for shelter. Cho Lin noticed with a slight pang of guilt the bruised face of the man she'd struck down in the woods as he sped past her, his gaze pointedly turned away from her. Well, he *had* tried to capture her.

Despite the threat of the approaching storm, Cho Lin found her heart lightening as she talked with Seril. The magister had a purity to her that touched Cho Lin – she had been around too many harsh men over the past few months. The past few years, really. The monks of Red Fang emptied their souls of all emotions, even empathy, in their quest for the Nothing. The Skein were a savage people, obsessed with violence and glory. Seril was different. She asked questions about the Empire of Swords and Flowers, its customs and its people, absorbing what Cho Lin told her with wide-eyed wonder. She had the soul of a scholar, not a soldier. The queen must have emptied her school of sorcerers if she had brought this innocent young woman on the march.

Cho Lin, in turn, asked about Seril's life in Herath, both before and during her tenure in the Scholia. The young woman had been born to an ancient and rich house, and she had displayed a deep passion for books and learning at a young age. It had seemed almost like a foregone conclusion, she told Cho Lin with a shrug, when one of the magisters who periodically visited their manse noticed the spark within her and invited her to return with him to Saltstone.

Seril did not offer up any insights about their companions, and Cho Lin did not pry, despite her curiosity. She did not want to do anything that might break this bond that was slowly forming between them – it had been too long since she had spoken with someone as nothing more than a friend.

A friend. The very idea that in the waning days of a quest that could end with another Raveling she had found something as frivolous as a friendship was ridiculous. Cho Lin discovered she didn't care, though, when she pried deeper into her feelings on the matter.

The storm began as a few slow, fat flakes drifting down from the gray sky. Soon, the mountains swelling in front of them were obscured by a swirling veil of white, and then even the forest-covered slopes of the foothills vanished. Cho Lin's trickling unease strengthened into a real fear that they would be caught out in the open. Beside her, Seril stumbled and fell, her arms vanishing up to her elbows in the snow.

"It's so cold," the magister murmured as Cho Lin helped her back to her feet, panic edging her voice.

"We'll need to find shelter," Cho Lin said, squinting into the storm.

She saw them, then, shadows swelling in the depths of the storm. Moments later the Dymorian rangers emerged from the white and made straight for their commander. After a hurried conversation, he turned to the rest of them.

"There's a good place to wait this out," he yelled, his words barely rising over the wind. "Keep together. It's easy to get lost." The commander said something more quietly to the ranger beside him, and with a curt nod the man plunged back into the storm. Then the commander made a motion for the others to follow him before also vanishing.

"Best hurry," Cho Lin said as Seril slipped again. She caught her arm and the magister clutched at her like a piece of driftwood in the middle of the ocean. "We don't want to fall behind."

A light drew her attention, and Cho Lin turned to find the arrogant sorceress drifting past them on her flying circle. She'd summoned a great sphere of blazing radiance and set it to hover above her head, bright enough to penetrate the murk of the snowstorm. Cho Lin couldn't help but curl her lip in mild distaste when she saw how relaxed the sorceress appeared, stretched out on the strange device like she was reclining on a divan in the tearoom of her manse. Her face was bored, her eyes heavy-lidded, and the thickening snow did not appear to be reaching her dusky skin. This was a useful application of her sorcery, as a beacon to give the rest of them something to follow, but Cho Lin had found Alyanna's casual displays garish. The warlocks of Shan would never have shown their power so crassly.

The sorceress glanced at Cho Lin as she willed her floating palanquin after the ranger. Her eyes widened slightly, flicking from Cho Lin to the magister who clutched at her for support, and a flash of annoyance came and went in her face. Then she turned, leaving them behind, her roiling light dwindling as her flying circle quickened.

Cho Lin had developed an immediate dislike for the sorceress. She seemed to treat the rest of them, even those that who clearly older than her, as little more than children, with a sort of annoyed exasperation. Cho Lin wondered if she had been right to give the shards of her family sword to the sorceress for study. She still wanted to hold on to a flicker of hope that the blade could be reforged, even though she knew that was foolish. Cho Lin patted her furs above her heart, where she had slipped the only fragment of the Sword of Cho that wasn't on the flying circle with the sorceress. It was the same one in which she had glimpsed the face of the Shan concubine. It gave her comfort knowing it was there.

With Seril still leaning on her, Cho Lin followed the sorceress's light through the strengthening storm. The magister must have turned her ankle, as she was limping slightly as they slogged through the snow. Soon the ground became more uneven, the trees sparser, until finally they reached a stony cleft in the side of a great boulder. The space was large enough for all of them to shelter under, if they squeezed together, and so deep that the inner recesses were free of snow. Cho Lin brought Seril over to a rock and helped her to sit as the remaining soldiers stumbled from the swirling white, snow clotting their beards. With exhausted groans, they found dry spaces under the overhang and let their packs slip from their backs, then stretched out themselves. The Dymorian commander moved among them, counting to make sure none of the soldiers were still lost out there in the storm. When he was satisfied he cleared his throat to seize everyone's attention.

"Enjoy your rest, scrappers," he said loudly, turning to meet as many pairs of eyes as possible. "We'll stay here the night; by morning, the storm should've passed. It'll be hard going in the fresh snow, but we knew this wasn't going to be easy. Our queen is out there, captive of these barbarian bastards. Word is that we're close, might be even tomorrow we find where they've camped. So sleep, if you can. There'll be fighting soon." With that, he nodded curtly and strode away.

Cho Lin watched the faces of the men. There were no cheers following the commander's pronouncement, no raised fists or swords. The soldiers were hollow-eyed and sunken-cheeked, tired beyond endurance. The events of the last few weeks would have broken the resolve of most any soldier, Cho Lin admitted. Now this tiny band was about to try to rescue Cein d'Kara from a Skein horde of unknown size. And what if they succeeded? They would be trapped in the far north, hunted by a hostile people. It was a suicide mission, and from the looks of it, most of the men here knew this. Yet there had been no desertions, to her knowledge. It was a testament to the discipline of the Dymorian army and the affection with which the Crimson Queen was held by her subjects.

The other magister, Vhelan, began to circulate between the pockets of soldiers as they worked to set up some semblance of a camp. Cho Lin watched the way he squeezed the shoulders of some men and slapped the backs of others, smiling and laughing. In his wake, the men he spoke to seemed to straighten, some of the bleakness in their faces replaced by grim resolve. Here was their true leader, Cho Lin realized. The young Dymorian commander might have the authority because of rank and noble blood, but it was the magister who was keeping their frayed morale from unraveling completely.

She wasn't sure how long she sat there, her thoughts drifting in a numb cloud of exhaustion and cold, before suddenly she felt a presence beside her.

"Hello," said the boy who usually stayed in the company of the senior magister. He crouched beside her, his dark eyes fixed on her with obvious interest.

Cho Lin nodded in greeting. "Well met, I am Cho Lin."

"Keilan," the boy said, touching his chest lightly.

Seril had fallen asleep, her head leaning against Cho Lin's shoulder, and she stirred awake at the sound of their voices.

"Oh, I'm so sorry, Magister," Keilan said, his face flushing.

Seril straightened, shaking her head slightly as if to clear it of cobwebs. "It's nothing, apprentice. I should go lie down." Putting her hand on Cho Lin's shoulder, she stood, wincing, and then limped away to find a space to spread her bed-roll.

"Apprentice?" Cho Lin said while watching the magister depart. "You are a sorcerer?"

"I'm a student in the Scholia," Keilan said. "Or I was, for a time. I ran away, so I'm not certain if I am anymore."

Cho Lin gestured with her chin at where Vhelan was smiling and chuckling with a group of soldiers. "I've seen you with him. It seems like the magisters still accept you."

"I've known Vhelan and Nel longer than I've been an apprentice in the Scholia. They were the ones who first found me and brought me to Dymoria."

Keilan lapsed into silence, as if remembering something. His gaze became unfocused as he stared beyond their shelter at the thickly falling snow.

"I met a Shan once," he finally said, surprising Cho Lin.

"Oh?"

"He was very polite. He gave me tea." Keilan's voice became distant. "I watched him die."

Cho Lin studied the face of the boy. There was a deepness to him, she decided. Despite his youth, he'd suffered great losses. These events had not broken him, but they weighed heavily upon his soul.

Like her, he had been forced to grow up too soon.

"Did you enjoy the tea?" she asked lightly, and this seemed to jar Keilan from his melancholy.

"I did," Keilan said with a slight smile, as if he knew what she was trying to do. "It was bitter, but nowhere near as bitter as what we drink in my village. There were flowers floating in it!"

Cho Lin grinned. "Flower tea is my favorite," she said, then raised her eyes to stare at the rock above. "By the Four Winds, I would look beyond the veil for a cup of jasmine or tiger-ear tea."

"Tiger-ear tea?" Keilan said, and Cho Lin had to cover her mouth to hide her laughter at his horrified expression.

"It's a kind of lotus flower," she told him when her mirth had subsided.

"Ah," Keilan said, smiling sheepishly. He swallowed, as if trying to work up the courage to ask her something.

"Yes?" Cho Lin said, raising her eyebrows.

"Tell me about Shan," Keilan said, his tone almost begging.

"What do you want to know?"

He opened his mouth, then paused, as if trying to decide what he should ask. Finally, he shrugged. "Everything, I suppose. Tell me everything."

And for the second time that day, she did.

They talked well into the night while the storm raged outside, eventually moving to where a few of the soldiers had managed to coax a fire to life. The boy had a ravenous curiosity, and his questions meandered the length and breadth of her homeland. They talked about the food in Shan, the emperor and his Jade Court, the spirits her people prayed to and the cataclysm that had driven them across the World Sea and into the ruins of the Kalyuni Imperium. He was especially interested in the warlocks of Tsai Yin, his eyes widening as she told him about how the sorcerers of Shan dwelled in great towers of bone scavenged from the corpses of the giant turtles that had ferried them across the ocean.

After a time, the small woman who moved with the balance of a trained warrior came and sat near them. She said nothing, watching Cho Lin with shadowed eyes. Cho Lin nodded at her in greeting, but she did not respond, and eventually she stood again and retreated to where the others had spread their bedrolls. Watching her settle beside the senior magister made Cho Lin realize how exhausted she herself was, and she held up her hand to stop the boy's incessant questions.

He dropped his eyes sheepishly, as if he knew that they should be taking the opportunity to rest.

"We may speak again on the morrow, Keilan," she said, standing and stretching her tired limbs.

The storm had abated by the time the gray dawn lightened the sky outside their shelter. The drifts were deep, and the soldiers grumbled as they broke camp to continue the journey north. A year ago, Cho Lin would have found the thick white blanket draped over the trees to be beautiful, magical even, but now she shared the Dymorian's exasperation with the weather. Why had men ever settled in these lands, when a thousand *li* to the south it never snowed and fruits hung from branches all year round?

The journey was arduous, not only because of the fresh snow, but also because the land was growing more rumpled as they ascended into the foothills of the northern Bones. Jagged peaks now rose around them, tapering into sword points that pierced the brilliant blue above. A pair of black shapes were etched against the sky, lazily drifting on invisible currents high above. At first Cho Lin thought they must be birds, but then she realized just how large these creatures must be, and a shiver went through her. Whatever they were, she thought they could easily carry a man away. She remembered the dead wyvern the Skein king had returned from his hunt with, and wondered if those distant wings were covered in scales rather than feathers.

Cho Lin thought Keilan might seek her out the next day, but he lingered towards the rear of their column, walking beside the sorceress on her magic circle. They were deep in conversation, and every once in a while Cho Lin saw a little flare of light as the boy summoned some sorcery. A few of the soldiers glanced back nervously when a particularly vivid or loud spell split the monotony of the march, but for the most part the displays did not bother them. The Dymorians had been conditioned to accept sorcery, which surprised Cho Lin. She had thought that all the north feared and hated magic, and yet here was evidence to the contrary. What would the empire of Menekar and its paladins think about this? The emperor had waged several wars against the Empire of Swords and Flowers because of the Shan's open acceptance of their warlocks – how could he abide such behavior in a kingdom north of the Broken Sea?

She was trudging along lost in her thoughts when a commotion began ahead of her. A Dymorian ranger had just emerged from the woods, his face flushed, and she quickened her pace to hear what news he had to report.

"—it's them," the scout was saying, and her breath caught in her throat. "The Skein are there, m'lord. Outside a door big as a castle, set in the side of a hill. And the door . . . the door is open, m'lord."

26: ALYANNA

THE SKEIN WERE as motionless as the dead.
They had camped near the base of the hill that climbed up to the great door, a dozen blackened campfires encircled by small wagons. The horses were still yoked to their harnesses, as if the barbarians were ready to flee at any moment. At this distance, from the top of a wooded ridge looking down on the valley below, the men around the campfires were little bigger than insects. None were moving that she could see.

They were still alive, though, she was fairly certain of that. The gnawing in her head from the Worm had strengthened the closer they'd gotten to its resting place, until it actually felt like something was slowly burrowing its way through her skull. It was discomforting, but the sense was exacerbated among those without Talent; the rest of their band, save Keilan, were constantly shaking their heads and grimacing, as if trying to clear their thoughts after a night of drunken revelry. The Talented could sense the Ancients from farther away, but the effects were far more pronounced for those without sorcery the closer they had approached. Alyanna imagined that the Skein down there were lost in a numb haze, unable to understand the alien dreams that were infringing upon their minds.

Had the opening of the door strengthened the emanations flowing from within the Burrow? Despite her cloak of warmth, she couldn't hold back a shiver staring into that yawning darkness. She had seen illustrations of this place in books, and always the slab of featureless stone had been closed; in the histories of Min-Ceruth, when the Worm was slowly thrashing awake, the sorceress queen of Nes Vaneth and her trusted companions had opened the door and ventured within. They had not described the things they'd seen under the Burrow, or what had happened, but they had managed to quiet the Worm, then sealed the door again. Whatever was inside had claimed the lives of most of the Talents. It had proven dangerous to tread into the realm of a sleeping god. After, though, the Worm had remained quiet for thousands of years, and the door had remained closed.

Until now.

"That Skein sorcerer down there?"

Alyanna turned. The Dymorian commander had come alongside her. He looked as if he was suffering from a terrible headache.

"I have sought him out as gently as I can, and I have not found him. Nor do I believe the queen is in that camp."

D'Venish frowned. "Then that means . . ."

"Yes. They've already gone inside."

"Do you really believe there's some great monster in there?" His skepticism was evident.

Alyanna returned his look evenly. "I know there is, Commander. And how can you doubt it? You can feel the gnawing in your head, can't you? A presence pressing down on you, vast and terrible?"

"Enough," d'Venish said, cutting the air sharply with his hand. He tried to hide his true feelings behind a mask of anger and contempt, but Alyanna saw his fear.

He composed himself. "We are ready to attack. Our rangers killed their lookouts and we should be able to catch them completely unawares."

"Good. Then there is no time to waste."

"But they outnumber us four times over," d'Venish continued. "And my men are exhausted from the march. We cannot win if we charge them now. Perhaps if we wait until the night . . ."

Alyanna shook her head. "If the Skein sorcerer is not there, then they are cattle ready for the slaughter." With a flicker of sorcery, she lifted herself from the snow. Power surged along her limbs, crackling like lightning. The Dymorian hurriedly stepped back. "Sound the attack, Commander."

She ascended higher into the sky before he could attempt to argue with her. She wondered in passing if he would dare refuse to commit his troops now. It would not matter anyway, truly. These were mortal men, and she was so much more.

Still, she was satisfied when she heard the commander's horn rise up behind her.

The Skein began to stir as she drifted closer. At first, they moved sluggishly, as if unsure what she was or the threat she represented, but by the time she hovered over their fires they were scrambling to reach their weapons, pointing up at her and screaming in their harsh tongue. Men in filthy furs with long ragged hair, their faces inked with barbaric designs. Alyanna sneered. This was what the glory of the north had been reduced to? These savages?

A dozen of the Skein had drawn bows and were kneeling in the snow, and when a barked command came, they loosed a volley towards her. Some of the arrows snapped when they struck her invisible wards, while others skittered away and fell among the warriors milling below. One of the brutes hurled an ax of black iron high enough that it clanged only a few span from her face; with a thought, Alyanna wrapped the weapon in lines of force, then sent it tumbling end over end back towards the thrower. Alyanna smirked as he toppled over, the blade buried in his skull.

More shouts and cries from the Skein, but now she could hear their panic. Good. She was a goddess, and they were nothing.

Alyanna drew from the Void until her body thrummed with sorcery. Then she unleashed death.

Ropes of shimmering power unspooled from her hands. Bodies were torn asunder, flesh blackened and sloughed away from bones, blood hissed and sizzled. The barbarians shrieked in pain and fear, scrambling to evade her wrath. Snow and earth fountained into the sky as her sorcery churned the ground. Laughing, Alyanna raked the fleeing Skein, engulfing their wagons with flame as they sought shelter within. The horses screamed and kicked, straining against their halters, desperate to escape. The thought occurred to Alyanna that there was a slim possibility that Cein d'Kara or even Jan might be inside one of the wagons, perhaps collared to hide them from her senses, so with a thought she dampened the fire. The Dymorians could root out any that had hidden inside.

Alyanna revolved slowly in the air, gazing down at the smoking devastation she had wrought. The Skein had scattered, and no more arrows reached her wards. It should be a simple matter for the soldiers to kill the survivors. Pleased, she began to descend, but then hissed when she glanced below.

One of the Chosen stood among the dismembered corpses of the men she'd slain. Its white face was tilted upwards to watch her, though Alyanna didn't know what it saw, as this was one of the children whose eyes had been gouged out. Black veins writhed beneath its pale skin like worms wriggling through its flesh. Alyanna glanced around quickly, looking for the demon's brethren. She couldn't see any, but that didn't mean they weren't out there.

Her heart beating fast, she resumed her descent, until she stood in the snow a few dozen paces from the creature. It did not move or speak as she drew more and more strength from the Void, reinforcing her wards. Around her, beyond the boundary formed by the wagons, the sounds of battle swelled as the Dymorians fought the remnants of the Skein. She kept the entirety of her attention focused on the Shan demon.

"Let's see if you bleed," she snarled, her fingers tightening around the ebony handle of her flail.

Cho Lin charged across the snow, her butterfly swords unsheathed. Around her surged the remnants of the Dymorian army – haggard men in tattered armor, bellowing unintelligible war cries, their gazes fixed on the flashes of color rising up from within the ring of wagons. She reached for the Nothing, but the crackling hum in her head that had been swelling for the last few days kept her from falling into the deepness of the Self. Complete and total concentration was required, and the presence of this . . . this thing slumbering here in the north was making that impossible.

No matter. She had still been trained by the greatest swordsmen of Shan, and she did not require the Nothing to exact her vengeance.

Skein streamed around the wagons, fleeing the death the sorceress was hurling down from above. They staggered towards the Dymorians, more than a few with faces blackened and smoke drifting from their furs and hair. The Skein who still held their axes and swords raised them as the soldiers of the queen smashed into their midst, hacking and slashing. Cho Lin knocked aside a half-hearted swing from a bow that one of the Skein was wielding like a club, then buried her blade in his stomach. The man's eyes, set within an elaborately inked face of some snarling beast, widened in shock. Another took his place when he slumped in the snow, a man cradling the stump of his arm as he blundered past her. She let him go, but a few steps later one of the Dymorian rangers sent a black-fletched arrow through his throat.

Not a single soldier had fallen in this first skirmish, and a dozen of the Skein now lay dead. It had been a slaughter – the dazed barbarians had almost thrown themselves on the Dymorians' swords to escape the charnel field the sorceress had made within the circled wagons.

"Swords ready, scrappers!" shouted d'Venish, his face streaked with blood as he pointed his own blade towards where a larger band of Skein had appeared. These warriors did not seem as panicked as the ones who had already fallen.

"For the queen!" the commander bellowed, and echoing cries rose up as the Dymorians resumed their charge.

Cho Lin followed the screaming soldiers, though she was nearly thrown from her feet as a terrible explosion sounded from where the sorceress had vanished; it shook the ground and left her head ringing. A few of the Dymorians did slip and fall in the snow, but the blast knocked down just as many Skein. There was a frozen moment while all the warriors recovered, casting uncertain glances at the wagons that hid the sorceress from view. The shriek and crash of Alyanna's sorceries had momentarily abated, as if she had killed all the Skein that had dared remain before her.

A roar went up from the barbarians, surprising Cho Lin, and then they were rushing across the snow. The first Skein they had encountered must have been the cowards who had fled when the sorceress first attacked; these warriors, they were the ones who had only retreated when it had become clear that they could not stand before Alyanna.

Steel shrieked as the two sides came together with jarring force. She saw a Dymorian soldier take a spear in the throat, nearly severing his head. His companion screamed and bashed that Skein in the face with the buckler around his arm, then plunged his short sword into the barbarian's chest as he stumbled backwards. Elsewhere, a giant of a man, the knotted ropes of his blond beard swinging, held off a pair of soldiers by sweeping his great black ax in vicious arcs.

A Skein appeared before Cho Lin, his face painted white save for smudged black rings about his eyes, screaming incoherently as he thrust with his sword. She twisted out of the way, letting his momentum take him stumbling forward a step, then with a sweeping cut sent his head bouncing into the snow.

All discipline had broken down – the battle was swirling chaos, a collection of small skirmishes. Men screamed in rage and pain and terror, their voices rising above the constant sound of swords clashing and metal sinking into flesh.

Cho Lin found herself in a pocket of calm. She glanced around, looking for anywhere the Skein seemed on the verge of overwhelming the soldiers, preparing to throw herself into that fight. Cho Lin was not the only one with this idea – the Dymorian commander d'Venish and a few of his soldiers were making their way towards a knot of barbarians. As they smashed into that line of Skein, a gap opened in their ranks and Cho Lin glimpsed who stood behind them – Hroi, the thane of the White Worm and the king of the Frostlands. He wore the mottled cloak of the Skin Thief, and a circlet of black bone lay upon his brow. Hroi showed no concern as d'Venish hurtled closer with his curving officer's sword upraised, and at the last moment, the thane brought his own dark-bladed sword sweeping up to meet the commander's sword. D'Venish followed his initial strike with a flurry of flashing blows, but Hroi met and turned each away with an almost casual disdain.

Cho Lin began to run towards them, her heart sinking. The Dymorian commander was not a terrible swordsman, but she could tell that the Skein king was an entirely different breed of warrior. D'Venish must have realized this as well, but the Dymorian nevertheless pressed harder, hammering the Skein king's guard with desperate blows.

She knew what was about to happen, but she could do nothing to stop it. Hroi turned aside d'Venish's sword, then stepped forward and slashed the Dymorian's neck. Cho Lin burst through the fighting, arriving next to the commander just as he crumpled to the snow with his fingers scrabbling weakly at his ravaged throat.

The Skein king was already stalking towards her, and she raised her butterfly swords as she found her footing in the snow. A dark smile twisted Hroi's face.

"The Shan," he said, no hate or anger in his voice. He might have been addressing her back in the Bhalavan as she stood before his throne.

She flicked her swords in a quick pattern, loosening her wrists. He must have seen something in her crisp movements, as his expression hardened. He reached up and unclasped his cloak of cured flesh, letting it fall to the snow.

Cho Lin saw now that there was a second sword at his side, and Hroi's other hand went to the hilt. He drew it smoothly, with no hint of awkwardness. This one was in stark contrast to the dark blade he already held, a length of rippling silver inscribed with runes. He cut the air with the sword, as if testing its balance, and a jewel red as heartsblood flashed in its pommel as it caught the sunlight.

Then he attacked.

Alyanna paced in the snow, walking a wide circuit around the demon child. It did not move, yet somehow it was always facing her, radiating cold malice. Even though it lacked eyes, she felt its awareness following her. Alyanna's hand stayed on the hilt of her flail, and she felt the presence inside the ancient artifact questing out to understand the nature of the Chosen.

"Where are your brothers and sisters?" Alyanna asked mockingly, never taking her eyes from the demon.

She had not expected an answer, and was surprised when it replied in its ragged whisper.

inside. they go to wake the old one. you are too late, mistress.

Something was different. Every other time the Chosen had spoken she'd heard a chorus of hoarse voices. But this time there had been only one, and the inflections were that of a small girl.

Alyanna glanced at the Burrow looming above them. The gaping hole set in its side drank the sunlight, revealing nothing of what was within.

"Am I? I don't feel the Ancient stirring." She continued circling the demon. "You didn't know what was inside, did you? Jan of course never read those histories, the fool." Her fingers stroked the icy handle of the flail. "A dozen true Talents delved into the depths when the Worm was waking two thousand years ago. Five returned. Do you think two hobbled sorcerers, an ignorant savage, and a few pathetic ghosts of murdered children can survive what is within?" She snorted. "The rules of this world change inside the Burrow." Alyanna lowered her voice. "You can't feel them anymore, can you? The bonds have been sundered. You are alone."

The Chosen did not respond, but Alyanna saw one of its blackened fingers twitch. She pressed on, hoping her guess was correct.

"His power over you is broken. You can be free again."

wan ying is only one of five. his hate is my hate.

Alyanna kept her disappointment from showing. Instead, she sneered, drawing forth her flail. Strands of shadow coalesced from nothing, twisting and snapping in the air like living creatures. The flail strained against her will, pleading to be unleashed.

"Let us make Wan Ying one of four."

With a thought, she let slip the restraints, and the tendrils of darkness leapt forward, rippling towards the Chosen. The strands crossed the distance between them in an eyeblink, but the child demon twisted out of the way, contorting its body unnaturally so that the ravenous arms of the flail slipped past it without sinking into its dead flesh. Alyanna grunted in frustration and swung the ebony hilt sharply, whipping the tendrils through the air. Again, the Chosen avoided most of the lashing tendrils, but one managed to sink into its arm. For a moment it was trapped, and the flail seized this chance to wrap a half-dozen more of its arms around where the first had fastened itself to the Chosen. Alyanna let loose with a cry of triumph. She gripped the handle tightly with both hands, pulling hard as she willed her sorcery to strengthen the tendrils. The Chosen leaned its body away from the flail as the weapon dragged it towards Alyanna, its heels skidding in the snow.

Wisps of darkness were leaking from where the tendril's barbed ends had punctured skin, the coils constricting as the flail crushed the Chosen's arm.

"Die, you bastard," Alyanna hissed, straining to rip the limb away. The tension was swelling towards a breaking point, and she pulled harder.

Then she was stumbling backwards, barely able to keep herself upright. Cold surprise washed over her. She still held the ebony hilt of the flail, but the dark tendrils had been uprooted like weeds; they squirmed wildly, leaking shadows that stained the air. With a growl, the Chosen ripped the coils away and tossed them aside, where they writhed in the snow.

"By the dead gods . . ." she whispered, numb with shock. Then she jumped as her wards shuddered violently. The Chosen had leapt forward faster than she could see, slamming itself against her invisible shield. Its blackened fingers, tipped with long ragged nails, raked her wards; to anyone else it would look like the child demon was flailing against the air, but Alyanna could see the great gouges the creature was scooping from her sorcerous shield. Desperately, she poured more of her strength into the ward, reinforcing it. She still held the ebony handle, but the ancient soul that had infused the artifact had slipped into oblivion. Now she grasped nothing more than a hunk of cold dead wood. She hurled it to the snow, still having trouble comprehending what had just happened.

The Chosen had been hurt, though. It was hurling itself again and again at her wards, scrabbling to break through, but Alyanna could see that the arm the flail had seized was hanging oddly, as if whatever passed for its bones had been crushed and only its flesh was keeping it attached to its shoulder. There was blackness leaking from the wound as well, curling in the air, but Alyanna wasn't certain if that was the Chosen's blood or the remnants of whatever had spilled from the broken tendrils.

Her wards buckled again, and she was forced to channel more sorcery to keep them from collapsing.

Alyanna struggled to control her rising fear.

"What are you?" she murmured.

Hroi lunged at Cho Lin, stabbing at her with his dark blade. She crossed her butterfly swords and caught the length of clouded amber, the strange metal ringing like a struck bell. The force of the strike drove her back a pace, and she feared for a moment that her swords might shatter, but the ancient steel held. The Skein king followed with a broad sweep of the longer silver blade, and she leapt away, feeling the tip graze the furs covering her stomach. She had barely found her footing before he was pressing her again, lashing out with both blades. Her butterfly swords swept up to meet and turn aside the king's blows as they came in rapid succession. The other Skein had been sluggish, almost dazed by their time in the shadow of the mountain, but not Hroi.

Cho Lin was driven backwards as she desperately warded away the flickering blades, and she had to keep some small measure of concentration on keeping her footing in the snow. She gritted her teeth as she barely caught the amber sword before it found her belly, her wrist aching as it absorbed the force of the cut. Cho Lin had never seen a warrior wield two long blades as well as the Skein king – usually swordsmen preferred a shorter, parrying dagger to accompany a longer blade for striking, though her own pairing of identical butterfly swords was not unheard of.

Hroi's skill was frightening; he lacked the precision and agility of a Red Fang master, but his strength and speed were almost unnatural. Craftiness, too – several times he nearly lulled her into a fatal mistake, pretending to overextend on a slash and offering her a tantalizing opening to rush forward, but she restrained herself, and then he snapped his swords back into their guard with no suggestion that he had ever truly lost his balance. At times she tried to steal the initiative, launching her own flurry of strikes, but his blades met her own with disconcerting ease.

Her arms were tiring and her wrists burned. Without the strength of the Nothing flowing through her she would soon be exhausted. Despair crept into her heart, and her sword faltered, a heartbeat late. The tip of the silver sword grazed her thigh, opening a line of fire on her leg. She grunted in pain and hopped back a few steps, trying to buy herself a few moments to find her composure again, but the Skein king followed her with a vicious grin, his dark eyes exultant. Frantically, she turned away his eager slashes, avoiding a more serious injury by luck as much as skill.

Out of the corner of her eye she glimpsed a man wrapped in blue flames stumbling through the snow. Skein or Dymorian, she couldn't tell. His screams penetrated the fog in her head, and then she noticed more sounds, thunder grumbling loudly and the crack of ice shattering. She wanted to turn and see what was happening, but Hroi was coming at her again, swords whirling. He must have seen what she could not, as his mouth was set in a grim, determined line as he attacked. Her butterfly sword deflected the amber blade with a ringing clash, but her wounded leg gave out and she slipped to one knee in the snow with a pained cry. Hroi chopped down with his silver sword and she caught it with the guard of her own sword, but the force jarred the hilt from her hand. The Skein snarled something fierce and kicked out, his boot striking her in the chest. The breath was knocked from her as she went sprawling, and she lost her grip on her other sword.

A lance of crimson sorcery struck the Skein king in the chest, sending him tumbling backwards. Cho Lin drew in a shuddering breath and rolled onto her side, wincing at the grating pain in her ribs. Seril stood a few dozen paces away, her slim hand upraised, her eyes wide with surprise. Behind her, the fighting still raged, but a quick glance told Cho Lin that the Skein were nearly finished – the few barbarians still standing were surrounded by several soldiers, and she saw a volley of flashing green darts flash from elsewhere and disappear into one of the warriors. He roared, dropping his great sword to slap at his furs like he had been stung by a swarm of bees, and the pair of soldiers that had been kept at bay by his huge blade closed on him with flashing steel.

Cho Lin rolled to her feet and scooped one of her swords from the snow. She hobbled over to where the king of the Skein lay sprawled on his back; his dark eyes stared sightlessly at the blue sky, and a hole had been charred in the furs draped over his chest. Cho Lin stepped over him and saw that the red lance had also blasted a hole through the chain armor and flesh beneath.

Seril's strained voice came from just behind her. "I didn't . . . that was the first . . . is he dead?"

"Very dead," Cho Lin said, turning to the ashen-faced magister. Seril was staring at the dead king in horror, as if she couldn't believe what she had done.

Cho Lin took a step closer and wrapped her in an embrace.

"I didn't mean to kill him," Seril whispered.

"Thank the Four Winds you did," Cho Lin told her. "Else I would be dead."

She pulled away. Seril tugged on a lock of her golden hair, staring at the dead king in dread fascination. They turned as a final rending crash signaled the end of the battle, the lone remaining Skein warrior felled by a crackling green bolt. Cho Lin looked around to find the magister Vhelan sauntering through the corpses, emerald fire limning his hands.

He saw them and smiled broadly. "Victory!" He noticed Hroi's prone body and his eyebrows rose. "And well done, Magister d'Kalla. We'll make a battlemage of you yet."

"No," Seril said softly with a shudder. "I am not that kind of sorceress."

Vhelan paused, glancing around. "Speaking of those kinds of sorceresses . . . where is Alyanna?"

The demon stalked the perimeter of Alyanna's wards, the oily black blood leaking from its ravaged arm uncoiling in the air like smoke. Despite its eyes having been gouged out, Alyanna could somehow sense its burning, hateful stare, and it made her skin prickle. The black veins beneath its corpse-skin writhed, and she shuddered. Whatever it had once been, this child was tainted by powers beyond this world.

"What was your mother like?" Alyanna called out as it prowled around her.

The Chosen ignored her taunt, its face blank, continuing its circuit. Suddenly it attacked, clawing at her wards. In her mind's eye Alyanna saw the rent the creature's fingers had left in the invisible barrier, and she poured sorcery into the gap to seal it as quickly as possible.

Such strength! A dragon's lashing tail would have done less damage to her wards – had, in fact. Either the Chosen was far stronger than it looked, or whatever Void essence had corrupted its body was helping to corrode her sorcery. It struck again, nearly breaking through. Alyanna let out a shuddering breath. It was only a matter of time before the demon succeeded, and once it was within her wards, she had no illusions about how long she'd last. She needed to attack.

With the bulk of her strength devoted to maintaining her shield, she could only summon forth a lesser sorcery – dreadfire would have been her first choice, but that spell drained all Talents of their reserves, and if she missed or it proved ineffective the Chosen would be through her wards and tearing out her throat before the next moment had passed. Instead, she conjured a sphere of blue fire and thrust it crackling at the demon; it exploded when it struck the Chosen, gobbets of azure flame raining down, and the creature staggered back a step. Yet it appeared unharmed, and even its hair and ragged clothes failed to ignite. Alyanna honestly wasn't certain if even dreadfire would have the slightest effect on this thing.

The warlocks had been right – it would take a special weapon to slay the demons. Her hand slipped to the handle of the black knife and a cold thrill went through her. *Please, by all the dead gods, let Niara's genius be borne out this one last time.*

Alyanna's heart quickened. She would have to drop her wards, and then stab it before it could tear her apart. Sweat slickened her grip on the handle.

One chance.

Her life spun on the end of a fraying rope.

The Chosen raked her wards, slicing away another chunk. She could feel it pressing itself against the barrier, as cold as iron in winter.

Three. Two. One.

Alyanna dropped the ward, and she almost thought she saw surprise in the child's sunken face as it stumbled forward a step. She surged forward, stabbing with the knife she'd drawn from her belt.

The dark-threaded blade plunged towards the Chosen's throat. She was too close; it couldn't move in time, the edge was going to open whatever passed for an artery in its neck and spill its vile contents—

She missed.

The Chosen jerked its head away faster than she thought possible, then slapped at her hand. Alyanna screamed; it felt like a huge rock had struck her fingers. The knife was lost, spinning away through the air. Moaning, cradling her hand, Alyanna staggered backwards. For a moment the Chosen watched the knife where it had fallen, as if intrigued by something it saw, and then its lips pulled back from its blackened teeth as it lunged at her.

Screaming in terror, Alyanna summoned a final, desperate ward, just as the Chosen struck her and bore her to the snow. It was a thin shell barely a span from her body, and so fragile she felt it tremble as the demon slashed at her again and again. It was so close she could smell it now – the Chosen stank of holes deep under the earth where things rotted in the dark. She gagged, her tenuous hold on her ward slipping through her fingers as the demon straddling her struck again and again.

The last vestige of her ward turned to mist. "No!" she cried, throwing out her arms, expecting to feel the claws or fangs of the demon tearing at her flesh.

The Chosen shuddered, arching its back and raising its face to the sky. Alyanna scrabbled for her sorcery, trying to grasp enough that she could reform her shattered defenses. A rattling hiss escaped from the Chosen as it slowly lowered its head to stare down at her. Black tears streaked its pallid cheeks, leaking from the gaping holes where once its eyes had been. The demon's mouth opened, as if it was about to say something, and then it toppled off her.

On the edge of panic, Alyanna pushed herself away from the slumped Chosen, slipping and falling as she tried to stand.

Then she saw it – the hilt of the black knife protruding from between its bony shoulder blades.

A dozen paces away, Nel stood with her arm still frozen in the act of throwing, her eyes wide as she stared at the sprawled child-demon.

Alyanna fought back the terror that had nearly overwhelmed her. Taking a steadying breath she mastered herself again.

"Is it dead?" Nel asked.

"It was already dead," Alyanna replied, trying to hide how close she had been to breaking. She edged closer to the motionless demon, finally finding the power to weave a fragile ward; the demon would likely tear her sorcery apart like steel through silk if it leapt at her again, but still it made her feel more confident knowing it was there.

The Chosen was changing; it was lying face down, with one arm folded beneath its chest, but the other lay outstretched, half sunk in the snow. The color of the demon's pallid flesh was subtly shifting, and Alyanna could no longer see the distended black veins. For the first time, the Chosen's tangled hair was stirring in the breeze. Then its body and its ragged clothes began to blacken and shrivel, crumbling away. In the span of a few breaths there was nothing but the ashy outline of a small child upon the white snow. In its center, apparently untouched, lay the black knife.

"Well done, Niara," Alyanna whispered. She turned her attention to the magister's servant. "And I've decided to forgive you for your earlier transgressions."

Nel snorted and looked away.

Alyanna knelt beside the remains of the Chosen and gently lifted the black knife. The dark strands threading the metal might have lightened slightly, but perhaps that was her imagination.

"Sorceress!"

She glanced up from her examination of the dagger. The Shan girl was approaching, still holding her blood-streaked swords.

"Where were you?" Cho Lin asked accusingly, her jaw clenched. She seemed to have been wounded, as she was favoring her right leg.

"Finishing what we came here to do," Alyanna replied with a sniff, pointing the tip of the dagger at the ash smeared across the snow.

Cho Lin glared at her, and then comprehension slowly broke across her face. "Wait, that was—" She glanced at Nel, as if asking for confirmation. After the Lyrish thief nodded, Cho Lin sheathed her swords and hobbled over to the Chosen's ashes, sinking to her knees.

Cho Lin reached out, hesitated, and then scooped up a handful of the black grit. She let it sift through her fingers, her uptilted eyes wide with wonder as some of it was carried away by the breeze.

"It was just one?" she said softly.

"The others are inside the Burrow."

Cho Lin glanced sharply at Alyanna. "How do you know this?"

"The Chosen spoke with only one voice; it had been cut off from its brethren. The layers of sorcery separating the Burrow from the outside world must have severed their bond."

Cho Lin rose, wincing. "Truly, this weapon is a gift from the gods. How did you use it?"

Nel cleared her throat. "I was the one who stabbed the demon."

Cho Lin narrowed her eyes. "So no sorcery is required to wield the knife."

"None. Shove the point in and the demon falls apart."

The Shan turned to Alyanna. "Let me have the knife. There is no one here more deadly with a blade."

Nel opened her mouth as if to argue this, then shrugged. "True," she said grudgingly. "I saw her fighting the Skein." Then she smirked at Alyanna. "And you're useless. You looked like a butcher trying to hack up a piece of meat." Nel pantomimed an awkward chop with an imaginary knife.

Alyanna scowled, but she knew the idiot girl was right. She was no warrior.

She measured the Shan girl carefully. Young and slight, but there was a hardness about her. Her family had hunted the Chosen for a thousand years. And she was a disciple of Red Fang, the crucible known for forging the finest warriors in the world.

Alyanna drew the knife and offered it to the girl hilt first.

Cho Lin accepted it with a bow of her head. She stared at the black-threaded metal for a long moment; then she said something in Shan, a rapid tumble of strange words, and slipped the knife away.

Nel had also approached to examine the Chosen's remains. "Was this . . . was this the child connected to Keilan?"

Alyanna shook her head. "I don't think so. It felt different to me. But it gave me another name: the leader of these demons."

Cho Lin blinked. "Names? You know their names?" She sounded incredulous.

"Yes. There is a girl whose name was Ko Yan. And this demon mentioned another, their brother. The strongest of them, I believe." Alyanna thought back to the hoarse, sibilant whisper of the Chosen, trying to remember what it had said. "Wan Ying. He is the one dominating the others. If we can destroy him first, the corruption sustaining the rest of them might fail."

Cho Lin shook her head. "Wan Ying. That is not a name in Shan."

"I am certain that is what I heard."

Cho Lin grimaced. "It must be, for those words do have meaning. If it is the demon's name, it might have forgotten who it once was. Wan Ying means the Shadow King."

The crunch of boots slogging through the snow drew their attention. Vhelan and a handful of the Dymorian soldiers came hurrying through a gap between the wagons; the magister's face brightened when he saw them, but to Alyanna it seemed like something was wrong. At least a few of the soldiers looked disturbed, their faces pale.

"Ah!" he cried in relief. "I'm glad to see you ladies all survived the battle unscathed. A great victory." He smiled, but it did not touch his eyes. "Mistress Alyanna," he said formally, "would you mind accompanying me, please? There's something you must see."

Puzzled, Alyanna followed the magister as he turned away, the soldiers falling in behind them. She glanced back at Cho Lin, who had returned to crouch beside the ashes. Was she right to trust the Shan girl? She still felt uneasy giving up such a powerful artifact.

Vhelan led them across a snowy field towards where a lone wagon waited. A few Skein corpses were here, feathered by arrows, but the bulk of the fighting seemed to have happened elsewhere. Alyanna hoped nothing had befallen Keilan – he was supposed to have stayed far away from the fighting, but she knew that the blood of young men sometimes ran hot.

The magister turned back to her when they arrived at the wagon. His face was troubled, and Alyanna reflexively summoned a ward. He jerked his head in the direction of the wagon. "It's in there."

"What is?"

For once, the sorcerer seemed at a loss for words. He chewed his lip for a moment, then sighed. "I think you should see for yourself."

Preparing herself for anything, Alyanna crept up the stairs at the back of the wagon and eased open the door. Once, it had been secured by a great metal bolt, but now it was slightly cracked.

The first thing that struck her was the smell. It was the musty reek of a stable that hadn't been mucked in far too long: the sickening stench of an animal wallowing in its own waste and sweat. And rot – something had died in here recently, or was dying. Alyanna smelled corrupted flesh and stale blood. She nearly gagged, covering her nose and mouth with her hand. Straw covered the floor, and the only light in this space was what was spilling in from behind her. She couldn't even see the far wall, though she sensed something was there, shifting in the darkness.

With a thought, she summoned her wizardlight.

"Mistresss."

Alyanna recoiled, her wards flaring, a nimbus of killing light swelling around her upraised fist. She came within a heartbeat of unleashing her sorcery, and only stayed her hand because she saw the miserable state of her old slave.

The genthyaki slouched against the far wall, draped in layers of iron chains sunk into the floor of the wagon. Its skeletal horsehead lay pillowed on its sunken chest, which was laced with wounds, some of which were scabbed and others that still leaked black blood. Half of the shape-changer's head was scarred by fire, but she knew that had been caused by Keilan long ago. She found what her own dreadfire had done to the beast – one of its long arms ended in a stump, and Alyanna shuddered when she saw tiny white maggots squirming in the glistening black flesh. Metal spikes had also been driven into the genthyaki's spread wings, nailing the strips of ragged flesh to the wall like it was a specimen in the insect collection she had once seen in the Reliquary of Ver Anath.

If she hadn't heard its voice, she would have thought the genthyaki was dead.

"You look terrible," she said, taking a step inside the wagon.

The ancient creature rasped a wet chuckle. "You always find me at my worst, mistress. Though it seems you are deteriorating as well. Is that a gray hair I see? Both our stolen lives are finally nearing an end." It chuckled wetly.

Alyanna outwardly ignored this jab, but the creature's words still struck true. The last of her ancient sorcery was fading, and she was aging again.

"Who did this to you?"

The genthyaki raised its head slightly, baring long yellow fangs. "The shaman of the Skein. Lask, it calls itself."

There was something chilling in how the shape changer said the sorcerer's name. "It?"

The genthyaki clacked its teeth, its tail thumping.

"You should fear it, mistress."

"Why?"

"It is a *nas'achek*."

She knew that word – it was one she had come across in the oldest written records, used to describe sorcerers whose natures were so attuned to the ravenous Void that they became something more and less than mortal. The Kalyuni had another name for such a creature: a Hunger.

The coldness in her chest deepened. "Impossible. That is a legend."

The tail thrashed harder, splintering the wood, and Alyanna had to stop herself from taking a step back.

"They are no legend! One ruled in Menekar, during the age of the old empire."

The Warlock King.

"I was there, in the court," the genthyaki continued in its ragged voice. "I looked into its eyes and I knew that that human was no longer prey. It had become a predator, like my people. It had changed, as we once did."

"What do you mean?"

The genthyaki hacked a wad of vile green pus into the rushes near her feet, and she flinched away in disgust.

"I know the Skein is a *nas'achek*," it said, and Alyanna heard its madness, "because we became *nas'achek* as well. It was how we conquered death, mistress. The greatest sorcerers of my kind embraced the Void. We brought that hunger upon ourselves, so that we could consume the weak, and the ravages of time would not fall upon us."

"You ate your own people," she said, not bothering to hide her distaste, "and when they were gone, you turned to us."

The genthyaki wheezed with hissing laughter. "As you did."

Alyanna's sorcery swelled within her, outlining her hand in crackling green light. She wanted to wipe the stain of this creature from the world, but she held back for a moment.

"The Skein sorcerer. You say he is like you?"

"As much as any of you pathetic worms could be. It does not understand what it truly is, but it knows that by consuming others it stays young and grows stronger."

"Like the old emperor of Menekar." She had always suspected the ancient stories had exaggerated the evils of the imperial court – how the Warlock King had practiced cannibalism and dark blood magic to fuel his sorcery and dreams of immortality. But it seemed there had been more than a kernel of truth to them.

"I knew him to be a *nas'achek*. I thought it meant that your species was walking the same path as mine . . . but then the Pure emerged, and the Warlock King was slain, and those of my kind who dwelled in the court were driven back into the shadows." A line of drool hung suspended from the genthyaki's jaw. It did not seem to even have the strength to wipe it away. "Now another *nas'achek* has come. And it means to feed upon the carcass of this world."

The genthyaki lapsed into silence, its slitted black eyes staring at the floor. Alyanna could hear nothing save the buzz of the insects feasting on its ravaged stump. If not for the very slight rise and fall of its chest, she would have thought its spirit had finally slipped away.

Staring at this dying creature, Alyanna felt a welter of emotions. Hatred, yes, for the humiliation and pain it had caused her beneath the Selthari Palace. But there was something else as well. The genthyaki had been the tool she had used to bring about the end of the old world. Its soul had been twined with hers for a thousand years.

It had done what it needed to survive, just as she had.

She felt a presence appear beside her.

"What is that?" Cho Lin asked, disgust and fear twisting her voice.

The genthyaki's head slowly rose, nictating lids sliding rapidly across its eyes as it tried to focus on the newcomer. Then it smiled horribly. The shape-changer's flesh trembled, and for a moment the visage of a Shan in his middle years briefly overlaid its fire-ravaged face.

Cho Lin gasped.

"Shan. Come to avenge your father?"

Alyanna blinked in surprise, a coldness swelling in her stomach. *Oh, no.*

"I will make his spirit smile, monster," Cho Lin said, steel rasping as she drew one of her swords.

The genthyaki grated another chuckle. "Then cut off *her* head, Shan." It raised a trembling claw and pointed towards Alyanna. "She was the one who commanded me to kill your father."

Cho Lin whirled to face Alyanna.

By the dead gods. "Lying monster," she hissed, raising her hand. Blue flames erupted from her palm, billowing out to envelop the genthyaki. It screeched, thrashing in pain as her sorcery charred its flesh. Whatever pity she felt for the genthyaki had vanished.

Alyanna turned and clattered down the steps of the wagon, Cho Lin a step behind her. Tongues of eldritch flame licked the air as her sorcery spread with unnatural speed, until the genthyaki's prison was a raging inferno. She could hear the dwindling screams of the monster as it clung tenaciously to life. Then the sound stopped, and she knew that it was finally dead.

Cho Lin gripped her arm, turning Alyanna to look at her. "What did it mean? About my father?"

Alyanna shook her head. "I do not know. Its nature is lies."

Cho Lin let go of her, but her face was troubled. Alyanna kept her own expression one of grim resolve. Beside them, the roof of the wagon collapsed in a rush of flames, spraying blue sparks into the sky.

27: KEILAN

KEILAN WATCHED THE battle unfold from afar.

At first it was almost serenely beautiful, with ribbons of colored light falling from where Alyanna hovered, but then the sounds of rending explosions and pained screams began to drift across the field. Moments later, the first Skein stumbled out from among the circled wagons; some collapsed after taking only a few staggering steps, while others left behind dark trails in the snow as they fled the devastation. These warriors were barely able to lift their weapons before the charging Dymorian soldiers overwhelmed them. Despite the success of the ambush, Keilan wished he could be there; but as Alyanna had rightly pointed out, his control over his sorcery was tenuous, and he was as likely to strike down an ally as a foe. So instead he had stayed behind with the few soldiers who were too wounded to join the attack, hoping that none of his friends would die in the battle below.

The Skein did not look like they would last long.

"Right tired, aren't they?" growled the grizzled ranger crouched beside Keilan. He had lost three of the fingers on his sword-hand, but Keilan had heard he was still the finest hunter among the Dymorians, and it was his snares that had caught much of the small game they'd eaten on their journey north.

"They look like they've been drinking," Keilan replied, surprised at how slow and clumsy the Skein warriors appeared as they reeled across the snow.

The ranger cleared his throat noisily and spat. "Could be, lad. They certainly didn't expect a fight this deep in their land. But I think it's that." Keilan followed the Dymorian's outstretched hand and his lone finger that indicated the hole in the side of the mountain. "You sorcerers can feel it as well, eh?"

Keilan nodded. The scrabbling in his head had intensified as the mountain swelled larger and larger. But the Skein down below actually seemed disorientated, as if many of them could barely keep their feet.

"Might get worse the longer one stays in the shadow of this place," the ranger mused, rubbing his stubbled cheek with the hand that still had all its fingers.

He could be right, Keilan thought. Most of the Skein were now sprawled in the snow, and the Dymorian soldiers that moved among them finishing off the dying did seem more sluggish than even a few moments before. The largest knot of Skein warriors had been broken, and only a handful remained, each swarmed by Dymorians. It had been the arrival of the magisters that had extinguished any hope of the tide being turned – Vhelan and Seril had been well behind the initial charge, but when they had arrived, they had struck with glittering sorceries, slaying the few Skein who had been putting up resistance.

"Come on, lad. Fighting's done." The ranger rose and began to pick his way down the rocky slope.

As they followed the path of churned snow, Keilan noticed that several of the Skein wagons now crawled with sorcerous flames. One of the wagons that was set slightly apart from the rest had been almost entirely consumed, reduced to a blackened shell by the ravenous blue fire. Vhelan and Alyanna were slogging through the drifts as they left this wagon behind them, and Keilan angled his approach to intercept them before they rejoined the gathering of surviving Dymorians. As he neared them, he saw that Cho Lin there as well, though she had lingered behind to watch the fire finish devouring the wagon.

Vhelan turned to him as Keilan arrived beside them. The magister's smile was broad, but Keilan could see the strain he carried.

"A magnificent victory, my boy!" Vhelan said. "The Skein king is dead, and one of the Shan demons has been destroyed."

"Truly?" Keilan replied, hope rising in him.

"Aye," Vhelan said with what sounded like forced cheer, laying a hand on Keilan's shoulder and squeezing it hard. "The knife you brought sent the demon back to the abyss!"

"That is heartening to hear," Keilan said. It had been a long time since he'd allowed himself to dare believe that their quest could succeed, that the vision he had glimpsed could be averted. He glanced at Alyanna, expecting to see triumph in the sorceress's face, but instead a shadow lay over her, as if she was turning over something troubling. As Keilan watched, she examined a handful of her dark hair, then with a grimace ripped several of the strands loose and let them flutter free.

"What about the rest of the demons? And the queen, is she here?"

Vhelan's gaze drifted to the hole scooped from the mountain's side. Alyanna had called it a door, but if that was true it must have swung inward, as now it simply looked like the opening to a great cave. "They have already passed within," the magister said, and from his tone it was clear he feared what the queen had found inside.

"We must follow," Alyanna said, finally emerging from her reverie. "And quickly. The old histories speak of a chamber where the Min-Ceruthans laid down ancient magic to keep the

Ancient asleep. If the demons reach that room and unravel the weaves, we will have no hope of repairing what they destroy."

Keilan's trepidation rose as he stared at the breached entrance. What would they find inside? What traps had the Min-Ceruthans left behind to ensure no one could ever wake the godbeast of the north?

The surviving soldiers waited for them near where they had defeated the Skein. The flames that had spread in Alyanna's initial attack had subsided, and most of the wagons had escaped with little more than a light scorching. A few of the Dymorians were already dragging supplies from some of the wagons, haunches of dried meat and earthenware jugs. Keilan's stomach growled at the sight of food – they'd been on tight rations since leaving the cave near the battlefield, and the small game the rangers had caught had not been enough to keep him from going to bed hungry nearly every night. From what he could see, the Skein had expected to camp here for quite a while. It was strange, though, that they hadn't joined their shaman in venturing inside the Burrow. Perhaps the Skein king had found the limits of his warrior's bravery here.

Nel was in conversation with one of the Dymorian soldiers, an older veteran who served as Lord d'Venish's advisor. A small rush of relief went through him at the sight of Nel – he knew she could take care of herself, but still the swirl and chaos of battle was dangerous. The thought of a stray arrow or an unlucky sword catching her made his blood run cold. Nel raised her hand to forestall whatever the soldier was about to say; it looked like he wanted to argue about something, but instead she left him frowning behind her as she approached Vhelan.

"Boss, we lost eight men, including Lord d'Venish. Another three have suffered wounds that might kill them, especially since we don't have a trained chirurgeon with us. Galen has agreed to take command, though he's a bit hesitant. The others respect him well enough, but he does not see himself as worthy of leading."

"Well, he'll have to overcome his misgivings. There isn't much choice at this point." Vhelan shaded his eyes, squinting up at the Burrow. "We need to bring as many as we can inside. Leave those who are best at field dressing to care for the wounded, and another few to guard against wild beasts. And Seril. Where we're going is no place for her."

"We leave *now*?" Nel's tone was incredulous.

"Now," Vhelan said grimly.

Nel frowned in obvious disagreement, but still she turned away and made again towards the veteran soldier. Galen, he presumed.

A flash of light caught Keilan's eye – the chavenix, floating from where Alyanna had left it hidden high up among the tree line. It settled beside her and she pulled her sack from among the rest of their bags and began to rummage through it. Keilan drifted closer, curious what other wonders she had brought with her. He saw her secrete a slim ivory wand among her robes and then slip on a pair of jeweled rings. She caught him watching her.

"I'm not dragging this bag through the mountain." She paused, admiring a circlet of twisted golden threads before dropping it back into her sack. "A weapon or two, and a few other surprises for whatever we find inside."

"I'll carry it," Keilan offered, but Alyanna shook her head.

"To be true with you, I don't want to bring most of what's here within. I'm afraid of having to leave it all behind if we are forced to flee." She withdrew a large ring of bladed metal, with a handle set into its curving edge that, when gripped, would create a crescent of gleaming silver above her fist. This weapon also disappeared into the folds of her robes, and it must have been the last of the items she wished to take because she cinched the drawstring of her sack shut and then tossed it in the snow. With a flicker of sorcery, she unceremoniously swept the rest of their bags off the chavenix, molded the disc back into a sphere, and then dropped it inside her sack of treasures.

"I'm ready," she said, then arched an eyebrow at the Dymorians who had been watching her sidelong as she went through her artifacts. "And those of you not coming with us, don't touch anything I've left behind. It would be rather . . . incendiary."

"We must plan for spending a few days inside the mountain," Nel said, changing the topic. "That means food and water. I know we want to hurry after the queen, but we should gather what we need for an expedition. I don't want to be down there in the dark with nothing to eat or drink."

Mutters of assent rippled among the soldiers. Alyanna pursed her lips in disapproval, but she must have agreed somewhat, as she voiced no opposition.

"My knife is correct," Vhelan said, sounding resigned. "It would be foolish to brave the mountain without being prepared. Galen, have your men gather enough food and water for a few days. And torches, as well."

No one moved after the magister had finished speaking, so he clapped his hands together sharply. "Quickly, Dymorians! Your queen is waiting for you."

With characteristic efficiency, the soldiers scavenged what they could from the Skein stores and added it to their own supplies. Keilan watched them as they worked, and it was obvious that the longer they stayed in the shadow of the Burrow, the more they were affected by whatever slept below. Movements were becoming more sluggish, faces pinched as if by pain or exhaustion, and tempers had begun to fray. A tussle over a cloudy bottle of Dymorian wine that must have been looted from the queen's stores nearly came to drawn swords, until Galen put himself between the men and gave them a tongue-lashing that taught Keilan several new Dymorian curses.

The scrabbling in his own head did not seem to be getting worse; if anything, he was learning to live with the strange feeling of having a great presence hovering on the edge of his awareness. It had almost begun to feel familiar, which was frightening. But the headaches and joint pain the soldiers were grousing about did not afflict him – or Alyanna, by the looks of it. He approached the sorceress while she waited for the soldiers to finish their preparations; she was stretched out on the reformed chavenix like a bored cat, watching from under heavy-lidded eyes.

"This is not a place for those without Talent," she explained, her gaze lingering contemptuously on the soldiers. "The Ancients are not entirely of this world. I suspect they were birthed from the Void, or dwelled in it for ages, as they are infused with its essence. You and I have our own connection with the realm beyond. It was why we could feel the Ancient from so far away, but being close now does not affect us to the degree it does those who have never experienced the Void's caresses."

A thought occurred to Keilan, and he swallowed nervously. "Will they . . . will they be able to accompany us inside?"

Alyanna shrugged. "We shall see."

That troubled him, and he wandered away to crouch in the snow to consider what the sorceress had said. He knew, in his heart, that the swords and shields of the soldiers would be of little use against the sorcery of the demons, but he felt safe among the Dymorians. What if only he and Alyanna could enter the Burrow? The thought made his heart beat faster. What if the fate of the world rested on him? Keilan scratched at the cut on his arm, struggling to keep his breathing calm.

He was not the only one who seemed troubled. Cho Lin waited away from the rest of them, kneeling in the snow, her chin lifted so that she was staring up at the great gaping maw set in the side of the mountain. The hood of her furs had been thrown back, and the cold wind was making her long black hair dance. She was holding something in her hands: a length of gleaming metal. She looked deep in thought, and they were not pleasant thoughts. As he watched, she glanced at where Alyanna perched atop her chavenix, and the look she gave the sorceress chilled Keilan. Something had happened between them. He could only hope it wouldn't endanger the already difficult task ahead.

The first soldier faltered before they'd made it halfway to the door. The going was difficult, steep and stony with patches of ice hidden beneath the snow, but they had overcome similarly harsh terrain during their trek north. Keilan saw how the soldiers were struggling and feared that one would topple backwards and crack their skull or start a cascade of rocks and snow, but the soldier who collapsed merely sank to his knees before flopping face-first into a drift. His companions pulled him out, cursing him in the colorful language of the Dymorian army. He did not seem to hear them, staring straight ahead with glazed eyes.

When the second soldier stumbled and fell, hurting his wrist as he tried to catch himself, Galen called for a halt. The grizzled veteran looked exhausted, his face creased with pain as he approached Vhelan. Behind him his men found places for a respite; most found rocks to perch on, their heads hanging, while others braced themselves against the harsh wind with their hands on their knees. Galen took a moment to collect himself before he addressed Vhelan, as he was visibly swaying.

"Magister Vhelan," Galen began, his voice thick. "The men . . . they need to rest. We're going to start losing them. Half can barely walk, and the . . . the evil that's coming outta that hole is just getting worse." He licked his lips. "Maybe . . . maybe we can try again tomorrow. Go back down, sleep for a night. Get our strength back."

Keilan saw the glance Vhelan cast towards Nel, and the barely perceptible shake of her head that she returned. The magister put his hand on the old soldier's shoulder, nearly causing him to lose his balance. Vhelan smiled, though Keilan could see the strain he was under as well.

"All of you are truly men of the queen, Captain. But this is not a fight that will be won with steel, and I believe this foulness afflicting you will only get worse." He leaned in closer to Galen, holding his gaze. "Return to the Skein camp and wait for us. We will rescue Cein d'Kara, I promise."

Tears trickled down the soldier's pockmarked cheeks. "My lord magister, we just need to rest . . ."

"No," Vhelan said firmly, grabbing the back of Galen's neck and giving him a slight shake. "It was foolish to believe that those without sorcery could enter the Burrow. That was no doubt why the Skein warriors were camped below. Now, I command you – go back down and wait for us."

Galen hesitated, and he looked like he might argue further, but then he nodded in resignation and turned away. The other soldiers watched him with hollow eyes as he explained that they would head back down the slope; Keilan wasn't sure what reaction he was expecting from the Dymorians – shame or relief, he supposed – but most of them just looked on blankly. With some effort, they slid from where they'd been resting and began to shuffle back the way they'd come.

Vhelan watched them depart with pursed lips. Then he shook his head, as if trying to clear it.

"How are you?" Keilan asked, and the magister sighed deeply.

"Truly, Keilan, I am suffering as well. The pain in my head . . . it is like a metal spike has been driven into my skull."

"It will only get worse," Alyanna said. She had observed what had happened between Galen and Vhelan, and now she drifted closer. "There was a reason only Min-Ceruthans with

Talent could enter the Burrow. By the time you passed through that door you'd be a gibbering wreck."

"What about them?" Keilan asked, pointing at Nel, who had scrambled up a small outcropping to get a better view of the path ahead, and Cho Lin, who was hovering nearby, her face turned away from them.

"I'm not sure," Alyanna said, and from her tone she was curious why they hadn't suffered as much as the soldiers. "Shan!" she said loudly, and Cho Lin slowly turned to face them. Keilan sucked in his breath when he saw her sunken features and the dried blood crusted beneath her nose. Despite this, her black eyes were hard and glittering.

"I suffer, sorceress," Cho Lin said softly. "This place is not meant for mortals."

"Nel, come here," said Vhelan, gesturing for his knife to join them. Nel slid down the rocks she'd climbed and leapt lightly into the snow. Keilan was surprised to see how untroubled she looked – there was no indication of the strain that was affecting everyone save Alyanna and himself.

"Yes, boss?"

"The soldiers are turning back. Whatever is flowing from the mountain is causing them great distress. How do you feel?"

Nel shrugged. "Fine, I suppose. I mean, I feel *something* kind of hovering just out of sight, but it's not painful."

Vhelan's face crinkled in confusion. "How? You have no sorcery."

"But you do have something," Alyanna said, nodding with dawning realization. "You are wearing the fingerbone of Tethys, are you not?"

Nel's hand drifted to her furred collar. "Yes. To protect against you."

"A wise decision," Alyanna said blandly. "I do find you quite annoying."

Nel sighed, pulling from under her furs the silver chain and the chunk of yellowed bone. She ducked her head as she slipped it over her hood, and Keilan could immediately see a change come over her.

"Oh, gods," she murmured hoarsely. "This is what the rest of you have been feeling?" She dangled the amulet in front of her face, squinting at the bone as it slowly spun.

"Tethys was the first and the greatest of the Pure," Alyanna explained. "His power lingers here, protecting against what seeps in from the Void, whether that is sorcery or the dreams of a slumbering Ancient."

"Then I can accompany you inside?" Nel asked, raising the amulet as if to put it on again. She paused as Keilan held up his hand to stop her.

"Wait," he said. When she glanced at him quizzically, he pointed at Cho Lin, who was holding her sleeve to her nose. He saw that the fur was stained dark by fresh blood.

"She has the dagger. You said yourself that among us she is the most dangerous warrior."

Nel frowned, her face clouding. "Are *you* trying to protect *me*, Keilan? I'm the only one who has killed one of those things."

Keilan shook his head. "No. Cho Lin has spent her life training for this moment. We need her more than we need you."

He felt a little flush of shame when he saw the hurt in her face. Of course he was trying to keep her safe – he'd already lost Pelos and Xin and Lady Numil – but if he was going to convince Nel, he'd have to appeal to her reason.

The knife turned to Cho Lin, who was still dabbing at her nose as she watched this exchange. "Can you withstand the pain?"

Cho Lin's pale face showed no emotion. "I am going inside, with or without whatever magic you have."

"You'll die," Alyanna said with finality. "I did not know how strong these emanations would be; already you are bleeding, and it will only get stronger when we pass within. You brain will rupture long before we find the Chosen."

"The Betrayers," Cho Lin said through gritted teeth. Despite the sorceress's words, she did not look deterred.

"Give her the amulet," Keilan urged, seeing the conflict in Nel's face.

"And let you go inside by yourself?" Nel hissed angrily, her eyes flashing. "It wasn't so long ago I found you draped like a sack of grain across the paladin's saddle. You're no warrior. You're no sorcerer. Not yet, anyway. You're a fisherman's son, Keilan! What can you do in there?" She looked at Alyanna almost imploringly. "He's a boy, sorceress."

"He is a Talent," she replied evenly. "One of the few in the world who can enter the Burrow." Her gaze slid over to Keilan. "And I need his help."

"I'm going inside," he said, stepping closer to Nel and reaching out to touch her arm. To his surprise, he thought he saw tears in her eyes. She scowled, pulling away to wipe at her face angrily.

"It's not fair, Keilan," she said. "This shouldn't be your duty."

There wasn't much he could say to that, so he merely shrugged helplessly. He certainly wouldn't have chosen to venture inside. He remembered the sensation when he'd disturbed the Ancient deep under the ocean – just the briefest flicker of its attention had felt like being flayed alive. But he had no choice. He was different; he had power that others lacked. He would go into the Burrow and stop the children from waking this creature, because if he did not, everyone he cared about would die.

Nel seemed to see that in his face. She thrust the amulet towards Cho Lin. "Here," she said softly. "Please keep him alive, Shan."

Cho Lin accepted the artifact solemnly, ducking her head to show she understood Nel's concerns. Hesitating for only the briefest of moments, she slipped the chain over her head and tucked the chunk of bone beneath her furs. As soon as the amulet settled against her skin, her eyes widened and she breathed in sharply. Her brow smoothed and her jaw unclenched. She said something in Shan, blinking rapidly.

"You feel better," Vhelan stated.

Cho Lin nodded, drawing herself up. Keilan hadn't realized she'd been holding herself hunched over, probably from pain. "Yes. My mind is clear." She closed her eyes, and when she opened them again after a long moment she smiled in fierce exultation. "I feel unsullied by the taint of this place."

Nel was clearly suffering now. She put a hand out to steady herself on Keilan's shoulder, her face ashen.

"Go back down," he said softly. Vhelan appeared beside her and gently shifted her weight from Keilan to himself. The magister seemed to be dealing with the oppressive emanations better than those without sorcery, but the strain was still showing. He reached out to clasp Keilan's forearm.

"May fortune favor you," he said simply, offering Keilan a strained smile. "We'll be waiting for you."

He began to guide Nel back down the slope, but before they had taken more than a few steps, she broke free of his grip and whirled around. "You come back from there, Keilan," she said fiercely. "Don't you dare do anything heroic. Remember that there's no shame in running away."

Keilan's lips twitched, and he had to struggle not to smile. "I'll remember," he said.

Nel likely would have continued holding his gaze to ensure he understood how serious this all was, but suddenly she doubled over and retched in the snow. If not for Vhelan's hold on her, she would have surely collapsed.

"I need to take her down," the magister said, and Keilan knew what he really meant was that he should continue up the slope, as Nel wasn't about to move first.

With a last look at his friends, he turned away. Alyanna and Cho Lin were already slightly ahead, picking their way among the tumbled scree. Taking a deep, steadying breath, Keilan followed them.

28: CHO LIN

ONE OF CHO Lin's earliest memories was of when she'd nearly drowned. She wasn't sure how old she had been at the time – old enough to walk and escape her minders, at least, but before her father had gained the ear of the old emperor and moved his household into the imperial district of Tsai Yin. She remembered peering at him from between tangled branches as he sat in the pagoda at the center of the Cho gardens, studying an unrolled scroll in the early morning light. In her hand she'd clutched a handful of rice stolen from the kitchens, and as stealthily as she could she had crept close to one of the koi ponds and tossed it into the water. The red and white fish – which usually drifted so serenely – had churned the murk in a frenzy, and she'd crouched at the edge of the pond to watch. Their fins and scales had broken the water as they thrashed, and she'd always wanted to know what these felt like, so she'd leaned out and tried to brush her fingers against the fish.

She'd lost her balance, toppling forward into the water, and the koi had instantly scattered. Through her terror and shock she distinctly remembered feeling indignation that they would abandon her when she'd always shown them such kindness. She had flailed her arms, trying to rise back up through the darkness, but the water had poured into her mouth and nose and she'd sunk deeper and deeper, her panic and pain blotting out everything else. A great weight had crushed her, both inside and out. Her vision had faded; the last thing she clearly remembered was the sunlight dappling the water's surface above her like a scattering of golden coins.

Her father had pulled her from the water soon after. She had only indistinct, stuttering images of him sitting her down on the stone pathway and pounding her back until she coughed up the darkness clotting in her chest. She remembered his face, though. Before that day, she had only seen two emotions from him: approval and disapproval. Anger, joy, affection – these were the province of her brother and the *aya* that cared for her. But that day, as she struggled to breathe while spitting up what she'd swallowed, she'd seen such fear in her father's face that she'd known, in a moment of clarity, that he truly did love her.

That feeling – of a terrible pressure lifting as she expelled what had been suffocating her – was the closest she could come to describing what it was like when the bone amulet settled against her skin. She had been drowning, then wrenched from the depths. The fog that had settled over her thoughts since this cursed place had appeared on the horizon had lifted almost immediately. She was whole again, untainted by the evil of this place.

Despite this, she still felt some trepidation when they finally stood on the threshold of the great door. Its size defied all reason – why would anyone bother creating an entrance so vast? Was there actually something so large that this door had been necessary? It soared a thousand span high, at least, and she suspected that the tiny shapes turning gyres far up where the doorway merged with the rock of the mountain were the same great northern falcons the Skein had kept as hunting birds in Nes Vaneth.

The scale of the Burrow's entrance was not the only reason it was so unnerving. She could see no hinges on the great doors, and everywhere she looked the stone was as smooth and unblemished as if it were freshly hewn. Yet this place was many thousands of years old, she'd heard Alyanna say, older than the oldest of the holdfasts.

The sun had risen further as they ascended, and the threshold of the entrance was almost perfectly demarcated by the unnaturally straight shadow of the lintel high above. They hesitated before crossing this line. A tunnel stretched away, and it seemed to dwindle in front of them before finally terminating in a tiny circle of hazy light. Cho Lin couldn't tear her eyes from the unseen depths, imagining the Betrayers crouched in the darkness waiting to ambush them as they passed. She held tight to the Nothing, her fingers curled around the hilt of the black knife.

The shadows suddenly fled as the sorceress summoned a roiling sphere of pale wizardlight, revealing the walls that had been hidden; they were as smooth and featureless as the doors, bereft of cracks or ornamentation.

The floor, though, was very different. Straight, shallow channels were incised into the stone, wide enough for a man to walk down, as if water had once flowed through this vast antechamber. And the paths between were inlaid with spiraling designs made of smooth black and white stones. Every dozen paces or so a glistening dark gem was set at the center of one of these strange arrangements.

As they crept down the passage, she watched the sorceress sidelong. Cho Lin's thoughts had been so muddled earlier that she hadn't been able to truly consider what the demon shapechanger had claimed in the confusion of the battle's aftermath. She'd been shocked to see it there, her tormentor, wrapped in chains and near death. The monster had said *Alyanna* had been responsible for her father's death? That the sorceress had been trying to *protect* the Betrayers by murdering her father? No. That was impossible. She had seen the ashes in the snow. Alyanna was not an ally of the children – she was trying to destroy them. The nature of demons was to lie, to sow discord. And yet . . .

Cho Lin shook her head to banish these thoughts. She had to be completely focused.

They had traversed about half the length of this long entranceway when Alyanna's wizardlight suddenly sputtered and went out. Cho Lin tensed, drawing the black knife, her awareness sharpening as she seized the Nothing. But no demons lunged from the darkness, and after a moment the pale ball of light swelled again.

"What happened?" Keilan asked.

"I don't know," Alyanna replied. She sounded perfectly calm, which Cho Lin suspected meant that she was actually quite unnerved.

"Then you didn't intend to do that?"

"No. My sorcery simply . . . failed, for a moment."

That unsettled Cho Lin. "Does such a thing happen often?"

"It does not," Alyanna replied with a trace of irritability. "Keilan, summon your wizardlight. Let us see if that happens again."

Keilan nodded and his own wizardlight appeared. While the sorceress's sphere was smooth and unblemished, his rippled with crackling energy, and Cho Lin could see the concentration in his face necessary for maintaining the spell. He had nowhere near the same mastery as Alyanna.

They continued on, the illuminated doorway ahead of them swelling larger. It looked like one of the curved moon gates that were popular in the gardens of her homeland. They had nearly reached it when again they were plunged into darkness, both wizardlights extinguished simultaneously. Keilan let out a surprised gasp when his sorcery fizzled.

"It was just gone," he murmured as Alyanna crafted a new wizardlight.

"There are strange forces surging here," the sorceress said. "Leaking through from the Void . . . and perhaps elsewhere. There was once speculation that the Ancients persist in several different realms of existence at once, and the rules of this world might not be the only ones that hold sway here. Whatever it is, our power is being disrupted. We must be cautious." She started forward again, then turned back to Keilan. "Set your ward, Keilan. If it falters, remake it when you can. I do not know what we will find within."

They had their sorcery, and Cho Lin had the Nothing within the Self. For the last hundred paces before they arrived at the doorway, she kept her mind empty except for the mantra of Red Fang. *The self my nothing, the self my nothing . . .* Whatever awaited them, she would be ready.

It was not what she expected. Alyanna was first through the rounded doorway, preceded by her wizardlight. Cho Lin followed close behind, brandishing the black knife, and she nearly collided with the sorceress, who had suddenly halted.

"By all the dead gods," Alyanna breathed, awed by the immensity of what lay before them.

They stood on a ledge overlooking a vast cavern. No, not a cavern – it seemed like the entirety of the Burrow had been purposefully hollowed, as the walls stretching away from either side of them were unnaturally smooth. How high the space soared Cho Lin couldn't see, as the ceiling was lost to the darkness. It was almost like looking up at the sky on a starless night, such was the immensity. The light they'd seen earlier came from a softly glowing mist blanketing the floor far below them. It roiled like it was being blown about by a wind she could not feel. And half-submerged in this luminous fog was a stone city, the likes of which she had never seen before. There were no towers, or rooftops, or any other kind of structure that she had encountered on her travels. Most of the buildings were featureless stone spheres of various sizes, the tops of their curving domes emerging from the mist like bubbles on a witch's cauldron. In the distance she could vaguely see that the far wall rising up over this subterranean city was a different color, a sort of grayish white.

"That is where we need to go," Alyanna said, pointing across the sweeping expanse of the city spread below them.

"How do you know?" Cho Lin asked.

"That's a glacier, isn't it?" Keilan said, stepping to the edge of the ledge and peering at the distant discolored wall.

"It's not ice," Alyanna said softly. Then she cocked her head to one side, her eyes narrowing. "Listen."

Cho Lin concentrated. Yes; there was a sound rising up from below. Some kind of steady, rhythmic pounding. Now that she noticed it, her whole body seemed to be pulsing in time to that deep cadence. "Drums? Someone has seen us?"

The sorceress shook her head. "No." She pursed her lips, crouching beside where Keilan stood and peering over the edge. "Ah!" she exclaimed. "There are holds cut into the rock here. Perhaps from when the Min-Ceruthans first breached this place. We can climb down that way."

"Why don't you just fly?" Keilan asked.

"You saw what happened to our wizardlight," Alyanna replied, already swinging over the side and lowering herself until her feet found something to stand on. "What if my sorcery fails mid-flight?"

"Wait," Cho Lin said, unnerved by the sea of churning mist and what could be hiding within its depths. "What *is* that sound?"

Alyanna paused her descent, looking back up at Cho Lin. "The heartbeat of a god, Shan." She indicated the far wall with her chin. "And that is its flesh. It's where we must go to find the Chosen."

29: KEILAN

KEILAN HAD NEVER known he had a fear of heights, but he had also never clung to the side of a sheer rock wall far above a dead city. The holds that had been cut into the stone were easy to grasp, and there were small ledges as well for his feet, but still he had to pretend that he was not one missed step away from plunging to his death, or he might have frozen, unable to continue. As it was, his hands were growing disconcertingly slick, and he had to keep wiping them on his furs when he reached down for the next hold. He wished they could have used the chavenix, but Alyanna had made it clear she wasn't sure if the disc would be affected by the strange sorcerous currents that had earlier extinguished their wizardlights.

Cho Lin had insisted she precede him down the wall, and she must have sensed his nervousness, as she kept talking to him soothingly as they descended. If the foothold was shallower than the others, she told him. If the handholds were spaced farther than usual, she let him know. The Shan sounded perfectly calm, as if she was used to scaling such dizzying heights.

"Think of nothing except the feel of the stone under your fingers and toes," she said, her words floating up from below.

"Make sure your grip is sure before you step down again. Are you doing all right?"

"Yes," he replied, fighting to keep his voice steady.

"Good. We are almost halfway."

That was meant to cheer him, he knew, but instead Keilan's heart fell. He hadn't looked down since starting this descent, and he had kept his spirits up by imagining that they were nearing the bottom.

He breathed out slowly and gingerly lowered his leg, searching for the next ledge.

A sound came from beneath them, and before Keilan could catch himself, he glanced down. He saw Cho Lin, right below him, and beyond her was Alyanna, and far, far beneath the sorceress was the swirling, glowing mist, its surface broken by the rounded tops of the stone city's buildings.

And something else. His attention was drawn to a patch of mist roiling more fiercely than the rest, as if stirred by something within . . .

A black shape erupted from the depths, great wings churning the mist.

"Hold to the rock!" Cho Lin screamed, and he tore his gaze from the rising creature. He clung as tightly as he could to the wall, his cheek pressed against the stone.

Keilan expected a piercing shriek as the thing surged higher, but it kept so silent that he could hear the leathery flap of its wings. He whimpered, the strength draining from his arms and legs. Then he was buffeted by winds as it passed him, and something hard struck his shoulder. Pain lanced down his arm, and his fingers slipped from the hold. He was falling; Keilan screamed as the emptiness closed around him.

A hand seized his wrist and his plunge was abruptly arrested, though his momentum sent him swinging hard into the wall. Pain erupted in his face and shoulder, and his vision was consumed with flashes of light. When these cleared a moment later, he glanced up, dazed. Cho Lin was hanging from the wall by one hand; with the other she had grabbed his wrist. Through the fog of his thoughts, Keilan struggled to understand how his weight hadn't torn her from the wall and sent them both plummeting.

"Find a grip on the wall," Cho Lin said, and though her face was calm he could hear the strain in her voice.

Keilan scrabbled for purchase with his free hand, his feet scraping stone as they sought for a ledge. A moment later he found one, and he immediately saw the relief in her face as his weight vanished.

"Are you ready for me to let go?"

"Yes." He pressed his forehead to the stone, his head still ringing. The thought of what had almost happened was seeping into his consciousness, and his stomach felt like it was full of ice.

"What was that thing?" he called up, not quite ready yet to continue the descent.

"I don't know," Cho Lin said. "It looked like a snake with wings. A big snake. The tip of its tail struck your shoulder as it went by."

Keilan peered past Cho Lin into the darkness obscuring the ceiling. Would that thing come swooping down to try and knock them off again? His hands were shaking now, and it took all his willpower to make them stop.

Alyanna seemed to hear his thoughts. "Hurry, Keilan," the sorceress called up from below. "You're in the middle now. If that thing returns, it will go for the Shan, not you."

He guessed he was supposed to find comfort in that, but he knew he couldn't grab Cho Lin if she came tumbling past.

"I'll be fine," the Shan said. "I promise. Just keep moving."

The flying creature did not reappear, and after what seemed like an eternity the first tongues of cool mist licked his exposed skin, making his hands even slicker than they already were. Soon he was enveloped entirely, and Cho Lin was just a hazy dark shape above him. He couldn't help but imagine other creatures lurking in the fog, waiting to strike, but he did not hear the stirring of wings. His arms and fingers were burning, and he couldn't imagine having to pull himself back up the same way.

"I'm at the bottom." The sorceress's voice was muffled, but Keilan knew she wasn't too far ahead of him, and he felt a great swell of relief.

He glanced down after descending a bit farther and there she was, her beautiful upturned face emerging from the mist.

"That must have been terrifying for you," she said when he finally stood on solid ground again, steadying him with a hand on his shoulder as he stumbled slightly. "I saw you fall. The Shan is stronger than she looks."

"I almost died," Keilan said shakily.

"Oh, no. I was prepared to catch you with sorcery."

Keilan scowled. "Why not tell me that?"

Alyanna chuckled at his evident annoyance. "Because there was a chance my sorcery would fail, as our wizardlights did in the entrance hall. Also, I wanted to test your mettle. Both of you."

Cho Lin had almost reached the bottom as well, and she dropped the last few span, landing lightly. She must have heard what Alyanna said, as she snorted.

"You need not worry about me, sorceress," she said, then jerked her head towards Keilan. "Or him. He made that climb without your sorcery or my training. Your only concern should be finding the Betrayers."

Rubbing his aching arms, Keilan turned away from the sorceress and the Shan. The thick mist obscured their surroundings, but he saw dark shapes looming out of the gloom – the buildings he had seen from above, he assumed. Some were small and completely shrouded by the mist, but others were surprisingly large, as big as the gatehouses of the great cities he had passed through in his travels. The rock beneath his boots was not like the cave where the Dymorians had hidden after their defeat; the ground here was made of interlocking stones that had been smoothed and leveled. It looked like one of the main thoroughfares in Vis or Lyr, though fashioned by stonemasons of even more exquisite skill.

"What is this place?" Keilan asked, peering into the mist.

Alyanna came to stand beside him. "A relic from before the age of man. Built by creatures that have long since vanished."

Keilan thought back to his lessons with his grandmother, reclining on a faded velvet couch while she explained how the millstone of time had ground countless other races to dust.

"What happened to them?" Keilan asked.

Alyanna shrugged. "Who knows? But I have some theories as to why they built this place."

"And those are?" Cho Lin said, appearing next to Keilan.

"They feared the Ancient would wake, just as we do now. Perhaps they also worshipped it as a god. Or maybe they wished to mine the strange energies that swirl around the beast. It seems to infringe upon other realities, and something of those places leaks through. First and foremost, though, they must have known that if it woke, their world would end. So they constructed this city here, and filled it with their most powerful sorcerers, to soothe the Worm back to sleep when it threatened to wake."

"Are there dangers here?" Cho Lin asked, her hand on the hilt of one of her swords.

"I would expect so," Alyanna said, and Keilan felt her strengthening the weave of her ward. "But I have no idea what they might be."

"Which way?" Keilan asked, and Alyanna let out a long breath.

"That way?" the sorceress replied, gesturing vaguely into the glowing murk. "I tried to get a sense of the way we should go before we descended into the mist, but I must confess I don't think I'll be able to guide us perfectly."

"To the Worm," Keilan said, remembering the great wall of white flesh.

"Yes."

He sighed, straightening his shoulders. "Let us be off, then."

The stone city reminded him of the lichyard in Theris. There was no sign that it had ever been inhabited by the living; he peered inside the rounded doorways of one of the spherical buildings and found it completely empty, without any sort of furniture or other fragments of everyday life, the walls bereft of design or decoration. A ramp without a railing or balustrade spiraled higher onto a second story, but neither Alyanna nor Cho Lin seemed interested in exploring this place, and so he pulled himself away from the abandoned structure and hurried to keep up with them as they pushed onward through the luminescent mist.

Aside from the buildings, there were a few other oddities that they encountered. At the confluence of several streets, a sculpture had been erected – it looked like a great stone tree, its empty branches covered in thorns. Curled around the base of the trunk was a great centipede, and for a moment Keilan thought it was part of the statue as well. Then the centipede lifted its head drowsily, fixed its slitted yellow eyes on them, and clacked a warning with its serrated mandibles. Keilan felt sorcery surge in Alyanna, but before she could weave an attack the centipede uncoiled itself from the tree and slithered off into the mist.

"Keep your wards up, Keilan," Alyanna told him as they skirted the petrified tree and started down a different street than the one where the creature had vanished.

They passed more of the bulbous structures, with nothing except their size to differentiate them, and before long Keilan felt like they were revisiting the same ground. The clotting mist made it almost impossible to know whether they were walking in circles or slowly traversing this sprawling city; Alyanna was keeping up a veneer of confidence, but Keilan caught her hesitating more and more often as she chose one path over another.

"We should have already reached the far wall," Cho Lin finally said, her gaze lingering on an open doorway that was squared rather than rounded. Keilan knew she was thinking they'd already seen the same building – he suspected the same.

"This place does not follow the rules we know," Alyanna said, and Keilan heard the frustration in her voice. Whether it was with what Cho Lin had said or the nature of the stone city he wasn't sure. "Time and distance are fluid here, ebbing and flowing."

Alyanna seemed like she was about to say more, but a shiver of movement from the mist-choked mouth of a nearby alley made her step back in alarm, her wards flaring. Keilan scrabbled to strengthen his own weave as a trio of shapes emerged. They moved hesitatingly out into the broader street, then froze when they noticed they were not alone.

The creatures were tall and thin and walked on two legs like men, their long arms hanging down nearly to their knees. They were dressed in elaborate finery, lush robes and long dresses trimmed with fur, and gold glittered around their arms and necks. Each also wore thin silver diadems, with large, colorful jewels resting on their brows. The creatures did not move, watching them silently, but Keilan felt a surge of sorcery as they lashed together their own protective wards. The strength of their weave reminded him of Alyanna or Cein. These were powerful sorcerers; the equal of Talents.

Keilan found he couldn't breathe, staring at these creatures. He knew what they were; he'd seen them before.

Wraiths.

They looked different than the beasts that had ambushed the caravan along the Way – their hair was not matted and wild, but rather intricately bound into braids threaded with beads, and the long curving claws he remembered had been filed down to blunted points. There was the matter of their eyes, as well, and the intelligence Keilan saw glittering in their black depths.

"*Gaitunpan*," he heard Cho Lin whisper beside him. It sounded like she recognized these creatures, too.

Slowly, the wraith in front of the others raised his hands, showing them his open palms. He wore an elaborate headdress, plumes of plum-colored silk falling from the top of a pointed hat to veil his face. Then, cautiously, he began to retreat back into the alley from which they'd come, keeping his hands up. The other wraiths followed him, until they were all again swallowed by the mists.

For a few long moments after the creatures had vanished, no one said anything, and Alyanna kept her wards raised, as if she expected a trick.

"Those were wraiths," Keilan said finally, letting the strands of sorcery he held go slack.

"Not the wraiths you know," Alyanna replied. "From a different age."

"The past?"

"Perhaps."

"Why were those beasts dressed in clothes?" Cho Lin asked, and Keilan saw that she had drawn her swords.

"They were not always beasts," Alyanna said. "They ruled these lands for thousands of years before the first men came here."

"But how can they still be alive?"

Alyanna shrugged at Cho Lin's question, then resumed going the way they had been traveling before encountering the wraiths. Tendrils of glowing mist swirled around her, clutching at her legs. "They evidently became lost," she said over her shoulder. "Pray that the same does not happen to us."

They progressed through the dead city for what felt like an eternity. His legs ached and he wanted to rest, but Keilan knew that sand was trickling through the hourglass, and the longer they wandered the more likely it was that the Chosen would find a way to wake the slumbering Ancient. Alyanna did let them stop for brief snatches, enough time to choke down strips of salted meat and swallow some water, but he never felt refreshed when she commanded they continue their march.

The second time she called for a halt was when they reached a broad plaza speckled with small round stone eggs, and while Alyanna and Cho Lin seated themselves on these strange ornamentations, Keilan meandered towards one of the larger avenues that emptied into this space. He didn't expect to be able to see anything, but suddenly the thick mist swirled and eddied, as if disturbed by a strong wind he could not feel. A strange scene was revealed: three small fox-men encircled a creature that resembled the centipede they'd seen earlier curled around the tree. This one was much larger, though, and the upper half of its body was vaguely man-like, with a half-dozen limbs emerging from its long torso. Perched on its sloping shoulders was a gray, hairless head with a single slitted eye and a circular, leech-like mouth ringed by fangs. The fox-creatures chittered and danced around the creature, prodding at it with silver tridents, and the centipede-man roared angrily and swiped at his tormentors, but they were too quick to catch. For a moment Keilan was frozen, staring in shock, and then the mists rushed in again.

"Alyanna," he hissed, beckoning for the sorceress to come over. With a look of concern, she did just that, coming to stand beside him and peering where he indicated.

"What is it?"

"We are not alone," he replied, but then the mists shifted again and the street stretching before them was empty.

"I saw something," he said quickly, turning to Alyanna. "And there was a sound. A roar like an animal. You *must* have heard it from just over there."

The sorceress watched him solemnly for a long moment, then slowly shook her head. "I heard nothing."

"But it was so loud! There was a monster and three little fox-men—"

She held up her hand to stop him from explaining further. "I believe you saw something, Keilan, do not doubt that. Echoes of other times. Ghosts and fragments. They are only distractions right now for us, though."

Keilan swallowed, watching where the strange vision had been revealed, but it did not return. Finally, reluctantly, he turned away, and let her guide him back to where Cho Lin waited with a raised eyebrow and a questioning look.

"Wait," Alyanna said sometime later, motioning for them to stop. Keilan glanced at Cho Lin, and from her expression the Shan had also heard the edge of concern – maybe even fear – in the sorceress's voice.

They had found themselves on the widest and grandest of any avenue they'd yet traversed. The rounded buildings here were also the largest they'd seen, packed so tightly together that it would have been difficult to squeeze between them. And that was why Alyanna's command sent a shiver of fear through him – there was really nowhere to run if danger emerged from the mists.

"What?" Keilan asked, but instead of answering Alyanna grabbed him roughly by his furs and dragged him towards the open doorway of one of the buildings.

"Quiet," she hissed, practically throwing him within the structure. The great space was as empty as the rest, though the spiraling ramp leading to the higher floors had been shattered, reduced to chunks of stone. "Hide," she continued, pressing herself against the wall that abutted the street. Keilan and Cho Lin did the same. He knew Alyanna was reinforcing her wards, but he could not sense her doing it; she must have been taking great pains to conceal her sorcery. He followed her lead and did not grasp his own power, as he could not hide it like she could. Clearly she was afraid that something would notice she was here.

They stayed that way, breathing quietly, long enough for Keilan to wonder if Alyanna had been mistaken. He opened his mouth at one point to ask her something, but she shook her head fiercely, so he remained silent.

Then he heard it. It was a scraping, like a vast bulk was being dragged over stone. He wanted to peek around the edge of the doorway and see what was approaching, but when he shifted slightly Alyanna reached out to restrain him and he sank back again. She looked stricken, her face emptied of color and her eyes wide and terrified. To see such fear in the sorceress was in truth more unnerving than the sound coming from outside. A smell drifted to Keilan – it was the smell of dead sea things rotting in the sun; the beach at low tide after the water had retreated, but many times stronger. The wall he was pressed against creaked, and it almost felt like it buckled slightly, as if a great weight was pushing against the other side. He stayed silent, not daring to breathe.

The scraping continued for longer than he would have imagined possible. Either the thing was moving extremely slowly, or it was as long as a wagon train. Finally, the sound faded into the distance, and the noxious smell diminished, although it did not vanish entirely.

Cho Lin was the first to speak. "What was that?"

Alyanna was still pale and shaken. "I do not know. But I've felt its like before. It reeked of the Void."

"How can there be *creatures* in the Void?" Keilan had always conceived of the Void as a place of raw energy, the material that sorcerers drew forth to weave into spells.

Alyanna didn't answer him, staring at nothing. He sensed she was reliving some dark memory, and he left her to her recollections.

Finally, she shook her head and pushed herself from the wall. She looked composed again, and Keilan felt a surge of relief. If she broke here, he didn't think they would ever find their way out of this cursed place.

"We must be on our way," she said, and strode from the building.

The flesh of the White Worm materialized from the mist like sorcery. It soared upwards into the gloom, white and craggy, laced with the faded remnants of scars and covered in places with broad patches of something that resembled lichen. As his gaze lingered on those ancient wounds, Keilan couldn't help but wonder what sort of creature could inflict such damage on a beast as large as a mountain. The heartbeat that had been gradually swelling louder during their journey was now so strong he felt himself tremble with every deep reverberation.

Beside him, Alyanna hissed in triumph. "I did it," she said. "I have led us through the city."

Steel rasped as Cho Lin drew one of her Shan swords. "Are the Betrayers in there?" she asked, pointing with the tip of the blade at a strange black structure grafted onto where the wall of white flesh disappeared into the stone floor. It was the only building pressed up against the Ancient's bulk, and it did not resemble any other that they had passed: while the rest of the city was rounded, with curving doorways and roofs, this structure was all sharp edges, like a great heap of mismatched swords and lances forged into one spiny whole. An entrance was set into the side of the building, infringed by tapering black-metal points so that it resembled a fanged mouth, and a river of the glowing mist was issuing forth from this doorway, coiling and twisting in the streets before slithering away.

"They must be," Alyanna said softly, slowly approaching the structure's gaping maw. Keilan felt her tightening the weave of her wards, and he did the same.

"Do they know we're here?" Keilan whispered, eyeing the doorway's spines nervously.

"I hope not," the sorceress answered quietly. Keilan saw that she had drawn the ivory wand. Cho Lin appeared beside him, brandishing a Shan sword in one hand and the glistening black knife in the other. "Strike fast, strike true," Alyanna said, raising the wand. Then she plunged forward, into the mist-shrouded doorway, and they followed her.

30: ALYANNA

THE MIST ENVELOPED her, and for a terrifying moment she was blind. She still sensed Keilan on her right as she rushed into the building, the weave of his ward rough but strong – well, strong enough, she hoped. The Shan must be beside him, though Alyanna couldn't sense her, as she was protected from sorcery by the artifact of Tethys. Alyanna had considered trying to craft an ambush, but had discarded that idea in favor of boldness. If the Chosen knew they were coming, they would expect subtlety and prepare accordingly. If they were unaware, a fast, brazen attack might prove overwhelming. In truth, they just needed to close any distance quickly so that the Shan could use the knife on the demons. Alyanna would distract the Chosen and the Skein shaman by presenting herself – a Talent wielding powerful artifacts – as the greatest threat, while Cho Lin sought her chance to end this nightmare.

The dimensions of the space they had entered seemed disproportionate to what they had seen from the outside. Alyanna couldn't see the walls, nor did she see the white flesh of the Ancient rising up in front of her. She floundered her way forward, peering into the mist for a flash of corpse-flesh or tangled black hair, struggling to restrain the roiling sorcery in the wand she held. Her heart leapt as she glimpsed something dark deeper in the murk, and she lunged in that direction, but then slowed to a halt when she realized it had vanished.

She whirled around, snarling, sorcery singing in her veins. The mist eddied and swirled, so thick she could barely see more than a few span in front of her face.

It was then that she realized she was alone. "Keilan," she hissed, casting about with her senses. The boy's fumbling attempts at a ward should have flared like a candle in the dark, but she could feel nothing. Foolish; why would he dispense with his protections?

"Keilan!" she repeated, louder than before. "Where are you?" Tendrils of cool mist brushed her skin, raising gooseflesh.

She saw movement again out of the corner of her eye, and turned quickly to confront whatever was lurking out there. With a trembling hand she raised her wand, preparing to unleash the fury of its bound soul.

The swirling murk parted, and Demian was revealed. She gasped, staggering backwards. The swordsinger watched her with sad eyes, one hand resting on the hilt of his cursed sword. His pale face glistened from the cool mist, damp black curls plastered to his brow and neck. It looked like he had been waiting here for a long time.

"Demian?" she whispered, not trusting what she was seeing.

"Weaver," he replied.

It sounded like him. His expression of calm detachment was one she had seen countless times.

But this was impossible – he was dead. She'd killed him.

"It can't be you."

He cocked his head to one side, his thin lips pursed. "It is." She felt it then, the sorcery swelling inside him. Bright and hot, a vastness only a Talent could summon. What was this? How could this be? Alyanna quested out with her own power, but instead of investigating Demian, she explored the aura of his sword. Malazinischel was as unique and powerful an artifact as had ever been forged, and she had spent enough time in the corrupted blade's presence to be certain whether or not it was a forgery. She felt the presence within the cracked sword tremble with anticipation, swirling with unfettered hatred for her, the same as it always had. Dazed, she withdrew her sorcery. An illusion could be crafted to deceive the eyes and the mind, but it was impossible to fool her sorcerous senses.

Emotions surged within Alyanna, her vision blurring. She blinked away her tears, struggling with what she should say. She hated herself for what she had done, the guilt a hollow ache in her chest . . . yet she knew she would do it all again if the stakes were the same.

"Why have you come?" she asked, her voice cracking.

"The same reason I always came," he replied in the calm and measured voice she knew so well. "Because you need me."

"But . . . I saw you die."

Demian's thin lips curved into a weary smile. "No, you didn't, Weaver. I became the vessel for another. But that shadow has lifted, from both myself and the mountain. It has returned to where it came from. And so I sought you out again."

"For revenge?" she whispered. It was what was just, she knew.

"No. To help you."

She had never deserved Demian.

"We need your help," she said, her words tumbling out in a rush. "A Talent and the Chosen are trying to wake this Ancient. With your strength, we can stop them, I know it."

He stepped forward, his dark eyes holding hers. "You have always been pure, Weaver. True to your nature. I understand you better than anyone. And that is why I am offering you a chance to escape death yet again."

Keilan pushed through the swirling mist, trying his best to maintain his wards. The sorcery was slippery, threatening to squirm out of his grasp, and it took all his concentration just to keep his ragged shield from failing. He was so distracted that it was several moments before he realized that he could no longer sense the sorceress beside him.

"Alyanna?" he cried, blundering towards where she should have been. The mists swirled, stirred by his outstretched hands, but did not part to reveal the immortal sorceress. His breathing quickened as his panic rose. Where had she gone? Had the Chosen somehow seized her already?

"Cho Lin?" he tried, dreading the thought that he could be alone in this terrible place.

No answer. Keilan tried to calm himself, focusing on keeping his wards strong. Perhaps this mist deadened sound, and they were really just a few span from him, also calling out his name. Swallowing away his fear, Keilan began to push through the mist. If they all did the same, they would meet where the back of this structure pressed up against the flesh of the Ancient.

His unease grew when he realized he should have already hit the far wall. The building had looked to be no more than fifty paces deep from the outside, yet he'd gone twice that distance and there was nothing in front of him except this Shael-cursed mist. He was just about to turn back and try to retrace his steps when a woman emerged from the churning murk.

"Keilan," his mother said, and his insides turned to water.

"Ma," he managed numbly.

"Oh," she murmured, and whatever else she was going to say was lost in a choked sob. Her cheeks glistened as she rushed towards him, her arms wide.

This was a trick. A trap. But before he could summon his sorcery or draw his sword she had reached him, enfolding him in an embrace.

"You're so tall," she whispered into his shoulder, her hands clutching at his back. He could feel her hot tears trickling down his neck, pooling in the hollow of his collarbone. With shaking hands, he gripped her shoulders and pushed her away. This thing smelled just like his mother. Even the way she cocked her head slightly to one side as she gazed at him was the same, her unbound silver hair falling over one shoulder.

"You're not my mother," he said hoarsely, and despite knowing this was true he still felt a stab of pain in his chest as her face crumbled at his words.

"I am," she said, holding his arms tightly.

"She died."

"I did. I'm so sorry."

"Are you a ghost?"

A flicker of confusion passed across his mother's face. "I . . . I don't know. I remember drowning, the water filling my chest." She blinked, taking in a shuddering breath, and then she focused on him again. "My last thoughts were of you. You must know that."

He couldn't help himself. Illusion or spirit or whatever, the question he had always wanted to ask forced its way out. "Why did you go with them?" he asked, his voice breaking.

"Oh," his mother said softly. She let go of his arm and reached up to touch the side of his head. He thought he would flinch away; he did not want to not give in to whatever this thing was, but he could not help himself. "I was so scared for you. I could see the murder in their eyes. If I fought, if I tried to run, I knew it would only bring their blood up. I told them . . . I told them I would let them take me down to the sea and I wouldn't scream or fight, but they had to leave you alone."

Keilan bowed his head, tears coursing down his cheeks. His mother's hand moved behind his head, stroking the nape of his neck, just like she used to do when he was small.

"Why are you here?"

She raised a finger to catch his tears, her soft eyes filled with love. "To save you, Keilan."

The others were gone. With her senses augmented by her grasp on the Nothing, their sudden absence had been jarring. It had happened in a heartbeat – one moment she had heard them blundering through the mist beside her: Keilan's heavy breathing, the rustle of Alyanna's robes, the scuff of their footsteps on stone . . . and then nothing. Only a silence like that which descends after the fall of a headsman's ax. They were simply no longer here . . . or, she supposed, she was no longer where she had been. Were they casting about in the mists looking for her even now? Or were they dead?

Well, there was little she could do now except find her way through this cursed mist. She should have already reached the far wall, so some other strangeness was happening. Quickening her pace, she held the strange black knife in front of her so that its glistening point carved the thick murk.

Soft footsteps disturbed the quiet. It did not sound like the scrape of Keilan or Alyanna's leather boots – rather, this was the slither of fabric on stone as someone glided closer. The Betrayers? Only those already dead could wear silken slippers in this frozen land. Cho Lin tensed, ready to lash out if one of those demon children emerged from the mist.

A shape swelled within the haze. Too large to be one of the Betrayers – could it be one of her companions? She was just about to call out when it spoke.

"Lin."

She nearly dropped the knife in shock.

"Father?" she whispered.

He stepped from the mist, glowing tendrils clinging to his imperial robes and circular scholar's cap, his hands thrust into his long sleeves.

Cho Lin staggered back, her hold on the Nothing dissipating. This was impossible.

"Who are you?" she hissed, brandishing the black knife menacingly.

Her father watched her with the same look of calm judgement she had seen countless times before, his thin lips set in a considering line.

"I am Cho Yuan. You dishonor me by not recognizing your own father."

"You were killed."

The thing that looked like her father inclined its head slightly. It was a mannerism she was familiar with.

"I am dead."

"Then how are you here?"

Cho Yuan withdrew his hands from his robes and passed them in front of his face, rippling the mist. "This place, it is a crossroads. The Veil infringes upon the living world here, and so my spirit can speak with you. Before, I could only watch."

"You have been watching me?" she said softly.

Again the small nod, the tassel of his cap slipping forward. "Our ancestors have watched everything you've done."

She had to remember this was not real. Yet still she found herself responding to the apparition like it was truly her father. "And what do you think of what is happening?"

Her father held her fast with the strength of his gaze. "We are shamed."

Despite her attempt to harden her heart against whatever this thing said, still she felt a pang of sorrow at its words.

Her father shook his head sadly. "You gave up the Sword of Cho willingly, and it was destroyed. You were captured by the Betrayers and proved too weak to escape their prison." His jaw hardened, anger flaring in his eyes. "And now you ally yourself with the one who ordered my murder!"

"She is trying to stop them," Cho Lin said numbly.

"The sorceress freed them! She was the one who stole the chest from the bone-shard towers. She unleashed this plague upon the world for her own petty ends! Yet you stand beside her, follow her commands, and would fight to save her if she was in danger. You disgrace the Cho name."

Cho Lin's thoughts whirled. She had suspected that Alyanna had been responsible for more than she claimed ever since the shapechanger's cryptic comments, but she had held fast to the idea that the monster had been trying to sow discord between them. If what this spirit said was true, though, then she had truly failed her family and her father.

"What would you have me do?" she said bitterly. "I cannot stop the Betrayers by myself. I need the sorceress's strength."

"Leave this place," he replied with harsh conviction. "Take the weapon they gave you and return to Shan. Present it to the emperor and the warlocks and let them give it in turn to the greatest warrior in the empire, so that he can slay the Chosen."

He. Of course.

"But they will wake another Raveling!" Cho Lin cried, stepping closer to her father.

"In the north!" her father spat back. "Shan is on the other side of the Broken Sea, and this creature cannot cross the water. It was how our ancestors fled the destruction long ago. The northerners brought this calamity down upon themselves, and your loyalty must be to Shan!"

"You want me to flee?" Alyanna said, a shiver of cold surprise going through her as she met Demian's placid gaze.

"I want you to survive, Weaver," replied the swordsinger. "This is not a fight you can win. The Ancient is already stirring; nothing can stop its awakening now. The Chosen and the Skein sorcerer are too strong for you alone to oppose." She retreated as he moved forward a step. "Please. You will die if you stay here."

"I will die if I leave," she spat back.

"Only if you stay in Araen. This land is doomed, but remember what the Shan did long ago. They fled the ravages of an Ancient and found a new life on distant shores. You can do the same. Go to Xi and explore the ruins hidden deep in the dark jungles. Travel south to the burning oases of the black sand deserts. Sail the western ocean to the Sunset Lands and see what mysteries wait there to be discovered."

"And let the world I know be destroyed?"

A slight smile quirked the shadowblade's lips. "As you did before. Except then, you were the one that wielded the sword."

"I knew it would not all be lost, and that much would survive."

"The same will happen here," Demian replied calmly. "The Ancients are like fires in the forest. When too much bracken and dead wood chokes the land, keeping new life from growing, the Ancient scourges it clean. It is the natural way of things. Other creatures will rise to take the place of man. It has happened countless times before."

Something about what Demian had said did not ring true. "Wait," she said, gathering her sorcery. "You once told me that you chose immortality because you wanted time to discover the meaning of existence. And now you suggest it is nothing but a cycle of death and rebirth."

Demian shrugged. "I was wrong. There is no great mystery. All we can do is hold out against the darkness."

"Those are *my* words," Alyanna said, stalking closer. The sorcery thrummed within her, wanting to be released. "You know what I wish to hear. But it is not Demian who would say such things. *You* are not Demian."

"Weaver—" the phantasm began, but Alyanna had already unleashed a wave of shimmering sorcery. When it struck Demian he wavered, his face contorting, and then he dissolved into colorless wisps that quickly merged with the eddying mist.

Alyanna drew in a deep, steadying breath. Whatever that thing had been, it had preyed on her guilt over what she had done to Demian and had tried to use her secret innermost thoughts to turn her from her path. It had known her so intimately. She couldn't conceive of how that was possible. What if she found Keilan or the Shan, and they were in truth simply flawless simulacra intent on stopping her?

The mist in front of her roiled and fled, revealing a wall of mottled white flesh broken by a ragged wound. Black metal barbs had been sunk into the skin to keep the injury from scarring over, and from the gray-green crusting of scabs at its fringes Alyanna could tell that this wound was ancient, perhaps as old as this city. No blood or ichor leaked forth, and there seemed to be emptiness beyond it. Alyanna approached cautiously. She ran her hand lightly over the pebbled wall; it felt like lichen-spotted stone, but she knew she was touching flesh, and she couldn't hold back a shiver.

She ducked down, peering within the open wound. There was no mist, but a dull light infused the space beyond, radiating from everywhere and nowhere. It revealed a tunnel crudely hacked from the flesh, curving away into the distance. Black pustules hung from the ceiling like corrupted fruit, and a bile-green liquid flowed behind one of the walls in rhythmic pulsings. Far away a distant, mighty heartbeat thundered.

She slipped one leg through the gaping wound, her boot sinking slightly into the soft floor. The air was much different here – the coolness of the mist-shrouded city was gone, replaced by a slick, oppressive humidity and the smell of freshly butchered meat.

Steeling herself, Alyanna pulled herself fully inside the great beast.

"Save me from what?" Keilan asked, closing his eyes as his mother's fingers continued to stroke the back of his neck.

"From all this," she said softly. "You've done so well, Keilan. And so much. But you're just a boy. This place would be dangerous to the greatest of sorcerers – even my mother would have feared to tread here. You must flee while you still can."

Keilan grimaced, looking at her again. "I can't. There are so many who will die if we cannot stop the Chosen."

"You will die!" his mother cried, her voice wrenched by fear and sorrow. "What can you do, my son? The sorceress has power that has been refined for a thousand years. The Shan has a weapon forged to end the miserable existence of those tainted children. You have nothing!"

"I have something," Keilan said, and held out his forearm so that his mother could see the faint black lines spidering beneath his skin.

Pity swelled in her face, fresh tears glimmering. She withdrew her hand from his neck and lightly traced the swollen veins with her finger. "Oh, my sweet son. What have they done to you?"

"I am bound to one of them. I have felt its rage and fear and confusion. She's lost and lonely. Maybe I can help her."

"You were always so kind," his mother murmured, enfolding his hand in hers. "And for a soul so pure it is hard to see the wickedness in others. But there is evil in this world, and however innocent these children once were, they have been corrupted beyond redemption. They will kill you if you go forward."

"Then I will go to my death," Keilan said sadly, pulling away from this thing that might have been his mother. "I cannot run from this."

"Please, Keilan!" his mother cried, and he felt her fingers clutching at him as he moved past her. "Please!" Her sobbing ripped at his heart, but he forced himself to ignore it. Even if this truly was her, he must continue. The lives of Nel and Sella and his father hung in the balance.

After a few steps, he turned and saw only swirling mist where his mother had been. But he thought he could still hear her anguished cries somewhere far away, pleading with him to turn back.

"I'm sorry," he whispered as the mist suddenly cleared and he found himself staring at the blackened, festering edges of a great wound set into white flesh.

Cho Lin stepped away from this creature that looked like her father, her lip curling in contempt. "Your words betray you. My father would never show such callousness, even towards the northern barbarians."

"You do not truly know me, Lin," the phantasm said angrily. "I thought of Shan above all else. The counsel I gave the emperor was always for the benefit our people. Why should I care what happens to these savages?"

"And you believe allowing the Raveling to come again would be in the best interest of the empire?" Cho Lin stepped closer to her father, scorn dripping from her words. "Allow millions of innocents to perish while we ready our fleets to abandon this land as well? You think I should turn away when our ancient foe is here, and I have a weapon that can end their curse forever?"

The creature drew itself up taller, glowering down at her with the same expression of disappointment she had seen countless times when she was young. The familiarity of this look sent a shiver through her, but she held fast to her belief that this thing in front of her was not truly her father's spirit. "Such disrespect! You must obey me, Lin!"

"You are trying to turn me away," Cho Lin said. "And it will not work."

Holding the creature's outraged gaze, she stalked forward, her butterfly sword extended in front of her, but before the point could touch its robes the phantasm trembled and split apart into shreds of coiling mist.

Cho Lin slashed angrily at the drifting tendrils. How dare they try to use the memory of her father against her? But she was not so easily fooled; whatever tricks and traps infested this cursed place, she would persevere. Even if it killed her.

A few steps beyond where the illusion of her father had vanished, she caught sight of the wall she had expected to reach much earlier. A fissure large enough for her to slip inside marred the mottled white flesh, held open by barbs of black metal.

"Keilan!" she shouted once more into the mists, though she did not expect an answer. They were not here anymore, and she did not have the time to search for them. She would push on, towards where the Betrayers waited, and hope that if her companions still lived they would do the same.

31: KEILAN

SEATED UPON A glistening black knob that sprouted from the spongy floor of the tunnel, Keilan stared at the wound he had passed through and wondered if he had made a terrible mistake. He had been praying to every god he knew of: the Deep Ones, Ama, the Silver Lady, the Ten – even the Four Winds he had heard Cho Lin entreating, though he wasn't sure if those were actually divine beings – hoping that the Shan or the sorceress would emerge from the roiling murk and join him inside the Ancient. Yet there was no sign of his vanished companions, and the fear wriggling within him was growing harder to ignore.

Inside the Ancient. The thought that he was sitting on a chunk of organic matter in a space carved from the flesh of a beast was almost beyond his comprehension. This place was a nightmare made real, seething with life. Iridescent beetles the size of his fist scuttled across the craggy walls, and webs of ropy filaments spread across the ceiling. Clusters of dark, broad-capped fungi shivered in the steamy air, and black globes swollen with foulness hung ponderously above his head. More noxious liquid flowed behind the walls in places where they grew membrane-thin, gurgling and hissing as it rushed past.

His own body was vibrating slightly in time to the heartbeat of the beast, and the oppressive presence in his thoughts seemed to be squatting just behind his eyes. He kept shaking his head, as if that could clear it. A silvery centipede that looked to be of the same ilk – only much smaller – as the creature they had seen in the stone city slithered across his foot and disappeared into a tear in the wall.

Keilan shivered. He stared at the churning mist that stopped at the threshold of the Worm and willed the others to appear. He considered venturing outside again, but he was afraid of what else he might encounter in the mist. Continuing deeper into these tunnels was not an option. Without Alyanna's sorcery or Cho Lin's strength, there was no way he could stop the Shan demons.

Had they also encountered something within the mist and been turned away? Or had they already arrived where he sat now, and after waiting for him had finally decided to push on? Alyanna had said it was only a matter of time before the Chosen successfully roused the Ancient. But surely she and Cho Lin would have left some note or marker so that he would know they had been here? Should he do the same? Keilan peered down the curving passage, its far reaches choked by feathery fronds stirring in a breeze he could not feel, wondering if he dared press on without them.

He froze, coldness creeping up his spine. It almost looked like something was crouched among the drifting fronds, watching him. His unease grew as he continued to stare at that patch of shadows recessed among the stalks. Finally, he could take it no longer and he grasped his sorcery, summoning a ball of wizardlight. Pale radiance filled the tunnel, dispelling the gloom. All along the walls small creatures scurried into holes, and even the odd flora seemed to shy away from the light. With a thought, Keilan sent his sorcery floating down the corridor.

The leaves shivered as one of the Chosen stepped out into the light. Shocked, Keilan's hold on his sorcery slipped, and the tunnel plunged into twilight again, the demon's ragged shape merging with the darkness.

Panic rising, Keilan fumbled to weave his wards, letting out a triumphant cry as they shimmered into existence.

He waited, barely breathing, and stared at the shadows where he had seen the Chosen. Could it have been a phantasm like his mother? His mind playing tricks? Perhaps it—

His ward shivered, buckling. He had barely begun to scream before the demon pushed through his sorcery and the darkness swallowed him.

Cho Lin stepped through the wound and into the humid interior of the Ancient. It was like entering a jungle cave overgrown with vegetation: traceries of vines clung to the ceiling, and strange plants and fungi crawled along the walls, drooping with unnatural blossoms. Small lizards skittered away from her approach, and a huge insect uncased silver wings and whirred into the air with thrumming urgency. Overlaying all this was the distant, maddening drumbeat of the great beast's heart. That reminded her that the ceiling was not stone but flesh, and the latticework of vines was actually strands of organic matter. The creatures that inhabited this realm were parasites on a vast host.

A crackling far down the tunnel drew her attention. In the vague, dusky light that permeated everything she saw a shape crouched among a profusion of curling stalks and broad leaves.

"Alyanna!" she cried, and the sorceress rose, turning to look at her.

Cho Lin peered down the tunnel. Where was Keilan? Had he not yet pushed his way through the mist?

"Shan," Alyanna said, carefully stepping over a small puddle of yellowish liquid as she approached Cho Lin. "You made it past the guardian."

"The thing that looked like my father?" she asked, squinting at the glowing mist on the other side of the wound. It roiled and eddied, prevented from entering this place by some invisible barrier.

"Yes. The complexity of the sorcery took me by surprise, but now that I can consider what I experienced I've concluded that it was something fashioned to dissuade us from entering. Unlike any sort of sorcery I've ever known, but the Burrow was made by creatures very different than us, and in many ways very far beyond our capabilities."

"Did Keilan make it through?"

Alyanna stooped down to examine a shining black knob of something that looked vaguely like bone. "He did," she said, running her hand along the surface of the protrusion and then sniffing her fingers.

Cho Lin looked around again. "Well, where is he?"

"I'm not sure. I think he arrived first. But there's another smell here . . . a foulness I know. The Chosen."

"They must have come through the rift as well."

Alyanna pressed her palm into the soft flesh of the ground and closed her eyes. "Keilan's sorcery is . . . messy. There's a residue here that suggests he summoned as much as he could hold, and then that was slapped away from him, spilling everywhere."

"So you are saying . . ."

"The demons have him, if he's still alive." Alyanna straightened, staring down the length of the tunnel. "The Chosen taint their surroundings with their passage. It's a trail I think I can follow."

"Is that how you discovered them in the warlocks' tower?"

"No," Alyanna replied distractedly, still focused on whatever clues the Chosen had left behind. "I was experimenting with the sorcery of dreams and they called out to me."

Cho Lin reacted without thinking. She seized Alyanna by her robes and smashed her against the wall. The sorceress gave a pained yelp as her head struck a twisted black vine.

"You *were* the one who freed them!" Cho Lin cried, shaking Alyanna like a doll. "You lied to me! The shapechanger spoke the truth!"

Rage contorted the sorceress's face. "Filthy Shan!" she hissed, and the gloomy tunnel suddenly grew darker. "You dare touch me?"

"You killed my father," Cho Lin said coldly, then slammed Alyanna again into the soft wall. Bits of debris rained down from above, tangling in her hair.

The sorceress stared at her hatefully. "Fool," she spat. Tendrils of purple light coalesced from nothing, reaching out to wrap around Cho Lin's arms and neck.

Yet when the sorcery touched her, it shimmered and vanished. Cho Lin felt the bone amulet pulse with warmth.

Shock replaced the anger in Alyanna's face, her eyes widening.

"You unleashed the Betrayers," Cho Lin said, throwing the sorceress to the ground. Alyanna broke her fall with her outstretched arms, but one of her hands landed on a flower with gleaming, shard-like petals and she shrieked with pain. She rolled onto her back, cradling her bleeding hand. "This horror is all because of you!"

A wave of blue flame billowed up from where Alyanna sprawled, but the sorcery melted away before it reached Cho Lin.

"You need me!" screamed Alyanna, fear lacing her words.

"I cannot trust you," Cho Lin replied, and she found that her hand was on the hilt of her butterfly sword. "Will you destroy the Betrayers, or try to use them for your own ends, as you did before?"

"Idiot girl," Alyanna snarled. "If I have to be the one to wield the black knife, I will."

"You will have to take it from me."

"I'll take it from your cold fingers!" Alyanna cried, then swept her arm across her body in a cutting motion. A scythe of crimson energy erupted from her hand, consuming Cho Lin's vision. Where it struck her there was no effect, the bone upon her chest throbbing, but she realized belatedly that she was not the true target. With a wet ripping sound, the membrane stretched taut across the wall beside her ruptured, and a surge of cold liquid knocked her from her feet.

Cocooned in a shell of sorcery, Alyanna could only watch in mute astonishment as the ichor she had unleashed flowed in pulsing waves. It was like she was a stone at the bottom of a fast-flowing river, staring up at the water rushing above. She hadn't expected a flood like this; she had been hoping merely to send the Shan tumbling, maybe render her senseless so she could remove that damnable Pure artifact from around her neck. Clearly, though, she had punctured some deep pocket of whatever this substance was, and it was draining into the tunnel.

The world lurched. Alyanna screamed as she was flung about with jarring force, and only her wards kept her from smashing hard into the walls. Even still, black spots swam in her vision as more spasms rocked the tunnel, tossing her back and forth. An earthquake . . . but this was not under the earth.

The tremors subsided as quickly as they had started, though the dark liquid continued to gush from where she'd pierced the wall. Gradually even that started to slow, until finally it was no longer coursing over her in a torrent. With some effort she stumbled to her feet, swaying. The tunnel was flooded by the black ichor; it came well up past her knees, and was still slowly flowing. Her gorge rose at the smell. The sundered membrane hung in ragged strips, and beyond it was a vast, dark cavity.

Had she hurt the Ancient? Was it even now rousing from its dreams, or had whatever flicker of pain she'd caused already been forgotten?

And where was Cho Lin?

She must have been swept down the tunnel and out of sight. *Hopefully she cracked her skull open,* Alyanna thought as she slogged through the black liquid. She needed Niara's knife – why had she allowed Cho Lin to carry it? She cursed her foolishness, though it was true she'd never expected the Shan to turn on her, even if she'd somehow realized the truth of what happened with her father. Idiot spider-eating savage, more obsessed with her family honor than her own life. With all their lives.

Alyanna turned down the bend in the flooded tunnel, and her heart sank. The floor in front of her was riven by a chasm about a dozen paces across, and the liquid flowing around her legs was tumbling over the edge. She crept closer and peered down into the abyss; the same vague radiance as in the tunnel illuminated the depths, and she could glimpse a river of black far below.

Oh, by all the dead gods. The Shan must have been carried down there and swept away. She was never going to be able to find her now. A numb hopelessness spread through Alyanna as she stood on the lip of the chasm and gazed down at the ichor or blood or bile of the Ancient. Alyanna stumbled and nearly fell as another tremor, smaller than before, shivered the White Worm. She glanced back the way she'd come. The Chosen had taken Keilan in that direction; presumably, they were bringing him to wherever Jan and the queen and the Skein shaman had gone. It must be a place where the beast could be woken. Alyanna fingers brushed the ivory handle of her wand. She may not have the knife, but she was still a Talent. She could not destroy the Chosen anymore, but to rouse the Ancient the dark children must need the power of the sorcerers – otherwise why bring them inside? Perhaps if she killed the other Talents the Chosen's madness could still be stopped.

Vhelan was just picking himself up when a second, stronger tremor struck, knocking him back down into the snow. A tremendous crack sounded, and he glanced up the slopes of the Burrow as a sheet of stone broke free. Luckily, they were not in its path, and he gave silent thanks for this as he watched the avalanche gather ice and snow and scree as it swept down the side of the Burrow.

"That's not good," Nel said, helping Seril to her feet. The magister was staring up at the Burrow, her face a welter of emotions.

"What if they need our help?" Seril asked.

"There is little we can do," Vhelan said with a sigh. "Except perhaps to get farther away."

"We can try to enter," the younger magister suggested. "Maybe once we get inside the effects of the Worm are lessened."

Vhelan shook his head slowly. Seril's newfound bravery cheered him, but he had no illusions about what they could do to aid the two Talents that had already gone inside.

"It looks like whatever is under there is waking up, boss," Nel said uneasily.

"Hope that it doesn't," Vhelan replied. He turned back to the rest of the soldiers, most of whom were staring at him like he knew what to do. "In the meantime, let us retreat back to the ridge. At least get somewhere we won't be crushed by falling rocks."

"What about the supplies and horses?" Seril asked, waving her arm in the direction of the half-burned Skein wagons.

"Help the men salvage what you can; we'll need the food if we're going to survive the journey out of the Frostlands." *If we ever get that chance*, he thought with a grimace. "But be quick about it. We don't know what is coming next."

With some effort, Keilan swam back up towards the light. He cracked open his eyes and saw the mottled walls rushing past him in a blur. His cheek rested on something cold and hard and his arms were wrapped around the body of a thin and gaunt child, held in place by fingers that gripped his wrists as solidly as iron manacles. Pain lanced from his knees and shins as his legs knocked against the bulging growths emerging from the uneven ground.

Realization of what was happening slowly wormed into his awareness: he was being carried by one of the Shan demons. Terror rose in him and Keilan tried to pull his hands free, but it was like straining against a mountain. A scream bubbled up, but all that escaped his lips was a broken whimper. He could feel the sharp shoulder blades and each individual knob of the demon's spine digging into his flesh as he squirmed, trying to free himself.

The Chosen ignored him as it hurtled down the tunnels.

Where was it taking him? What was it—

The world spasmed.

Keilan tumbled through the air, his head smashing against something hard. The darkness returned, and he struggled to keep from slipping into unconsciousness. He coughed, moving his arms feebly. Where was the Chosen? He tried to sit up, but it was like there was a great weight pressing against his chest. The ground beneath him shivered again, and he groaned. What was happening?

Cold fingers touched his wrist. He forced his eyes open, and after a moment the blurry shape hunched over him sharpened. The Chosen was crouched beside him; it had lifted his limp arm, and seemed to be examining it. Terror swelled in Keilan again as he saw clearly its corpse-pale features and the black holes beneath its tangled hair. It had been a girl once, he thought from the shape of its face, but it was difficult to tell for sure. Its attention flickered from his arm to its own. Mustering all his strength, Keilan lifted his head slightly so he could better see what it was looking at. Black veins were etched stark against its white flesh, and the exact same pattern was visible on his own arm. As he watched, one of the dark lines in the Chosen's arm twitched, and as if in a mirror he saw the same movement under his own skin.

"No," he mumbled, unable to accept what he was seeing.

The Chosen wrenched its attention from their arms and bared its sharpened teeth at him, hissing.

Then he was being lifted again, as easily as if he were a child, and the Chosen resumed its flight through the tunnels of the Worm.

The rushing darkness carried her along. When she'd first struck the surface after her fall, Cho Lin had accidentally swallowed a mouthful of the cold, viscous liquid, and it had burned all the way down her throat. It wasn't water, whatever it was, but it also hadn't killed her. Her stomach ached a little, and her skin was tingling as the ichor seeped into the wounds she'd taken. Now she was just trying to keep her head above the surface of the black substance as the walls of the tunnel flashed past.

A muted rumbling slowly began to swell, and by the time she realized what it was she was being carried over the edge of a small waterfall. She screamed, fearing that something hard or sharp waited for her at the bottom, but luckily she ended up plunging into a deep pool. She surfaced, spluttering, wiping the black liquid from her eyes. She was floating in the middle of a large cavern, or cavity, or whatever one would call such a space inside a great beast. While the first tunnels they'd entered had appeared to have been hacked from the flesh, this place gave her the impression of having been naturally formed, channels carved by this liquid as it flowed through the Worm.

She began to swim with awkward strokes – it had been some years since her father had insisted she learn following her fall into the koi pond, and the thick liquid was more difficult to move through than water. The only reason she wasn't panicking was because she could see that a strip of dry flesh fringed the edges of this pool. There even appeared to be a hole set in the wall, which hopefully would provide an exit. She couldn't think of a worse way to die than being trapped down here, slowly withering away, unable to escape.

Finally, she heaved herself onto the shore, her hands and arms sinking into the ground. Tiny crab creatures skittered away from her as she rolled onto her back and stared at the soaring rib-like structures that met at a point far above her.

She felt disgusting. The liquid clung to her, oozing along her skin and pooling inside her clothes. With a shudder, she shrugged out of her furs and then began to try and scrape the substance from her body, dressed only in the light garments of the southern lands. It was warm inside the great beast, and glancing at the sodden heap of furs she realized there was nothing that could get her to wear those again. She did find the black knife and the shard of her father's sword within the discarded furs and secured them in the belt that cinched her tunic. Then she staggered to her feet, wishing fervently for a way to wash this foulness from her hair, and set off towards the gap that she prayed would give her a way to return to the tunnels above.

Just before she entered the crack in the wall, something shifted within its depths, and then she stumbled back as a small shadow stalked from the darkness.

Keilan had the vague sense that the tunnels the Chosen had been rushing through had opened up into a much larger space, and then he was unceremoniously dumped onto the ground. He lay there, too drained to look up, his cheek pressed against the flesh of the Worm as the reverberations of its heartbeat echoed in his skull. The sound had been swelling for a while now. He imagined a gnarled black heart the size of a great castle suspended in the semi-darkness, awash with the ichor that he had seen flowing behind the translucent tunnel walls.

"Is he what we need?" a man said, his accent grating and harsh.

the boy has powerful sorcery.

This was the hoarse whisperings of many children roughly layered over each other. He'd heard the same voices once before in the ruins of the Selthari Palace, as a broken sky bled above a temple of twisted corpses.

Keilan struggled to his knees and looked around, swaying.

The chamber was large, but it still seemed constricted given the size of the black iron door set into the far wall. The door was round and covered with strange, swirling designs that had been incised into the dark metal, fairly blazing with sorcery in his mind's eye. Keilan wasn't sure if this power was bound up within the door, or if it was originating beyond it and leaking out from around the edges, but it was so overwhelming he had to look away.

When he saw what else was in the room, he moaned. A cadaverously thin man in threadbare robes stood close to the iron door, staring at Keilan. The skin stretched taut over his skull was smooth and unlined, but Keilan could not believe this sorcerer – and this was the Skein shaman, he was certain – was as young as he looked. The soul staring out from his unnaturally blue eyes had an ancient, terrible weight. With some effort, Keilan looked away from the Skein and at the other figures in the room.

Jan and Cein d'Kara were, like him, also kneeling in the chamber, though their backs were arched and their heads thrown back, as if gripped by a terrible force. They both stared forward sightlessly, their lips slightly parted, and beneath their sallow skin were the shadows of dark lines. Behind each of them stood one of the Chosen, their hands reaching around to rest upon their faces. Where those corpse-pale fingers were splayed, the black veins were darkest, radiating out like cracks in broken porcelain.

"Your Highness?" Keilan whispered, but the queen made no indication that she could hear him. Her once-beautiful red hair was matted and snarled, and dirt smudged her pale cheeks. If it were not for the tattered remnants of her royal finery, just noticeable beneath the furs draped over her, she would have looked like one of the ragged street urchins Keilan had seen in the streets of Herath.

"Jan?" he tried, but the immortal was lost in the same dark sorcery as the queen. He was barely recognizable as the handsome, confident sorcerer who had cut such a dashing figure in Saltstone. He looked to have aged a decade in the months since Keilan had last seen him, his bones etched stark against his skin and his one visible eye deeply sunken. Livid red scars covered half of his face; Vhelan had told Keilan how the Chosen had struck Jan down beneath Nes Vaneth, but the wounds were worse than he'd imagined.

"He was the only one following us?" the Skein shaman asked.

the scent of the sorceress who first freed us is heavy on him. she is here as well.

"She must have power, to enter the Worm. This child could not survive the city on his own."

she is dangerous. after the barrier is breached we will hunt for her.

"And will I be rewarded with her as well?"

Sharp hissing rose from the Chosen. *no. consume these sorcerers, but she is ours.*

The shaman inclined his head, but Keilan caught the faintest trace of a grimace on his lips.

she will be coming here. we must finish quickly.

"Then let us begin," the shaman said, turning away as he faced the great door.

Keilan tried to stand, but a small hand fell upon his shoulder and forced him back to his knees. He cried out as his bones creaked under the crushing strength; he felt the presence of the Chosen standing behind him, but he could not see what it was doing. He ignored the pain and reached for his sorcery, but he lost all semblance of control as another of the demon's hands reached around to touch him on the cheek. Searing cold flooded his body and he tried to scream, but he could summon nothing past his numb lips. Shadows gathered on the edges of his vision, squirming like the tendrils of monstrous things. He could *feel* the Chosen. It was inside him, wriggling beneath his skin, reveling in his terror and helplessness. Against his will he was falling within himself, tumbling into nothing, the chamber at the center of the Worm becoming a dwindling point of light.

It guttered and went out, and the darkness consumed him.

---

daughter of cho xin.

The words were Shan, spoken with an archaic lilt. Cho Lin retreated as the Betrayer stepped from the shadows, drawing her black knife and holding it like she would one of her butterfly swords.

"Daughter of Cho Yuan," she corrected it, as calmly as she could with her heart thundering in her chest. She wasn't sure what she had expected – something monstrous, given what these creatures had done. Yet it looked like nothing more than the drowned corpse of a child, its pale flesh marred by swollen black veins, its dark clothes hanging in tattered strips.

daughter of shan.

"I am," she agreed fiercely. "And I am your doom, demon."

The Betrayer's blackened lips curled back from yellow teeth. It brushed away the ragged dark hair covering its face, and Cho

Lin saw the empty pools of darkness where its eyes had once been. As it lifted its head slightly, she also glimpsed the ragged wound across its neck where a blade had sliced its flesh, purple and livid.

She remembered memories that were not her own. An ancient sorcerer in snow-white robes leading a small boy towards a blood-stained rock. The flash of a dagger and the child's life spilling out in that terrible cavern. A ghost huddled in the darkness, sobbing.

"You are him," she said softly. "The last of them. The one that freed the others. You started all this."

we did not start anything. we are the end, not the beginning.

"The Shadow King. Do you call yourself that because you do not know your own name?"

The veins beneath the child's skin writhed. *everything we had was stolen.*

Its bare feet whispered as it approached her with slow, measured steps. Cho Lin reached for the Nothing within her Self, every detail of this moment sharpening. Behind her, she heard the rumble of the waterfall as it emptied into the lake. The clotting rot of this thing filled her nose, sickly sweet beneath the pungent, festering smell of the Worm's flesh.

She lunged, slashing with the black knife.

Keilan floated in the emptiness.

He had been here before, or somewhere very much like it. A vast, oppressive darkness, though it was total no longer, as the hovering point of light had flared again. If he concentrated on this pinprick, peering at the scene beyond, he could see a man standing in front of a great black door, his arms upraised.

This was important, though it took him a frustrating moment to remember why.

The shaman and the Worm. One of the monstrous children had touched him and he'd fallen within himself. Into the Deep, where monsters dwelled.

And one was here with him now.

Keilan could sense something drifting nearby, lost in the blackness. Pulses of cold air washed over him, and he had the feeling of being observed.

"Hello?" Keilan cried out, and his voice returned to him in a hollow echo.

The pale face of a child emerged from the dark, followed by a black-threaded hand. It reached out and gripped his arm; he tried to pull away, but the fingers were sunk into his flesh. No blood welled up, nor did he feel any pain.

"What are you doing?" he cried, frantically attempting to escape. The child ignored his struggles, pulling him closer, and for the first time he clearly saw the face behind the tangled hair.

He knew it.

"Ko Yan," he stammered, but there was no flicker of recognition in the child's face. "Please. Don't do this."

The Chosen brought its other hand up, reaching towards his head.

"Stop. I know you're in there . . . stop!"

Clammy fingers touched his lips. He turned his head away, trying to keep his mouth closed. Keilan battered at the Chosen, prying desperately at the demon's fingers, but it was like trying to bend iron. With implacable strength it worked first its fingers into his mouth, then its entire hand. Keilan gagged, overwhelmed by the horror of what was happening.

The Chosen reached down his throat and seized his sorcery.

Slowly, it withdrew its arm, and when its hand slipped free, Keilan saw that it gripped a shimmering strand, and he knew this extended back down into his gut, into his core where the forces of the Void welled up. He felt his sorcery unspool deep inside him, drawn forth by the child demon, and then it was fed into the mote of light hovering in the darkness. Something on the other side grabbed it roughly and yanked hard.

His sorcery was no longer his own.

The hand on his arm disappeared, but he was still firmly in the grip of the demon.

"Ko Yan," he cried, surprised he could still talk with the torrent of sorcery flowing from his mouth. "You had a brother! You went swimming with him in the river! Your mother sang to you!"

Keilan trembled as the fire swelled inside him. He reached out to the blank face of the Chosen, but its dead eyes watched him without mercy.

The Betrayer leapt away with preternatural quickness, and the black knife carved the air a half-span from its savaged neck. It landed on all fours, its limbs bent awkwardly, and scuttled backwards before rising to its feet again. Even with Cho Lin's hold on the Nothing the child seemed to move with frightening speed. It watched the dark-threaded blade in her hand with wary caution as it began to circle her.

"You fear this?" she taunted, flourishing the knife. "It has already ended one of you today."

it smells like our flesh and blood. the old blood, the first flesh.

"From when you were just children. Innocents. Apprentices of Lo Jin."

The Betrayer's face contorted, the black lines that fractured its face writhing. *he said he was our father*

"And he murdered you. I saw. It was a terrible crime."

the anger, the hate. It burned a hole in our prison and we were changed by what we found on the other side.

Cho Lin licked her lips, edging closer. *Keep it talking.* If she could distract the demon for just a moment she could end this nightmare. She tensed, the strength of the Nothing coiling inside her like a serpent ready to strike.

"You have had your revenge. You killed Lo Jin. Every Shan who was alive when your spirits were first bound is now dead."

the rage still burns. it will not be extinguished until all men suffer like we do.

The bone amulet suddenly pulsed, warmth spreading from where it lay against her skin. The Betrayer had tried to use some sorcery, but this relic of the northern god had protected her. Cho Lin thought she saw the child hesitate, as if surprised that its power had slid away from her, and she used that moment to explode forward. All her years of training – in the gardens of the emperor by the Tainted Sword her father had hired, in the halls of Red Fang against the finest warriors in the world – were channeled into this one strike. She had never moved faster in her life, the world blurring around her, every shred of her being focused on the corpse child.

The Betrayer flowed out of the way. Cho Lin stumbled forward, caught off balance by the sudden movement. She lashed out awkwardly with the blade, hoping to catch it by surprise, but again struck nothing.

Long nails raked her arm and the black knife was ripped from her fingers. It tumbled end over end and splashed into the dark pool, instantly vanishing. Cho Lin barely had enough time to comprehend what had just happened when more burning lines opened in her belly. She fell, landing flat on her back, her hands going to her stomach.

"Oh," she said softly, trying to keep her insides from sliding out. Warmth gushed between her fingers, making them sticky.

She stared up at the ceiling of the chamber, her vision fading, and then the Chosen was there, crouched above her. She felt herself being pulled into the endless black abyss of its eyes. Cold fingers pushed past her hands, reaching into her belly.

I'm sorry, Father.

He had been emptied, hollowed out. All the sorcery that had pooled deep within him had been drawn forth and fed into the man outside. The point of light had swelled larger even as the thread of power grew more attenuated, until Keilan could clearly see what was happening in the chamber with the iron door. The emaciated Skein blazed with the power of four Talents, a roiling maelstrom of sorcery. Near him, their faces sallow and slack, Jan and the queen stared sightlessly. Even drained of their power, the Chosen were still holding them in thrall.

The Skein began to weave, braiding countless strands of sorcery into a shimmering tapestry. Keilan was awed by the skill the sorcerer displayed; somehow, he was keeping track of hundreds of threads simultaneously. His movements became faster, the spell reaching a crescendo, and then he extended his arms towards the door and a hurricane of raw power erupted from his outstretched hands.

The door shattered. Glowing cracks spread through the black iron, and then it crumbled, chunks of metal spilling across the floor. The Skein swayed and then fell to one knee. Wearily, he raised his head, and Keilan could see his back rising and falling like he was taking great, gulping breaths. The raging sorcery that had filled him was gone; he must have thrown all his strength – and the strength of Keilan, Jan and the queen – against the barrier. Slowly he rose to his feet.

Keilan couldn't see what had been revealed beyond the door – the sorcerer was partly blocking his view – but it looked like a black tunnel. He strained towards the light, yet the grip on his arm was unrelenting. He had a terrible sense that once the Skein passed beyond the broken door there could be no way to stop the cataclysm he had seen in the coral temple.

"Ko Yan," he pleaded, turning away from the light and staring into the child's empty eyes. "Let me go. Wan Ying wants this, not you. Not you."

Her hold did not slacken.

"You are Ko Yan," he continued, desperate. "We stood on a beach." Keilan reached down, searching for the hand that hung at her side. He found her cold fingers and twined them with his own, as he'd done in the dream they'd shared on the shore of the Broken Sea. Surprisingly, she did not pull away.

"You said it was beautiful."

The light suddenly swelled until it enveloped him, and when he blinked away the spots in his vision he realized that he was again kneeling in the chamber. His mind had been returned to his body.

The feeling of the Chosen's fingers on his cheek was gone, but he could sense its cold presence. A quick glance to his side showed him that Jan and the queen were still lost to the demons hovering behind them, their skin threaded with blackness and their eyes staring blankly ahead.

The Skein shaman had paused for a brief moment at the threshold to examine the glowing remnants of the door he had just split asunder.

Keilan lurched to his feet.

The sound made the Skein whirl around, and he brought up his hands as Keilan stumbled across the chamber towards him.

Keilan screamed in rage, expecting to be enveloped in flame or struck down by lightning, but nothing flashed from the Skein's fingers.

The shaman must have used all his sorcery to tear down the door, Keilan realized, ripping his sword from its sheath. He had done what Alyanna had warned Keilan never to do – pour all his strength into a single spell.

The unnaturally blue eyes of the Skein widened in shock as Keilan plunged his blade into the sorcerer's chest. There was a moment of resistance as the point of the sword struck something hard, then that gave way and the length of steel sank halfway to its hilt. Keilan lost his grip on the sword as the sorcerer was driven backwards a few steps and then tripped over one of the scraps of metal that had once been the door. The Skein went sprawling, the blade pushed entirely through his thin body. Blood poured from the wound, darkening his already black robes; the sorcerer's fingers were wrapped around the hilt, as if he was trying to pull the sword from his chest, but whatever strength was in his thin limbs had fled. When he realized the blade would not move, he raised his head, staring at Keilan with blazing hatred and baring red-stained teeth.

Then a shudder passed through him, his hands slipping from the outstretched silver wings of the sword's hilt.

Keilan stood over the sorcerer, his chest heaving. He had reacted without thinking, desperate to keep the Skein from passing through the shattered door.

Slowly, Keilan turned back to the Chosen. He let out a long, shuddering breath, certain that the demons would end his life in the next heartbeat.

But they had remained where they were. Two of the Chosen still stood behind Jan and the queen, but they had turned their heads and were now staring at their sister, the one who had released Keilan. And she was staring back at them, her dead face expressionless.

The pain was unbearable. It rippled through her in pulsing waves, radiating from the hand that had been plunged into her abdomen. Cold fingers fluttered inside her, plucking and prodding at things that were not meant to be touched. Cho Lin mewled from the agony, weakly pulling at the Betrayer's arm with blood-stained hands. The demon ignored her. Its thin lips were pursed and its empty eye sockets slightly narrowed, as if it were a master artisan concentrating to ensure its work turned out perfect.

She realized she was crying when the tears fell from her cheeks and trickled down her throat. There was a flame in her belly, eating away at her from the inside. She was going to be consumed, burned to ash by this thing, this monster that had haunted her family for a thousand years. Cho Lin moaned, turning her head to stare out upon the glistening black lake. Her father stood in the liquid up to his waist; he had unbound his long hair, and it fell in a dark river over his shoulders. Behind him were arrayed a dozen more figures, all men. All silent, all watching.

"I'm sorry," Cho Lin whispered, then closed her eyes and moaned as a sharper pain pierced her stomach. She felt the Betrayer's hand withdraw from her.

Fighting back the haze that was threatening to carry her away, she focused on the demon crouched above. The hand that had been inside her now hung suspended over her, dribbling gore onto her tunic. The Betrayer looked distracted. It had turned its head, peering into the shadows of the chamber, its corpse-pale face creased in confusion. But there was nothing there. Somewhere else, something unexpected had happened.

Cho Lin slipped her shaking hand to her waist. Her fingers sought and found what she'd thrust into her belt. Metal sliced her flesh, and fresh blood flowed forth. The Betrayer did not seem to notice, continuing to stare at something only it could see.

Cho Lin withdrew the last shard of the Sword of Cho and with all her remaining strength jabbed it into the hand of the Betrayer.

The sorceress had said its power was gone. That the soul of the poor girl who had helped usher in the Raveling a thousand years ago had finally gone to her rest. Cho Lin expected nothing except for the demon to realize that she was not broken, not bowed. That she would pass beyond the Veil raging against the dark.

The Betrayer twisted its head to look at her again, its lips parted slightly, and she heard it truly speak for the first time. Not in hoarse, layered whispers, but in the voice of a surprised child.

"No."

It broke apart into tattered strips of darkness. The fragments dwindled, fading into nothing.

The piece of the sword slipped from her fingers. Without the hand of the Betrayer filling the wound in her belly the blood was pumping out of her in great gouts. She felt the warmth of it even as the rest of her body grew cold and numb. She turned her head back to the lake. Her father was closer now, nearly to the edge. The liquid barely reached up to his ankles, though his long robes were somehow dry. She blinked, trying to understand how this was possible. Even more strange, he was smiling at her, something she hadn't seen since she was a small girl. Slowly, he raised his hand, beckoning her to come to him.

In another chamber hollowed from the flesh of the Ancient, the last three creatures that called themselves the Chosen dissolved into mist and shadow.

32: KEILAN

"YOUR HIGHNESS!" KEILAN cried as the queen let out a shuddering cough and fell forward. Cein d'Kara caught herself with splayed hands before she struck the ground and stayed like that for a long moment, her tangled red curls veiling her face. Beside her, Jan had doubled over, his arms folded across his chest and his eyes closed. Suddenly his body was wracked by violent heaving and he spat up a clump of glistening darkness.

Keilan hurried over to the queen, offering to help her up as she slowly raised her head. She ignored him, struggling to her feet with a look of grim determination, then stumbled towards where the Skein lay.

The sorcerer was not yet dead, to Keilan's great surprise – he'd managed to prop himself up against one of the larger chunks of the broken iron door, his arms and legs hanging limp and his skull-like head lolling to one side. A line of blood trickled from the corner of his mouth. The only indication that he was alive was his ragged breathing, his chest rising and falling despite the sword embedded in his ribs.

He did not lift his head as the queen came to loom over him. She swayed, then steadied herself and leaned over to grip the silver hilt of Keilan's sword with two hands. With a grunt she pulled hard, nearly toppling backwards as the blade slid from the sorcerer's body. He coughed as a fresh wash of darkness stained his robes, but still he did not look up at the queen.

"Don't be afraid, Skein," Cein d'Kara said. "After all, life is a circle." Then she swung the sword. Blood erupted from the stump of the Skein's neck as his corpse toppled to the side, and Keilan had to jump back as the head of the sorcerer bounced close to his boots.

The queen turned back to Keilan, holding out his sword for him to take. The Skein's blood speckled her pale face. He accepted the sword with a nervous bob of his head, trying to avoid staring at the gore-streaked blade or the queen's satisfied smile.

"The . . . Chosen," Jan gasped, and they turned to him. The Min-Ceruthan was on his knees again, staring around the chamber. "Where did they go?"

"They just . . . broke apart," Keilan answered. He felt the queen lash together a sorcerous weave and send it questing outwards.

"They're gone," she said. "Destroyed, we can hope."

"Look!" Jan cried, pointing.

A ghostly haze surrounded the Skein's severed head, leaking from his eyes and mouth. As it dissipated, Keilan saw that the hair of the sorcerer was fading to gray, and his skin – once youthful and unblemished – was now creased by wrinkles. The queen gazed at this transformation for a long moment, her face unreadable. It did not look to Keilan like she was surprised by what had just occurred.

"The Chosen might be dead," Keilan said, tearing his eyes from what was happening to the Skein's corpse. "Or more dead than before. Cho Lin was carrying a weapon that could kill them."

"Cho Lin is here?" Jan blurted, finally finding the strength to stand.

Keilan nodded. "And Alyanna—"

"*Alyanna* as well?" The Min-Ceruthan looked dazed, as if he couldn't believe what he was hearing.

"Yes. We came here to rescue you, but we got separated. And then I was ambushed by one of the Chosen and it brought me here." There was so much more to tell, but it would have to wait. "Alyanna believed the Chosen were connected, all of them bound together by the will of the most powerful of the children. The Shadow King, he called himself. It was his hate and anger that drove them to punish the world for what had happened to them long ago. Perhaps somewhere in this place Cho Lin managed to strike him down, and the rest of them followed his spirit into oblivion."

The queen was looking at him strangely. "You are not the same boy who ran away from Saltstone," she said, shaking her head.

"Much has happened, Your Highness," Keilan replied, embarrassed by her scrutiny.

"Clearly," she said, turning away from him to stare at the tunnel that had been revealed when the door was destroyed. "And there will be time later for the telling of stories." She stepped over a still-smoldering chunk of black iron as she approached the threshold.

"Wait," Jan cried. She glanced at him, one eyebrow raised, and he seemed to realize the impertinence of giving her a command. "Your Highness, that door was a Min-Ceruthan artifact of incredible power. It was never meant to be breached. They wanted to keep whatever is behind it hidden away forever."

The queen stared at him for a long moment, her face inscrutable. "I cannot turn away now," she finally said, taking another step towards the tunnel.

It was like walking inside a hollow length of polished black bone, Keilan decided. Which it might actually be, he admitted, though he hadn't seen anything like this before in the body of the Worm. He'd read somewhere that the bones of dragons were black as obsidian – perhaps the Min-Ceruthans had brought the remains of one of those legendary creatures here . . . or maybe the Ancient had swallowed one thousands of years ago.

It was likely something else entirely. He wanted to ask Jan and the queen what they thought, but he couldn't bring himself to break the eerie silence that had descended. Even the heartbeat of the Worm was muffled, when just a short while ago his teeth had fairly chattered with the pounding. His companions also seemed to be baffled by the tunnel, if their expressions were any indication. The queen's pace was slow and measured as she trailed her fingers against the smooth black walls; her brow was knitted and her eyes were narrowed, suggesting she was lost in deep thought. Jan looked more nervous, his hands clenching and unclenching as he followed a few steps behind the queen.

The tunnel stretched arrow-straight, until it terminated far ahead in a hazy white glow. Gradually, this patch of light grew, until Keilan saw that it was another chamber. The heartbeat of the Worm swelled again here, its walls and ceiling the same mottled white flesh threaded with organic filaments he had seen before. The entrance to another black-sheathed tunnel was across from the one they had just traversed, but between them and this passage was something strange.

It hovered in the center of the circular chamber: a sphere larger than a man carved of some opalescent substance. Keilan was reminded of the pearls that divers risked their lives to gather in the rocky coves near his village. Washes of shimmering color crawled across its surface, as if it was reflecting light from some hidden source. A thin stream of sorcery, visible in Keilan's mind's eye, extended from the sphere and vanished down the tunnel across from them.

Cein d'Kara approached the strange artifact, her hands clasped behind her back, and made a slow circuit as she studied it carefully. A tendril of sorcery flickered out from the queen to gently caress the sphere, but she must have learned nothing, or what she did learn simply confused her, as after her investigations she pursed her lips, frowning.

"Do you know what this is?" she asked Jan, who had edged closer than her to the floating pearl.

"I . . . think so," he said slowly, though he did not sound at all certain. "There are . . . echoes of something I've felt before. Perhaps if I . . ." As he reached out his hand the queen cried a warning, but it was too late. His palm found the gleaming surface, and for a brief moment the energy coruscating across the pearl infused Jan, his hair lifting slightly and sparks dancing from his fingertips.

The queen muttered a curse, her wards flaring into existence.

Jan shivered as he pulled away a moment later, the crackling power dissipating.

"Yes, it is," he said softly, his voice raw. He cleared his throat and spat out another wad of blackness. "It's what I thought it was."

"And?" the queen asked with a hint of impatience.

"A soul jewel. Or something very much like one."

The queen's brow furrowed. "Wait. The same sort of artifact you and the other Talents used to gather the lives necessary for your immortality?"

Jan nodded grimly. "Alyanna forged her jewel in the black kiln, the lost workshop of the Warlock King, following instructions set down by that ancient sorcerer. This artifact is much older, I believe. Different, but perhaps the same principles. It is an artifact designed to absorb lives and transform them into energy that can be harnessed for great acts of sorcery." His eyes were sad, Keilan thought, as he stared into the roiling sphere. "There are lives in this one still, though they are not human."

"Not human?" Keilan blurted. "What are they, then?"

Jan gestured at the artifact, as if inviting him to touch it. "See for yourself. It won't harm you."

Keilan and the queen shared a quick glance, and then they stepped forward and laid their hands on the sphere.

The brightness scalded her skin. It hurt to raise her eyes so she kept them fixed on what was below, the great writhing mass of her people. They filled the huge pit that had been scooped from the mountain, mothers and elders and young, their sobs and screeches carrying up the slope to where she clung. She had been one of the last to be herded into the pit, prodded along by the metal claws of the savage men, and so she had not been forced by the crush of bodies to go deeper, as had happened to the rest.

Where were the fathers? They were supposed to protect. What had happened, that the people could be pulled from under the mountain and brought here, to suffer beneath the blazing fire fixed to the roof of the outside?

A roar split the air, and hissing in fear she glanced up at the ridge above the pit. Light rippled across silver scales as the great wyrm reared back and spread wide its wings. The men in their metal shirts raised their claws and gave answering, triumphant cries. She moaned, scraping her cheeks raw with the filed ends of her talons, tearing at the silken ribbon the elder had tied around her neck for luck on her spawning day.

Five shining points hovered in the air above the great pit – Wielders, but men, which she had been told by one of her mothers long ago was impossible. Men could not Wield, as they were little more than beasts. Lines of fire connected the five Wielders, forming a burning pattern in the sky. Her mother had been wrong.

Another roar, and the wyrm leapt from its perch on the ledge. She glimpsed the terrible queen of these men, her golden hair flowing behind her as she held tight to a spine on the wyrm's back. The wyrm circled the pit, its wings churning the air.

Where were the fathers? Where were the Wielders? Where was the king and his broodmates?

The wyrm banked again, its sinuous neck twisting so that it faced the people huddled below. How many thousands were shrieking in fear under that merciless gaze?

The wyrm's maw opened, and flame consumed everything.

Keilan's fingers slipped from the surface of the pearl and he was thrust back into the chamber, the edges of the scene he had just witnessed – so vivid and distinct only moments ago – already beginning to blur.

"Wraiths," he said softly, meeting the eyes of the queen as she lowered her own hand from the sphere. "I was a wraith child. A girl."

"And I was an elder," Cein said. "I could not breathe because there were so many others crushed against me.

"You saw the moment of their death," Jan said, his face troubled. "The last of their memories before their souls were drawn into this artifact."

"Men did this," the queen said. "I saw them on the cliffs above."

"It was my people," Jan murmured. "Min-Ceruthans. That dragon . . . I recognized her. It was Kalixias, the Mother Drake, though in my time she was ancient, her scales tarnished and her spines yellowing. She was the first of the great dragons to be tamed by a sorceress queen of Nes Vaneth." He looked overwhelmed by what he had just witnessed. "And that woman on her back must have been Galiana, the one who waged war against the wraiths and tore down their mountain kingdoms. She was revered as the queen who first made the holdfasts mighty."

"She murdered the helpless," Keilan said, harsher than he intended.

Jan said nothing, but his gaze turned to the black tunnel where the thread of sorcery from the sphere vanished.

"Why did the Min-Ceruthans do this?" the queen said, joining him as he stared into the darkness. "What is feeding on this sorcery?"

Jan shook his head to suggest he didn't know. "We can still walk away from here, Your Highness. Seal up this place as best we can and pray that the Worm returns to its slumber."

Cein gave no indication that she had heard the bard. She took a step in the direction of the tunnel, and Jan's hand shot out to grab her by the wrist. The queen turned back towards him, her eyebrows rising.

"Do you know why Alyanna feared you?" Jan said, his voice almost desperate. "Because you and she are the same. You both push forward, heedless of the consequences, and others die because of your ambitions." Cein watched him without expression. "She freed the Chosen, despite the dangers she knew must come with ushering such demons back into the world. She ended the old empires because she saw no other way to cheat death. *You* broke through the barriers that had been erected in my mind because you had to know what was behind them, even though the risks of prying at an unknown sorcery were great." Keilan thought he saw a flicker of emotion in the queen's face when Jan said this. "And *she knew* you would do this – that is why she sent me to Herath. She knew this because she understands you; she realizes you are like her. Alyanna has accepted herself and embraced her nature. But you . . . you still have a choice. You can step back from the edge."

Jan fell silent, and the queen studied him for a long moment. She searched his face, seemingly looking for something, and then she pulled her wrist from his grip.

"You truly believe that," she said, her voice tinged with sadness. "You think it is ambition that drives me forward. The pursuit of power." She ran a hand through her tangled red hair, smoothing out some of the snarls. "We live in a time of ignorance, Jan. The candles that once illuminated the dark corners of this world have guttered and gone out. And there are ancient things out there, in the shadows, watching us. Dangerous threats. Creatures like Alyanna. The Chosen." She spread her arms, indicating the flesh of the Ancient that they stood within. "The White Worm. I do not press against the boundaries of what we know because I want to gather more for myself; I do it because that is the only way I can reveal what lurks beyond the light. I do it to protect my people; in truth, I do it to protect all men." Her voice was rising, growing more strident. "We are a weak and fragile species, and only the most recent of many to walk this world. The rest have all vanished. What was their undoing? How can it be prevented?" Cein returned her gaze to the tunnel. "To know this, I have to bring light to the darkness." With a flicker of sorcery her wizardlight swelled in the tunnel, the pale radiance sliding along the polished black walls. "The Kalyuni sorceress and I are very different. It saddens me if you cannot see this."

She moved forward, into the tunnel, walking directly beneath the thread of sorcery emanating from the soul sphere. Jan watched her with his shoulders slumped, as if he had failed at something of great importance. Then he sighed deeply and followed her.

"If only you could talk," Alyanna mused, addressing the head she was holding up by its brittle hair. Intensely blue eyes bored into her, glazed by death. She brushed a finger against the yellowing, parchment-like skin stretched tight over the skull, grimacing at the strange, oily residue of sorcery that clung to it. These remains reeked of the Void. This must have been the Skein sorcerer, and she remembered what the genthyaki had said. A Hunger, tainted by powers beyond this world. Perhaps the shapechanger had been telling the truth, mad as it was.

She glanced around the chamber, taking in the headless corpse with the brutal stab wound in its chest, the chunks of iron smoldering with potent sorcery, and the black tunnel stretching into oblivion. No sign of the Chosen or the other Talents, although there were two unclasped collars lying on the ground. Her gaze lingered on the dead Skein. His head had been hacked off with a sword, which would suggest that it had been done by Keilan. As prisoners, Jan and Cein certainly wouldn't have had any weapons. Did that mean the Chosen had been destroyed? She stretched out her senses, searching for their vile presence, but found nothing except a fading trace.

It truly seemed that they were no longer here.

This would suggest the Crimson Queen was free once more, and that instead of fleeing this place she had decided to push even deeper into the Worm.

How interesting. Alyanna allowed herself a crooked smile, and then tossed the head over her shoulder. She concentrated, spending a moment tucking away all traces of her sorcery, folding her power deep within herself.

Slipping her ivory wand into her hand, Alyanna entered the black tunnel.

Keilan's breath caught as the tunnel they followed emptied into a vast, astonishing space. He had witnessed so many wonders since being dragged from his village, and in truth he had been preparing himself to be awed again by whatever awaited them, but even still he struggled to accept what was before him.

The chamber was much larger than any he had yet seen carved from the Worm's flesh. It was roughly circular, the walls rising up to curve into a dome that could have contained the tallest towers of Vis. But this was not why he couldn't stop looking at what was above. At a certain point the solid flesh of the walls transitioned into a translucent membrane, so that it was possible to see what was beyond the chamber. It was like staring up into murky gray-green water while lying at the bottom of the sea. There were shapes drifting through this great emptiness, and bridges of organic matter spanning the void, but what dominated everything else, black and pendulous and distended by bulging folds of flesh, was the heart of a god, swelling above them like a mountain.

It moved, and with every one of its rhythmic pulsings the room trembled, though the sound Keilan had been expecting was muffled, just as in the black-sheathed tunnels.

Probably, he decided, for the benefit of those who had once dwelled here, in the sanctum of the Worm.

Five tall pillars of some glistening green material rose in a circle at the center of the room, each crowned by a jagged chair. Four of these thrones were inhabited by the desiccated husks of strange creatures – Keilan realized with a jolt that he'd seen one like them before, in the stone city, being taunted by a trio of fox-men. These centipede-men were much larger, though. Their insect-like lower halves, bristling with legs, spiraled several times around the pillars, reaching halfway to the floor. The arm-rests of the thrones were broad enough to accommodate the six segmented limbs that protruded from their upper bodies. The single great eye above each circular, leech-like mouth was closed, as if they were sleeping. Vines or tendrils wrapped their bodies, binding them to the thrones and keeping them from toppling off the pillars.

A man sat in the last throne. He looked tiny, as if a small child had climbed up into its father's chair. The same filaments covered his body, and to Keilan it appeared that some of the strands actually vanished into his flesh. He was naked, except for the blue runes scribed all over his skin and a necklace of what looked to be curved claws. His sandy hair was wild and unkempt, falling down past his shoulders, but the rest of his tattooed face and body was bereft of hair. The thread of sorcery they had followed into this place plunged into the base of the man's pillar and vanished.

"By the dead gods," Jan murmured as he stared upwards, his wards flaring.

The man's golden eyes were open, and he was watching them.

"Keilan, stand back," the queen said calmly, motioning for him to get behind her. The wards she wove were slightly expanded so that he would also gain some protection from her sorcery.

Slowly, the man on top of the pillar stood. He looked to be in good health, but his movements were stiff and pained, as if he had not raised himself from his chair for a very long time. He stared down at them with his brow furrowed, and then his own glittering wards leapt into existence.

Keilan was no expert in judging the relative power of sorcerers, but from the shining lines of sorcery the man had braided so skillfully he guessed that he was a Talent at least as strong as the queen.

Everyone in the chamber stayed as they were, taking the measure of the other, as the heartbeat of the Worm thundered.

It was the stranger who finally broke the silence. He called something down in a language Keilan had never heard before. From his tone he did not sound angry, or aggressive, which heartened Keilan, though his voice was stern. Keilan truly did not want any sorcerous duels to erupt in this place.

After a brief pause, Jan responded in the same tongue, and Keilan could see some of the tension leak from the man's face and posture. He said something more, and it almost looked like the ghost of a smile touched his lips.

"What is he saying?" asked Cein.

Jan turned back to Keilan and the queen. "He's Min-Ceruthan, but his style of speaking is very old. He asked who we were, and I told him. He seems relieved that I'm one of his people."

"He's coming down," Keilan said nervously as the man stepped from the top of the pillar and into empty air. As he floated to the ground, a few of the tendrils remained embedded in his body, tethering him to the throne he had just vacated.

Jan and Keilan took instinctive steps back as the Min-Ceruthan alighted less than a dozen paces away, but the queen remained where she was, her head held high as she met the stranger's gaze. His golden eyes were unsettling, their shape and color more befitting an animal than a man. The rest of his appearance was just as striking: every bit of his skin was covered in the same style of runes that Keilan had once seen carved onto the Min-Ceruthan saga bones. He wondered what story the blue, squirming writing told.

The sorcerer directed a question towards Jan, though he never shifted his attention from Cein. He did not seem the least bit embarrassed that he was unclothed.

"He asks if you are a queen, Your Highness."

Cein d'Kara crooked a smile. "Tell him I am."

Jan said this, and the man nodded in evident satisfaction that his guess was correct. Then he spoke again, with Jan translating when he finished.

"He says you remind him of his own queen." Excitement colored Jan's words. "Galiana duth Seraval, of Nes Vaneth." The bard shook his head in wonder. "This man is very old, Your Highness. When he was born, the Warlock King still ruled in Menekar. Two thousand years ago, at least."

"He makes you seem positively youthful, Jan," the queen murmured, her eyes drifting to the shimmering thread of sorcery that terminated at the base of the stranger's pillar. Keilan swallowed as he realized the purpose of the poor, trapped souls he had brushed against back in the chamber with the sphere.

The man asked another question, his voice hardening slightly. This started a rapid back and forth between Jan and the Min-Ceruthan, until finally the man pressed his fists together and bowed slightly in their direction.

"He asked if we were the ones disturbing the Worm's dreams," Jan explained. "This sorcerer . . . his purpose here is to soothe the Ancient back to sleep when it begins to wake. And he says that the Worm has been troubled recently. It must have been the influence of the Chosen. But so long as he remains here, connected to the Worm, it will not rouse from its slumber. I told him we were also trying to keep the Worm sleeping, and that the ones who wished for it to wake are now dead. He is grateful."

"He has been here for all this time?" Keilan asked, unable to comprehend how this could be true.

Jan nodded. "He says he has been sleeping, sharing the dreams of the Worm. He knows he has been here for a great length of time, but to him it does not feel so long. The chair he sits in nourishes him and brings him into communion with the Ancient."

Cein raised her hands to indicate the chamber. "Ask him the purpose of this place and how he came to be here."

The man listened to the bard relay the queen's question, and then launched into a lengthy explanation that Jan occasionally interrupted for clarification. When the Min-Ceruthan finally stopped speaking Jan stepped back, shaking his head. Keilan thought he looked overwhelmed, but nevertheless he gamely attempted to communicate what the man had explained.

"It's . . . difficult for me to understand, Your Highness. He says that in his time, the ground began to shake and the sorcerers of his people felt a great disturbance was coming. They traced these . . . emanations back to the Burrow of the Worm. They had been warned never to breach the door by the Vaneshalii, which I believe is an old, old name for the creatures we now know as wraiths. But the quakes were getting worse, so Queen Galiana opened the Burrow and found the Worm and the stone city. The man says only a few of the great sorcerers who entered survived the dangers of the city and entered the flesh of the Ancient. They discovered this room, and one of these creatures" —here Jan gestured at the centipede men lashed to their thrones— "breathing its last. The artifact that was sustaining it – the pearl we saw earlier – had exhausted all the lives it had once contained. The Min-Ceruthans realized somehow that a great sorcerous Talent would have to stay here. This man remained behind, and Galiana departed the Burrow to find the lives necessary for him to remain alive as long as possible."

"And they found them in the wraith kingdoms," Keilan said quietly. "My grandmother and Alyanna both told me that the wraiths of the Frostlands had once been as civilized as men, but that their race had slipped into barbarism. They did not slip, though. They were dragged down."

"A sad story," the queen said. "Yet the Worm has remained sleeping for two thousand years."

"Does it justify what was done?" Keilan asked bitterly.

The queen turned to him. "I cannot judge them. Many died so countless could live. Sometimes hard choices must be made . . . it is the burden of wearing a crown."

Keilan bit back on the reply he wanted to make, looking away from Cein so she wouldn't see the disagreement in his face. Who was he to question a queen? He was merely a—

Wait. Keilan blinked, wondering if what he was seeing could be true. He reached for his sorcery, cold power swelling within him.

Jan had been speaking to the Min-Ceruthan in their tumbling language, but as he felt Keilan grasp his sorcery he suddenly paused. "What is the matter?"

Keilan ignored him, his unease rising as he slowly walked towards the pillar that the sorcerer had been perched upon. He stretched out his senses, hoping he was wrong.

The stream of sorcery flowing from the soul sphere and into the pillar had stopped.

He whirled around just as the Min-Ceruthan sorcerer clutched at his chest, his golden eyes widening. Jan shouted in alarm, rushing closer and taking him by his arm as he staggered and cried out. The queen took a quick step back, her face aghast, as the sorcerer began to change. His hair darkened, then faded to gray, while at the same time wrinkles emerged on his tattooed skin. His broad shoulders sloped, his back becoming more hunched as his muscles dwindled. He clutched at Jan's arm, his face sinking in upon itself, his eyes receding into his skull and his skin sloughing from his bones in a cascade of gray dust.

Two thousand years passed in the span of a few heartbeats. Skeletal fingers slipped from Jan's arm as the man collapsed into a pile of bones; the bard could only reach out helplessly as the ancient sorcerer dissolved. He stared in shock at the pile that had been a young man only moments before, and then jumped as something twitched in the sorcerer's remains. The fibrous tendrils that had been sunk into the man's flesh squirmed in the dust, as if searching for what had just vanished, and then they retracted with blinding speed back to the throne.

"What . . . what happened?" Jan whispered, staring at Cein helplessly.

The queen said nothing, but then her face paled. She whirled and began running back towards the tunnel. Jan and Keilan shared a glance as they hurried to follow her.

The first tremor hit before they were halfway to the chamber of the soul sphere, sending the queen crashing into the smooth black wall. Keilan had managed to keep from falling and he held out his arm for her, but she struggled to her feet on her own, then continued her headlong dash down the tunnel. Another, smaller shiver struck, cracks beginning to spider along the walls. If the Worm woke fully, would the labyrinth carved from its flesh be crushed? The thought was terrifying.

They spilled into the chamber of the soul sphere, Cein in front, and as she skidded to a halt Keilan had to twist himself to avoid running into her. Jan did bump into him, nearly sending both of them sprawling, but they caught each other before they tumbled into the mess strewn before them. The pearl that had housed the lives of the ancient wraiths had been shattered into countless opalescent shards, the largest as long as his forearm, the smallest no more than a gleaming speck. He quested out with his sorcery, searching for the power he had felt roiling in the sphere, but the artifact was cold and dead. The souls were gone.

Keilan tore his gaze from the ruin on the floor and found that Cein and Jan were already looking at him. For a moment they were silent, and then the queen gave voice to the name they were all thinking.

"Alyanna," she said, just before the Worm gave a wrenching spasm, and they were smashed violently against the walls.

It felt like the world was shaking itself to pieces.

Vhelan braced himself against a tree as the ground continued to tremble; they had retreated back to the ridge overlooking the valley of the Burrow when the first of the quakes had struck, and there had been a long enough period of stability that he'd hoped the danger had passed. His prayers had not been answered, however, as the tremors had returned. They'd begun as a grumble and had now swelled to the point where he couldn't stand without help. Down on the plains below, great fissures had opened up in the snow as the ground beneath broke apart. The Burrow looked like it was disintegrating before his eyes: great chunks of stone were cascading down its slopes, and the doorway was so full of rubble he feared it was now impassable.

Keilan and Alyanna had failed. The thing beneath the mountain had awoken. He found Nel a few paces from him, kneeling in the snow. She was staring at the unfolding destruction in shock.

"We need to get away from here!" he cried over the sound of the Burrow collapsing.

Nel looked at him with empty eyes. "Does it matter? They're dead."

She began to turn away, but Vhelan grabbed her roughly and spun her back to face him. "We're not. These men followed us here, and we owe it to them to try and escape what's coming!"

She nodded unsteadily and let him drag her to her feet. Just then a stronger quake struck, and he had to pull her close so she wouldn't go sprawling among the roots of the trees they were sheltering beneath.

"Galen!" he cried, getting the attention of the grizzled veteran. The soldier and his men were clinging to trees or rocks, dazed by what was happening. Galen glanced at him with frightened eyes, and Vhelan tried to project as much confidence and calmness as he could muster, given the circumstances. "Gather everyone and order a retreat! I want us moving as fast as we can! Leave any supplies that will slow us down. Understood?"

At first Galen's face was blank, as if he was indeed having trouble parsing out what Vhelan was shouting over the sounds of the world breaking, but then he nodded jerkily.

"Good. And where is Seril? Have you seen her?" he asked, craning his neck to search for the magister.

Galen nodded again, but now confusion creased his face. "Pardon, my lord, but I thought you knew."

"Knew what?"

"She ain't here."

"What?" Vhelan clutched at the branches around him, steadying himself as a stronger tremor struck. "Where did she go?"

Galen pointed at the Burrow. "She was going the other way when we was headed up here. I asked her why an' she said she had to try and help. Last I saw she had started climbing the hill towards the door."

Vhelan's head was whirling. What had that fool girl been thinking? She knew the Worm's presence wouldn't let her enter. "Why didn't you stop her?"

"Ain't my place to question magisters, lord. And to be true, I thought you must have sent her."

"No, I—"

"Boss!"

Nel's anguished cry made him follow where she was looking, back across the valley at the Burrow.

Fear washed through him, leaving him tingling and numb. The hill was heaving. No longer did it look like it was shaking itself to pieces; rather, it seemed like something was pushing up from below—

A crack like the world fracturing echoed among the Bones. Stone and dust fountained high into the sky, and then a great white shape lifted from the earth. The size of the thing was beyond Vhelan's comprehension; a mountain had come to life. Rocks sifted from a massive head as it raised itself skyward, blindly questing – at least, Vhelan thought it was a head. There were no eyes that he could see, just mottled flesh tapering to a blunted point. Perhaps this was the tail of the Worm? Then its mouth opened like a fist unclenching, five great jaws spreading wide, the inside of each covered with thousands of thorny protrusions. The Worm swung its head through the air, and Vhelan saw for a brief moment directly down its throat. The sight numbed him – it was a black abyss that could swallow cities.

At the edges of his vision he could see the soldiers fleeing, stumbling backwards in panic, but he could not tear his gaze from the awesome sight of this ancient creature. The Worm's head came down, dislodging another great avalanche, and then a shiver went through it as it heaved more of its bulk from the gaping hole it had made in the side of the hill.

Vhelan fell to his knees. He felt Nel's arm slip through his own, and a moment later her head was resting on his shoulder. Across from them, as the world broke apart, the Worm's bulk continued to slither into the light.

33: KEILAN

KEILAN FOUGHT HIS way back to awareness.

Dazed, he lay on the ground and stared at the organic strands covering the ceiling. Every part of his body was sore, from the soles of his feet to his throbbing head. He rolled onto his side, moaning, his fingers sinking into the soft flesh of the Worm as he tried to push himself to his hands and knees.

What had happened? He remembered being flung about as the chamber shook, smashing into the walls until the darkness had come and taken him away. The Worm had been thrashing as it woke. Now, though, everything was still. He spent a few long moments gathering his strength, and then struggled to his feet. He swayed, glancing around the chamber. The remnants of the soul sphere were still scattered about – he had been lucky he hadn't been pierced by any of the shards. Where were Jan and the queen?

He saw her after taking a few stumbling steps. She was crumpled in a heap a little way down the tunnel leading to the heart chamber.

"Your Highness," Keilan cried as he rushed over to her, nearly toppling as a wave of dizziness washed over him.

He had a horrible premonition that she was dead, but as he touched her shoulder she rolled onto her back, coughing. Her face was swollen, stained by a mass of bruises, and it took her glazed eyes a moment to focus on him.

"Keilan," she murmured through bloody lips. "You look terrible."

Despite the pain lancing through his body he couldn't hold back a slight smile. "As do you, Your Highness."

She turned her head, spitting out a wad of blood. "Don't be rude . . . to your queen," she muttered, then used her arm to brace herself as she tried to stand. Keilan hurriedly moved to assist her, helping her rise. She leaned on his shoulder, her hair brushing his face.

"*Ng*," she cried, and he felt a shiver of pain go through her.

"Your Highness?"

"My ankle," she explained, her fingers tightening on his arm. "It hurts, but I don't think it's broken."

"Can you walk?"

She let go of him and took a few tottering steps, wincing every time her left foot came down. "Yes. But I'm going to requisition the use of your shoulder again."

"Of course," he said, ignoring his own soreness as he went to her again. She looped an arm around his neck and, after he hesitated a moment, grabbed his hand and put it on her waist so he could better support her weight.

"Let us forget propriety for a moment," she said. He hoped she was too close to see the blush burning his cheeks. Would anyone ever believe that a beautiful queen had once clung to him? He couldn't believe it, and it was happening right now.

"Why did the tremors stop, Your Highness?" Keilan asked, trying to distract himself from the warm presence pressed against him. She smelled surprisingly good given the terrible ordeal she had been through over the last few weeks. Or perhaps that was just in contrast to how he smelled.

"I have my suspicions," she replied. "We must find Jan."

"Do you think he's still alive?"

"I am almost certain he is." She jerked her chin in the direction of the chamber where they had encountered the golden-eyed Min-Ceruthan. "That way."

Together they hobbled down the length of the tunnel. Many of the black panes that had sheathed the walls had fallen and shattered, revealing the white flesh of the Worm beneath. The way seemed to have narrowed, as if the tunnel had constricted as the Ancient shifted. Keilan eyed the walls nervously, remembering his fears that the awakening beast would crush what had been carved from its body.

The heart chamber had also suffered during the tremors. Two of the great pillars had come crashing down, spilling the dried husks of the centipede men onto the floor, and on one side of the chamber a bulge of flesh like a tumescent growth now spilled into the room. Through the membrane stretched across the ceiling Keilan could see the great heart hanging in the emptiness, and the floor trembled with its reverberations. Whatever had stopped the Worm from moving, it was not its death.

It took Keilan a moment to find Jan, as he was nearly lost in the depths of the huge throne. He sat upon the same pillar the other Min-Ceruthan had once occupied, his back straight and his eyes closed.

"Jan!" he cried, but the bard did not stir. Was he asleep? Keilan suddenly realized that the filaments or vines that had wrapped around the ancient Min-Ceruthan now lashed Jan to the throne. Had they entered his body as well?

"Jan!" thundered the queen, so loud that Keilan thought she might have magically amplified her voice.

His face twitched.

"Jan duth Verala!" she boomed again, making Keilan's ears ring, and the bard's one eye slowly opened. It was tinged gold now, as the Min-Ceruthan's had been.

"Your Highness," he said, his voice hollow.

"What is this, Jan?" the queen yelled up at him.

Jan swallowed; he looked drugged, or trapped halfway between the dreaming and the waking world. Slowly, he raised his arm, examining the tendrils encircling his wrist.

"I couldn't see any other way," he murmured.

"You took the sorcerer's place," the queen said matter-of-factly.

His golden eye flicked to them again. "Yes. The Worm was writhing and you had both fallen. I was hurt, but I managed to return to this room." He looked around slowly, as if seeing the chamber for the first time. "How long have I been here?"

"Not long," the queen called back.

Jan's placid expression did not change. "I see. It feels like forever has passed, and also no time at all. I cannot describe it. I am so vast, yet so small . . ." His voice trailed away, as if his attention was being drawn elsewhere.

"What can we do? How can we save you?" the queen cried.

Jan returned to himself, shaking his head slowly. "I've lured the Worm back into its slumber, but it will wake if I leave. I cannot go."

"There must be a way," the queen said, the frustration clear in her voice.

"Perhaps if one of you took my place?" Jan said, and it took Keilan a moment to realize he was jesting. After the silence had stretched for a moment, he continued. "Do not mourn me. This will be my atonement for what happened long ago. And it is not so terrible. I will close my eyes and share the dreams of a god."

The queen growled something under her breath, then spoke again, her words growing more impassioned. "I will find a way to free you, Jan. There must be another way to soothe this beast. I promise you, I will return."

Jan's golden eye closed, and for a moment Keilan thought he had slipped back into the dreams of the Ancient. Then it opened again, except this time it gleamed with a new resolve.

"I thank you, Your Highness. But if you truly wish to grant me a boon, there is something else I would ask."

The souls roiled within her as she paced the tunnels of the Worm. Alyanna felt swollen, gorged; it was the same as a thousand years ago, except that this time the torrent of emotions and memories that had washed over her were utterly alien. She had worried for a brief moment that the lives of wraiths would not be able to sustain her, but as they settled inside her, a hot flush of warmth making her skin tingle and her blood surge, she knew that those fears were unfounded.

She was again immortal.

The tremors that had followed her destruction of the soul jewel had eventually abated; for a short while there she had been sure the Worm would not return to its slumber. The thought of being trapped inside the awoken beast had been terrifying, though in retrospect – unless the tunnels collapsed – this might in truth be one of the safest places she could shelter. Thank the dead gods that eventually either Cein or Jan had realized one of them would have to remain in the inner sanctum to ensure the Worm remained asleep, since whatever ancient Talent that had been keeping the Worm asleep must have perished when she had absorbed the souls.

Alyanna threw back her head and laughed, startling a sleeping pod of bat-like creatures clinging to the tunnel's ceiling. Their wings fluttered like falling leaves in the humid air, and then they were gone. What a remarkable turn of events. She had refilled the well of immortality within her, and forced one of her rivals to exile themselves forever from the world. The traitorous Chosen were defeated, and the power of Dymoria and the Crimson Queen was broken. The symbol sticks had fallen perfectly for her yet again.

Now if she could only find her way out of the maze. She was sure she'd retraced her steps perfectly, but she had never seen these tunnels before. The walls were darker here, and there was no vegetation or fungi feeding on the mottled flesh. She must have taken a wrong turn, and she considered doubling back, but then discarded the idea. The two Talents who had not stayed to placate the Worm were somewhere behind her. Cein and Keilan, she guessed. Jan had always been the sort for grand, tragic sacrifices.

She didn't want to risk a sorcerous battle when the Worm was so unsettled, so she pushed forward. Perhaps another way to exit the tunnels would emerge, or the tunnel she followed would loop back to where they'd first entered the Ancient.

When she first heard the sobbing, she thought her mind was playing tricks. But the sound continued to swell as she followed the curve of the tunnel, and then she rounded a bend and the source was revealed.

A young woman was on her knees, bent forward as if in pain, her fingers tangled in her honey-colored hair. She was rocking back and forth, clearly lost in the trauma this place inflicted on those who were not Talents.

"Seril?" Alyanna asked, and the magister raised her pretty, tear-streaked face to stare at her in abject misery.

"Alyanna . . ." Seril gasped, and then let out a low moan of pain. Her mind must be shredded if she'd managed to come this far – it was surprising that the girl was even conscious.

"What are you doing here?" Alyanna asked, coming closer and crouching beside the magister.

"I had to come. I had to . . ." Seril resumed her rocking, and Alyanna wondered if there was enough of her left to save.

She'd found the magister intriguing, and it was true that she had gotten used to having companions. At the very least, Seril might be able to guide her back to the entrance.

She put her hand on the magister's shoulder. If there was going to be any hope of salvaging her sanity, they had to go now. "We should leave."

Seril drew in a deep, shuddering breath. Her large dark eyes focused on Alyanna, and her confusion seemed to lift.

"Yes . . . we should leave . . . mistress. Together."

Something hard and sharp slid into Alyanna's back. She gasped, glancing down as a curving black barb emerged glistening from her belly. Beneath her fingers Seril's robes twisted, rippling, and then suddenly she was touching hard, gnarled flesh studded with thorns. The magister's face melted away to reveal a skeletal horse-head, blistered bones showing where the skin had fallen away. The genthyaki wheezed, its breath gurgling in its lungs.

Alyanna shuddered as the creature's barbed tail withdrew from her abdomen. Her left hand drifted down to the wound, feeling hot pulses as the lives she'd recently consumed slipped from her to patter upon the tunnel floor. Her other hand slowly moved from the genthyaki's shoulder to its blackened cheek. Its flesh flaked away beneath her fingers, but the creature only rubbed its head harder against her open palm, nuzzling her as it whined.

Alyanna swallowed back the blood that was creeping up her throat. The genthyaki was staring at her with its empty black eyes . . . begging her. Alyanna grasped her sorcery, channeling burning power down her arm and out through the hand touching her old slave. Shining cracks webbed the genthyaki's skull, and then its head collapsed, motes of light spewing from its eye sockets. The creature sagged in death, sliding to the ground, its flesh bubbling and hissing.

Alyanna swooned. Her hand was soaked from holding back the tide of blood trying to escape. She gritted her teeth, battered by waves of pain. The dark walls of the tunnel seemed to shift and writhe.

She couldn't die here. This was not her time – she had ten thousand lives burning inside her.

"Demian," she moaned. *Come for me again. Save me.*

She reached out to the shadows, imploring the shape that watched from the gathering darkness.

Blackness had been poured into the wound in the Worm's side since last she'd stood here.

Strange as that was, elation still surged in Cho Lin at the sight of the entrance, which was so welcome after the endless mottled gray and white walls of the tunnels. She had started to worry that she would never find her way out of this labyrinth.

Was this actually the same tear in the Worm that she and Keilan and Alyanna had once passed through? She wasn't sure, to be honest. It looked similar, down to the barbs of black metal keeping the flaps of skin pinned open, but as she rushed forward she wondered where the roiling, glowing mists had gone. Then she skidded to a halt, gasping as she clutched at the ragged edges of the wound.

On the other side was emptiness.

She smelled clean mountain air, and took several gulping breaths. It was so incredibly refreshing after the fetid stench of the tunnels that she nearly laughed with joy. Stars were scattered above her, gleaming cold and sharp, and in the distance brooded the shadows of the Bones. Below her, the exterior of the Worm curved away into darkness. How high up was she? The thrashing that had nearly shaken her to pieces earlier must have been the Ancient breaching the Burrow, she realized. Cho Lin dispatched an earnest thanks to the Four Winds for this great luck; she had been dreading having to brave the stone city by herself.

To celebrate she pulled out her wine skin. She'd been saving the last swallow of the healing water until she knew she had found her way out of the Worm. With a toast to Heaven above she finished the skin and dropped it over the edge of the wound. She counted six heartbeats before she heard the faint sound of it striking rock.

Not for the first time, she was left in awe at the size of this beast.

A thought occurred to her, and she searched the blackness below for the twinkle of fires. As she suspected, there was nothing. The Dymorians must have already departed; Cho Lin wasn't sure how long she'd slept while recovering from the wounds inflicted on her by the Betrayer, but she suspected it had been several days at least, given how thirsty she'd been when she'd finally awoken. She had wanted to guzzle the little bit of the healing water that she'd forced herself to save, but she'd managed to resist the temptation. Her hand drifted to where the demon's claws had sliced her open; the scabbed wound on her belly was still slightly sore, but she wouldn't be surprised if even that pain was gone when next she woke.

Cho Lin dragged her gaze from the seamless darkness below to the star-spattered one above. She found the constellation of the Monk, lurching drunkenly across the sky, and followed the direction his staff was thrusting. That would be south, the way back to the Empire of Swords and Flowers. The thought of seeing the jagged green hills and gentle rivers of her home sent a pang of bittersweet longing through her. She swallowed that feeling and shifted slightly, staring to the southeast.

That was where she must go. To Menekar, the ancient enemy of Shan. Jan had told her he had seen the rosewood chest of the Betrayers in the pleasure garden of the Menekarian emperor.

That was where their spirits must have fled after she'd stabbed the one that called itself the Shadow King. The legends were very clear: the sword of her family only forced the spirits of the Betrayers back into the chest. She'd won a great victory, as great as any since her ancestor Cho Xin had first bound the demons, but she could not rest now. Her fingers brushed the handle of the black knife, still slightly slick from spending so long at the bottom of the dark pool. She had a weapon that could finally end the Betrayers, so she had to finish the hunt. When that was done, then she could return to Shan.

Suffused with fresh resolve, Cho Lin swung herself over the edge of the wound and began to descend the outside of the Worm.

EPILOGUE

THE AX-HEAD HISSED as Senacus dragged it through the withered leaves blanketing the barren orchard. It was a wicked thing, a great hunk of curving black iron that he suspected had been forged with the intention of splitting skulls rather than wood. He had watched Marialle struggle with it from the doorway of the farm when he'd first mustered the strength to leave his pallet, every swing difficult as she cut logs for the night's fire. The first thing he had done when he could walk again – or hobble, at least – was to take over this duty from her. She had tried to dissuade him, telling him that he was still too weak, but he had insisted.

As he stumped through the orchard, he was mindful of the twisting roots hidden beneath the fallen leaves. He had not yet regained full control over his left leg, and once already he had gone sprawling when his foot had come down awkwardly. In truth, he wasn't sure if it would ever be as it was before. The healing power of the Pure was legendary, but the claws of the shapechanger had severed tendons that, if he was a normal man, would have crippled him for life.

He arrived at the tree Marialle had told him about, its ancient trunk blackened from a lightning strike. Hefting the ax onto his shoulder, he stepped forward, considering the best angle to take down this grizzled old man of the forest. A pair of emerald-green birds watched him from on high, their heads tilted to the side as if trying to figure out his purpose here.

"Apologies," he said to them, laying the edge of the ax against the scarred bark. "I'm afraid you'll have to find a new home."

"Talking to the birds, paladin?" a voice called out from behind him, faintly mocking.

Senacus whirled around, the ashwood handle slipping from his hands. Nel sat in a nearby branch, her back pressed to the trunk, watching him with an impish smile. One of her legs was drawn up to her chest, and the other dangled down, higher than a man could reach. He realized it was the same position she had been in the first time they'd met, and he couldn't hold back a grin.

"Nel!" he cried, dragging his leg behind him as he hurried closer to where she perched. "Thank the Radiant Father. How is Keilan? Did you succeed?"

"The demons are gone," she called down. "Keilan is safe in Herath. The future we saw in the Oracle's temple has been averted."

The knot that Senacus had been carrying around in his chest for months suddenly loosened. "Thank the Radiant Father," he breathed.

Nel twisted so that she sat on the edge of the branch, both legs now hanging down. She leaned forward, her hair falling around her face. "I'm not sure he had much to do with it."

"He works in mysterious ways," Senacus assured Nel, and even from where he stood he could see her eyes roll.

"Well, maybe he sent me back to you, then," she said.

"This isn't just a visit between friends?"

Nel shook her head. "I came to see if you're well enough to travel. Queen Cein has extended you an invitation to her court."

"Truly? The Pure in a city of sorcerers?"

A dagger appeared in Nel's hand and she idly flipped it in the air, then caught it with a flourish. "Do you still consider yourself one of the Pure? Even after the leaders of your faith cast you out?"

Senacus felt a twinge of sadness at this reminder. "You speak of worldly things, and my loyalty has always been foremost to Ama himself. Men can be corrupted, but not the divine."

"And that, in a roundabout way, is why I'm here." Nel spun her dagger again, the blade glittering in the light filtering through the branches. "The queen believes war is coming. Dymoria is weakened after what happened in the north. Her army was lost and most of the magisters perished. Whispers from the east say that the legions of Menekar are preparing to march over the Spine, intent on another Cleansing."

"What can I do about this? As you said, the High Mendicant has named me apostate."

"Return with me to Herath," Nel said. "Show the world that sorcerers and the faithful of Ama need not be enemies."

"I still believe sorcery is dangerous."

"Believe me, I know that to be true as well. So does the queen, perhaps more than before."

Senacus considered what she said, his gaze drifting to the farmhouse, just visible through the maze of trees. What had happened over the last year had taught him many lessons, but two were of particular importance. The first was that sorcery was not by its nature evil. It was a tool – a dangerous tool – and while it could be used for wicked ends, far more important was the nature of the one that wielded it. A sword was much the same: it could be swung to take or to protect. And the second truth he now understood was that sorcery could not be suppressed. The paladins of Ama had spent a thousand years scouring the land of magic, yet that had not stopped ancient threats like the Chosen from returning, or new powers such as the Crimson Queen from emerging. Perhaps Ama intended for him to help guide the rebirth of sorcery in this new age.

"I will pray on what you've said," he said quietly. Senacus saw that Marialle had appeared under the eaves of the farmhouse, peering into the orchard. No doubt she was curious as to why she couldn't hear the sound of chopping wood.

Leaves crunched as Nel dropped to the ground. He turned back to her and found that she was staring at the farmhouse now with a strange look.

"Why haven't you left this place, Senacus? I see you're still injured, but it looks like you could sit a horse."

He cleared his throat, trying to hide the flush he felt coming on by bending to retrieve the ax he'd dropped. "I . . . have found something here."

Nel arched an eyebrow, a playful smile curving the edges of her lips. "The farmer's wife?"

When she saw his expression, she burst out laughing. "Oh, Senacus. How scandalous!"

"She's not a farmer's wife anymore," he said quickly. "Marialle has been a widow for three years."

Nel's brow creased in confusion. "But she told us her husband was gone bringing fruit to market . . ."

"A falsehood. Better to let strangers think a man could return at any time. In truth, he died of the Weeping and she and her boys have been on their own ever since."

"Hm," Nel grunted, and then she shrugged. "It seems you do have decisions to make. But eventually word will get out that you are here, and the mendicants and your brothers will come looking. The woman and her sons could accompany you to Herath; I'm sure the queen's offer extends to them as well."

Senacus bowed his head in gratitude. "Thank you, Nel. I will consider what you have said." He held out his arm, and she clasped it firmly.

"I hope to see you again in Herath, paladin."

A gentle knocking pulled Keilan from the depths of the dusty tome. Blinking, he glanced at the window and saw that night had fallen; he had no recollection of lighting the candles on his desk, but he must have done it some time ago as a fair amount of fresh-melted wax had collected at the base of their holders. He sat back, rolling his neck to alleviate the soreness. The knocking came once more, slightly more insistent. He must have missed supper again, and this would be the steward Haephus delivering a tray. His stomach squirmed at the thought of food; apparently, his body had made an agreement with his mind not to disturb him when he was immersed in his reading, but once he surfaced from the words on the page he was expected to immediately attend to the needs he had been ignoring. A visit to the chamber pot would also be in order.

"Keilan! Are you there?"

That wasn't Haephus. Keilan came to his feet and quickly crossed his chamber, then flung open his door.

"My apologies, Magister Vhalus," he said, ducking his head and gesturing for Vhelan to enter.

The sorcerer sauntered inside, a book of cracked red leather pressed to his chest. "Vhelan is fine when we're not around the apprentices," he murmured distractedly, raising his eyebrows as he took in the state of Keilan's room.

"Are you in the process of moving the entirety of the queen's library here?"

Keilan flushed as he hurried to drag a chair closer to the head magister. He gestured for him to take a seat, but the magister waved the invitation away.

"Thank you, Keilan, but I'm late for a tzalik match with the Keshian ambassador. I was just stopping by to drop off this." He thrust out the red book, and Keilan graciously accepted it. Vhelan's gaze traveled over the haphazardly constructed castle of books rising from his desk and the other piles of parchment and folios spread around his chamber. "Though only the Silver Lady knows where you're going to put it."

Keilan carefully shifted a yellowing scroll from a side table and laid the book down. While he was doing this, he glimpsed the lettering on the spine and gasped. "Eschaton's history of the wraithhold wars! The librarian said it was missing!"

Vhelan smiled indulgently, evidently enjoying Keilan's excitement. "Texts written in High Kalyuni have a habit of being misplaced. That tends to happen when there's no one around who can read them."

"Thank you, Vhelan," Keilan said earnestly. So many questions had been gnawing at him since he had touched the wraithchild's memories. Maybe here he would find some answers.

Vhelan noticed Keilan's eyes wandering back to the book he had just set down and chuckled. "I see your thoughts are already somewhere else. I'll let you get back to your studies, but first I have a bit of news as well. A bird flew in from Theris today."

Keilan's attention snapped back to Vhelan. "Nel?"

The magister nodded. "She's about to start on the Wending. If she spends a few days in Vis, that would mean she'd return in a month or so."

"And my father?"

"He's well. Nel says he and his wife moved up north into the town near your village – Chale, is it? – and they are living with a woman named Amela. You know her, I believe?"

Keilan nodded, emotions swelling within him. Happiness, certainly, to hear about his da, but also sadness when his thoughts turned to Pelos.

"Nel has the books you left with Amela. Though I don't think you are lacking in material to read."

Keilan smiled ruefully. "They are all I have left of my mother. It will be good to have them here."

Vhelan suddenly noticed the smear of dust the book had left on his robes and attempted to wipe it away, frowning as he only ended up making it worse. "Well, I'll leave you to the company of these dead men and their musings. Get some rest – when the queen returns, she'll expect you fresh for the great works she has planned." He strode to the door, but then paused and turned back. "Oh, I should tell you that Nel has convinced me that every magister should have a knife like her for protection. It seems she's under the impression it's the only reason I'm still breathing."

Keilan kept his face blank, but inwardly he agreed with that assessment.

"In her letter, Nel said she's returning with a promising candidate for just such a position. Some fierce girl with mismatched eyes, if you can believe that. She said I should let you know this."

Then with a wink Vhelan was gone, the door clicking shut behind him.

Lessa stalked her prey, drifting like a ghost between the trees. Every step she took she slid into the snow carefully, making sure not to crack the thin layer of ice that had formed atop the drifts. Upwind from her, the deer continued stripping bark from the trees, the harshness of this winter evidenced by the ribs showing clearly along their dappled flanks. Yet even when treading the edge of starvation the deer would be wary, she knew, poised to flee at the slightest hint of danger.

Silently, she reached over her shoulder and drew forth an arrow, then raised her bow and nocked the shaft, briefly closing her eyes to better sense the breeze. Slightly to the right, so she shifted her aim a bit; yes, that was perfect. Now she visualized the path her gray-fletched arrow would take, from the length of taut sinew she held without the slightest trembling beside her ear to the gap between the second and third rib, where she knew the deer's heart to be. Brend had taught her that, how seeing an action before you attempted it made it easier to do, though Lessa had found the technique worked much better with shooting arrows than other things. Cooking, for one.

The smallest of the deer raised its head, surveying the surrounding woods. Lessa held her breath. Now! She should shoot now! And yet she did not. Instead, she remained perfectly still, until the fawn bent again to its feeding.

Ever so slowly, she crouched and set her bow down. Then she wriggled her feet from her boots, curling her toes in the snow, enjoying the icy prickle as the cold crept up her legs. She could do it. Brend said it was impossible, but Lessa had come close before, within only a few handspans, and she would give anything to see the look on Grandfather's face if she managed to return with a still-living deer slung across her shoulders. They had enough venison to last the remainder of the winter, anyway, whether she brought home game today or not.

With agonizing patience she crept closer, leg muscles tensed, ready to dash forward if the deer spotted her approach. Yes, they were careless today, intent; with their tails down and the hair flat against their backs Lessa could tell how safe they felt. Just a few more steps . . .

One of the deer, the larger doe, looked up in alarm, reacting to something Lessa hadn't heard. She stared into its deep brown eyes and could almost taste the animal's surge of panic; then it was moving, bounding away, and her own legs were churning the snow in pursuit. The doe's white tail flashed up and instantly the two fawns scattered, leaping in opposite directions. The last doe hesitated, and Lessa angled towards it, running so fast she felt as if she skimmed across the snow, her bare feet having no time to sink into the drifts.

Left, right, left again. Snow sprayed up as the deer jagged back and forth over fallen logs and bushes, muscles rippling. Lessa pursued, pushing off from a rock half-sunk in the snow, reveling in her strength and the exhilaration of the chase. Branches clawed at her face, but the white tail hovered so tantalizingly close, an arm's length away . . . she just needed to reach out—

Her foot skidded. She was falling, and with a frustrated cry Lessa made one last attempt to grab the doe; her fingers brushed the tawny fur, so smooth, and then the deer was gone, vanishing into the thicket.

She lay panting, tasting snow in her mouth as she listened to the fading crash of the deer's flight through the woods. Lessa rolled onto her back, staring at the fast-moving clouds through the skeletal tree limbs. So close! Next time, next time . . .

She heaved herself to her feet and retraced her steps to where she'd dropped her belongings. Freija would be incensed if she saw Lessa standing out here without her boots; the poor woman still refused to accept that the cold did not bother Lessa as much as it did others. It was best not to invite trouble, though, so Lessa scraped the snow from between her toes and slipped into her boots again. She scooped up her bow, and was just about to sling it over her shoulder when a prickling on the back of her neck made her turn.

A figure stood across the clearing from her.

"Ho!" Lessa cried in alarm, quickly nocking another arrow and aiming it at the stranger. "Who goes there?"

The figure did not reply, drifting closer. It was a woman, she thought, from the shape of the robes she wore, though a fur-trimmed cowl hid her face. Lessa swallowed nervously when she realized how little the stranger was wearing; her slim white arms were even bare below the elbows, and this was on a day when one of the syrup trees outside her home had burst from the cold.

"Stop, or I will loose!" she said, and the stranger must have heard the resolve in her voice because she did halt her approach.

"Are ye from the Iron clan?" Lessa asked, still not lowering her bow. The Iron dwelled on the other side of these mountains, though they rarely ventured into these forests. Brend had told her they thought her grandfather was possessed by spirits; she could understand why, in truth, as Algeirr was like a thunderstorm: dark and brooding, with occasional flashes of intense, frightening anger. Never directed at her, though, thank the Stormforger.

"I am not," the stranger said. It was a woman's voice, quiet yet strong, and flavored with a strange accent. She was not valley-born; Lessa wondered if she was even from the Frostlands. The stranger drew back her cowl and red curls tumbled past her shoulders. She had pale, unblemished skin and brilliant green eyes, and she held Lessa's gaze confidently.

"I come bearing a gift for you," she said, and then she withdrew a sheathed sword from the inner recesses of her robes. It looked finely wrought, and a fist-sized red jewel burned in its hilt. Lessa found that she was holding her breath.

Slowly, the woman crouched and laid the sword in the snow. "It belonged to your father. When you wish to learn more about him, come find me in Herath."

Lessa glanced over her shoulder as a crack sounded, but it was only a frozen branch falling.

When she turned back, the woman was gone.

ACKNOWLEDGMENTS

Thank you so very much to all the readers who came on this journey with me. I really appreciate your support. I believe we are living in a golden age of fantasy writing, and I am immensely grateful and humbled that you would spend your reading hours wandering through my worlds. I hope you'll accompany me on future adventures.

ABOUT THE AUTHOR

Alec Hutson grew up in a geodesic dome and a bookstore, and he currently lives in Shanghai, China. To sign up for his mailing list, please go to authoralechutson.com.

Made in the USA
Monee, IL
06 February 2021